PRAISE FOR

Neverwhere

"Some of the best pure storytelling around.... Consistently witty, suspenseful, and hair-raisingly imaginative."

—*Kirkus Reviews*

"*Neverwhere* displays the kind of wit, mythological invention, and attention to the odd detail that will be familiar to anyone who has read Gaiman's groundbreaking comic series, *The Sandman*."

—*San Francisco Examiner*

"There are plenty of laughs as geography takes on a mythical dimension and the Underground transforms into a house of mystery and imagination. You'll never look at the Tube the same way again."

—*Wired*

"[A] strange place where dark, fabulous worlds collide with mundane reality."

—*Seattle Times*

"Readers will find themselves as unable to escape this tale as the characters themselves. Highly recommended."

—*Library Journal*

"Neil Gaiman is undoubtedly one of the modern masters of fantasy writing.... American readers can experience this spellbinding, magical world the way that Neil Gaiman wanted us to all along."

—Huffington Post

Neverwhere

Author's Preferred Text

Also by Neil Gaiman

Novels
The Ocean at the End of the Lane
Graveyard Book
Anansi Boys
Coraline
American Gods
Stardust
Neverwhere
Good Omens (with Terry Pratchett)

Collections
The Neil Gaiman Reader: Selected Fiction
Trigger Warning
Fragile Things
Smoke and Mirrors

Illustrated Stories
The Truth Is a Cave in the Black Mountains
(illustrated by Eddie Campbell)
The Sleeper and the Spindle (illustrated by Chris Riddell)

For Younger Readers
Fortunately, the Milk (illustrated by Skottie Young)
Hansel and Gretel (illustrated by Lorenzo Mattotti)
Instructions (illustrated by Charles Vess)
Odd and the Frost Giants (illustrated by Brett Helquist)
Crazy Hair (illustrated by Dave McKean)
Blueberry Girl (illustrated by Charles Vess)
The Dangerous Alphabet (illustrated by Gris Grimly)
M Is for Magic (illustrated by Teddy Kristiansen)

Nonfiction
Art Matters (illustrated by Chris Riddell)
Make Good Art
The View from the Cheap Seats

Neverwhere

Author's Preferred Text

NEIL GAIMAN

WILLIAM MORROW

An Imprint of HarperCollinsPublishers

For Lenny Henry, friend and colleague,
who made it happen all the way;
and Merrilee Heifetz, friend and agent,
who makes everything good

I have never been to St John's Wood. I dare not. I should be afraid of the innumerable night of fir trees, afraid to come upon a blood red cup and the beating of the wings of the Eagle.

The Napoleon of Notting Hill, G. K. CHESTERTON

> *If ever thou gavest hosen or shoon*
> *Then every night and all*
> *Sit thou down and put them on*
> *And Christ receive thy soul*

> *This aye night, this aye night*
> *Every night and all*
> *Fire and fleet and candlelight*
> *And Christ receive thy soul*

> *If ever thou gavest meat or drink*
> *Then every night and all*
> *The fire shall never make thee shrink*
> *And Christ receive thy soul*

The Lyke Wake Dirge, TRADITIONAL

INTRODUCTION
TO THIS TEXT

⸻ ⋅◆⋅ ⸻

I T'S A GOOD BET that even if you've read *Neverwhere* before, you haven't read this version of *Neverwhere* before.

Neverwhere began life, in the way these things do, as a television series I was asked to write for the BBC. And while the show that was broadcast was not necessarily a bad television series, I kept finding myself bumping up against the fact that what one saw on-screen simply wasn't what I had in my head. A novel seemed the easiest way to get what I had had in my head into the insides of other people's heads. Books are good that way.

Neverwhere as a novel began for me as we started making the BBC TV series of the same name, more or less as a way to keep my sanity.

With every scene that was cut, every line that vanished, everything that was simply changed, I'd announce, "Not a problem. I'll put it back in the novel," and thus regain my equilibrium. This went on until the day that the producer came over and said, "We're cutting the scene on page twenty-four, and if you say *I'll put it back in the novel* I'll kill you."

After that, I only thought it.

What I wanted to do was to write a book that would do for adults what the books I had loved when younger, books like *Alice in Wonderland,* or the Narnia books, or *The Wizard of Oz,* did for me as a kid. And I wanted to talk about the people who fall through the cracks, to talk about the dispossessed—using the mirror of fantasy, which can sometimes show us things we have seen so many times that we never see them at all—for the very first time.

I started writing the novel on the day we started shooting the TV series, in January, in the kitchen of the South London flat in which we were filming. I finished it in May, in a hotel in a small town in Southern California.

It was published in August of that year, by the BBC. When Avon Books wanted to publish it, I jumped at the chance to, in essence, do a second draft of the novel. I locked myself in a hotel room in New York City's World Trade Center, and I wrote for a week, adding material for Americans who might not know where Oxford Street was or what you'd find if you walked down it, and enjoying the opportunity to revisit the text, expanding and deepening it wherever I could. My editor at Avon Books, Jennifer Hershey, was a terrific and perceptive editor; our major disagreement was the jokes. She didn't like them and was con-

vinced that American readers would not be able to cope with jokes in a book that wasn't meant solely to be funny. She wanted the second prologue gone, too, in which we got to meet Croup and Vandemar for the first time, before the story began, and although I missed it, I decided that she was right and moved the description of them into the text. (It's reprinted here, at the back, in its original form, for the curious.)

By the time I was finished, I'd added around twelve thousand words and cut several thousand different words. Some of the words I was happy to lose. Others I missed.

This version of *Neverwhere,* assembled from the various drafts of the book with the aid of Pete Atkins from Hill House Publishers, combines the original UK text and the U.S. text, and then I removed a few of the redundancies and created a new, and I hope definitive, version of *Neverwhere,* along with a headache for bibliographers.

I don't write sequels. Still, the world of *Neverwhere* is one that I hope, one day, I'll return to. In a book called *The Lost Rivers of London,* I read about a brass bed found one day in a sewer. To this day, nobody knows where it came from or how it got there.

I bet de Carabas knows.

NEIL GAIMAN

The LONDON UNDERGROUND (Detail)

WARWICK AVENUE
Opened 1/31/1915

LORD'S
Opened as St. John's
Wood Road 4/13/1868
Closed 11/19/1939

EDGWARE ROAD
Opened 6/15/1907

MARYLEBONE
Opened as Great
Central 3/27/1907

BAKER
Opened

Opened as Paddington
(Bishop's Road) 1/10/1863
PADDINGTON

EDGWARE ROAD
Opened 1/10/1863

BAKER
STREET
Opened 5/

ROYAL OAK
Opened 10/30/1871

WESTBOURNE PARK
Opened 11/1/1871

Westbourne Park
Opened 2/1/1866
Closed 10/31/1871

PADDINGTON
Opened 12/1/1913

EDGWARE ROAD
Opened 11/1/1926

BAKER STREET
Opened 1/10/1863

BAKER STR
Opened 4/12
Closed 3/7/1
Reopened 1/
Closed 5/19
Reopened 7/

LADBROKE GROVE
Opened as Notting Hill
6/13/1864

PADDINGTON
Opened as Paddington (Praed Street) 11/1/1926

PADDINGTON
Opened as Paddington (Praed Street) 10/1/1868

REGENT
Opened 3/

LATIMER ROAD
Opened 12/16/1868

BAYSWATER
Opened 10/1/1868

BAYSWATER
Opened as Bayswater (Queen's Road)
& Westbourne Grove 11/1/1926

Uxbridge Road
Opened 11/1/1869
Closed 10/19/1940

NOTTING HILL GATE
Opened 7/30/1900

QUEENSWAY
Opened as Queen's Road 7/30/1900

MARBLE ARCH
Opened 7/30/1900

BOND STREET
Opened 5/1/1979

OXFORD C
Opened 3/10

HOLLAND PARK
Opened 7/30/1900

NOTTING HILL GATE
Opened 11/1/1926

LANCASTER GATE
Opened 7/30/1900

BOND STREET
Opened 9/24/1900

NOTTING HILL GATE
Opened 10/1/1868

HIGH STREET KENSINGTON
Opened as Kensington
(High Street) 10/1/1868

HIGH STREET KENSINGTON
Opened as Kensington (High Street) 7/3/1871

GREEN PARK
Opened 5/1/1979

GREEN PARK
Opened as Dover Street (St. James's) 12/15/1906

GREEN
Opened

Down Street
Opened as Down Street (Mayfair) 3/15/1907
Closed 5/21/1932

HYDE PARK CORNER
Opened 12/15/1906

Kensington (Addison Road)
Opened as Kensington 7/1/1864
Closed 10/19/1940

KENSINGTON (Olympia)
Opened 12/19/1946

KNIGHTSBRIDGE
Opened 12/15/1906

Opened as Brompton
(Gloucester Road) 10/1/1868
GLOUCESTER ROAD

Brompton Road
Opened 12/15/1906
Closed 7/29/1934

Opened 12/15/1907
Closed 8/30/1987
Reopened 5/21/1989
GLOUCESTER ROAD

SOUTH KENSINGTON
Opened 1/8/1907

Opened 12/24/1868
SOUTH KENSINGTON

VICTORIA
Opened 3/7/1969

EARL'S COURT
Opened 12/15/1906

EARL'S COURT
Opened 2/1/1878

Earl's Court
Opened 10/30/1871
Closed 1/31/1878

GLOUCESTER ROAD
Opened as Brompton
(Gloucester Road) 4/12/1869

SOUTH KENSINGTON
Opened 7/10/1871

SLOANE SQUARE
Opened 12/24/1868

VICTORIA
Opened 12/24/1868

ST. JAMES'S
Opened 12/24

LEGEND

Central Line	Piccadilly Line
District Line	Victoria Line
Northern Line	Jubilee Line
Metropolitan Line	British Rail
Bakerloo Line	

Neverwhere

Author's Preferred Text

PROLOGUE

———⁕———

THE NIGHT BEFORE HE went to London, Richard Mayhew was not enjoying himself.

He had begun the evening by enjoying himself: he had enjoyed reading the good-bye cards, and receiving the hugs from several not entirely unattractive young ladies of his acquaintance; he had enjoyed the warnings about the evils and dangers of London, and the gift of the white umbrella with the map of the London Underground on it that the lads had clubbed together to buy him; he had enjoyed the first few pints of ale; but then, with each successive pint of ale he found he was enjoying himself significantly less; until now he was sitting and shivering on the sidewalk outside the pub in a small Scottish town, weighing the conflicting

merits of being sick and not being sick, and not enjoying himself at all.

Inside the pub, Richard's friends continued to celebrate his forthcoming departure, with an enthusiasm that, to Richard's way of thinking, was beginning to border on the sinister. He sat on the sidewalk and held on tightly to the rolled-up umbrella, and wondered whether going south to London was really a good idea.

"You want to keep an eye out," said a cracked old voice. "They'll be moving you on before you can say Jack Robinson. Or taking you in, I wouldn't be surprised." Two sharp eyes stared out from a beaky, grimy face. "You all right?"

"Yes, thank you," said Richard. He was a fresh-faced, boyish young man, with dark, slightly curly hair and large hazel eyes; he had a rumpled, just-woken-up look to him, which made him more attractive to the opposite sex than he would ever understand or believe.

The grimy face softened. "Here, poor thing," she said, and pushed a fifty-pence piece into Richard's hand. " 'Ow long you been on the streets, then?"

"I'm not homeless," explained Richard, embarrassed, attempting to give the old woman her coin back. "Please—take your money. I'm fine. I just came out here to get some air. I go to London tomorrow."

She peered down at him suspiciously, then took back her fifty pence and made it vanish beneath the layers of coats and shawls in which she was enveloped. "I've been to London," she confided. "I was married in London. But he was a bad lot. Me mam told me not to go marrying outside, but I was young and

beautiful, although you'd never credit it today, and I followed my heart."

"I'm sure you did," said Richard, embarrassed. The conviction that he was about to be sick was starting, slowly, to fade.

"Fat lot of good it done me. I been homeless, so I know what it's like," said the old woman. "That's why I thought you was. What you going to London for?"

"I've got a job," he told her proudly.

"Doing what?" she asked.

"Um, securities," said Richard.

"I was a dancer," said the old woman, and she tottered awkwardly around the sidewalk humming tunelessly to herself. Then she teetered from side to side like a spinning top coming to rest, and finally she stopped, facing Richard. "Hold out your hand," she told him, "and I'll tell yer fortune." He did as he was told. She put her old hand into his, and held it tightly, and then she blinked a few times, like an owl who had swallowed a mouse that was beginning to disagree with it. "You got a long way to go . . . ," she said, puzzled.

"London," Richard told her.

"Not just London . . ." The old woman paused. "Not any London I know." It started to rain, then, softly. "I'm sorry," she said. "It starts with doors."

"Doors?"

She nodded. The rain fell harder, pattering on the roofs and on the asphalt of the road. "I'd watch out for doors if I were you."

Richard stood up, a little unsteadily. "All right," he said, unsure of how one ought to treat information of this nature. "I will. Thanks."

The pub door was opened, and light and noise spilled out into the street. "Richard? You all right?"

"Yeah, I'm fine. I'll be back in a second." The old lady was already wobbling down the street, into the pelting rain, getting wet. Richard felt he had to do something for her; he couldn't give her money, though. He hurried after her, down the narrow street, the cold rain drenching his face and hair. "Here," said Richard. He fumbled with the handle of the umbrella, trying to find the button that opened it. Then a click, and it blossomed into a huge white map of the London Underground network, each line drawn in a different color, every station marked and named.

The old woman took the umbrella, gratefully, and smiled her thanks. "You've a good heart," she told him. "Sometimes that's enough to see you safe wherever you go." Then she shook her head. "But mostly, it's not." She clutched the umbrella tightly, as a gust of wind threatened to tug it away from her, or pull it inside out. She wrapped her arms around it, and bent almost double against the rain and the wind. Then she walked away into the rain and the night, a round white shape covered with the names of London Tube stations, Earl's Court, Marble Arch, Blackfriars, White City, Victoria, Angel, Oxford Circus . . .

Richard found himself pondering, drunkenly, whether there really was a circus at Oxford Circus: a real circus with clowns and beautiful women, and dangerous beasts. The pub door opened once more: a blast of sound, as if the pub's volume control had just been turned up high. "Richard, you wanker, it's your bloody party, and you're missing all the fun." He walked back in the pub, the urge to be sick lost in all the oddness.

"You look like a drowned rat," said someone.

"You've never seen a drowned rat," said Richard.

Someone else handed him a large whisky. "Here, get that down you. That'll warm you up. You know, you won't be able to get real Scotch in London."

"I'm sure I will," sighed Richard. Water was dripping from his hair into his drink. "They have everything in London." And he downed the Scotch, and after that someone bought him another, and then the evening blurred and broke up into fragments: afterward he remembered only the sense that he was leaving somewhere small and sensible that made sense for somewhere huge and old that didn't; and vomiting interminably into a gutter flowing with rainwater, somewhere in the small hours of the morning; and a white shape marked with strange-colored symbols, like a little round beetle, walking away from him in the rain.

The next morning Richard got on the train to London for the six-hour journey south that would bring him to the strange Gothic spires and arches of St. Pancras Station. His mother gave him a small walnut cake that she had made for the journey and a thermos flask filled with tea; and Richard Mayhew went to London feeling like hell.

1

S HE HAD BEEN RUNNING for four days now, a harum-scarum tumbling flight through passages and tunnels. She was hungry, and exhausted, and more tired than a body could stand, and each successive door was proving harder to open. After four days of flight, she had found a hiding place, a tiny stone burrow, under the world, where she would be safe, or so she prayed, and at last she slept.

MR. CROUP HAD HIRED Ross at the last Floating Market, which had been held in Westminster Abbey. "Think of him," he told Mr. Vandemar, "as a canary."

"Sings?" asked Mr. Vandemar.

"I doubt it; I sincerely and utterly doubt it." Mr. Croup ran a hand through his lank orange hair. "No, my fine friend, I was thinking metaphorically—more along the lines of the birds they take down mines." Mr. Vandemar nodded, comprehension dawning slowly: yes, a canary. Mr. Ross had no other resemblance to a canary. He was huge—almost as big as Mr. Vandemar—and extremely grubby, and quite hairless, and he said very little, although he had made a point of telling each of them that he liked to kill things, and he was good at it; and this amused Mr. Croup and Mr. Vandemar, much as Genghis Khan might have been amused by the swagger of a young Mongol who had recently pillaged his first village or burnt his first yurt. He was a canary, and he never knew it. So Mr. Ross went first, in his filthy T-shirt and his crusted blue jeans, and Croup and Vandemar walked behind him, in their elegant black suits.

There are four simple ways for the observant to tell Mr. Croup and Mr. Vandemar apart: first, Mr. Vandemar is two and a half heads taller than Mr. Croup; second, Mr. Croup has eyes of a faded china blue, while Mr. Vandemar's eyes are brown; third, while Mr. Vandemar fashioned the rings he wears on his right hand out of the skulls of four ravens, Mr. Croup has no obvious jewelry; fourth, Mr. Croup likes words, while Mr. Vandemar is always hungry. Also, they look nothing at all alike.

A rustle in the tunnel darkness; Mr. Vandemar's knife was in his hand, and then it was no longer in his hand, and it was quivering gently almost thirty feet away. He walked over to his knife, and picked it up by the hilt. There was a gray rat impaled on the blade, its mouth opening and closing impotently as the life fled. He crushed its skull between finger and thumb.

"Now, there's one rat that won't be telling any more tales," said Mr. Croup. He chuckled at his own joke. Mr. Vandemar did not respond. "Rat. Tales. Get it?"

Mr. Vandemar pulled the rat from the blade and began to munch on it, thoughtfully, head first. Mr. Croup slapped it out of his hands. "Stop that," he said. Mr. Vandemar put his knife away, a little sullenly. "Buck up," hissed Mr. Croup, encouragingly. "There will always be another rat. Now: onward. Things to do. People to damage."

THREE YEARS IN LONDON had not changed Richard, although it had changed the way he perceived the city. Richard had originally imagined London as a gray city, even a black city, from pictures he had seen, and was surprised to find it filled with color. It was a city of red brick and white stone, red buses and large black taxis (which were often, to Richard's initial puzzlement, gold, or green, or maroon), bright red postboxes, and green grassy parks and cemeteries.

It was a city in which the very old and the awkwardly new jostled each other, not uncomfortably, but without respect; a city of shops and offices and restaurants and homes, of parks and churches, of ignored monuments and remarkably unpalatial palaces; a city of hundreds of districts with strange names—Crouch End, Chalk Farm, Earl's Court, Marble Arch—and oddly distinct identities; a noisy, dirty, cheerful, troubled city, which fed on tourists, needed them as it despised them, in which the average speed of transportation through the city had not increased in three hundred years, following five hundred years of fitful road widening and unskillful compromises between the needs of traf-

fic, whether horse-drawn or, more recently, motorized, and the needs of pedestrians; a city inhabited by and teeming with people of every color and manner and kind.

When he had first arrived, he had found London huge, odd, fundamentally incomprehensible, with only the Tube map, that elegant multicolored topographical display of underground railway lines and stations, giving it any semblance of order. Gradually he realized that the Tube map was a handy fiction that made life easier, but bore no resemblance to the reality of the shape of the city above: like belonging to a political party, he thought once, proudly, and then, having tried to explain the resemblance between the Tube map and politics, at a party, to a cluster of bewildered strangers, he had decided in the future to leave political comment to others.

He continued, slowly, by a process of osmosis and white knowledge (which is like white noise, only more informative), to comprehend the city, a process which accelerated when he realized that the actual City of London itself was no bigger than a square mile, stretching from Aldgate in the east to Fleet Street and the law courts of the Old Bailey in the west, a tiny municipality, now home to London's financial institutions, and that was where it had all begun.

Two thousand years before, London had been a little Celtic village on the north shore of the Thames which the Romans had encountered and settled in. London had grown, slowly, until, roughly a thousand years later, it met the tiny Royal City of Westminster immediately to the west, and, once London Bridge had been built, London met the town of Southwark directly across the river; and it continued to grow, fields and woods and marshland slowly vanishing beneath the flourishing town, and

it continued to expand, encountering other little villages and hamlets as it grew, like Whitechapel and Deptford to the east, Hammersmith and Shepherd's Bush to the west, Camden and Islington in the north, Battersea and Lambeth across the Thames to the south, absorbing all of them as it grew, just as a pool of mercury encounters and incorporates smaller beads of mercury, leaving only their names behind.

London grew into something huge and contradictory. It was a good place, and a fine city, but there is a price to be paid for all good places, and a price that all good places have to pay.

After a while, Richard found himself taking London for granted; in time, he began to pride himself on having visited none of the sights of London (except for the Tower of London, when his Aunt Maude came down to the city for a weekend, and Richard found himself her reluctant escort).

But Jessica changed all that. Richard found himself, on otherwise sensible weekends, accompanying her to places like the National Gallery and the Tate Gallery, where he learned that walking around museums too long hurts your feet, that the great art treasures of the world all blur into each other after a while, and that it is almost beyond the human capacity for belief to accept how much museum cafeterias will brazenly charge for a slice of cake and a cup of tea.

"Here's your tea, and your éclair," he told her. "It would have cost less to buy one of those Tintorettos."

"Don't exaggerate," said Jessica, cheerfully. "Anyway, there aren't any Tintorettos at the Tate."

"I should have had that cherry cake," said Richard. "Then they would have been able to afford another van Gogh."

"No," said Jessica, accurately, "they wouldn't."

Richard had met Jessica in France, on a weekend break in Paris two years earlier; had in fact discovered her in the Louvre, while trying to find the group of his office friends who had organized the trip. Staring up at an immense sculpture, he had stepped backward into Jessica, who was admiring an extremely large and historically important diamond. He tried to apologize to her in French, which he did not speak, and so gave up, and began to apologize in English, and then tried to attempt to apologize in French for his having to apologize in English, until he noticed that Jessica was about as English as it was possible for any one person to be, by which time she had him buy her an expensive French sandwich and some overpriced fizzy apple juice, by way of apology, and, well, that was the start of it all, really. He had never been able to convince Jessica that he wasn't the kind of person who went to art galleries after that.

On weekends when they did not go to art galleries or to museums, Richard would trail behind Jessica as she went shopping, which she did, on the whole, in affluent Knightsbridge, a short walk and an even shorter taxi ride from her flat in a Kensington mews. Richard would accompany Jessica on her tours of such huge and intimidating emporia as Harrods and Harvey Nichols, stores where Jessica was able to purchase anything, from jewelry, to books, to the week's groceries.

Richard had been awed by Jessica, who was beautiful, and often quite funny, and was certainly going somewhere. And Jessica saw in Richard an enormous amount of potential, which, properly harnessed by the right woman, would have made him the perfect matrimonial accessory. If only he were a little more focused, she would murmur to herself, and so she gave him

books with titles like *Dress for Success* and *A Hundred and Twenty-Five Habits of Successful Men,* and books on how to run a business like a military campaign, and Richard always said thank you, and always meant to read them. In Harvey Nichols's men's fashion department she would pick out for him the kinds of clothes she thought that he should wear—and he wore them, during the week, anyway; and, a year to the day after their first encounter, she told him she thought it time that they went shopping for an engagement ring.

"Why do you go out with her?" asked Garry, in Corporate Accounts, eighteen months later. "She's terrifying."

Richard shook his head. "She's really sweet, once you get to know her."

Garry put down the plastic troll he had picked up from Richard's desk. "I'm surprised she still lets you play with these."

"The subject has never come up," said Richard, picking up one of the creatures from his desk. It had a shock of Day-Glo orange hair and a slightly baffled expression, as if it were lost.

The subject had indeed come up. Jessica had, however, convinced herself that Richard's troll collection was a mark of endearing eccentricity, comparable to Mr. Stockton's collection of angels. Jessica was in the process of organizing a traveling exhibition of Mr. Stockton's angel collection, and had come to the conclusion that great men always collected something. In actuality Richard did not really collect trolls. He had found a troll on the street outside the office and, in a vague and pretty vain attempt at injecting a little personality into his working world, he had placed it on his computer monitor. The others had followed over the next few months, gifts from colleagues who had

noticed that Richard had a penchant for the ugly little creatures. He had taken the gifts and positioned them strategically about his desk, beside the telephones and the framed photograph of Jessica. Today, the photograph had a yellow Post-it note stuck to it.

It was a Friday afternoon. Richard had noticed that events were cowards: they didn't occur singly, but instead they would run in packs and leap out at him all at once. Take this particular Friday, for example. It was, as Jessica had pointed out to him at least a dozen times in the last month, the most important day of his life. Not the most important day of her life, of course. That would come one day in the future, when, Richard had no doubt, they would make her Prime Minister, or Queen, or God. But it was, without question, the most important day of his life. So it was unfortunate that, despite the Post-it note Richard had left on his fridge door at home, and the other Post-it note he had placed on the photograph of Jessica on his desk, he had forgotten about it completely and utterly.

Also, there was the Wandsworth Report, which was overdue and taking up most of his head. Richard checked another row of figures; then he noticed that page 17 had vanished and he set it up to print out again; and another page down, and he knew that if he were only left alone to finish it . . . if, miracle of miracles, the phone did not ring . . . It rang. He thumbed the speakerphone.

"Hello? Richard? The Managing Director needs to know when he'll have the report."

Richard looked at his watch. "Five minutes, Sylvia. It's almost wrapped up. I just have to attach the P & L projection."

"Thanks, Dick. I'll come down for it." Sylvia was, as she liked to explain, "the MD's PA," and she moved in an atmosphere of

crisp efficiency. He thumbed the speakerphone off; it rang again, immediately. "Richard," said the speaker, with Jessica's voice, "it's Jessica. You haven't forgotten, have you?"

"Forgotten?" He tried to remember what he could have forgotten. He looked at Jessica's photograph for inspiration, and found all the inspiration he could have needed in the shape of a yellow Post-it note stuck to her forehead.

"Richard? Pick up the telephone."

He picked up the phone, reading the Post-it note as he did so. "Sorry, Jess. No, I hadn't forgotten. Seven P.M., at Ma Maison Italiano. Should I meet you there?"

"Jessica, Richard. Not Jess." She paused for a moment. "After what happened last time? I don't think so. You really could get lost in your own back garden, Richard."

Richard contemplated pointing out that *anyone* could have confused the National Gallery with the National Portrait Gallery, and that it wasn't *she* who had spent the whole day standing in the rain (which was in his opinion every bit as much fun as walking around either place until his feet hurt), but he thought better of it.

"I'll meet you at your place," said Jessica. "We can walk down together."

"Right, Jess. Jessica—sorry."

"You *have* confirmed our reservation, haven't you, Richard."

"Yes," lied Richard earnestly. The other phone on his desk had begun to ring, shrilly. "Jessica, look, I—"

"Good," said Jessica, and she broke the connection. The largest amount of money Richard had ever spent on anything had been spent on Jessica's engagement ring, eighteen months ear-

lier, at one of Harrods' many jewelry concessions. He picked up the other phone.

"Hi, Dick," said Garry. "It's me, Garry." Garry sat a few desks down from Richard. He waved at Richard from his own, gleamingly troll-free, desk. "Are we still on for drinks? You said we could go over the Merstham account."

"Get off the bloody phone, Garry. Of course we are." Richard put down the phone. There was a telephone number at the bottom of the Post-it note; Richard had written the Post-it note to himself, several weeks earlier. And he *had* made the reservation: he was almost certain of that. But he had not confirmed it. He had kept meaning to, but there had been so much to do and Richard had known that there was plenty of time. But events run in packs . . .

Sylvia was now standing next to him. "Dick? The Wandsworth Report?"

"Almost ready, Sylvia. Look, just hold on a sec, can you?"

He finished punching in the number, breathed a sigh of relief when somebody answered, "Ma Maison. Can I help you?"

"Yes," said Richard. "A table for three, for tonight. I think I booked it. And if I did I'm confirming the reservation. And if I didn't, I wondered if I could book it. Please." No, they had no record of a table for tonight in the name of Mayhew. Or Stockton. Or Bartram—Jessica's surname. And as for booking a table . . .

It wasn't the words that Richard found so unpleasant: it was the tone of voice in which the information was transmitted. A table for *tonight* should certainly have been booked years before, perhaps, it was implied, by Richard's parents. A table for *tonight* was impossible: if the Pope, the Prime Minister and the President

of France arrived this evening without a confirmed reservation, even they would be turned out into the street with a continental jeer. "But it's for my fiancée's boss. I know I should have phoned before. There are only three of us, can't you *please*—"

They had put down the phone.

"Richard?" said Sylvia. "The MD's waiting."

"Do you think," asked Richard, "they'd give me a table if I phoned back and offered them extra money?"

IN HER DREAM THEY were all together in the house. Her parents, her brother, her baby sister. They were standing together in the ballroom, staring at her. They were all so pale, so grave. Portia, her mother, touched her cheek, and told her that she was in danger. In her dream, Door laughed, and said she knew. Her mother shook her head: no, no—now she was in danger. *Now.*

Door opened her eyes. The door was opening, quietly, quietly; she held her breath. Footsteps, quiet on the stone. *Perhaps he won't notice me*, she thought. *Perhaps he'll go away.* And then she thought, desperately, *I'm hungry.*

The footsteps hesitated. She was well hidden, she knew, under a pile of newspapers and rags. And it was possible that the intruder meant her no harm. *Can't he hear my heartbeat?* she thought. And then the footsteps came closer, and she knew what she had to do and it scared her. A hand pulled the covers off her, and she looked up into a blank, utterly hairless face, which creased into a vicious smile. She rolled, then, and twisted, and the knife blade, aimed at her chest, caught her in the upper arm.

Until that moment, she had never thought she could do it.

Never thought she would be brave enough, or scared enough, or desperate enough to dare. But she reached up one hand to his chest, and she *opened* . . .

He gasped, and tumbled onto her. It was wet and warm and slippery, and she slithered and staggered out from under the man, and she stumbled out of the room.

She caught her breath in the tunnel outside, narrow and low, as she fell against the wall, breathing in gasps and sobs. That had taken the last of her strength; now she was spent. Her shoulder was beginning to throb. *The knife,* she thought. But she was safe.

"My, oh my," said a voice from the darkness on her right. "She survived Mister Ross. Well I never, Mister Vandemar." The voice oozed. It sounded like gray slime.

"Well I never either, Mister Croup," said a flat voice on her left.

A light was kindled and flickered. "Still," said Mr. Croup, his eyes gleaming in the dark beneath the earth, "she won't survive us."

Door kneed him, hard, in the groin, and then she began, randomly, to run, her right hand holding her left shoulder.

And she ran.

"Dick?"

Richard waved away the interruption. Life was almost under his control, now. Just a little more time . . .

Garry said his name again. "Dick? It's six thirty."

"It's *what?*" Papers and pens and spreadsheets and trolls were tumbled into Richard's briefcase. He snapped it shut and ran.

He pulled his coat on as he went. Garry was following. "Are we going to have that drink, then?"

"Drink?"

"We were meant to be getting together this evening to talk about the Merstham account. Remember?"

That was tonight? Richard paused for a moment. If ever, he decided, they made disorganization an Olympic sport, he could be disorganized for Britain. "Garry," he said, "I'm sorry. I blew it. I have to see Jessica tonight. We're taking her boss out to dinner."

"Mister Stockton? Of Stocktons? *The* Stockton?" Richard nodded. They hurried down the stairs. "I'm sure you'll have fun," said Garry, insincerely. "And how is the Creature from the Black Lagoon?"

"Jessica's from Ilford, actually, Garry. And she remains the light and love of my life, thank you very much for asking." By which time they were in the lobby, and Richard made a dart for the automatic doors, which spectacularly failed to open.

"It's after six, Mister Mayhew," said Mr. Figgis, the building's security guard. "You have to sign out."

"I don't need this," said Richard to no one in particular, "I really don't."

Mr. Figgis smelt vaguely of medicinal liniment and was widely rumored to have an encyclopedic collection of soft-core pornography. He guarded the doors with a diligence that bordered upon madness, never quite having lived down the evening when an entire floor's worth of computer equipment upped and left, along with two potted palms and the Managing Director's Axminster carpet.

"So our drink's off, then?"

"I'm sorry, Garry. Is Monday okay for you?"

"Sure. Monday's fine. See you Monday."

Mr. Figgis inspected their signatures and satisfied himself they had no computers, potted palms or carpets about their persons, then he pressed a button under his desk, and the door slid open.

"Doors," said Richard.

THE UNDERWAY BRANCHED AND divided; she picked her way at random, ducking through tunnels, running and stumbling and weaving. Behind her strolled Mr. Croup and Mr. Vandemar, as calmly and cheerfully as Victorian dignitaries visiting the Crystal Palace exhibition. When they arrived at a crossroads, Mr. Croup would kneel, and find the nearest spot of blood, and they would follow it. They were like hyenas, exhausting their prey. They could wait. They had all the time in the world.

LUCK WAS WITH RICHARD, for a change. He caught a black taxi, driven by a particularly enthusiastic taxi driver who took Richard home by an unlikely route involving streets Richard had never previously noticed, while holding forth, as Richard had discovered all London taxi drivers will hold forth—given a living, breathing, English-speaking passenger—on London's inner-city traffic problems, how best to deal with crime, and thorny political issues of the day. Richard jumped out of the cab, leaving a tip and his briefcase behind, managed to flag down

the cab again before it made it into the main road and so got his briefcase back, then he ran up the stairs and into his flat. He was already shedding clothes as he entered the hall: his briefcase spun across the room and crash-landed on the sofa; he took his keys from his pocket and placed them carefully on the hall table, in order to ensure he did not forget them.

Then he dashed into the bedroom. The buzzer sounded. Richard, three-quarters of the way into his best suit, launched himself at the entryphone.

"Richard? It's Jessica. I hope you're ready."

"Oh. Yes. Be right down." He pulled on a coat and he ran, slamming the door behind him. Jessica was waiting for him at the bottom of the stairs. She always waited for him there. Jessica didn't like Richard's flat; it made her feel uncomfortably female. There was always the chance of finding a pair of Richard's underwear, well, anywhere, not to mention the wandering lumps of congealed toothpaste on the bathroom sink: no, it was not a Jessica kind of place.

Jessica was very beautiful; so much so Richard would occasionally find himself staring at her, wondering, *How did she end up with me?* And when they made love—which they did at Jessica's mews flat in fashionable Kensington, in Jessica's brass bed with the crisp white linen sheets (for Jessica's parents had told her that eiderdowns were decadent)—in the darkness, afterward, she would hold him very tightly, and her long brown curls would tumble over his chest, and she would whisper to him how much she loved him, and he would tell her he loved her and always wanted to be with her, and they both believed it to be true.

"Bless me, Mister Vandemar. She's slowing up."

"Slowing up, Mister Croup."

"She must be losing a lot of blood, Mister V."

"Lovely blood, Mister C. Lovely wet blood."

"Not long now."

A click: the sound of a switchblade opening, empty and lonely and dark.

"Richard? What are you doing?" asked Jessica.

"Nothing, Jessica."

"You haven't forgotten your keys again, have you?"

"No, Jessica." Richard stopped patting himself and pushed his hands deep into the pockets of his coat.

"Now, when you meet Mister Stockton tonight," said Jessica, "you have to appreciate that he's not just a very important man. He's also a corporate entity in his own right."

"I can't wait," sighed Richard.

"What was that, Richard?"

"I can't wait," said Richard, rather more enthusiastically.

"Oh, do step lively," said Jessica, who was beginning to exude an aura of what, in a lesser woman, might almost have been described as nerves. "We mustn't keep Mister Stockton waiting."

"No, Jess."

"Don't call me that, Richard. I loathe pet names. They're so demeaning."

"Spare any change?" The man sat in a doorway. His beard was yellow and gray, and his eyes were sunken and dark. A

hand-lettered sign hung from a piece of frayed string around his neck, and rested on his chest, telling anyone with the eyes to read it that he was homeless and hungry. It didn't take a sign to tell you that; Richard, hand already in his pocket, fumbled for a coin.

"Richard. We haven't got the time," said Jessica, who gave to charity and invested ethically. "Now, I do want you to make a good impression, fiancé-wise. It is vital that a future spouse makes a good impression." And then her face creased, and she hugged him for a moment, and said, "Oh, Richard. I *do* love you. You do know that, don't you?"

And Richard nodded, and he did.

Jessica checked her watch and increased her pace. Richard discreetly flicked a pound coin back through the air toward the man in the doorway, who caught it in one grimy hand.

"There wasn't any problem with the reservations, was there?" asked Jessica. And Richard, who was not much good at lying when faced with a direct question, said, "Ah."

SHE HAD CHOSEN WRONGLY——— The corridor ended in a blank wall. Normally that would hardly have given her pause, but she was so tired, so hungry, in so much pain . . . She leaned against the wall, feeling the brick roughness against her face. She was gulping breath, hiccuping and sobbing. Her arm was cold, and her left hand was numb. She could go no further, and the world was beginning to feel very distant. She wanted to stop, to lie down, and to sleep for a hundred years.

"Oh, bless my little black soul, Mister Vandemar, do you see what I see?" The voice was soft, close: they must have been

nearer to her than she had imagined. "I spy, with my little eye, something that's going to be—"

"Dead in a minute, Mister Croup," said the flat voice, from above her.

"Our principal will be delighted."

And the girl pulled whatever she could find deep inside her soul, from all the pain, and the hurt, and the fear. She was spent, burnt out, and utterly exhausted. She had nowhere to go, no power left, no time. *"If it's the last door I open,"* she prayed, silently, to the Temple, to the Arch. *"Somewhere . . . anywhere . . . safe . . . ,"* and then she thought, wildly, *"Somebody."*

And, as she began to pass out, she tried to open a door.

As the darkness took her, she heard Mr. Croup's voice, as if from a long way away. It said, "Bugger and blast."

JESSICA AND RICHARD WALKED down the street toward the restaurant. She had her arm through his, and was walking as fast as her heels permitted. He hurried to keep up. Streetlights and the fronts of closed stores illuminated their path. They passed a stretch of tall, looming buildings, abandoned and lonely, bounded by a high brick wall.

"You are honestly telling me you had to promise them an extra fifty pounds for our table tonight? You are an idiot, Richard." Jessica, dark eyes flashing, was not even slightly amused.

"They had lost my reservation. And they said all the tables were booked." Their steps echoed off the high walls.

"They'll probably have us sitting by the kitchen," sighed Jessica. "Or the door. Did you tell them it was for Mister Stockton?"

"Yes," replied Richard.

Jessica sighed. She continued to drag him along, as a door opened in the wall, a little way ahead of them, and someone stepped out and stood swaying for one long terrible moment, and then collapsed to the concrete. Richard shivered and stopped in his tracks. Jessica tugged him into motion.

"Now, when you're talking to Mister Stockton, you must make sure you don't interrupt him. Or disagree with him—he doesn't like to be disagreed with. When he makes a joke, laugh. If you're in any doubt as to whether or not he's made a joke, look at me. I'll . . . mm, tap my forefinger."

They had reached the person on the sidewalk. Jessica stepped over the crumpled form. Richard hesitated. "Jessica?"

"You're right. He might think I'm bored," she mused. "I know," she said brightly, "if he makes a joke, I'll rub my earlobe."

"Jessica?" He could not believe she was simply ignoring the figure at their feet.

"What?" She was not pleased to be jerked out of her reverie.

"Look."

He pointed to the sidewalk. The person was facedown, and enveloped in bulky clothes; Jessica took his arm, and tugged him toward her. "Oh. I see. If you pay them any attention, Richard, they'll walk all over you. They all have homes, really. Once she's slept it off, I'm sure she'll be fine." *She?* Richard looked down. It was a girl. Jessica continued, "Now, I've told Mister Stockton that we—" Richard was down on one knee. "Richard? What are you doing?"

"She isn't drunk," said Richard. "She's hurt." He looked at his fingertips. "She's bleeding."

Jessica looked down at him, nervous and puzzled. "We're going to be late," she pointed out.

"She's *hurt*."

Jessica looked back at the girl on the sidewalk. Priorities; Richard had no priorities. "Richard. We're going to be late. Someone else will be along; someone else will help her."

The girl's face was crusted with dirt, and her clothes were wet with blood. "She's hurt," he said, simply. There was an expression on his face that Jessica hadn't seen before.

"Richard," she warned, and then she relented, a little, and offered a compromise. "Dial 999 and call an ambulance then. Quickly, now."

Suddenly the girl's eyes opened, white and wide in a face that was little more than a smudge of dust and blood. "Not a hospital, please. They'll find me. Take me somewhere safe. Please." Her voice was weak.

"You're bleeding," said Richard. He looked to see where she had come from, but the wall was blank and brick and unbroken. He looked back to her still form, and asked, "Why not a hospital?"

"Help me?" the girl whispered, and her eyes closed.

Again he asked her, "Why don't you want to go to the hospital?" This time there was no answer at all.

"When you call the ambulance," said Jessica, "don't give your name. You might have to make a statement or something, and then we'd be late, and I'm not having this evening ruined by . . . Richard? What are you doing?"

Richard had picked the girl up, cradling her in his arms. She was surprisingly light. "I'm taking her back to my place, Jess. I

can't just leave her. Tell Mister Stockton I'm really sorry, but it was an emergency. I'm sure he'll understand."

"Richard Oliver Mayhew," said Jessica, coldly. "You put that young person down and come back here this minute. Or this engagement is at an end as of now. I'm warning you."

Richard felt the sticky warmth of blood, soaking into his shirt. Sometimes, he realized, there is nothing you can do. He walked away.

Jessica stood there on the sidewalk, watching him ruin her big evening, and her eyes stung with tears. After a while he was out of sight, and then, and only then, did she say, loudly and distinctly, an unladylike "Shit," and fling her handbag as hard as she could onto the ground, hard enough to scatter her mobile phone and her lipstick and her planner and a handful of tampons across the concrete. And then, because there was nothing else to do, she picked them all up and put them back into her handbag and walked back down to the restaurant, to wait for Mr. Stockton.

Later, as she sipped her white wine, she tried to come up with plausible reasons why her fiancé was not with her, and found herself wondering desperately whether or not she could simply claim that Richard was dead.

"It was very sudden," said Jessica, wistfully, under her breath.

RICHARD DID NOT, AT any point on his walk, stop to think. It was not something over which he had any volition. Somewhere in the sensible part of his head, someone—a normal, sensible

Richard Mayhew—was telling him how ridiculous he was being: that he should just have called the police, or an ambulance; that it was dangerous to lift an injured person; that he had really, seriously, properly upset Jessica; that he was going to have to sleep on the sofa tonight; that he was spoiling his only good suit; that the girl smelled quite dreadful . . . but Richard found himself placing one foot in front of the other, and, arms cramping and back hurting, and ignoring the looks he got from the passersby, he just kept walking. And after a while he was at the ground-floor door of his building, and he was stumbling up the staircase, and then he was standing in front of the door to his flat and realizing that he had left his keys on the hall table, inside . . .

The girl reached out one filthy hand to the door, and it swung open.

Never thought I'd be pleased that the door hadn't latched properly, thought Richard, and he carried the girl in—closing the door behind him with his foot—and put her down on his bed. His shirt front was soaked in blood.

She seemed semi-conscious; her eyes were closed, but fluttering. He peeled off her leather jacket. There was a long cut on her left upper arm and shoulder. Richard caught his breath. "Look, I'm going to call a doctor," he said, quietly. "Can you hear me?"

Her eyes opened, wide and scared. "Please, no. It'll be fine. It's not as bad as it looks. I just need sleep. No doctors."

"But your arm—your shoulder—"

"I'll be fine. Tomorrow. Please?" It was little more than a whisper.

"Um, I suppose, all right," and with sanity beginning to assert itself, he said, "Look, can I ask—?"

But she was asleep. Richard took an old school scarf from his closet, and wrapped it firmly around her left upper arm and shoulder; he did not want her to bleed to death on his bed before he could get her to a doctor. And then he tiptoed out of his bedroom and shut the door behind him. He sat down on the sofa, in front of the television, and wondered what he had done.

2

H E IS SOMEWHERE DEEP *beneath the ground: in a tunnel, perhaps, or a sewer. Light comes in flickers, defining the darkness, not dispelling it. He is not alone. There are other people walking beside him, although he cannot see their faces. They are running, now, through the inside of the sewer, splashing through the mud and filth. Droplets of water fall slowly through the air, crystal clear in the darkness.*

He turns a corner, and the beast is waiting for him.

It is huge. It fills the space of the sewer: massive head down, bristled body and breath steaming in the chill of the air. Some kind of boar, he thinks at first, and then realizes that that must be nonsense: no boar could be so huge. It is the size of a bull, of a tiger, of a car.

It stares at him, and it pauses for a hundred years, while he lifts his spear. He glances at his hand, holding the spear, and observes that it is not his hand: the arm is furred with dark hair, the nails are almost claws.

And then the beast charges.

He throws his spear, but it is already too late, and he feels the beast slice his side with razor-sharp tusks, feels his life slip away into the mud, and he realizes he has fallen facedown into the water, which crimsons in thick swirls of suffocating blood. And he tries so to scream, he tries to wake up, but he can breathe only mud and blood and water, he can feel only pain . . .

"Bad dream?" asked the girl.

Richard sat up on the couch, gasping for breath. The curtains were still drawn, the lights and the television still on, but he could tell, from the pale light coming in through the cracks, that it was morning. He fumbled on the couch for the remote control, which had wedged itself into the small of his back during the night, and turned off the television.

"Yes," he said. "Sort of."

He wiped away the sleep grit that crusted his eyes, and took stock of himself, pleased to notice that he had at least taken off his shoes and jacket before he had fallen asleep. His shirt front was covered with dried blood and with dirt. The homeless girl didn't say anything. She looked bad: pale, beneath the grime and brown-dried blood, and small. She was dressed in a variety of clothes thrown over each other: odd clothes, dirty velvets, muddy lace, rips and holes through which other layers and styles could be seen. She looked, Richard thought, as if she'd done a midnight raid on the History of Fashion section of the Victoria

and Albert Museum, and was still wearing everything she'd taken. Her short hair was filthy, but looked like it might have been a dark reddish color under the dirt.

If there was one thing Richard really hated, it was people who stated the obvious: the kind of people who came up to him and said things that he was incapable of failing to notice for himself, such as, for example, "It's raining," or "The bottom just dropped out of your shopping bag and your food just fell into that puddle," or even, "Ooh. I bet that hurts."

"You're up, then," said Richard, and hated himself.

"Whose barony is this?" asked the girl. "Whose fiefdom?"

"Um. Sorry?"

She looked around her suspiciously. "Where am I?"

"Flat Four, Newton Mansions, Little Comden Street . . ." He stopped. She had opened the curtains, blinking at the cold daylight. The girl stared out at the rather ordinary view from Richard's window, astonished, peering wide-eyed at the cars and the buses and the tiny sprawl of shops—a newsagent's, a baker's, a chemist's and an off-licence liquor store—below them.

"I'm in London Above," she said, in a small voice.

"Yes, you're in London," said Richard. *Above what?* he wondered. "I think maybe you were in shock or something last night. That was a nasty cut on your arm." He waited for her to say something, to explain. She glanced at him, and then looked back down at the buses and the shops. Richard continued: "I, um, found you on the pavement. There was rather a lot of blood."

"Don't worry," she said, seriously. "Most of the blood was someone else's."

She let the curtain fall back. Then she began to unwrap the scarf, now bloodstained and crusted, from her arm. She examined the cut, and made a face. "We're going to have to do something about this," she said. "Do you want to give me a hand?"

Richard was beginning to feel a little out of his depth. "I don't really know too much about first aid," he said.

"Well," she said, "if you're really squeamish you only have to hold the bandages and tie the bits I can't reach. You do have bandages, don't you?"

Richard nodded. "Oh yes," he said. "In the first aid box. In the bathroom. Under the sink." And then he went into his bedroom, and changed his clothes, and wondered whether the mess on his shirt (his best shirt, bought for him by, oh God, Jessica, she would have *kittens*) would ever come off.

THE BLOODY WATER REMINDED him of something, some kind of dream he had once had, perhaps, but he could no longer for the life of him remember exactly what. He pulled the plug, let the water out of the sink, and filled it with clean water again, to which he added a cloudy splash of Dettol liquid disinfectant: the sharp antiseptic smell seemed so utterly sensible and medicinal, a remedy for the oddness of his situation, and his visitor. The girl leaned over the sink, and he splashed warm water over her arm and shoulder.

Richard was never as squeamish as he thought he was. Or rather, he was astonishingly squeamish when it came to blood on-screen: a good zombie movie or even an explicit medical drama would leave him huddled in a corner, hyperventilating,

with his hands over his eyes, muttering things like "Just tell me when it's over." But when it came to real blood, real pain, he simply got on and did something about it. They cleaned out the cut—which was much less severe than Richard remembered it from the night before—and bandaged it up, and the girl did her very best not to wince in the process. And Richard found himself wondering how old she was, and what she looked like under the grime, and why she was living on the streets and—

"What's your name?" she asked.

"Richard. Richard Mayhew. Dick." She nodded, as if she were committing it to memory. The doorbell rang. Richard looked at the mess in the bathroom, and the girl, and wondered how it would look to a sensible outside observer. Such as, for example . . . "Oh, Lor'," he said, realizing the worst. "I bet it's Jess. She's going to kill me." *Damage control. Damage control.* "Look," he told the girl. "You wait in here."

He shut the door of the bathroom behind him and walked down the hall. He opened the front door, and breathed a huge and quite heartfelt sigh of relief. It wasn't Jessica. It was—what? Mormons? Jehovah's Witnesses? The police? He couldn't tell. There were two of them, at any rate.

They wore black suits, which were slightly greasy, slightly frayed, and even Richard, who counted himself among the sartorially dyslexic, felt there was something odd about the cut of the coats. They were the kind of suits that might have been made by a tailor two hundred years ago who had had a modern suit described to him but had never actually seen one. The lines were wrong, and so were the grace notes.

A fox and a wolf, thought Richard, involuntarily. The man

in front, the fox, was a little shorter than Richard. He had lank, greasy hair, of an unlikely orange color, and a pallid complexion; and as Richard opened the door, he smiled, widely, and just a fraction too late, with teeth that looked like an accident in a graveyard. "A good morrow to you, good sir," he said, "on this fine and beautiful day."

"Ah. Hello," said Richard.

"We are conducting a personal inquiry of a delicate nature as it were, door to door. Do you mind if we come in?"

"Well, it's not very convenient right now," said Richard. Then he asked, "Are you with the police?" The second of the visitors, a tall man, the one he had thought of as a wolf, his gray and black hair cut bristle-short, stood a little behind his friend holding a stack of photocopies to his chest. He had said nothing until now—just waited, huge and impassive. Now he laughed, once, low and dirtily. There was something unhealthy about that laugh.

"The police? Alas," said the smaller man, "we cannot claim that felicity. A career in law and order, although indubitably enticing, was not inscribed on the cards Dame Fortuna dealt my brother and me. No, we are merely private citizens. Allow me to make introductions. I am Mister Croup, and this gentleman is my brother, Mister Vandemar."

They did not look like brothers. They did not look like anything Richard had seen before. "Your brother?" asked Richard. "Shouldn't you have the same name?"

"I am impressed. What a brain, Mister Vandemar. Keen and incisive isn't the half of it. Some of us are so sharp," he said as he leaned in closer to Richard, went up on tiptoes into Richard's

face, "we could just cut ourselves." Richard took an involuntary step backward. "Can we come inside?" asked Mr. Croup.

"What do you want?"

Mr. Croup sighed, in what he obviously imagined was a rather wistful manner. "We are looking for our sister," he explained. "A wayward child, willful and headstrong, who has close to broken our poor dear widowed mother's heart."

"Ran away," explained Mr. Vandemar, quietly. He thrust a photocopied sheet into Richard's hands. "She's a little . . . funny," he added, and then he twirled one finger next to his temple, to indicate that the girl was in fact a complete lunatic.

Richard looked down at the paper.

It said:

HAVE YOU SEEN THIS GIRL?

Beneath that was a photocopy-gray photograph of a girl who looked to Richard rather like a tidier, cleaner, longer-haired version of the young lady he had left in his bathroom.

Under that it said:

ANSWERS TO THE NAME OF DOREEN. BITES AND KICKS. RUNAWAY. TELL US IF YOU SAW HER. WANT HER BACK. REWARD PAYED.

And below that, a telephone number. Richard looked back at the photograph. It was definitely the girl in his bathroom. "No," he said. "I haven't seen her, I'm afraid. I'm sorry."

Mr. Vandemar, however, was not listening. He had raised his head, and was sniffing the air, like a man smelling something odd or unpleasant. Richard reached out to give him back his piece of paper, but the big man simply pushed past him, and walked into the flat, a wolf on the prowl. Richard ran after him. "What do you think you are doing? Will you stop that? Get out. Look, you can't go in there—" Because Mr. Vandemar was headed straight for the bathroom. Richard hoped that the girl—Doreen?—had had the presence of mind to lock the bathroom door. But no; it swung open at Mr. Vandemar's push. He walked in, and Richard, feeling like a small and ineffectual dog yapping at the heels of a postman, followed him in.

It was not a large bathroom. It contained a bath, a toilet, a sink, several bottles of shampoo, a bar of soap and a towel. When Richard had left it, a couple of minutes before, it had also contained a rather dirty, bloody girl, a very bloody sink, and an open first aid kit. Now it was gleamingly tidy.

There was nowhere the girl could have been hiding. Mr. Vandemar walked out of the bathroom, and pushed open Richard's bedroom door, walked in, looked around. "I don't know what you think you're doing," said Richard. "But if you two don't get out of my flat this minute, I'm phoning the police."

Then Mr. Vandemar, who had been in the process of examining Richard's living room, turned back toward Richard, and Richard suddenly realized he was very, very scared, like a small dog who had just discovered that what he had thought to be a postman was in fact an enormous dog-eating alien from the kind of film that Jessica had no time for. Richard found him-

self wondering whether Mr. Vandemar was the kind of person to whom you said, "Don't hurt me," and, if he was, whether it would do any good.

And then foxy Mr. Croup said, "Why yes, whatever can have come over you, Mister Vandemar? It's grief for our dear sweet sibling, I'll wager, has turned his head. Now apologize to the gentleman, Mister Vandemar."

Mr. Vandemar nodded, and pondered for a moment. "Thought I needed to use the toilet," he said. "Didn't. Sorry."

Mr. Croup began to walk down the hall, pushing Mr. Vandemar in front of him. "There. Now, you'll forgive my errant brother his lack of social graces, I trust. Worry over our poor dear widowed mother, and over our sister, whom even as we speak is wandering the streets of London unloved and uncared for, has nigh unhinged him, I'll be bound. But for all that, he's a good fellow to have at your side. Is't not so, stout fellow?" They were out of Richard's flat now, into the stairwell. Mr. Vandemar said nothing. He did not look nigh unhinged with grief. Croup turned back to Richard, and essayed another foxy smile. "You will tell us if you see her," he said.

"Good-bye," said Richard. Then he closed the door and locked it. And, for the first time since he had lived there, he attached the security chain.

"I'm not fat," said Mr. Vandemar.

Mr. Croup, who had cut Richard's phone line at the first mention of calling the police, and was starting to wonder whether he had cut the right cord or not, twentieth-century telecommuni-

cations technology not being his strongest point, took a handbill from Vandemar.

"I never said you were," he said. "Spit!"

Mr. Vandemar hawked a mouthful of phlegm from the back of his throat, and spat it neatly onto the back of the handbill. Mr. Croup slapped the handbill hard onto the wall, next to Richard's door. It stuck immediately and stuck hard.

HAVE YOU SEEN THIS GIRL? it asked.

"Said 'stout fellow.' Means fat."

"Stout also means strong, sound, sturdy, stanch, lusty, vigorous, brave, resolute and intrepid," said Mr. Croup. "Do you believe him?"

They turned back down the stairs. "Do I buggery," said Mr. Vandemar. "I could smell her."

RICHARD WAITED BY HIS front door until he heard the main door slam, several floors below. He was walking down the hallway, back toward the bathroom, when the phone rang loudly, startling him. He sprinted back down the hall, and picked up the handpiece. "Hello?" said Richard. "Hello?"

No sound came out of the handpiece. Instead, there was a click, and Jessica's voice came out of the answering machine on the table next to the phone. Her voice said, "Richard? This is Jessica. I'm sorry you're not there, because this would have been our last conversation, and I did so want to tell you this to your face." The phone, he realized, was completely dead. The handpiece trailed a foot or so of cord, and was then neatly cut off. He shouted into it anyway, saying things like "Jessica," and "I am here," and "Please don't hang up."

"You embarrassed me very deeply last night, Richard," the voice continued. "As far as I'm concerned our engagement is at an end. I have no intention of returning the ring, nor indeed of ever seeing you again. I trust you and your lame duck will rot in hell. Buh-bye."

"Jessica!" shouted Richard, hoping, perhaps by sheer volume, to penetrate the telecommunications network. The tape stopped turning, there was another click, and the little red light began to flash.

"Bad news?" asked the girl. She was standing just behind him, in the mini-kitchen part of the flat, with her arm neatly bandaged. She was getting out teabags, putting them in mugs. The kettle was boiling.

"Yes," said Richard. "Very bad." He walked over to her, handed her the HAVE YOU SEEN THIS GIRL? poster. "That's you, isn't it?"

She raised an eyebrow. "The photograph's me."

"And you are . . . Doreen?"

She shook her head. "I'm Door, Richardrichardmayhewdick. Milk and sugar?"

Richard was feeling utterly out of his depth by now. And he said, "Richard. Just Richard. No sugar." Then he said, "Look, if it isn't a personal question, what happened to you?"

Door poured the boiling water into the mugs. "You don't want to know," she said, simply.

"Oh, well, I'm sorry if I—"

"No. Richard. Honestly, you *don't* want to know. It wouldn't do you any good. You've done more than you should have already."

She removed the teabags, and handed him a mug of tea. He

took it from her and realized that he was still carrying around the telephone handset. "Well. I mean. I couldn't just have left you there."

"You could have," she said. "You didn't." She pressed herself up against the wall and peered out of the window. Richard walked over to the window and looked out. Across the street, Mr. Croup and Mr. Vandemar were coming out of the newsagent's, and HAVE YOU SEEN THIS GIRL? was stuck in a place of prominence in the newsagent's window.

"Are they really your brothers?" he asked.

"Please," said Door, unimpressed. "Give me a break."

He sipped his tea, and tried to pretend that everything was normal. "So where were you?" he asked. "Just now?"

"I was here," she said. "Look, with those two still around we have to get a message to—" She paused. "To someone who can help. I don't dare leave here."

"Well, isn't there somewhere you could go? Someone that we could phone?"

She took the dead handset from his hand, cut wire trailing, and shook her head. "My friends aren't on the telephone," she said. She put the phone back down in its cradle, where it sat, useless and lonely. Then she smiled, fast and wicked. "Breadcrumbs," she said.

"Sorry?" said Richard.

THERE WAS A LITTLE window in the back of the bedroom which looked out on an area of roof tiles and gutters. Door stood on Richard's bed to reach it, opened the window and sprinkled

the breadcrumbs around. "But I don't understand," said Richard.

"Of course you don't," she agreed. "Now, shush." There was a flutter of wings, and the purple-gray-green sheen of a pigeon. It pecked at the breadcrumbs, and Door reached out her right hand and picked it up. It looked at her curiously but made no complaint.

They sat down on the bed. Door got Richard to hold the pigeon, while she attached a message to its leg, using a vivid blue rubber band that Richard had previously used to keep his electricity bills all in one place. Richard was not an enthusiastic holder of pigeons, even at the best of times. "I don't see the point in this," he explained. "I mean, it's not a homing pigeon. It's just a normal London pigeon. The kind that craps on Lord Nelson."

"That's right," said Door. Her cheek was grazed, and her dirty reddish hair was tangled; tangled, but not matted. And her eyes . . . Richard realized that he could not tell what color her eyes were. They were not blue, nor green, nor brown, nor gray; they reminded him of fire opals: there were burning greens and blues and even reds and yellows that vanished and glinted as she moved. She took the bird from him, gently, held it up, and looked it in the face. It tipped its head on one side and stared back at her with bead-black eyes. "Okay," she said, and then she made a noise that sounded like the liquid burbling of pigeons. "Okay *Crrppllrr,* you're looking for the Marquis de Carabas. You got that?"

The pigeon burbled liquidly back at her.

"Attagirl. Now, this is important, so you'd better—" The pigeon interrupted her with a rather impatient-sounding bur-

ble. "I'm sorry," said Door. "You know what you're doing, of course." She took the bird to the window, and let it go.

Richard had watched the whole routine with some amazement. "Do you know, it almost sounded like it understood you?" he said, as the bird shrank in the sky and vanished behind some rooftops.

"How about that," said Door. "Now. We wait."

She went over to the bookshelf in the corner of the bedroom, found a copy of *Mansfield Park* Richard had not previously known that he possessed, and went into the living room. Richard followed her. She settled herself on his sofa and opened the book.

"So is it short for Doreen?" he asked.

"What?"

"Your name."

"No. It's just Door."

"How do you spell it?"

"D-o-o-r. Like something you walk through to go places."

"Oh." He had to say something, so he said: "What kind of a name is Door, then?"

And she looked at him with her odd-colored eyes, and she said, "My name." Then she went back to Jane Austen.

Richard picked up the remote control, and turned on the television. Then he changed the channel. Changed it again. Sighed. Changed it again. "So, what are we waiting for?"

Door turned the page. She didn't look up. "A reply."

"What kind of a reply?" Door shrugged. "Oh. Right." It occurred to him then that her skin was very white, now some of the dirt and blood had been removed. He wondered if she were

pale from illness, or from loss of blood, or if she simply didn't get out much, or was anemic. Maybe she'd been in prison, although she looked a bit too young for that. Perhaps the big man had been telling the truth when he said she was mad. "Listen, when those men came over—"

"Men?" A flash of the opal-colored eyes.

"Croup and, um, Vanderbilt."

"Vandemar." She mused, for a moment, then nodded. "I suppose you could call them men, yes. Two legs, two arms, a head each."

Richard kept going. "When they came in here, before. Where were you?"

She licked her finger and turned a page. "I was here."

"But—" He stopped talking, out of words. There wasn't anywhere in the flat that she could have hidden herself. But she hadn't left the flat. But—

There was a scratching noise, and a dark shape rather larger than a mouse scurried out from the mess of videotapes beneath the television. "Jesus!" said Richard, and he threw the remote control at it as hard as he could. It crashed into the videos with a bang. Of the dark shape there was no sign.

"Richard!" said Door.

"It's okay," he explained. "I think it was just a rat or something."

She glared at him. "Of course it was a rat. You'll have scared it now, poor thing." She looked around the room, then made a low whistling noise between her front teeth. "Hello?" she called. She knelt on the floor, *Mansfield Park* abandoned. "Hello?"

She flashed a glance back at Richard. "If you've hurt it . . . ,"

she threatened; then, softly, to the room, "I'm sorry, he's an idiot. Hello?"

"I'm not an idiot," said Richard.

"Shh," she said. "Hello?" A pink nose and two small black eyes peered out from under the sofa. The rest of the head followed, and it scrutinized its surroundings suspiciously. It was indeed much too big to be a mouse, Richard was certain of that. "Hi," said Door, warmly. "Are you okay?" She extended her hand. The animal climbed into it, then ran up her arm, nestling in the crook of it. Door stroked its side with her finger. It was dark brown, with a long pink tail. There was something that looked like a folded piece of paper attached to its side.

"It's a rat," said Richard, feeling that there were some times when a man could be forgiven for stating the obvious.

"Yes, it is. Are you going to apologize?"

"What?"

"Apologize."

Maybe he hadn't heard her properly. Maybe he was the one who was going mad. "To a rat?"

Door said nothing, fairly meaningfully.

"I'm sorry," said Richard, to the rat, with dignity, "if I startled you."

The rat looked up at Door. "No, he really does mean it," she said. "He's not just saying it. So what have you got for me?" She fumbled at the rat's side, and pulled out a much-folded piece of brown paper, which had been held on with something that looked to Richard rather like a vivid blue rubber band.

She opened it up: a piece of ragged-edged brown paper, with spidery black handwriting on it. She read it, and nodded.

"Thank you," she said, to the rat. "I appreciate all you've done." It scampered down onto the couch, glared up at Richard for a moment, and then was gone in the shadows.

The girl called Door passed the paper to Richard. "Here," she said. "Read this."

IT WAS LATE AFTERNOON in Central London, and, with autumn drawing on, it was getting dark. Richard had taken the Tube to Tottenham Court Road, and was now walking west down Oxford Street, holding the piece of paper. Oxford Street was the retail hub of London, and even now the sidewalks were packed with shoppers and tourists.

"It's a message," she said, when she gave it to him. "From the Marquis de Carabas."

Richard was sure he had heard the name before. "That's nice," he said. "Out of postcards, was he?"

"This is quicker."

He passed the lights and the noise of the Virgin Megastore, and the shop that sold tourists souvenir London police helmets and little red London buses, and the place next door that sold individual slices of pizza, and then he turned right.

"You have to follow the directions written on here. Try not to let anyone follow you." Then she sighed, and said, "I really shouldn't involve you this much."

"If I follow these directions . . . will it speed up getting you out of here?"

"Yes."

He turned into Hanway Street and, while he had taken only

a few steps from the well-lit bustle of Oxford Street, he might have been in another city: Hanway Street was empty, forsaken; a narrow, dark road, little more than an alleyway, filled with gloomy record shops and closed restaurants, the only light spilling out from the secretive drinking clubs on the upper floors of buildings. He walked along it, feeling apprehensive.

"*. . . turn right into Hanway Street, left into Hanway Place, then right again into Orme Passage. Stop at the first streetlight you come to . . .*"

"*Are you sure this is right?*"

"*Yes.*"

He did not remember an Orme Passage, although he had been to Hanway Place before: there was an underground Indian restaurant there of which Garry-from-work was quite fond. As far as Richard could remember, Hanway Place was a dead end. The Mandeer, that was the restaurant. He passed the brightly lit front door, the restaurant's steps leading invitingly down into the underground, and then he turned left . . .

He had been wrong. There *was* an Orme Passage. He could see the sign for it, high on the wall.

ORME PASSAGE W1

No wonder he hadn't noticed it before: it was scarcely more than a narrow alleyway between houses, lit by a sputtering gas jet. *You don't see many of those anymore,* thought Richard, and he held up his instructions to the gaslight, peering at them.

"*'Then turn around thrice, widdershins'?*"

"*Widdershins is anticlockwise, Richard.*"

He turned, three times, feeling stupid. "Look, why do I have to do all this, just to see your friend. I mean, all this nonsense—"

"It's not nonsense. Really. Just—humor me on this, okay?" And she had smiled at him.

He stopped turning. Then he walked down the alley to the end. Nothing. No one. Just a metal garbage can, and beside it something that might have been a pile of rags. "Hello?" called Richard. "Is anyone here? I'm Door's friend. Hello?"

No. There was no one there. Richard was rather relieved. Now he could go home and explain to the girl that nothing had happened. Then he would call in the appropriate authorities, and they would sort it all out. He crumpled the paper into a tight ball, and tossed it toward the bin.

What Richard had taken for a pile of rags unfolded, expanded, stood up in one fluid motion, and a hand caught the crumpled paper in midair.

"Mine, I believe," said the Marquis de Carabas. He wore a huge dandyish black coat that was not quite a frock coat nor exactly a trench coat, and high black boots, and, beneath his coat, raggedy clothes. His eyes burned white in an extremely dark face. And he grinned white teeth, momentarily, as if at a private joke of his own, and bowed to Richard, and said, "De Carabas, at your service, and you are . . . ?"

"Um," said Richard. "Er. Um."

"You are Richard Mayhew, the young man who rescued our wounded Door. How is she now?"

"Er. She's okay. Her arm's still a bit—"

"Her recovery time will undoubtedly astonish us all. Her family had remarkable recuperative powers. It's a wonder any-

one managed to kill them at all, isn't it?" The man who called himself the Marquis de Carabas walked restlessly up and down the alley. Richard could already tell that he was the type of person who was always in motion, like a great cat.

"Somebody killed Door's family?" asked Richard.

"We're not going to get very far if you keep repeating everything I say, now, are we?" said the Marquis, who was now standing in front of Richard. "Sit down," he ordered. Richard looked around the alley for something to sit on. The Marquis put a hand on his shoulder and sent him sprawling to the cobblestones. "She knows I don't come cheap. What exactly is she offering me?"

"Sorry?"

"What's the deal? She sent you here to negotiate, young man. I'm not cheap, and I never give freebies."

Richard shrugged, as well as he could shrug from a supine position. "She said to tell you that she wants you to accompany her home—wherever that is—and to fix her up with a bodyguard."

Even when the Marquis was at rest, his eyes never ceased moving. Up, down, around, as if he were looking for something, thinking about something. Adding, subtracting, evaluating. Richard wondered whether the man was quite sane. "And she's offering me . . . ?"

"Well. Nothing."

The Marquis blew on his fingernails and polished them on the lapel of his remarkable coat. Then he turned away. "She's offering *me*. Nothing." He sounded offended.

Richard scrambled back up to his feet. "Well, she didn't say

anything about money. She just said she was going to have to owe you a favor."

The eyes flashed. "Exactly what kind of favor?"

"A really big one," said Richard. "She said she was going to have to owe you a really big favor."

De Carabas grinned to himself, like a hungry panther sighting a lost peasant child. Then he turned on Richard. "And you left her alone?" he asked. "With Croup and Vandemar out there? Well, what are you waiting for?" He knelt down, and took a small metal object from a pocket, which he pushed into a manhole cover at the edge of the alley and twisted. The manhole cover came up, easily; the Marquis put away the metal object, and took something out of another pocket that reminded Richard a little of a long firework, or a flare. He held it in one hand, ran his other hand along it, and the far end erupted into scarlet flame.

"Can I ask a question?" said Richard.

"Certainly not," said the Marquis. "You don't ask any questions. You don't get any answers. You don't stray from the path. You don't even think about what's happening to you right now. Got it?"

"But—"

"Most important of all: no buts. Now, we have a damsel to undistress," said de Carabas. "And time is of the essence. Move." He pointed into the depths revealed by the open manhole cover. Richard moved, clambering down the metal ladder set into the wall beneath the manhole, feeling so far out of his depth that he would have needed a bathyscaphe to ever see the surface again.

RICHARD WONDERED WHERE THEY were. This didn't seem to be a sewer. Perhaps it was a tunnel for telephone cables, or for very small trains. Or for . . . something else. He realized that he did not know very much about what went on beneath the streets of London. He walked nervously, worried that he'd catch his feet in something, that he'd stumble in the darkness and break his ankle. De Carabas strode on ahead, nonchalantly, apparently uncaring of whether Richard was with him or not. The crimson flame cast huge shadows on the tunnel walls.

Richard ran to catch up. "Let's see . . . ," said de Carabas. "I'll need to get her to the market. The next one's in, mm, two days' time, if I recall correctly, as of course I unfailingly do. I can hide her until then."

"Market?" asked Richard.

"The Floating Market. But you don't want to know about that. No more questions."

Richard looked around. "Well, I was going to ask you where we are now. But I suppose you were going to refuse to tell me."

The Marquis grinned once more. "Very good," he said, approvingly. "You are in enough trouble already."

"You can say that again," sighed Richard. "My fiancée's dumped me, and I'll probably have to get a new telephone—"

"Temple and Arch. A telephone is the least of your troubles." De Carabas put the flare down on the ground, resting it against the wall, where it continued to sputter and flame, and he began to climb up some metal rungs set into the wall. Richard hesitated, and then followed him. The rungs were cold and rusted;

he could feel them crumbling roughly against his hands as he climbed, fragments of rust getting in his eyes and mouth. The scarlet light from below was flickering, and then it went out. They climbed in total darkness.

"So, are we going back to Door?" he asked.

"Eventually. There's a little something I need to organize first. Insurance. And when we get into daylight, don't look down."

"Why not?" asked Richard. And then daylight hit his face, and he looked down.

IT WAS DAYLIGHT (*How was it daylight? a tiny voice asked, in the back of his head. It had been almost night when he entered the alley, what, an hour ago?*), and he was holding on to a metal ladder that ran up the outside of a very high building (*but a few seconds ago he was climbing up the same ladder, and he had been inside, hadn't he?*), and below him, he could see . . .

London.

Tiny cars. Tiny buses and taxis. Tiny buildings. Trees. Miniature lorries. Tiny, tiny people. They swam in and out of focus beneath him.

To say that Richard Mayhew was not very good at heights would be perfectly accurate, but would fail to give the full picture; it would be like describing the planet Jupiter as bigger than a duck. Richard hated cliff tops, and high buildings: somewhere not far inside him was the fear—the stark, utter, silently screaming terror—that if he got too close to the edge, then something would take over, and he would find himself

walking to the edge of a cliff top and then he would just step off into space. It was as if he could not entirely trust himself, and that scared Richard more than the simple fear of falling ever could. So he called it vertigo, and hated it and himself, and kept away from high places.

Richard froze on the ladder. His hands clamped tightly to the rungs. His eyes hurt, somewhere behind the eyeballs. He started breathing too fast, too deeply. "Somebody," said an amused voice above him, "wasn't listening, was he?"

"I . . ." Richard's throat didn't work. He swallowed, moistening it. "I can't move." His hands were sweating. What if they sweated so much that he simply slipped off into the void . . . ?

"Of course you can move. Or, if you don't you can stay here, hanging on to the side of the wall until your hands freeze and your legs buckle and you tumble to a messy death a thousand feet below." Richard looked up at the Marquis. He was looking down at Richard, and still smiling; when he saw that Richard was watching him he let go of the rungs with both his hands, and waggled his fingers at him.

Richard felt a wave of sympathetic vertigo run through him. "Bastard," he said, under his breath, and he let go of the rung with his right hand and moved it up eight inches, until it found the next rung. Then he moved his right leg up one rung. Then he did it again, with his left hand. After a while he found himself at the edge of a flat roof, and he stepped over it, and collapsed.

He was aware that the Marquis was striding along the roof, away from him. Richard felt the rooftop with his hands, and felt the solid structure beneath him. His heart was pounding in his chest.

A gruff voice some distance away shouted, "You're not wanted here, de Carabas. Get away. Clear off."

"Old Bailey," he heard de Carabas say. "You're looking wonderfully healthy."

And then footsteps shuffled toward him, and a finger prodded him gently in the ribs. "You all right, laddie? I've got some stew cookin' back there. You want some? It's starling."

Richard opened his eyes. "No thank you," he said.

He saw the feathers first. He wasn't sure if it was a coat, or a cape, or some kind of strange covering that had no name, but whatever kind of outer garment it was, it was covered thickly and entirely in feathers. A face, kind and creased, with gray mutton-chop whiskers, peered out from the top of the feathers. The body beneath the face, where it was not covered with feathers, was wound round and about with ropes. Richard found himself remembering a theatrical performance of *Robinson Crusoe* he had been taken to, as a child: this was what Robinson Crusoe might have looked like, if he had been shipwrecked on a rooftop instead of a desert island.

"They call me Old Bailey, lad," said the Robinson Crusoe man. He fumbled at a battered pair of glasses, on a string around his neck, and pulled them on, staring through them at Richard. "I don't recognize ye. What barony do you give fealty to? What's your name?"

Richard pulled himself into a sitting position. They were on the roof of an old building, built of brown stone, with a tower above them. Weathered gargoyles, missing wings and limbs and, in a couple of cases, even heads, jutted sadly from the corners of the tower. From far below he could hear the wail of a police

siren, and the muted roar of traffic. Across the rooftop, in the shadow of the tower, was something that looked like a tent; an old brown tent, much-mended, spackled white with bird shit. He opened his mouth to tell the old man his name.

"You. Shut up," said the Marquis de Carabas. "Don't say another word." Then he turned to Old Bailey. "People who put their noses where they aren't wanted sometimes"—he snapped his fingers, loudly, beneath the old man's nose, making him jump—"lose them. Now. You've owed me a favor for twenty years, Old Bailey. A big favor. And I'm calling it in."

The old man blinked. "I was a fool," he said, quietly.

"No fool like an old fool," agreed the Marquis. He reached a hand into an inside pocket of his coat, and pulled out a silver box, larger than a snuff box, smaller than a cigar box, and a good deal more ornate than either. "Do you know what this is?"

"I wish I didn't."

"You'll keep it safe for me."

"I don't want it."

"You don't have any choice," said the Marquis. The old roof man took the silver box from him, and held it, awkwardly, in both hands, as if it were something that might explode at any moment. The Marquis prodded Richard gently with his square-toed black boot. "Right," he said. "We'd better get a move on, hadn't we?" He strode off across the roof and Richard got to his feet and followed, keeping well away from the side of the building. The Marquis opened a door in the side of the tower, beside a high cluster of chimneys, and they went down a poorly lit spiral staircase.

"Who was that man?" asked Richard, peering against the

dim light. Their footsteps echoed and reverberated down the metal stairs.

The Marquis de Carabas snorted. "You haven't heard a word I've said, have you? You're in trouble already. Everything you do, everything you say, everything you hear, just makes it worse. You had better pray you haven't stepped too far in."

Richard put his head on one side. "Excuse me," he said. "I know this is a personal question. But are you clinically insane?"

"Possible, but very unlikely. Why?"

"Well," said Richard. "One of us must be."

It was now completely dark, and Richard stumbled slightly as he reached the last of the steps and found himself looking for a step that wasn't there. "Mind your head," said the Marquis, and he opened a door. Richard banged his forehead into something hard, and said, "Ow," and then stepped out, through a low door, shielding his eyes against the light.

Richard rubbed his forehead, then he rubbed his eyes. The door they had just come through was the door to the broom closet in the stairwell of his apartment building. It was filled with brooms, and dusters, and an elderly mop, and a huge variety of cleaning fluids, powders and waxes. It had no stairs at the back of it, that he could see, just a wall, on which a stained old calendar hung, quite uselessly, unless 1979 ever came back around.

The Marquis was examining the HAVE YOU SEEN THIS GIRL? poster, stuck beside Richard's front door. "Not her best side," he said.

Richard shut the door to the broom closet. He took his keys from his back pocket, unlocked his front door, and he

was home. It was, he was rather relieved to see through the kitchen windows, nighttime once more.

"Richard," said Door. "You did it." She had washed herself while he was gone, and her layers of clothes looked like she had at least made an effort to get the worst of the filth and the blood off them. The grime was gone from her face and hands. Her hair, when washed, was a dark shade of auburn, with copper and bronze highlights. Richard wondered how old she was: fifteen? Sixteen? Older? He still couldn't tell.

She had put on the brown leather jacket she had been wearing when he had found her, huge and enveloping, like an old flying jacket, which somehow made her look smaller than she was, and even more vulnerable.

"Well, yes," said Richard.

The Marquis de Carabas went down on one knee to the girl, and lowered his head. "My lady," he said.

She seemed uncomfortable. "Oh, do get up, de Carabas. I'm pleased you came."

He stood, in one smooth movement. "I understand," he said, "that the words *favor, really,* and *big* have been used. In conjunction, and the right order."

"Later." She walked over to Richard, and took his hands in hers. "Richard. Thanks. I really appreciate everything you've done. I changed the sheets on the bed. And I wish there was something I could do to pay you back."

"You're leaving?"

She nodded. "I'll be safe now. More or less. I hope. For a little while."

"Where are you going now?"

She smiled, gently, and shook her head. "Uh-uh. I'm out of your life. And you've been wonderful." She went up on tiptoes then, and kissed him on the cheek, as friends kiss friends.

"If I ever need to get in touch with you—?"

"You don't. Ever. And . . ." And then she paused. "Look, I'm sorry, okay?"

Richard inspected his feet, in an awkward sort of way. "There's nothing to be sorry about," he said, and added, doubtfully, "It was fun." Then he looked up again.

But there was nobody there.

3

O N SUNDAY MORNING RICHARD took the Batmobile-shaped telephone he had been given for Christmas several years earlier by his Aunt Maude out from the drawer at the bottom of the wardrobe and plugged it into the wall. He tried telephoning Jessica, but without success. Her answering machine was turned off, as was her cellular phone. He supposed she had gone back to her parents' house in the country, and he had no desire to phone her there. Richard found Jessica's parents deeply intimidating, each in their separate ways. Neither of them had entirely approved of him as a future son-in-law: her mother had, in fact, on one occasion, mentioned to him, quite casually, how disappointed they

were by Richard and Jessica's engagement, and her conviction that Jessica could, if she wanted to, do so much better.

Richard's own parents were both dead. His father had died quite suddenly when Richard was still a small boy, of a heart attack. His mother had died very slowly after that, and once Richard had left home she had simply faded away: six months after he moved to London he had taken the sleeper back up to Scotland, and had spent her last two days in a small county hospital, sitting beside her bed. Sometimes she had known him; at other times she had called him by his father's name.

Richard sat on his couch, and he brooded. The events of the previous two days became less and less real, increasingly less likely. What was real was the message that Jessica had left on his machine, telling him she did not want to see him again. He played it, and replayed it, that Sunday, hoping each time that she would relent, that he'd hear warmth in her voice. He never did.

He thought about going out and buying a Sunday paper, but decided not to. Arnold Stockton, Jessica's boss, a many-chinned self-made caricature of a man, owned all the Sunday papers that Rupert Murdoch had failed to buy. His own papers talked about him, and so did the rest. Reading a Sunday paper would, Richard suspected, probably wind up reminding him of the dinner he had failed to attend on Friday night, so instead Richard had a long hot bath, and a number of sandwiches, and several cups of tea. He watched a little Sunday afternoon television and constructed conversations with Jessica in his head. At the end of each mental conversation they would make wild, angry, tear-stained and passionate love; and then everything would be all right.

On Monday morning Richard's alarm failed to go off. He came out onto the street at a run at ten to nine, briefcase swinging, staring up and down the road like a madman, praying for a taxi. Then he sighed with relief, because a big black car was heading down the road toward him, its yellow "TAXI" sign bright. He waved at it and yelled.

The taxi slid gently past him, ignoring him completely, turned a corner and was gone.

Another taxi. Another yellow for-hire light. This time Richard stepped out into the middle of the road to flag it down. It swerved past him and continued on its way. Richard began to swear under his breath. Then he ran for the nearest Tube station.

He pulled out a pocketful of coins, stabbed the button of the ticket machine for a single ticket to Charing Cross, and thumbed his change into the slot. Every coin he put in went straight through the guts of the machine and clattered into the tray at the bottom. No ticket appeared. He tried another ticket machine, with the same lack of result. And another. The ticket seller in the office was speaking to someone on the telephone when Richard went over to complain and to buy his ticket manually; and despite—or perhaps because of—Richard's cries of "Hey!" and "Excuse me!" and his desperate tapping on the Plexiglas barrier with a coin, the man remained resolutely on the telephone.

"Fuck it," announced Richard, and he vaulted the barrier. No one stopped him; no one seemed to care. He ran, breathless and sweating, down the escalator, and made it onto the crowded platform just as a train came in.

As a child, Richard had had nightmares in which he simply wasn't there, in which, no matter how much noise he made, no matter what he did, nobody ever noticed him at all. He began to feel like that now, as people pushed in front of him; he was buffeted by the crowd, pushed this way and that by commuters getting off, by others getting on.

He persisted, pushing and shoving in his turn, until he was almost on—he had one arm inside the train—when the doors began to hiss closed. He pulled his hand back, but his coat sleeve was trapped. Richard began to hammer on the door, and to shout, expecting the driver at least to open the door enough for him to free his sleeve. But instead the train began to move off and Richard was forced to run down the platform, stumbling, faster and faster. He dropped his briefcase onto the platform, pulled desperately at his sleeve with his free hand. The sleeve ripped, and he fell forward, scraping his hand on the platform, ripping his trousers at the knee. Richard climbed, a little unsteadily, to his feet, then walked back down the platform, and retrieved his briefcase.

He looked at his ripped sleeve and his grazed hand and his torn trousers. Then he walked up the stone stairs and out of the Underground station. Nobody asked him for a ticket on the way out.

"I'M SORRY I'M LATE," said Richard, to no one in particular in the crowded office. The clock on the office wall said that it was 10:30. He dropped his briefcase on his chair, wiped the sweat from his face with his handkerchief. "You wouldn't believe what it was like, getting here," he continued. "It was a nightmare."

He looked down at his desktop. There was something missing. Or, more precisely, there was everything missing. "Where are my things?" he asked the room, a little more loudly. "Where're my telephones? Where are my trolls?"

He checked the desk drawers. They were empty too: not even a Mars Bar wrapper or a twisted paper clip to show that Richard had ever been there. Sylvia was coming toward him, in conversation with two rather hefty gentlemen. Richard walked over to her. "Sylvia? What's going on?"

"I'm sorry?" said Sylvia, politely. She pointed the desk out to the hefty gentlemen, who each took an end of it, and began to carry it out of the office. "Careful now," she told them.

"My desk. Where are they taking it?"

Sylvia stared at him, gently puzzled. "And you are . . . ?"

I don't need this shit, thought Richard. "Richard," he said, sarcastically. "Richard Mayhew."

"Ah," said Sylvia. Then her attention slid off Richard, like water off an oiled duck, and she said, "No, not over there. For heaven's sakes," to the removal men, and hurried after them as they carried off Richard's desk.

Richard watched her go. Then he walked through the office until he got to Garry's workstation. Garry was answering e-mail. Richard looked at the screen: the e-mail Garry seemed to be writing was both sexually explicit and addressed to someone who was not Garry's girlfriend. Embarrassed, Richard moved around to the other side of the desk.

"Garry. What's going on? Is this a joke or something?"

Garry looked around, as if he had heard something. He flicked the keyboard, activating a screen saver of dancing hippopotami, then he shook his head as if to clear it, picked up the

telephone, and began to dial. Richard slammed his hand down on the phone, cutting Garry off.

"Look, this isn't funny, Garry. I don't know what everyone's playing at." Finally, to his enormous relief, Garry looked up at him. Richard continued, "If I've been fired then just tell me I've been fired, but all this pretending I'm not here . . ."

And then Garry smiled and said, "Hi. Yeah. I'm Garry Perunu. Can I help you?"

"I don't think so," said Richard, coldly, and he walked out of the office, leaving his briefcase behind him.

RICHARD'S OFFICES WERE ON the third floor of a big, old, rather drafty building, just off the Strand. Jessica worked about halfway up a large crystalline, mirrored structure in the City of London, fifteen minutes' walk up the road.

Richard jogged up the road. He got to the Stockton building in ten minutes, walked straight past the uniformed security guards on duty on the ground floor, stepped into the elevator, and went up. The inside of the elevator was mirrored, and he stared at himself as he went up. His tie was half-undone and askew, his coat was ripped, his trousers torn, his hair was a sweaty mess . . . God, he looked awful.

There was a fluting tone, and the elevator door opened. The floor of the Stockton building on which Jessica worked was quite opulent, in an under-decorated sort of way. There was a receptionist by the lift, a poised and elegant creature, who looked like her take-home pay beat Richard's hands-down. She was reading *Cosmopolitan*. She did not look up as Richard came over.

"I need to talk to Jessica Bartram," said Richard. "It's important. I have to speak with her."

The receptionist ignored him, intent upon examining her nails. Richard walked down the corridor until he got to Jessica's office. He opened the door, and went in. She was standing in front of three large posters, each advertising "Angels over England—A Traveling Exhibition," each with a different image of an angel on it. She turned as he came in, and she smiled warmly at him.

"Jessica. Thank God. Listen, I think I'm going mad or something. It started when I couldn't get a taxi this morning, and then the office and the Tube and—" He showed her his ragged sleeve. "It's like I've become some kind of non-person." She smiled at him some more, reassuringly. "Look," said Richard. "I'm sorry about the other night. Well, not about what I did, but about upsetting you, and . . . look, I'm sorry, and it's all crazy, and I don't honestly know what to do."

And Jessica nodded, and continued to smile sympathetically, and then she said, "You're going to think I'm absolutely awful, but I have a really dreadful memory for faces. Give me a second, and I know I'll get it."

And at that point, Richard knew that it was real, and a heavy dread settled in the pit of his stomach. Whatever madness was happening that day was really happening. It was no joke, no trick or prank. "It's okay," he said, dully. "Forget it."

And he walked away, out the door and down the corridor. He was almost at the lift when she called his name.

"Richard!"

He turned. It *had* been a joke. Some kind of petty revenge. Something he could explain.

"Richard . . . Maybury?" She seemed proud of herself for remembering that much.

"Mayhew," said Richard, and he got into the elevator, and the doors sang a sad fluting downward trill as they closed behind him.

RICHARD WALKED BACK TO his flat, upset and confused and angry. Sometimes he would wave at taxis, but never with any real hope that they would stop, and none of them did. His feet hurt, and his eyes stung, and he knew that soon enough he would wake up from today and a proper Monday, a sensible Monday, a decent, honest Monday would begin.

When he reached the flat, he filled the bathtub with hot water, abandoned his clothes on the bed, and, naked, walked through the hall and climbed into the relaxing waters. He had almost dozed off when he heard a key turn, a door open and close, and a smooth male voice say, "Of course, you're the first I've shown around today, but I've got a list of people as long as your arm who are interested."

"It's not as large as I imagined, from the details your office sent us," said a woman.

"It's compact, yes. But I like to think of that as a virtue."

Richard had not bothered locking the bathroom door. He was, after all, the only person there.

A gruffer, rougher male voice said, "Thought you said it was an unfurnished flat. Looks pretty damned furnished to me."

"The previous tenant must have left some of his accoutrements behind. Funny. They never told me anything about that."

Richard stood up in the bathtub. Then, because he was naked, and the people could walk in at any moment, he sat down in the bathtub. And then, rather desperately, he looked around the bathroom for a towel. "Oh look, George," said the woman in the hallway. "Someone's left a towel on this chair."

Richard inspected and rejected as poor towel substitutes a loofah, a half-empty bottle of shampoo, and a small yellow rubber duck. "What's the bathroom like?" asked the woman. Richard grabbed a wash cloth and draped it in front of his crotch. Then he stood up, with his back to the wall, and prepared to be mortifyingly embarrassed. The door was pushed open. Three of them walked into the bathroom: a young man in a camel-hair coat, and a middle-aged couple. Richard wondered if they were as embarrassed as he was.

"It's a bit small," said the woman.

"Compact," corrected the camel-hair coat, smoothly. "Easy to take care of." The woman ran her finger along the side of the sink, and wrinkled her nose. "I think we've seen it all," said the middle-aged man. They walked out of the bathroom.

"It *would* be very handy for everything," said the woman. A conversation continued in lower tones. Richard climbed out of the bath and edged over to the door. He spotted the towel on the chair in the hall, and he leaned out and grabbed it. "We'll take it," said the woman.

"You will?" said the camel-hair coat.

"It's just what we want," she explained. "Or it will be, once we've made it homey. Could it be ready for Wednesday?"

"Of course. We'll have all of this rubbish cleaned out of here tomorrow, no problem."

Richard, cold and dripping and wrapped in his towel, glared at them from the doorway. "It's not rubbish," he said. "It's my stuff."

"We'll pick up the keys from your office, then."

"Excuse me," said Richard, plaintively. "I live here."

They pushed past Richard on their way to the front door. "Pleasure doing business with you," said the camel-hair coat.

"Can you . . . can any of you hear me? This is my flat. I live here."

"If you fax contract details to my office—" said the gruff man, then the door slammed behind them, and Richard stood in the hallway of what used to be his flat, and he shivered, in the silence, from the cold. "This," announced Richard to the world, in direct defiance of the evidence of his senses, "is not happening." The Batphone shrilled, and its headlights flashed. Richard picked it up, warily. "Hello?"

The line hissed and crackled as if the call were coming from a long way away. The voice at the other end of the phone was unfamiliar. "Mister Mayhew?" it said. "Mister Richard Mayhew?"

"Yes," he said. And then, delighted, "You can hear me. Oh, thank God. Who is this?"

"My associate and I met you on Saturday, Mister Mayhew. I was inquiring as to the whereabouts of a certain young lady. Do you remember?" The tones were oily, nasty, foxy.

"Oh. Yes. It's you."

"Mister Mayhew. You said Door wasn't with you. We have reason to believe that you were embroidering the truth more than perhaps a little."

"Well, *you* said you were her brother."

"All men are brothers, Mister Mayhew."

"She's not here anymore. And I don't know where she is."

"We know that, Mister Mayhew. We are perfectly cognizant of both of those facts. And to be magnificently frank, Mister Mayhew—and I'm sure you want me to be frank, don't you?—were I you, I would no longer worry about the young lady. Her days are numbered, and the number in question isn't even in the double digits."

"Why are you calling me?"

"Mister Mayhew," said Mr. Croup, helpfully, "do you know what your own liver tastes like?" Richard said nothing. "Because Mister Vandemar has promised me that he's personally going to cut it out and stuff it into your mouth before he slits your sad little throat. So you'll find out, won't you?"

"I'm calling the police. You can't threaten me like this."

"Mister Mayhew. You can call anyone you wish. But I'd hate you to think we were making a threat. Neither myself nor Mister Vandemar make threats, do we, Mister Vandemar?"

"No? Then what the hell *are* you doing?"

"We're making a promise," said Mr. Croup through the static and the echo and the hiss. "And we do know where you live." And he hung up.

Richard held the Batphone tightly, staring at it, then he stabbed the nine key three times: Fire, Police and Ambulance. "Emergency services," said the emergency operator. "What service do you require?"

"Can you put me through to the police, please? A man just threatened to kill me, and I don't think he was joking."

There was a pause. He hoped he was being put through to

the police. After a few moments, the voice said, "Emergency ser-
vices. Hello? Is there anyone there? Hello?" And then Richard
put down the Batphone, and went into his bedroom, and put
his clothes on, because he was cold, and naked, and scared, and
there wasn't really anything else he could do.

EVENTUALLY, AND AFTER SOME deliberation, he took the black
sports bag from under the bed, and put socks into it. Underpants.
Some T-shirts. His passport. His wallet. He was wearing jeans,
sneakers, a thick sweater. He remembered the way the girl who
called herself Door had said good-bye. The way she had paused,
the way she had said she was sorry . . .

"You knew," he said to the empty flat. "You knew this would
happen." He went into the kitchen, took some fruit from the
bowl, put that into the bag. Then he zipped it up and walked out
onto the darkened street.

THE ATM TOOK HIS card with a whirr. PLEASE ENTER YOUR
PIN NUMBER, it said. Richard typed in his secret pin number
(D-I-C-K). The screen went blank. Then, PLEASE WAIT, it said.
Somewhere in the depths of the machine something grumbled
and growled.

THIS CARD IS NOT VALID. PLEASE CONTACT CARD ISSUER. There was
a chunking noise, and the card slid out again.

"Spare any change?" said a tired voice from behind him.
Richard turned: the man was short and old and balding, his
scraggly beard a matted tangle of yellow and gray, and the lines

of his face were etched deeply in black dirt. He wore a filthy coat over the ruin of a dark gray sweater. His eyes were gray as well, and rheumy.

Richard handed the man his cash card. "Here," he said. "Keep it. There's about fifteen hundred pounds in there, if you can get to it."

The man took the card in his street-blackened hands, looked at it, turned it over, and said, flatly, "Thanks a bunch. That and sixty pence'll get me a nice cup of coffee." He gave Richard his card back, and began to walk down the street.

Richard picked up his bag. And then he went after the man and said, "Hey. Hang on. You can see me."

"Nothing wrong with *my* eyes," said the man.

"Listen," said Richard, "have you ever heard of a place called 'the Floating Market'? I need to get there. There's a girl called Door—" But the man had begun, nervously, to back away from Richard. "Look, I really need help," said Richard. "Please?"

The man stared at him, without pity. Richard sighed. "Okay," he said. "I'm sorry I troubled you." He turned away, and, clenching the handle of his bag in both hands, so they hardly shook at all, he began to walk down the High Street.

"Oy," hissed the man. Richard looked back at him. He was beckoning. "Come on, down here, quickly, man." The man hurried down some steps on the derelict houses at the side of the road—garbage-strewn steps, leading down to abandoned basement flats, and Richard stumbled after him. At the bottom of the steps was a door, which the man pushed open. He waited for Richard to go through, and shut the door behind them. Through the door, they were in darkness. There was a scratch, and the

noise of a match flaring into life: the man touched the match to the wick of an old railwayman's lamp, which caught, casting slightly less light than the match had, and they walked together through a dark place.

It smelled musty, of damp and old brick, of rot and the dark. "Where are we?" Richard whispered. His guide shushed him to silence. They reached another door set in a wall. The man rapped on it rhythmically. There was a pause, and then the door swung open.

For a moment, Richard was blinded by the sudden light. He was standing in a huge, vaulted room, an underground hall, filled with firelight and smoke. Small fires burned around the room. Shadowy people stood by the flames, roasting small animals on spits. People scurried from fire to fire. It reminded him of Hell, or rather, the way that he had thought of Hell, as a schoolboy. The smoke scraped his chest, and he coughed. A hundred eyes turned, then, and stared at him: a hundred eyes, unblinking and unfriendly.

A man scuttled toward them. He had long hair, a patchy brown beard, and his ragged clothes were trimmed with fur—orange and white and black fur, like the coat of a calico cat. He would have been taller than Richard, but he walked with a pronounced stoop, his hands held up at his chest, fingers pressed together. "What? What is it? What is this?" he asked Richard's guide. "Who've you brought us, Iliaster? Talk-talk-talk."

"He's from the Upside," said the guide. (*Iliaster?* thought Richard.) "Was asking about the Lady Door. And the Floating Market. Brought him to you, Lord Rat-speaker. Figured you'd know what to do with him." There were now more than a dozen

of the fur-trimmed people standing around them, women and men, and even a few children. They moved in scurries: moments of stillness, followed by hasty dashes toward Richard.

The Lord Rat-speaker reached inside his fur-trimmed rags and pulled out a wicked-looking sliver of glass, about eight inches long. Some poorly cured fur had been tied around the bottom half of it to form an improvised grip. Firelight glinted from the glass blade. The Lord Rat-speaker put the shard blade to Richard's throat. "Oh yes. Yes-yes-yes," he chittered, excitedly. "I know *exactly* what to do with him."

4

M R. CROUP AND MR. Vandemar
had set up their home in the
cellar of a Victorian hospital,
closed down ten years earlier
because of National Health Service budget cut-
backs. The property developers, who had an-
nounced their intention of turning the hospital
into an unparalleled block of unique luxury-
living accommodations, had faded away as
soon as the hospital had been closed, and so it
stood there, year after year, gray and empty and
unwanted, its windows boarded up, its doors
padlocked shut. The roof was rotten, and rain
dripped through the empty hospital's interior,
spreading damp and decay through the build-

ing. The hospital was ranged around a central well, which let in a certain amount of gray and unfriendly light.

The basement world beneath the empty hospital wards comprised more than a hundred tiny rooms, some of them empty, others containing abandoned hospital supplies. One room contained a squat, giant metal furnace, while the next room housed the blocked and waterless toilets and showers. Most of the basement floors were covered with a thin layer of oily rainwater, which reflected the darkness and the decay back toward the rotting ceilings.

If you were to walk down the hospital steps, as far down as you could go, through the abandoned shower rooms, past the staff toilets, past a room filled with broken glass, where the ceiling had collapsed entirely, leaving it open to the stairwell above, you would reach a small, rusting iron staircase, from which the once-white paint was peeling in long, damp strips. And if you went down the staircase, and traversed the marshy place at the bottom of the steps, and pushed your way through a half-decayed wooden door, you would find yourself in the sub-cellar, a huge room in which a hundred and twenty years of hospital waste had accumulated, been abandoned and, eventually, forgotten; and it was here that Mr. Croup and Mr. Vandemar had, for the present, made their home. The walls were damp, and water dripped from the ceiling. Odd things moldered in corners; some of them had once been alive.

Mr. Croup and Mr. Vandemar were killing time. Mr. Vandemar had obtained from somewhere a centipede—a reddish-orange creature, almost eight inches long, with vicious, poisonous fangs—and was letting it run over his hands, watching it as it

twined between his fingers, vanished up one sleeve, appeared a minute later out of the other. Mr. Croup was playing with razor blades. He had found a whole box of fifty-year-old razor blades, wrapped in glassine paper, in a corner, and had been trying to think of things to do with them.

"If I might have your attention, Mister Vandemar," he said, at length. "Pipe your beady eyes on this."

Mr. Vandemar held the centipede's head delicately between a huge thumb and a massive forefinger, to stop it wriggling, and looked at Mr. Croup.

Mr. Croup put his left hand against a wall, fingers spread. He took five razor blades in his right hand, took careful aim, and threw them at the wall. Each blade stuck into the wall, between Mr. Croup's fingers; it was like a top knife-thrower's act in miniature. Mr. Croup took his hand away, leaving the blades in the wall, outlining the place his fingers had been, and he turned to his partner for approval.

Mr. Vandemar was unimpressed. "What's so clever about that, then?" he asked. "You didn't even hit *one* finger."

Mr. Croup sighed. "I didn't?" he said. "Well, slit my gullet, you're right. How could I have been such a ninny?" He pulled the razor blades out of the wall, one by one, and dropped them onto the wooden table. "Why don't you show me how it should have been done?"

Mr. Vandemar nodded. He put his centipede back into its empty marmalade jar. Then he put his left hand against the wall. He raised his right arm: his knife, wicked and sharp and perfectly weighted, was in his right hand. He narrowed his eyes, and he threw. The knife flew through the air like an extremely

large and sharp knife flying through the air very fast indeed. It thudded into the damp plaster wall blade-first, the blade having first hit and penetrated the back of Mr. Vandemar's hand on its way.

A telephone began to ring.

Mr. Vandemar looked around, satisfied, with the knife still through his hand. "*That's* how it's done," he said.

There was an old telephone in the corner of the room. An antique, two-part telephone, unused in the hospital since the 1920s, made of wood and Bakelite. Mr. Croup picked up the earpiece, which was on a long, cloth-wrapped cord, and spoke into the mouthpiece, which was attached to the base. "Croup and Vandemar," he said, smoothly, "the Old Firm. Obstacles obliterated, nuisances eradicated, bothersome limbs removed and tutelary dentistry."

The person at the other end of the phone said something. Mr. Croup cringed. Mr. Vandemar tugged at his left hand. It was pinned hard to the wall and wasn't coming free.

"Oh. Yes, sir. Yes, indeed. And might I say how your telephonic confabulation brightens up and cheers our otherwise dreary and uneventful day?" Another pause. "Of course I'll stop toadying and crawling. Delighted to. An honor, and—what do we know? We know that—" An interruption; he picked his nose, reflectively, patiently, then: "No, we don't know where she is at this precise moment. But we don't have to. She'll be at the market tonight and—" His mouth tightened, and, "We have no intention of violating their market truce. More of waiting till she has left the market and scrobbling her . . ." He was silent then, and listened, nodding from time to time.

Mr. Vandemar tried to pull the knife out of the wall with his free hand, but the knife was stuck quite fast.

"That might be arranged, yes," said Mr. Croup, into the mouthpiece. "I mean it will be arranged. Of course. Yes. I realize that. And, sir, perhaps we could talk about—" But the caller had hung up. Mr. Croup stared at the earpiece for a moment, then put it back on its hook. "You think you're so damned clever," he whispered. Then he noticed Mr. Vandemar's predicament, and said, "Stop that." He leaned over and pulled the knife out of the wall and out of the back of Mr. Vandemar's hand, and put it down on the table.

Mr. Vandemar shook his left hand, and flexed the fingers, then wiped the fragments of damp plaster from his knife blade. "Who was that?"

"Our employer," said Mr. Croup. "It seems the other one isn't going to work out. Not old enough. It's going to have to be the Door female."

"So we aren't allowed to kill her anymore?"

"That, Mister Vandemar, would be about the short and the long of it, yes. Now, it seems Little Miss Door has announced that she shall be hiring a bodyguard. At the market. Tonight."

"So?" Mr. Vandemar spat on the back of his hand, where the knife had gone in, and on the palm of his hand, where the knife had come out. He rubbed at the spit with a massive thumb. The flesh closed, knitted, was whole again.

Mr. Croup picked up his old coat, heavy, black, and shiny with age, from the floor. He put it on. "So, Mister Vandemar," he said, "shall we not also hire ourselves a bodyguard?"

Mr. Vandemar slid his knife back into the holster in his sleeve.

He put his coat on as well, pushed his hands deep into the pockets, and was pleasantly surprised to find an almost untouched mouse in one pocket. Good. He was hungry. Then he pondered Mr. Croup's last statement with the intensity of an anatomist dissecting his one true love; and, realizing the flaw in his partner's logic, Mr. Vandemar said, "We don't need a bodyguard, Mister Croup. We hurt people. We don't get hurt."

Mr. Croup turned out the lights. "Oh, Mister Vandemar," he said, enjoying the sound of the words, as he enjoyed the sound of all words, "if you cut us, do we not bleed?"

Mr. Vandemar pondered this for a moment, in the dark. Then he said, perfectly accurately, "No."

"A SPY FROM THE Upworld," said the Lord Rat-speaker. "Heh? I should slit you from gullet to gizzard and tell fortunes with your guts."

"Look," said Richard, his back against the wall, with the glass dagger pressed against his Adam's apple. "I think you're making a bit of a mistake here. My name is Richard Mayhew. I can prove who I am. I've got my library cards. Credit cards. Things," he added, desperately.

At the opposite end of the hall, Richard noticed, with the dispassionate clarity that comes when a lunatic is about to slit your throat with a piece of broken glass, people were throwing themselves to the ground, bowing low, and remaining on the floor. A small black shape was coming toward them along the ground. "I think a moment's reflection might prove that we're all being very silly," said Richard. He had no idea

what the words meant, just that they were coming out of his mouth, and that as long as he was talking, he was not dead. "Now, why don't you put that away, and—excuse me, that's my bag," this last to a thin, bedraggled girl in her late teens, who had taken Richard's bag, and was roughly tipping his possessions out onto the ground.

The people in the hall continued to bow, and to stay bowed, as the small shape came closer. It reached the group of people around Richard, although not a one of them noticed it. They were all looking at Richard.

It was a rat, which looked up at Richard, curiously. He had the bizarre and momentary impression that it *winked* one of its little black oil-drop eyes at him. Then it chittered, loudly.

The man with the glass dagger threw himself on his knees. So did the people gathered around them. So too, after a moment's hesitation, and a little more awkwardly, did the homeless man, the one they had called Iliaster. In a moment, Richard was the only one standing. The thin girl tugged at his elbow, and he, too, went down on one knee.

Lord Rat-speaker bowed so low his long hair brushed the ground, and he chittered back at the rat, wrinkling his nose, showing his teeth, squeaking and hissing, for all the world like an enormous rat himself.

"Look, can anybody tell me—" muttered Richard.

"Quiet!" said the girl.

The rat stepped—a little disdainfully, it seemed—into the Lord Rat-speaker's grubby hand, and the man held it, respectfully, up in front of Richard's face. It waved its tail languidly as it inspected Richard's features. "This is Master Longtail, of the

clan Gray," said the Lord Rat-speaker. "He says you looks exceeding familiar. He wants to know if he's met you afore."

Richard looked at the rat. The rat looked at Richard. "I suppose it's possible," he admitted.

"He says he was discharging an obligation to the Marquis de Carabas."

Richard stared at the animal more closely. "It's *that* rat? Yes, we've met. Actually, I threw the TV remote control at it." Some of the people standing round looked shocked. The thin girl actually squeaked. Richard hardly noticed them; at least something was familiar in this madness. "Hello, Ratty," he said. "Good to see you again. Do you know where Door is?"

"Ratty!" said the girl in something between a squeak and a horrified swallow. She had a large, water-stained red button pinned to her ragged clothes, of the sort that comes attached to birthday cards. It said, in yellow letters, I AM 11.

Lord Rat-speaker waved his glass dagger admonishingly at Richard. "You must not address Master Longtail, save through me," he said. The rat squeaked an order. The man's face fell. "Him?" he said, looking at Richard disdainfully. "Look, I can't spare a soul. How about if I simply slice his throat and send him down to the Sewer Folk . . ."

The rat chittered once more, decisively, and then leapt from the man's shoulder onto the ground, and vanished into one of the many holes that lined the walls.

The Lord Rat-speaker stood up. A hundred eyes were fixed on him. He turned back to the hall, and looked at his subjects, crouched beside their greasy fires. "I don't know what you lot are all looking at," he shouted. "Who's turning the spits, eh? You

want the grub to burn? There's nothing to see. Go on. Get—get away with the lot of you." Richard stood up, nervously. His left leg had gone numb, and he rubbed life into it, as it prickled with pins and needles. Lord Rat-speaker looked at Iliaster. "He's got to be taken to the market. Master Longtail's orders."

Iliaster shook his head, and spat onto the ground. "Well, I'm not taking him," he said. "More than my life's worth, that journey. You rat-speakers have always been good to me, but I can't go back there. You know that."

The Lord Rat-speaker nodded. He put his dagger away, in the furs of his robe. Then he smiled at Richard with yellow teeth. "You don't know how lucky you were, just then," he said.

"Yes I do," said Richard. "I really do."

"No," said the man, "you don't. You really don't." And he shook his head, and said, to himself, marveling, "Ratty."

The Lord Rat-speaker took Iliaster by the arm, and the two of them walked a little way out of earshot, and began to talk, darting looks back at Richard as they did so.

The thin girl was gulping down one of Richard's bananas in what was, Richard reflected, the least erotic display of banana eating he had ever seen. "You know, that was going to be my breakfast," said Richard. She looked up at him guiltily. "My name's Richard. What's yours?"

The girl, who, he realized, had already managed to eat most of the fruit that Richard had brought with him, swallowed the last of the banana, and hesitated. Then she half smiled, and said something that sounded a lot like Anaesthesia. "I was hungry," she said.

"Well, so'm I," he told her.

She glanced at the little fires across the room. Then she looked back at Richard. She smiled again. "Do you like cat?" she said.

"Yes," said Richard. "I quite like cats."

Anaesthesia looked relieved. "Thigh?" she asked. "Or breast?"

THE GIRL CALLED DOOR walked down the court, followed by the Marquis de Carabas. There were a hundred other little courts and mews and alleys in London just like this one, tiny spurs of old-time, unchanged for three hundred years. Even the smell of piss here was the same as it had been in Pepys's time, three hundred years before. There was still an hour until dawn, but the sky was beginning to lighten, turning a stark, leaden color. Strands of mist hung like livid ghosts on the air.

The door was roughly boarded up, and covered with stained posters for forgotten bands and long-closed nightspots. The two of them stopped in front of it, and the Marquis eyed it, all boards and nails and posters, and he appeared unimpressed; but then, unimpressed was his default state.

"So this is the entrance?" he said.

She nodded. "One of them."

He folded his arms. "Well? Say *open sesame,* or whatever it is that you do."

"I don't want to do this," she said. "I'm really not sure that we're doing the right thing."

"Very well." He unfolded his arms. "I'll be seeing you, then." He turned on his heel and began to walk back the way that they had come.

Door seized his arm. "You'd abandon me?" she asked. "Just like that?"

He grinned, without humor. "Certainly. I'm a very busy man. Things to see. People to do."

"Look, hold on." She let go of his sleeve, bit her lower lip. "The last time I was here . . ." She trailed off.

"The last time you were here, you found your family dead. Well, there you go. You don't have to explain it anymore. If we aren't going in, then our business relationship is at an end."

She looked up at him, her elfin face pale in the pre-dawn light. "And that's all?"

"I could wish you the best of luck in your future career, but I'm afraid I rather doubt you'll live long enough to have one."

"You're a piece of work, aren't you?"

He said nothing. She walked back toward the door. "Well," she said. "Come on. I'll take us in." Door put her left hand on the boarded-up door, and with her right hand she took the Marquis' huge brown hand. Her tiny fingers twined into his larger ones. She closed her eyes.

. . . something whispered and shivered and changed . . .

. . . and the door collapsed into darkness.

THE MEMORY WAS FRESH, only a few days old: Door moved through the House Without Doors calling, "I'm home," and "Hello?" She slipped from the anteroom to the dining room, to the library, to the drawing room; no one answered. She moved to another room.

The swimming pool was an indoor Victorian structure, constructed of marble and of cast iron. Her father had found it when

he was younger, abandoned and about to be demolished, and he had woven it into the fabric of the House Without Doors. Perhaps in the world outside, in London Above, the room had long been destroyed and forgotten. Door had no idea where any of the rooms of her house were, physically. Her grandfather had constructed the house, taking a room from here, a room from there, all through London, discrete and doorless; her father had added to it.

She walked along the side of the old swimming pool, pleased to be home, puzzled by the absence of her family. And then she looked down.

There was someone floating in the water, trailing twin clouds of blood behind him, one from the throat, one from the groin. It was her brother, Arch. His eyes were open wide and sightless. She realized that her mouth was open. She could hear herself screaming.

"THAT HURT," SAID THE Marquis. He rubbed his forehead, hard, twisted his head around on his neck, as if he were trying to ease a sudden, painful crick.

"Memories," she explained. "They're imprinted in the walls."

He raised an eyebrow. "You could have warned me."

"Ah," she said. "Right."

They were in a huge white room. Every wall was covered with pictures. Each picture was of a different room. The white room contained no doors, no openings of any kind. "Interesting décor," acknowledged the Marquis.

"This is the entrance hall. We can go from here to any room in the House. They are all linked."

"Where are the other rooms located?"

She shook her head. "I don't know. Miles away, probably. They're scattered all over the Underside."

The Marquis had managed to cover the whole room in a series of impatient strides. "Quite remarkable. An associative house, every room of which is located somewhere else. So imaginative. Your grandfather was a man of vision, Door."

"I never knew him." She swallowed, then continued, talking to herself as much as to him, "We should have been safe here. Nobody should have been able to hurt us. Only my family could move around it."

"Let's hope your father's journal gives us some clues," he said. "Where do we start looking?" Door shrugged. "You're certain he kept a journal?" he pressed.

She nodded. "He used to go into his study, and private the links until he'd finished dictating."

"We'll start in the study, then."

"But I looked there. I did. I *looked* there. When I was cleaning up the body . . ." And she began to cry, in low, raging sobs that sounded like they were being tugged from inside her.

"There. There," said the Marquis de Carabas, awkwardly, patting her shoulder. And he added, for good measure, "There." He did not comfort well.

Door's odd-colored eyes were filled with tears. "Can you . . . can you just give me a sec? I'll be fine." He nodded, and walked to the far end of the room. When he looked back she was still standing there, on her own, silhouetted in the white entrance chamber filled with pictures of rooms, and she was hugging herself, and shuddering, and crying like a little girl.

RICHARD WAS STILL UPSET about the loss of his bag.

The Lord Rat-speaker remained unmoved. He stated baldly

that the rat—Master Longtail—had said nothing at all about re-
turning Richard's things. Just that he was to be taken to market.
Then he told Anaesthesia that she was taking the Upworlder to
the market, and that, yes, it was an order. And to stop snivel-
ing, and to get a move on. He told Richard that if he, Lord Rat-
speaker, ever saw him, Richard, again, then he, Richard, would
be in a great deal of trouble. He reiterated that Richard did not
know how lucky he was, and, ignoring Richard's requests that
he return Richard's stuff—or at least the wallet—he led them to a
door, and locked it behind them.

Richard and Anaesthesia walked into the darkness side by
side.

She carried an improvised lamp, made of a candle, a tin,
some wire, and a wide-mouthed glass lemonade bottle. Rich-
ard was surprised how quickly his eyes became used to the near
darkness. They seemed to be walking through a succession of
underground vaults and storage cellars. Sometimes he thought
he could see movement, in far corners of the vaults, but whether
human, or rat, or something else altogether, it was always gone
by the time they reached the place it had been. When he tried
to talk to Anaesthesia about the movements, she hissed him to
silence.

He felt a cold draught on his face. The rat-girl squatted
without warning, put down her candle lamp, and tugged and
pulled hard at a metal grille set in the wall. It opened suddenly,
sending her sprawling. She motioned Richard to go through. He
crouched, edged through the hole in the wall; after about a foot,
the floor stopped completely. "Excuse me," whispered Richard.
"There's a hole here."

"It's not a big drop," she told him. "Go on."

She shut the grille behind her. She was now uncomfortably close to Richard. "Here," she said. She gave him the handle of her little lamp to hold, and clambered down into the darkness. "There," she said. "That wasn't that bad, was it?" Her face was a few feet below Richard's dangling feet. "Here. Pass me the lamp."

He lowered it down to her. She had to jump to take it from him. "Now," she whispered. "Come on." He edged nervously forward, climbed over the edge, hung for a moment, then let go. He landed on his hands and feet in soft, wet mud. He wiped the mud off his hands onto his sweater. A few feet forward, and Anaesthesia was opening another door. They went through it, and she pulled it closed behind them. "We can talk now," she said. "Not loud. But we can. If you want to."

"Oh. Thanks," said Richard. He couldn't think of anything to say. "So. Um. You're a rat, are you?" he said.

She giggled, like a Japanese girl, covering her face with her hand as she laughed. Then she shook her head, and said, "I should be so lucky. I wish. Nah. I'm a rat-speaker. We talk to rats."

"What, just chat to them?"

"Oh no. We do stuff for them. I mean"—and her tone of voice implied that this was something that might never have occurred to Richard unassisted—"there *are* some things rats *can't* do, you know. I mean, not having fingers, and thumbs, an' things. Hang on—" She pressed him against the wall, suddenly, and clamped a filthy hand over his mouth. Then she blew out the candle.

Nothing happened.

Then he heard distant voices. They waited, in the darkness and the cold. Richard shivered.

People walked past them, talking in low tones. When all sounds had died away, Anaesthesia took her hand from Richard's mouth, relit the candle, and they walked on. "Who were they?" asked Richard.

She shrugged. "It dun't matter," she said.

"Then what makes you think that they wouldn't have been pleased to see us?"

She looked at him rather sadly, like a mother trying to explain to an infant that, yes, *this* flame was hot, too. *All* flames were hot. Trust her, please. "Come on," she said. "I know a shortcut. We can nip through London Above for a bit." They went up some stone steps, and the girl pushed open a door. They stepped through, and the door closed shut behind them.

Richard looked around, puzzled. They were standing on the Embankment, that miles-long walkway which the Victorians built along the north shore of the Thames, covering the drainage system, and the newly created District Line of the Underground, and replacing the stinking mudflats which had festered along the banks of the Thames for the previous five hundred years. It was still night—or perhaps it was night once more. He was unsure how long they had been walking through the underplaces and the dark.

There was no moon, but the night sky was a riot of crisp and glittering autumn stars. There were streetlights too, and lights on buildings and on bridges, which looked like earthbound stars, and they glimmered, repeated, as they were reflected with the city in the night water of the Thames. *It's fairyland,* thought Richard.

Anaesthesia blew out her candle. And Richard said, "Are you sure this is the right way?"

"Yes," she said. "Pretty sure."

They were approaching a wooden bench, and the moment he set eyes on it, it seemed to Richard that that bench was one of the most desirable objects he had ever seen. "Can we sit down?" he asked. "Just for a minute."

She shrugged. They sat down at opposite ends of the bench. "On Friday," said Richard, "I was with one of the finest investment analysts in London."

"What's a investment an' a thing?"

"It was my job."

She nodded, satisfied. "Right. And . . . ?"

"Just reminding myself, really. Yesterday . . . it was like I didn't exist anymore, to anybody up here."

"That's 'cos you don't," explained Anaesthesia.

A late-night couple, who had been slowly walking along the Embankment toward them, holding hands, sat down in the middle of the bench, between Richard and Anaesthesia, and commenced to kiss each other, passionately. "Excuse me," said Richard to them. The man had his hand inside the woman's sweater, and was moving it around enthusiastically, a lone traveler discovering an unexplored continent. "I want my life back," Richard told the couple.

"I love you," said the man to the woman.

"But your wife . . . ," she said, licking the side of his face.

"Fuck her," said the man.

"Don' wanna fuck *her*," said the woman, and giggled drunkenly. "Wanna fuck you . . ." She put a hand on his crotch, and giggled some more.

"Come on," said Richard to Anaesthesia, feeling that the

bench had started to become a less desirable neighborhood, and they got up, and walked away. Anaesthesia peered back, curiously, at the couple on the bench, who were gradually becoming more horizontal.

Richard said nothing. "Something wrong?" asked Anaesthesia.

"Only everything," said Richard. "Have you always lived down there?"

"Nah. I was born up here." She hesitated. "You don't want to hear about me." Richard realized, almost surprised, that he really did.

"I do. Really."

She fingered the rough quartz beads that hung in a necklace around her neck, and she swallowed. "There was me and Mum and the twins . . . ," she said, and then she stopped talking. Her mouth clamped shut.

"Go on," said Richard. "It's all right. Really, it is. Honest."

The girl nodded. She took a deep breath, and then she began to talk, without looking at him as she talked, her eyes fixed on the ground ahead of her. "Well, Mum had me an' my sisters, but she got a bit funny in the head. One day I got home from school, and she was crying and crying, and she didn't have any clothes on, and she was breaking stuff. Plates and stuff. But she never hurt us. She never did. The lady from the social services came and took the twins away, an' I had to go and stay with my aunt. She was living with this bloke. I didn't like him. And when she was out of the house . . ." The girl paused; she was quiet for so long that Richard wondered if she had finished. Then she began once more, "Anyway. He used to hurt me. Do other stuff. In the

end, I told my aunt, an' she started hitting me. Said I was lying. Said she'd have the police on me. But I wasn't lying. So I run away. It was my birthday."

They had reached the Albert Bridge, a kitsch monument spanning the Thames, joining Battersea to the south with the Chelsea end of the Embankment, a fairy-tale bridge hung with thousands of tiny white lights.

"I didn't have anywhere to go. And it was so cold," said Anaesthesia, and she stopped again. "I slept on the streets. I'd sleep in the day, when it was a bit warmer, and walk around at night, just to keep moving. I was only eleven. Stealing bread an' milk off people's doorsteps to eat. Hated doing that so I started hanging around the street markets, taking the rotten apples an' oranges an' things people threw away. Then I got really sick. I was living under a flyover in Notting Hill. When I come to, I was in London Below. The rats had found me."

"Have you ever tried to return to all this?" he asked, gesturing. Quiet, warm, inhabited houses. Late-night cars. The real world . . . She shook her head. *All fire burns, little baby. You'll learn.* "You can't. It's one or the other. Nobody ever gets both."

"I'm sorry," said Door, hesitantly. Her eyes were red and she looked as if she had been vigorously blowing her nose, and scrubbing her tears from her eyes and cheeks.

The Marquis, who had been amusing himself playing a game of knucklebones with some old coins and bones he kept in one of the many pockets of his coat, looked up at her coldly. "Indeed?"

She bit her lower lip. "No. Not really. I'm not sorry. I've

been running and hiding and running so hard that . . . this was the first chance I've really had to . . ." She stopped.

The Marquis swept up the coins and the bones, and returned them to their pocket. "After you," he said. He followed her back to the wall of pictures. She put one hand on the painting of her father's study, and took the Marquis' large black hand with the other.

. . . reality twisted . . .

THEY WERE IN THE *conservatory, watering the plants. First Portia would water a plant, directing the flow of the water toward the soil at the base of the plant, avoiding the leaves and the blossoms. "Water the shoes," she said to her youngest daughter. "Not the clothes."*

Ingress had her own little watering can. She was so proud of it. It was just like her mother's, made of steel, painted bright green. As her mother finished with a plant, Ingress would water it with her tiny watering can. "On the shoes," she told her mother. She began laughing, then, spontaneous little-girl laughter.

And her mother laughed too, until foxy Mr. Croup pulled her hair back, hard and sudden, and cut her white throat from ear to ear.

"HELLO, DADDY," SAID DOOR, quietly.

She touched the bust of her father with her fingers, stroking the side of his face. A thin, ascetic man, almost bald. *Caesar as Prospero,* thought the Marquis de Carabas. He felt a little sick. That last image had *hurt.* Still, he was in Lord Portico's study. *That* was a first.

The Marquis took in the room, eyes sliding from detail

to detail. The stuffed crocodile hanging from the ceiling; the leather-bound books, an astrolabe, convex and concave mirrors, odd scientific instruments; there were maps on the walls, of lands and cities de Carabas had never heard of; a desk, covered in handwritten correspondence. The white wall behind the desk was marred by a reddish-brown stain. There was a small portrait of Door's family on the desk. The Marquis stared at it. "Your mother and your sister, your father, and your brothers. All dead. How did *you* escape?" he asked.

She lowered her hand. "I was lucky. I'd gone off exploring for a few days . . . did you know there are still some Roman soldiers camped out by the Kilburn River?"

The Marquis had not known this, which irritated him. "Hmm. How many?"

She shrugged. "A few dozen. They were deserters from the Nineteenth Legion, I think. My Latin's a bit patchy. Anyway, when I got back here . . ." She paused, swallowed, her opal-colored eyes brimming with tears.

"Pull yourself together," said the Marquis, shortly. "We need your father's journal. We have to find out who did this."

She frowned at him. "We know who did this. It was Croup and Vandemar—"

He opened a hand, waggled his fingers as he spoke. "They're arms. Hands. Fingers. There's a head that ordered it, that wants you dead too. Those two don't come cheap." He looked around the cluttered office. "His journal?" said the Marquis.

"It's not here," she said. "I told you. I looked."

"I was under the misapprehension that your family were skilled in locating doors, both obvious and otherwise."

She glowered at him. Then she closed her eyes, and put her

finger and thumb on each side of the bridge of her nose. Meanwhile, the Marquis examined the objects on Lord Portico's desk. An inkwell; a chess piece; a bone die; a gold pocket watch; several quill feathers; and . . .

Interesting.

It was a small statue of a boar, or a crouching bear, or perhaps a bull. It was hard to tell. It was the size of a large chess piece, and had been roughly carved out of black obsidian. It reminded him of something, but of what he could not say. He picked it up casually, turned it over, curled his fingers around it.

Door lowered her hand from her face. She looked puzzled and confused. "What's the matter?" he asked.

"It *is* here," she said, simply. She began to walk through the study, head turning first to one side and then to the other. The Marquis slipped the carving discreetly into an inside pocket.

Door stood before a high cabinet. "There," she said. She reached out a hand: there was a click, and a small panel in the side of the cabinet swung open. Door reached into the darkness, and removed something roughly the size and shape of a small cannonball. She passed it to the Marquis. It was a sphere, constructed of old brass and polished wood, inset with polished copper and glass lenses. He took it from her.

"This is it?"

She nodded.

"Well done."

She looked grave. "I don't know how I could have missed it before."

"You were upset," said the Marquis. "I was certain it would be here. And I am so rarely wrong. Now . . ." He held the little

wooden globe up. The light caught the polished glass and glinted from the brass and copper fittings. It galled him to admit ignorance about anything, but he said it anyway: "How does this work?"

ANAESTHESIA HAD LED RICHARD into a small park on the south side of the bridge, then down some stone steps, set beside a wall. She relit her candle-in-a-bottle, and then she opened a workman's door, and closed it behind them. They went down some steps, with the darkness all around them.

"There's a girl named Door," said Richard. "She's a bit younger than you. Do you know her?"

"The Lady Door. I know who she is."

"So which, um, barony is she part of?"

"No barony. She's of the House of the Arch. Her family used to be very important."

"Used to be? Why did they stop?"

"Somebody killed them."

Yes, he remembered the Marquis saying something about that, now. A rat ran across their path. Anaesthesia stopped on the steps, and performed a deep curtsey. The rat paused. "Sire," she said, to the rat. "Hi," said Richard. The rat looked at them for a heartbeat, then it darted off down the steps. "So," said Richard. "What is a floating market?"

"It's very big," she said. "But rat-speakers hardly ever need to go to the market. To tell the truth—" She hesitated. "Nah. You'll laugh at me."

"I won't," said Richard, honestly.

"Well," said the thin girl. "I'm a little scared."

"Scared? Of the market?"

They had reached the bottom of the steps. Anaesthesia hesitated and then turned left. "Oh. No. There's a truce in the market. If anyone hurt anyone there, the whole of London Below would be down on them like a ton of sewage."

"So what are you scared of?"

"Getting there. They hold it in a different place every time. It moves around. And to get to the place it'll be tonight . . ." She fingered the quartz beads around her neck, nervously. "We'll have to go through a really nasty neighborhood." She did sound scared.

Richard suppressed the urge to put an arm around her. "And where would that be?" he asked. She turned to him, pushed the hair from her eyes, and told him.

"Knightsbridge," repeated Richard, and he began to chuckle, gently.

The girl turned away. "See?" she said. "I said you'd laugh."

The deep tunnels had been dug in the early days of the Second World War. Troops had been quartered there in their thousands, their waste needing to be pumped up by compressed air to the level of the sewers far above. Both sides of the tunnels had been lined with metal bunk beds for the troops to sleep on. There had been plans to assimilate the tunnels into a high-speed extension to the underground system, but these plans came to nothing, and when the war ended the bunk beds had stayed in the tunnels, and on their wire bases cardboard boxes were stored,

each box filled with letters and files and papers: secrets, of the dullest kind, stored down deep, to be forgotten. Economies had closed the deep tunnels completely in the early 1990s. The boxes of secrets were removed, to be scanned and stored on computers, or shredded, or burned.

Varney made his home in the deepest of the deep tunnels, far beneath Camden Town Tube. He had piled abandoned metal bunk beds in front of the only entrance. Then he had decorated. Varney liked weapons. He made his own, out of whatever he could find, or take, or steal, parts of cars and rescued bits of machinery, which he turned into hooks, and shivs, crossbows and arbalests, small mangonels and trebuchets for breaking walls, cudgels, glaives, and knobkerries. They hung on the wall of the deep tunnel, or sat in corners, looking unfriendly.

Varney looked like a bull might look, if the bull were to be shaved, dehorned, covered in tattoos, and had suffered from complete dental breakdown. Also, he snored. The oil lamp next to his head was turned down low. Varney slept on a pile of rags, snoring and snuffling, with the hilt of a homemade two-bladed sword on the ground beside his hand.

A hand turned up the oil lamp.

Varney had the two-bladed sword in his hand, and was on his feet almost before his eyes were open. He blinked, stared around him. There was no one there: nothing had disturbed the pile of bunk beds blocking the door. He began to lower the sword.

A voice said, "Psst."

"Hh?" said Varney.

"Surprise," said Mr. Croup, stepping into the light.

Varney took a step back: a mistake. There was a knife at his

temple, the point of the blade next to his eye. "Further move-ments are not recommended," said Mr. Croup, helpfully. "Mister Vandemar might have a little accident with his old toad sticker. Most accidents do occur in the home. Is that not so, Mister Van-demar?"

"I don't trust statistics," said Mr. Vandemar's blank voice. A gloved hand reached down from behind Varney, crushed his sword, and dropped the twisted thing to the floor.

"How are you, Varney?" asked Mr. Croup. "Well, we trust? Yes? In fine form, fetlock and fettle for the market tonight? Do you know who we are?"

Varney did the nearest thing he could to a nod that didn't actually involve moving any muscles. He knew who Croup and Vandemar were. His eyes were searching the walls. Yes, there: the morning star: a spiked wooden ball, studded with nails, on a chain, in the far corner of the room . . .

"There is talk that a certain young lady will be audition-ing bodyguards this evening. Had you thought of trying out for the task?" Mr. Croup picked at his tombstone teeth. "Enunciate clearly."

Varney picked up the morning star with his mind. It was his Knack. Gentle, now . . . slowly . . . He edged it off the hook, and pulled it up toward the top of the tunnel arch . . . With his mouth, he said, "Varney's the best bravo and guard in the Un-derside. They say I'm the best since Hunter's day."

Varney mentally positioned the morning star in the shadows above and behind Mr. Croup's head. He would crush Croup's skull first, then he'd take Vandemar . . .

The morning star plunged toward Mr. Croup's head; Var-

ney flung himself down, away from the knife blade at his eye. Mr. Croup did not look up. He did not turn. He simply moved his head, obscenely fast, and the morning star crashed past him, into the floor, where it threw up chips of brick and concrete. Mr. Vandemar picked Varney up with one hand. "Hurt him?" he asked his partner.

Mr. Croup shook his head: *Not yet*. To Varney, he said, "Not bad. So, 'best bravo and guard,' we want you to get yourself to the market tonight. We want you to do whatever you have to, to become that certain young lady's personal bodyguard. Then, when you get the job, one thing you don't forget. You may guard her from the rest of the world, but when we want her, we take her. Got it?"

Varney ran his tongue over the wreck of his teeth. "Are you bribing me?" he asked.

Mr. Vandemar had picked up the morning star. He was pulling the chain apart, with his free hand, link by link, and dropping the bits of twisted metal onto the floor. *Chink.* "No," said Mr. Vandemar. *Chink.* "We're intimidating you." *Chink.* "And if you don't do what Mister Croup says, we're"—*chink*—"hurting you"—*chink*—"very badly, before we're"—*chink*—"killing you, even badlier."

"Ah," said Varney. "Then I'm working for you, aren't I?"

"Yes, you are," said Mr. Croup. "I'm afraid we don't have any redeeming features."

"That doesn't bother me," said Varney.

"Good," said Mr. Croup. "Welcome aboard."

———————

IT WAS A LARGE but elegant mechanism, built of polished wal-
nut and oak, of brass and glass, copper and mirrors and carved
and inlaid ivory, of quartz prisms and brass gears and springs
and cogs. The whole thing was rather larger than a wide-screen
television, although the actual screen itself was no more than
six inches across. A magnifying lens placed across it increased
the size of the picture. There was a large brass horn, like an ear
trumpet, coming out of the side—the kind you could find on an
antique gramophone. The whole mechanism looked rather like
a combined television and video player might look, if it had been
invented and built three hundred years ago by Sir Isaac Newton.
Which was, more or less, exactly what it was.

"Watch," said Door. She placed the wooden ball onto a plat-
form. Lights shone through the machine and into the ball. It
began to spin around and around.

A patrician face appeared on the small screen, vividly col-
ored. Slightly out of time, a voice came from the horn, crackling
in mid-speech. ". . . that two cities should be so near," said the
voice, "and yet in all things so far; the possessors above us, and
the dispossessed, we who live below and between, who live in
the cracks."

Door stared at the screen, her face unreadable.

"Still," said her father, "I am of the opinion that what crip-
ples us who inhabit the Underside is our petty factionalism. The
system of baronies and fiefdoms is both divisive and foolish."
The Lord Portico was wearing a threadbare old smoking jacket,
and a skullcap. His voice seemed to be coming to them across the
centuries, not days or weeks. He coughed. "I am not alone in this
belief. There are those who wish to see things the way they are.

There are others who wish the situation to worsen. There are those . . ."

"Can you speed it up?" asked the Marquis. "Find the last entry?"

Door nodded. She touched an ivory lever at the side: the image ghosted, fragmented, re-formed.

Now Portico wore a long coat. His skullcap was gone. There was a scarlet gash down one side of his head. He was no longer sitting at his desk. He was talking urgently, quietly. "I do not know who will see this, who will find this. But whoever you are, please take this to my daughter, the Lady Door, if she lives . . ." A static burst wiped across the picture and the sound. Then, "Door? Girl, this is bad. I don't know how long I've got before they find this room. I think my poor Portia and your brother and sister are dead." The sound and picture quality began to degrade.

The Marquis glanced at Door. Her face was wet: tears were brimming from her eyes, glistening down her cheeks. She seemed unaware that she was crying, made no attempt to wipe away the tears. She just stared at her father's image, listened to his words. *Crackle*. Wipe. *Crackle*. "Listen to me, girl," said her dead father. "Go to Islington . . . you can trust Islington . . . You must believe in Islington . . ." He ghosted. Blood had dripped from his forehead into his eyes, and he wiped it off. "Door? Avenge us. Avenge your family."

A loud bang came from the gramophone horn. Portico turned his head to look offscreen, puzzled and nervous. "What?" he said, and he stepped out of frame. For a moment, the picture remained unchanged: the desk, the blank white wall behind it.

Then an arc of vivid blood splashed across the wall. Door flicked a lever on the side, blanking the screen, and she turned away.

"Here." The Marquis passed her a handkerchief.

"Thanks." She wiped her face, blew her nose vigorously. Then she stared into space. Eventually, she said, "Islington."

"I've never had any dealings with Islington," said the Marquis.

"I thought it was just a legend," she said.

"Not at all." He reached across the desk, picked up the gold pocket watch, thumbed it open. "Nice workmanship," he observed.

She nodded. "It was my father's."

He closed the cover, with a click. "Time to go to market. It starts soon. Mister Time is not our friend."

She blew her nose once more, put her hands deep into the pockets of her leather jacket. Then she turned to him, elfin face frowning, odd-colored eyes bright. "Do you honestly think we can find a bodyguard who could deal with Croup and Vandemar?"

The Marquis flashed his white teeth at her. "There's been no one since Hunter who'd even be in there with a chance. No, I'll settle for someone who could give you the time you might need to get away." He fastened the fob of the watch chain to his waistcoat, slid the watch into his vest pocket.

"What are you doing?" asked Door. "That's my father's watch."

"He's not using it anymore, is he?" He adjusted the golden chain. "There. That looks rather elegant." He watched the emotions flicker across her face: grief, anger, and, finally, resignation.

"We'd better go," was all she said.

"THE BRIDGE ISN'T VERY far now," said Anaesthesia.

Richard hoped that was true. They were now on their third candle. He was astonished that they were still under London: he was half-convinced that they had walked most of the way to Wales.

"I'm really scared," she continued. "I've never crossed the bridge before."

"I thought you said you'd been to this market already," he asked, mystified.

"It's the *Floating* Market, silly. I told you already. It moves. Different places. Last one I went to was held in that big clock tower. Big . . . someone. And the next was—"

"Big Ben?"

"Maybe. We were inside where all the big wheels went around, and that was where I got this—" She held up her necklace. The candlelight glimmered yellow off the shiny quartz. She smiled, like a child. "Do you like it?" she asked.

"It's great. Was it expensive?"

"I swapped some stuff for it. That's how things work down here. We swap stuff." And then they turned a corner, and saw the bridge. It could have been one of the bridges over the Thames, five hundred years ago, thought Richard; a huge, stone bridge spanning out over a vast black chasm, into the night. But there was no sky above it, no water below. It rose into darkness. Richard wondered who built it, and when. He wondered how something like this could exist, beneath the city of London, without everyone knowing. He felt a sinking feeling in the pit of his

stomach. He was, he realized, deeply, pathetically scared of the bridge itself.

"Do we have to go across it?" he asked. "Can't we get to the market some other way?" They paused at the base of the bridge.

Anaesthesia shook her head. "We can get to the place it's in," she said. "But the market wouldn't be there."

"Huh? But that's ridiculous. I mean, something's either there or it's not. Isn't it? I mean, isn't it?"

She shook her head. There was a buzz of voices from behind him, and someone pushed Richard to the ground. He looked up: a huge man, crudely tattooed, dressed in improvised rubber and leather clothes that looked like they had been cut out of the inside of cars, stared back down at him, dispassionately. Behind the huge man were a dozen others, male and female: people who looked like they were on their way to a particularly low-rent costume party. "Somebody," said Varney, who was not in a good mood, "was in my way. Somebody ought to watch where he's going."

Once, as a small boy walking home from school, Richard had encountered a rat, in a ditch by the side of the road. When the rat saw Richard it had reared up onto its hind legs and hissed, and jumped, terrifying Richard. He backed away, marveling that something so small had been so willing to fight something so much larger than itself. Now Anaesthesia stepped between Richard and Varney. She was less than half his size, but she glared at the big man and bared her teeth, and she hissed like an angry rat at bay. Varney took a step backward. Varney spat at Richard's shoes. Then he turned away, and, taking the knot of people with him, he walked across the bridge and into the dark.

"Are you all right?" asked Anaesthesia, helping Richard back to his feet.

"I'm fine," he said. "That was really brave of you."

She looked down, shyly. "I'm not really brave," she said. "I'm still scared of the bridge. Even that lot were scared. That was why they all went over together. Safety in numbers. Big bullies."

"If you are crossing the bridge, I will go with you," said a female voice, rich as cream and honey, coming from behind them. Richard was never able to place her accent. At the time, he thought she might be Canadian, or American. Later he suspected she might have been African, or Australian, or even Indian. He was never able to tell. She was a tall woman, with long, tawny hair, and skin the color of burnt caramel. She wore dappled leather clothes, mottled in shades of gray and brown. She had a battered leather duffel bag over her shoulder. She was carrying a staff, and had a knife at her belt, and an electric flashlight strapped to her wrist. She was, also, without question, the most beautiful woman that Richard had ever seen.

"Safety in numbers. You're welcome to come with us," he said, after a moment's hesitation. "My name's Richard Mayhew. This is Anaesthesia. She's the one of us who knows what she's doing." The rat girl preened.

The leather woman looked him up and looked him down. "You're from London Above," she told him.

"Yes."

"Traveling with a rat-speaker. My word."

"I'm his guardian," said Anaesthesia, truculently. "Who are you? Who do you owe fealty to?"

The woman smiled. "I owe no man fealty, rat girl. Have ei-

ther of you crossed Night's Bridge before?" Anaesthesia shook her head. "Well," said the woman. "Isn't this going to be fun?"

They walked toward the bridge. Anaesthesia handed Richard her candle lamp. "Here," she said.

"Thanks." Richard looked at the woman in leather. "Is there anything, really, to be scared of?"

"Only the night on the bridge," she said.

"The kind in armor?"

"The kind that comes when day is over."

Anaesthesia's hand sought Richard's. He held it tightly. She smiled at him, squeezed his hand. And then they set foot on Night's Bridge, and Richard began to understand darkness: darkness as something solid and real, so much more than a simple absence of light. He felt it touch his skin, questing, moving, exploring—gliding through his mind. It slipped into his lungs, behind his eyes, into his mouth . . .

With each step they took the light of the candle became dimmer. He realized the same thing was happening to the leather woman's flashlight. It felt not so much as if the lights were being turned down, but as if the darkness were being turned up. Richard blinked, and opened his eyes on nothing—nothing but darkness, complete and utter. *Sounds.* A rustling, a squirming. Richard blinked, blinded by the night. The sounds were nastier, hungrier. Richard imagined he could hear voices: a horde of huge, misshapen trolls, beneath the bridge . . .

Something slithered past them in the dark. "What's that?" squeaked Anaesthesia. Her hand was shaking in his.

"Hush," whispered the woman. "Don't attract its attention."

"What's happening?" whispered Richard.

"Darkness is happening," said the leather woman, very qui-

etly. "Night is happening. All the nightmares that have come out when the sun goes down, since the cave times, when we huddled together in fear for safety and for warmth, are happening. Now," she told them, "now is the time to be afraid of the dark." Richard knew that something was about to creep over his face. He closed his eyes: it made no difference to what he saw or felt. The night was complete. It was then that the hallucinations started.

HE SAW A FIGURE falling toward him through the night, burning, its wings and hair on fire.

He threw up his hands: there was nothing there.

Jessica looked at him, with contempt in her eyes. He wanted to shout to her, tell her he was sorry.

Place one foot after another.

He was a small child, walking home from school, at night, down the one road with no streetlights. No matter how many times he did it, it never got any easier, never got any better.

He was deep in the sewers, lost in a labyrinth. The Beast was waiting for him. He could hear a slow drip of water. He knew the Beast was waiting. He gripped his spear . . . Then a rumbling bellow, deep in its throat, from behind him. He turned. Slowly, agonizingly slowly, it charged at him, through the dark.

And it charged.

He died.

And kept walking.

Slowly, agonizingly slowly, it charged at him, over and over, through the dark.

THERE WAS A SPUTTER, and a flare so bright it hurt, making Richard squint and stagger. It was the candle flame, in its lemonade-bottle holder. He had never known how brightly a single candle could burn. He held it up, gasping and gulping and shaking with relief. His heart was pounding and shuddering in his chest.

"We would appear to have crossed successfully," said the leather woman.

Richard's heart was pounding in his chest so hard that, for a few moments, he was unable to talk. He forced himself to breathe slowly, to calm down. They were in a large anteroom, exactly like the one on the other side. In fact, Richard had the strange feeling that it was the same room they had just left. Yet the shadows were deeper, and there were afterimages floating before Richard's eyes, like those one saw after a camera flash. "I suppose," Richard said, haltingly, "we weren't in any real danger . . . It was like a haunted house . . . a few noises in the dark . . . and your imagination does the rest. There wasn't anything to be scared of, was there?"

The woman looked at him, almost pityingly; and Richard realized that there was nobody holding his hand. "Anaesthesia?"

From the darkness at the crown of the bridge came a gentle noise, like a rustle or a sigh. A handful of irregular quartz beads pattered down the curve of the bridge, toward them. Richard picked one up. It was from the rat girl's necklace. "We'd better . . . We have to go back. She's . . ."

The woman raised her flashlight, shone it across the bridge. Richard could see all the way across the bridge. It was deserted. "Where is she?" he asked.

"Gone," said the woman, flatly. "The darkness took her."

"We've got to do something," said Richard urgently.

"Such as?"

He opened his mouth but, this time, he found no words. He closed it again. He fingered the lump of quartz, looked at the others on the ground.

"She's gone," said the woman. "The bridge takes its toll. Be grateful it didn't take you too. Now if you're going to the market, it's through here, up this way." She gestured toward a narrow passageway that rose up into the dimness in front of them, barely illuminated by the beam of her flashlight.

Richard did not move. He felt numb. He found it hard to believe that the rat girl was gone—lost, or stolen, or strayed, or . . .—and harder to believe that the leather woman was able to carry on as if nothing at all out of the ordinary had happened, as if this were utterly usual. Anaesthesia could not be dead . . .

He completed the thought. She could not be dead, because if she were, then it was his fault. She had not asked to go with him. He held the quartz bead so tightly it hurt his hand, thinking of the pride with which she had shown it to him, of how fond he had become of her in the handful of hours that he had known her.

"Are you coming?"

Richard stood there in the darkness for a few pounding heartbeats, then he placed the quartz bead gently into the pocket of his jeans. He followed the woman, who was still some paces ahead of him. As he followed her, he realized that he still did not know her name.

5

EOPLE SLIPPED AND SLID through the darkness about them holding lamps and torches, flashlights and candles. It made Richard think of documentary films he had seen of schools of fish, glittering and darting through the ocean . . . Deep water, inhabited by things that had lost the use of their eyes.

Richard followed the leather woman up some steps. Stone steps, edged with metal. They were in an Underground station. They joined a line of people waiting to slip through a grille, which had been opened a foot or so to uncover the door, which led out onto the pavement.

Immediately in front of them were a couple of young boys, each with a string tied around

his wrist. The strings were held by a pallid, bald man, who smelled of formaldehyde. Immediately behind them in the line waited a gray-bearded man with a black and white kitten sitting on his shoulder. It washed itself, intently, licked the man's ear, then curled up on his shoulder and went to sleep. The line moved slowly as, one by one, the figures at the end slipped through the space between the grille and the wall and edged into the night. "Why are you going to the market, Richard Mayhew?" asked the leather woman, in a low voice.

"I have friends I'm hoping to meet there. Well, just one friend, actually. I don't actually know many people from this world. I was sort of getting to know Anaesthesia, but . . ." He trailed off. Asked the question he had not dared to voice until this moment. "Is she dead?"

The woman shrugged. "Yes. Or as good as. I trust your visit to the market will make her loss worthwhile."

Richard shivered. "I don't think it could," he said. They were approaching the front of the queue. "What do you do?" he asked.

She smiled. "I sell personal physical services."

"Oh," he said. Then, "What kind of personal physical services?"

"I rent my body." She did not elaborate.

"Ah." He was too weary to pursue it, to press her to explain just what she meant; he had an idea, though. And then they stepped out into the night. Richard looked back. The sign on the station said KNIGHTSBRIDGE. He didn't know whether to smile or to mourn. It felt like the small hours of the morning. Richard looked down at his watch, and was not surprised to notice that the digital face was now completely blank. Perhaps the batteries had died, or, he thought, more likely, time in London Below had

only a passing acquaintance with the kind of time he was used to. He did not care. He unstrapped the watch and dropped it into the nearest waste bin.

The odd people were crossing the road in a stream, walking through the double doors facing them. "There?" he said, appalled.

The woman nodded. "There."

The building was large, and covered with many thousands of burning lights. Conspicuous coats of arms on the wall facing them proclaimed that it proudly sold all sorts of things by appointment to various members of the British Royal Family. Richard, who had spent many a footsore weekend hour trailing behind Jessica through every prominent shop in London, recognized it immediately, even without the huge sign proclaiming it to be—"Harrods?"

The woman nodded. "Only for tonight," she said. "The next market could be anywhere."

"But I mean," said Richard. "Harrods." It seemed almost sacrilegious to be sneaking into this place at night.

They walked in through the side door. The room was dark. They passed the *bureau de change* and the gift-wrapping section, through another darkened room selling sunglasses and figurines, and then they stepped into the Egyptian Room. Color and light broke over Richard like a wave hitting the shore. His companion turned to him: she yawned, cat-like, shading the vivid pinkness of her mouth with the back of her caramel hand. And then she smiled, and said, "Well. You're here. Safe and, more or less, sound. I have business to attend to. Fare you well." She nodded curtly, and slipped away into the crowd.

Richard stood there, alone in the throng, drinking it in. It

was pure madness. Of that there was no doubt at all. It was loud, and brash, and insane, and it was, in many ways, quite wonderful. People argued, haggled, shouted, sang. They hawked and touted their wares, and loudly declaimed the superiority of their merchandise. Music was playing—a dozen different kinds of music, being played a dozen different ways on a score of different instruments, most of them improvised, improved, improbable. Richard could smell food. All kinds of food: the smells of curries and spices seemed to predominate, with, beneath them, the smells of grilling meats and mushrooms. Stalls had been set up all through the shop, next to, or even on, counters that, during the day, had sold perfume, or watches, or amber, or silk scarves. Everybody was buying. Everybody was selling. Richard listened to the market cries as he began to wander through the crowds.

"Lovely fresh dreams. First-class nightmares. We got 'em. Get yer lovely nightmares here."

"Weapons! Arm yourself! Defend your cellar, cave or hole! You want to hit 'em? We got 'em. Come on, darling, come on over here . . ."

"Rubbish!" screamed a fat, elderly woman, in Richard's ear, as he passed her malodorous stall. "Junk!" she continued. "Garbage! Trash! Offal! Debris! Come and get it! Nothing whole or undamaged! Crap, tripe, and useless piles of shit. You know you want it."

A man in armor beat a small drum, and chanted as he did so, "Lost property. Roll up, roll up, and see for yourself. Lost property. None of your found muck here. Everything guaranteed properly lost."

Richard wandered through the huge rooms of the store, like

a man in a trance. He was unable even to guess how many people there were at the night market: a thousand? Two thousand? Five thousand?

One stall was piled high with bottles, full bottles and empty bottles of every shape and every size, from bottles of booze to one huge glimmering bottle that could have contained nothing but a captive djinn; another sold lamps, and candles, made of many kinds of wax and tallow; a man thrust what appeared to be a child's severed hand clutching a candle toward him, as he passed, muttering, "Hand of Glory, sir? Send 'em up the wooden hill to Bedfordshire. Guaranteed to work." Richard hurried past, not wishing to find out what a Hand of Glory was, nor how it worked; he passed a stall selling glittering gold and silver jewelry, another selling jewelry made from what looked like the valves and wires of antique radios; there were stalls that sold every manner of book and magazine; others that sold clothes—old clothes patched, and mended, and made strange; several tattooists; something that he was almost certain was a small slave market (he kept well clear of this); a dentist's chair, with a foot-operated manual drill, with a line of miserable people standing beside it, waiting to have their teeth pulled or filled by a young man who seemed to be having altogether too good a time; a bent old man selling unlikely things that might have been hats and might have been examples of modern art; something that looked very much like a portable shower facility; even a blacksmith's . . .

And every few stalls there would be somebody selling food. Some of them had food cooking over open fires: curries, and potatoes, and chestnuts, and huge mushrooms, and exotic breads. Richard found himself wondering why the smoke from the fires

didn't set off the building's sprinkler system. Then he found himself wondering why no one was looting the store: why set up their own little stalls? Why not just take things from the shop itself? He knew better, at this point, than to risk asking anyone . . . He seemed marked as a man from London Above, and thus worthy of great suspicion.

There was something deeply tribal about the people, Richard decided. He tried to pick out distinct groups: there were the ones who looked like they had escaped from a historical reenactment society; the ones who reminded him of hippies; the albino people in gray clothes and dark glasses; the polished, dangerous ones in smart suits and black gloves; the huge, almost identical women who walked together in twos and threes, and nodded when they saw each other; the tangle-haired ones who looked like they probably lived in sewers and who smelled like hell; and a hundred other types and kinds . . .

He wondered how normal London—*his* London—would look to an alien, and that made him bold. He began to ask them, as he went, "Excuse me? I'm looking for a man named de Carabas and a girl called Door. Do you know where I'd find them?" People shook their heads, apologized, averted their eyes, moved away.

Richard took a step back, and stepped on someone's foot. Someone was well over seven feet tall, and was covered in tufty ginger hair. Someone's teeth had been sharpened to points. Someone picked Richard up with a hand the size of a sheep's head, and put Richard's head so close to someone's mouth that Richard almost gagged. "I'm really sorry," said Richard. "I—I'm looking for a girl named Door. Do you know—" But someone dropped him onto the floor, and moved on.

Another whiff of cooking food wafted across the floor, and

Richard, who had managed to forget how hungry he was ever since he had declined the prime cut of roast cat—he could not think how many hours before—now found his mouth watering, and his thinking processes beginning to grind to a halt.

The iron-haired woman running the next food stall he came to did not reach to Richard's waist. When Richard tried to talk to her, she shook her head, drew a finger across her lips. She could not talk, or did not talk, or did not want to talk. Richard found himself conducting the negotiations for cottage cheese and lettuce sandwiches, and a cup of what looked and smelled like a form of home-brewed lemonade, in dumb-show. His food cost him a ballpoint pen, and a book of matches he had forgotten he had. The little woman must have felt that she had got by far the better of the deal, for, as he took his food, she threw in a couple of small, nutty biscuits.

Richard stood in the middle of the throng, listening to the music—someone was, for no reason that Richard could easily discern, singing the lyrics of "Greensleeves" to the tune of "Great Balls of Fire"—watching the bizarre bazaar unfold around him, and eating his sandwiches.

He realized as he finished the last of the sandwiches that he had no idea how anything he had just eaten had tasted, and he resolved to slow down, and chew the biscuits more slowly. He sipped the lemonade, making it last. "You need a bird, sir?" asked a cheery voice, close at hand. "I got rooks and ravens, crows and starlings. Fine, wise birds. Tasty *and* wise. Brilliant."

Richard said, "No, thank you," and turned around.

The hand-painted sign above the stall said

"OLD BAILEY'S BIRDS AND INFORMATION"

There were other, smaller, signs scattered about: "YOU WANTS IT, WE KNOWS IT!" and "YOU WON'T FIND A PLUMPER STARLING!!!!" and "WHEN IT'S TIME FOR A ROOK, IT'S TIME FOR OLD BAILEY!!" Richard found himself reminded of the man he had seen when he had first come to London, who used to stand outside Leicester Square Tube station with a huge hand-painted sandwich board which exhorted the world to "LESS LUST THROUGH LESS PROTEIN, EGGS, MEAT, BEANS, CHEESE AND SITTING."

Birds hopped and fluttered about small cages that looked like they had been woven out of television aerials. "Information, then?" continued Old Bailey, warming to his sales pitch. "Roof maps? History? Secret and mysterious knowledge? If I don't knows it, it's probbly better forgot. That's what I says." The old man still wore his feathered coat, was still wrapped about with ropes and cords. He blinked at Richard, then pulled on the pair of spectacles tied about his neck with string, and inspected Richard carefully through them. "Hang on. I knows you. You was with the Marquis de Carabas. On the rooftops. Remember? Eh? I'm Old Bailey. Remember me?" He thrust out his hand, pumped Richard's hand furiously.

"Actually," said Richard, "I'm looking for the Marquis. And for a young lady named Door. I think they're probably together."

The old man did a little jig, causing several feathers to detach themselves from his coat, and provoking a chorus of raucous disapproval from the various birds around them. "Information! Information!" he announced to the crowded room. "See? I told 'em. *Diversify,* I said. Diversify! You can't sell rooks for the stewpot forever—anyway they taste like boiled slipper. And they're so stupid. Thick as custard. You ever eaten rook?" Richard shook

his head. That was something he could be certain of, at any rate. "What'll you give me?" asked Old Bailey.

"Sorry?" said Richard, awkwardly leaping from ice floe to ice floe in the stream of the old man's consciousness.

"If'n I give ye your information. What'll I get?"

"I don't have any money," said Richard. "And I just gave my pen away." He began to pull out the contents of his pockets.

"There," said Old Bailey. "That!"

"My hankie?" asked Richard. It was not a particularly clean handkerchief; it had been a present from his Aunt Maude, on his last birthday. Old Bailey seized it and waved it above his head, happily.

"Never you fear, laddie," he sang, triumphantly. "Your quest is at an end. Go down there, through that door. You can't miss them. They're auditioning." He was pointing toward Harrods' extensive network of Food Halls. A rook cawed, maliciously. "None of your beak," said Old Bailey, to the rook. And, to Richard, he said, "Thank'ee for the little flag." He jigged around his stall, delighted, waving Richard's handkerchief to and fro.

Auditioning? thought Richard. And then he smiled. It didn't matter. His quest, as the mad old roof man had put it, was at an end. He walked toward the Food Halls.

FASHION, IN BODYGUARDS, SEEMED to be everything. They all had a Knack of one kind or another, and each of them was desperate to demonstrate it to the world. At this moment Ruislip was facing off against the Fop With No Name.

The Fop With No Name looked somewhat like an early-

eighteenth-century rake, one who hadn't been able to find real rake clothes, and had had to make do with what he could find at the Salvation Army store. His face was powdered to white, his lips painted red. Ruislip, the Fop's opponent, looked like the kind of dream one might have if one fell asleep watching sumo wrestling on the television with a Bob Marley record playing in the background. He was a huge Rastafarian who looked like nothing so much as an obese and enormous baby.

They were standing face-to-face, in the middle of a cleared circle of spectators and other bodyguards and sightseers. Neither man moved a muscle. The Fop was a good head taller than Ruislip. On the other hand, Ruislip weighed as much as four fops, each of them carrying a large leather suitcase entirely filled with lard. They stared at each other, without breaking eye contact.

The Marquis de Carabas tapped Door on the shoulder, and pointed. Something was about to happen.

One moment there were two men standing impassively, just looking at each other, then the Fop's head rocked back, as if he'd just been hit in the face. A small, reddish-purple bruise appeared on his cheek. He pursed his lips and fluttered his eyelashes. "La," he said, then stretched his rouged lips wide, in a ghastly parody of a smile.

The Fop gestured. Ruislip staggered, and clutched his stomach.

The Fop With No Name smirked outrageously, waggled his fingers, and blew kisses to several spectators. Ruislip stared angrily at the Fop, redoubling his mental assault. Blood began to drip from the Fop's lips. His left eye started to swell. He staggered. The audience muttered appreciatively.

"It's not as impressive as it looks," whispered the Marquis to Door.

The Fop With No Name stumbled, suddenly, going onto his knees, as if someone were forcing him down, and he fell, awkwardly, to the floor. Then he jerked, as if someone had just kicked him, hard, in the stomach. Ruislip looked triumphant. The spectators clapped, politely. The Fop writhed and spat blood onto the sawdust on the floor of Harrods' Meat, Fish, and Poultry Hall. He was dragged off into the corner by some friends, and was violently sick.

"Next," said the Marquis.

The next would-be bodyguard was again thinner than Ruislip (being about the size of two and a half fops, carrying but a single suitcase filled with lard between them). He was covered in tattoos, and dressed in clothes that looked like they had been stitched together from old car seats and rubber mats. He was shaven-headed, and he sneered at the world through rotten teeth. "I'm Varney," he said, and he hawked, and spat green on the sawdust. He walked into the ring.

"When you're ready, gentlemen," said the Marquis.

Ruislip stamped his bare feet on the floor, sumo-like, one-two, one-two, and commenced to stare hard at Varney. A small cut opened on Varney's forehead, and blood began to drip from it into one eye. Varney ignored it, and instead appeared to be concentrating on his right arm. He pulled his arm up slowly, like a man fighting a great deal of pressure. Then he slammed his fist into Ruislip's nose, which began to spurt blood. Ruislip drew one long, horrible breath, and hit the ground with the sound of half a ton of wet liver being dropped into a bathtub. Varney giggled.

Ruislip slowly pulled himself back to his feet, blood from his nose soaking his mouth and chest, dripping onto the sawdust. Varney wiped the blood from his forehead, and bared his ruined mouth at the world in an appalling grin. "Come on," he said. "Fat wanker. Hit me again."

"That one's promising," muttered the Marquis.

Door raised an eyebrow. "He doesn't look very nice."

"*Nice* in a bodyguard," lectured the Marquis, "is about as useful as the ability to regurgitate whole lobsters. He looks *dangerous*." There was a murmur of appreciation, then, as Varney did something rather fast and painful to Ruislip, something that involved the sudden connection of Varney's leather-bound knee and Ruislip's testicles. The murmur was the kind of restrained and deeply unenthusiastic applause one normally only hears in England on sleepy sunny Sunday afternoons, at village cricket matches. The Marquis clapped politely with the rest of them. "Very good, sir," he said.

Varney looked at Door, and he winked at her, almost proprietorially, before he returned his attention to Ruislip. Door shivered.

RICHARD HEARD THE CLAPPING, and walked toward it.

Five almost identically dressed, extremely pale young women walked past him. They wore long dresses made of velvet, each dress so dark it was almost black—respectively dark green, dark chocolate, royal blue, dark blood, and pure black. Each woman had black hair, and wore silver jewelry; each was perfectly coiffed, perfectly made up. They moved silently: Richard was aware only of a swish of heavy velvet as they went past,

a swish that sounded almost like a sigh. The last of the women, the one dressed all in utter black, the palest and the most beautiful, smiled at Richard. He smiled back at her, warily. Then he walked on toward the audition.

It was being held in the Meat, Fish, and Poultry Hall, on the open area of floor beneath Harrods' fish sculpture. The audience had their back to him, were standing two or three people deep. Richard wondered if he would easily be able to find Door and the Marquis, and then the crowd parted, and he saw them both, sitting on the glass top of the smoked-salmon counter. He opened his mouth to shout "Door," and as he did so, he realized why the crowd had parted, as an enormous dreadlocked man, naked but for a green, yellow, and red cloth wrapped like a diaper about his midriff, came catapulting through the crowd, as if tossed by a giant, and landed squarely on top of him.

"Richard?" she said.

He opened his eyes. The face swam in and out of focus. Fire opal–colored eyes, peering into his, from a pale, elfin face.

"Door?" he said.

She looked furious; she looked beyond fury. "Temple and Arch, Richard. I don't believe it. What are you doing here?"

"It's nice to see you, too," said Richard, weakly. He sat up, and wondered if he was suffering from a concussion. He wondered how he'd know if he was, and he wondered why he had ever thought that Door would have been pleased to see him. She stared intently at her nails, nostrils flaring, as if she did not trust herself to say anything else.

The big man with the very bad teeth, who had knocked

Richard over on the bridge, was fighting with a dwarf. They were fighting with crowbars, and the fight was not as unequal as one might have imagined. The dwarf was preternaturally fast: he rolled, he struck, he bounced, he dove; his every movement made Varney appear lumbering and awkward by comparison.

Richard turned to the Marquis, who was watching the fight intently. "What's happening?" he asked.

The Marquis spared him a glance, and then returned his gaze to the action in front of them. *"You,"* he said, "are out of your depth, in deep shit, and, I would imagine, a few hours away from an untimely and undoubtedly messy end. *We* on the other hand are auditioning bodyguards." Varney connected his crowbar with the dwarf, who instantly stopped bouncing and darting, and instantly began lying insensible. "I think we've seen enough," said the Marquis, loudly. "Thank you all. Mister Varney, if you could wait behind?"

"Why did you have to come here?" Door said to Richard, frostily.

"I didn't really have much choice," said Richard.

She sighed. The Marquis was walking around the perimeter, dismissing the various bodyguards who had already auditioned, distributing a few words of praise here, of advice there. Varney waited patiently, off to one side. Richard essayed a smile at Door. It was ignored. "How did you get to the market?" she asked.

"There are these rat people—" Richard began.

"Rat-speakers," she said.

"And you see, the rat who brought us the Marquis' message—"

"Master Longtail," she said.

"Well, he told them they had to get me here."

She raised an eyebrow, cocked her head slightly on one side. "A rat-speaker brought you here?"

He nodded. "Most of the way. Her name was Anaesthesia. She . . . well, something happened to her. On the bridge. This other lady brought me the rest of the way here. I think she was a . . . You know." He hesitated, then said it. "Hooker."

The Marquis had returned. He stood in front of Varney, who looked obscenely pleased with himself. "Weapons expertise?" asked the Marquis.

"Whew," said Varney. "Put it like this. If you can cut someone with it, blow someone's head off with it, break a bone with it, or make a nasty hole in someone with it, then Varney's the master of it."

"Previous satisfied employers include . . . ?"

"Olympia, the Shepherd Queen, the Crouch Enders. I done security for the May Fair for a bit, as well."

"Well," said the Marquis de Carabas. "We're all very impressed with your skill."

"I had heard," said a female voice, "that you had put out a call for bodyguards. Not for enthusiastic amateurs." Her skin was the color of burnt caramel, and her smile would have stopped a revolution. She was dressed entirely in soft mottled gray and brown leathers and Richard recognized her immediately.

"That's her," Richard whispered to Door. "The hooker."

"Varney," said Varney, affronted, "is the best guard and bravo in the Underside. Everyone knows that."

The woman looked at the Marquis. "You've finished the trials?" she asked.

"Yes," said Varney.

"Not necessarily," said the Marquis.

"Then," she told him, "I would like to audition."

There was a beat before the Marquis de Carabas said, "Very well," and stepped backward, leapt up to the smoked-salmon counter, and sat, comfortably watching the action.

Varney was undoubtedly dangerous, not to mention a bully, a sadist, and actively harmful to the physical health of those around him. What he was not, though, was particularly quick on the uptake. He stared at the Marquis as the penny dropped, and dropped, and kept on dropping. Finally, in disbelief, he asked, "I have to fight *her*?"

"Yes," said the leather woman. "Unless you'd like a little lie-down, first." Varney began to laugh: a manic giggle. He stopped laughing a moment later, when the woman kicked him, hard, in the solar plexus, and he toppled like a tree.

Near his hand, on the floor, was the crowbar he had used in the fight with the dwarf. He grabbed it, slammed it into the woman's face—or would have, had she not ducked out of the way. She clapped her open hands onto his ears, very fast. The crowbar went flying across the room. Still reeling from the pain in his ears, Varney pulled a knife from his boot. He was not entirely sure what happened after that, only that the world swung out from under him, and then he was lying, face-down, on the ground, with blood coming from his ears, and his own knife at his throat, while the Marquis de Carabas was saying,

"Enough!"

The woman looked up, still holding Varney's knife to his throat. "Well?" she said.

"Very impressive," said the Marquis. Door nodded.

Richard was thunderstruck: it had been like watching Emma Peel, Bruce Lee, and a particularly vicious tornado, all rolled into one and sprinkled with a generous helping of footage he had once seen on a wildlife program of a mongoose killing a king cobra. That was how she had moved. That was how she had fought.

Richard normally found displays of real violence unnerving. But he found watching this woman in action exhilarating, as if she were finding a part of him he had not known existed. It seemed utterly right, in this unreal mirror of the London he had known, that she should be here and that she should be fighting so dangerously and so well.

She was part of London Below. He understood that now. And as he thought that, he thought about London Above, and a world in which no one fought like this—no one needed to fight like this—a world of safety and sanity, and, for a moment, the homesickness engulfed him like a fever.

The woman looked down at Varney. "Thank you, Mister Varney," she said, politely. "I'm afraid we won't be needing your services after all." She got off him, and put his knife away in her belt.

"And you are called?" asked the Marquis.

"I'm called Hunter," she said.

Nobody said anything. Then Door said, hesitantly, *"The* Hunter?"

"That's right," said Hunter, and she brushed the dust of the floor from her leather leggings. "I'm back."

From somewhere a bell sounded, twice, a deep bonging noise

that made Richard's teeth vibrate. "Five minutes," muttered the Marquis. Then he said, to the remains of the crowd, "I think we've found our bodyguard. Thank you all very much. Nothing more to see."

Hunter walked over to Door, and looked her up and down. "Can you stop people killing me?" asked Door. Hunter inclined her head toward Richard. "I saved *his* life three times today, crossing the bridge, coming to the market."

Varney, who had stumbled to his feet, picked up the crowbar with his mind. The Marquis watched him do it; and he said nothing.

The ghost of a smile hovered about Door's lips. "That's funny," she said. "Richard thought you were a—"

Hunter never found out what Richard thought she was. The bar came hurtling toward her head. She simply reached out a hand, and caught it: it *thwapped,* satisfyingly, into the palm of her hand.

She walked over to Varney. "Is this yours?" she asked. He bared his teeth at her, yellow and black and brown. "Right now," said Hunter, "we're under Market Truce. But if you try something like that again, I'll waive the truce, and I'll break off both your arms and make you carry them home in your teeth. Now," she continued, bending his wrist behind his back, "say sorry, nicely."

"Ow," said Varney.

"Yes?" she said, encouragingly.

He spat it out as if it were choking him. "I'm sorry." She let him go. Varney backed away to a safe distance, plainly scared and furious, his face toward Hunter. And, when he reached the

door to the Food Halls, he hesitated, and shouted, "You're dead. You're fucking dead, you are!" in a voice that hovered on the edge of tears, and then he turned, and he ran from the room.

"Amateurs," sighed Hunter.

THEY WALKED BACK THROUGH the store the way that Richard had come. The bell was now tolling deeply and continually. When they came upon it, he saw that it was a huge brass bell, suspended on a wooden frame, with a rope suspended from the clapper. It was being tolled by a large black man, wearing the black robes of a Dominican monk, and it had been set up next to Harrods' gourmet jelly bean stand.

Impressive as the market had been to watch, Richard found it even more impressive to see the speed at which it was being dismantled, broken down and put away. All evidence that it had ever been there was vanishing: stalls were being taken apart, loaded onto people's backs, hauled off into the streets. Richard noticed Old Bailey, his arms filled with his crude signs and with bird cages, stumbling out of the store. The old man waved happily at Richard, and vanished off into the night.

The crowds thinned, the market vanished, and the ground floor of Harrods looked as usual, as sedate, as proper, and as clean as any time he had walked around it in Jessica's wake on a Saturday afternoon. It was as if the market had never existed.

"Hunter," said the Marquis. "I've heard of you, of course. Where have you been all this time?"

"Hunting," she said, simply. Then, to Door, "Can you take orders?"

Door nodded. "If I have to."

"Good. Then maybe I *can* keep you alive," said Hunter. "If I take the job."

The Marquis stopped. His eyes flickered over her, distrustfully. "You said, *if* you take the job . . . ?"

Hunter opened the door, and they stepped out onto the pavement of London at night. It had rained while they had been at the market, and the streetlights now glimmered on the wet tarmac. "I've taken it," said Hunter.

Richard stared at the glistening street. It all seemed so normal, so quiet, so sane. For a moment, he felt that all he needed to get his life back would be to hail a taxi and tell it to take him home. And then he would sleep the night through in his own bed. But a taxi would not see him or stop for him, and he had nowhere to go, even if one did.

"I'm tired," he said.

No one said anything. Door would not meet his eyes, the Marquis was cheerfully ignoring him, and Hunter was treating him as an irrelevance. He felt like a small child, unwanted, following the bigger children around, and that made him irritated. "Look," he said. "I don't want to be a bother or anything. I know you are all very busy people. But what about me?"

The Marquis turned and stared at him, eyes huge and white in his dark face. "You?" he said. "What about you?"

"Well," said Richard. "How do I get back to normal again? It's like I've walked into a nightmare. Last week everything made sense, and now nothing makes sense . . ." He trailed off. Swallowed. "I want to know how to get my life back," he explained.

"You won't get it back traveling with us, Richard," said Door. "It's going to be hard enough for you anyway. I . . . I really am sorry."

Hunter, in the lead, knelt down on the pavement. She took a small metal object from her belt, and used it to unlock the cover to a sewer. She pulled up the sewer cover, looked into it warily, climbed down, then ushered Door into the sewer. Door did not look at Richard as she went down. The Marquis scratched the side of his nose. "Young man," he said, "understand this: there are two Londons. There's London Above—that's where you lived— and then there's London Below—the Underside—inhabited by the people who fell through the cracks in the world. Now you're one of them. Good night."

He began to climb down the sewer ladder. Richard said, "Hang on," and caught the sewer cover before it could close. He followed the Marquis down. It smelled like drains at the top of the sewer—a dead, soapy, cabbagey smell. He expected it to get worse as he went down, but instead the smell quickly dissipated as he approached the sewer floor. Gray water ran, shallow but fast, along the bottom of the brick tunnel. Richard stepped into it. He could see the lights of the others up ahead, and he ran and splashed down the tunnel until he caught up with them.

"Go away," said the Marquis.

"No," he said.

Door glanced up at him. "I am really sorry, Richard," she said.

The Marquis stepped between Richard and Door. "You can't go back to your old home or your old job or your old life," he said to Richard, almost gently. "None of those things exist. Up there,

you don't exist." They had reached a junction: a place where three tunnels came together. Door and Hunter set off along one of them, the one that no water was coming down, and they did not look back. The Marquis lingered.

"You'll just have to make the best of it down here," he said to Richard, "in the sewers and the magic and the dark." And then he smiled, hugely, whitely: a gleaming grin, monumental in its insincerity. "Well—delightful to see you again. Best of luck. If you can survive for the next day or two," he confided, "you might even make it through a whole month." And with that he turned and strode off through the sewer, after Door and Hunter.

Richard leaned against a wall, and listened to their footsteps, echoing away, and to the rush of the water running past on its way to the pumping stations of East London, and the sewage works. "Shit," he said. And then, to his surprise, for the first time since his father died, alone in the dark, Richard Mayhew began to cry.

THE UNDERGROUND STATION WAS quite empty, and quite dark. Varney walked through it, keeping close to walls, darting nervous looks behind him, and in front of him, and from side to side. He had picked the station at random, had headed for it over the rooftops and through the shadows, making certain that he was not being followed. He was not heading back to his lair in the Camden Town deep tunnels. Too risky. There were other places in which Varney had cached weapons and food. He would go to ground for a little while, until this all blew over.

He stopped beside a ticket machine, and listened, in the dark-

ness: absolute silence. Reassured that he was alone, he allowed himself to relax. He stopped at the top of the spiral staircase and drew a deep breath.

A voice from beside him, oleaginous as sump oil, said conversationally, "Varney's the finest bravo and guard in the Underside. Everyone knows that. Mister Varney told us so himself."

And a voice from the other side of him responded, dully, "It's not nice to lie, Mister Croup."

In the pitch darkness, Mr. Croup warmed to his theme. "It isn't, Mister Vandemar. I have to say, I regard it as a personal betrayal, and I was deeply wounded by it. And disappointed. When you don't have any redeeming features, you don't take particularly kindly to disappointment, do you, Mister Vandemar?"

"Not kindly at all, Mister Croup."

Varney threw himself forward, and ran, headlong, in the dark, down the spiral staircase. A voice from the top of the stairs, Mr. Croup's: "Really," it said, "we ought to look upon it as a mercy killing."

The sound of Varney's feet clattered off the metal railings, echoed throughout the stairwell. He puffed, and he panted, his shoulders glancing off the walls, tumbling blindly downward in the dark. He reached the bottom of the steps, next to the sign warning travelers that there were 259 steps up to the top, and only healthy people should even think about attempting it. Everyone else, suggested the sign, should use the elevator.

The elevator?

Something clanked, and the elevator doors opened, magnificently slowly, flooding the passageway with light. Varney fumbled for his knife, cursed when he realized the Hunter bitch

still had it. He reached for the machete in his shoulder sheath. It was gone.

He heard a polite cough behind him, and he turned.

Mr. Vandemar was sitting on the steps, at the bottom of the spiral staircase. He was picking his fingernails with Varney's machete.

And then Mr. Croup fell upon him, all teeth and talons and little blades; and Varney never had a chance to scream. "Bye," said Mr. Vandemar, impassively, and he continued paring his nails. After that the blood began to flow. Wet, red blood in enormous quantities, for Varney was a big man, and he had been keeping it all inside. When Mr. Croup and Mr. Vandemar were finished, however, one would have been hard put even to notice the slight stain on the floor at the bottom of the spiral staircase.

The next time the floors were washed it was gone forever.

HUNTER WAS IN THE lead. Door walked in the middle. The Marquis de Carabas took up the rear. None of them had said a word since they had left Richard, half an hour earlier.

Door stopped, suddenly. "We can't do this," she said, flatly. "We can't leave him back there."

"Of course we can," said the Marquis. "We did."

She shook her head. She had felt guilty and stupid since she saw Richard, lying on his back beneath Ruislip, at the audition. She was tired of it.

"Don't be foolish," said the Marquis.

"He saved my life," she told him. "He could have left me on the sidewalk. He didn't."

It was her fault. She knew that was true. She had opened a door to someone who could help her, and help her he had. He had taken her somewhere warm, and he had cared for her, and he had brought her help. The action of helping her had tumbled him from his world into hers.

It was foolish to even think about bringing him with them. They could not afford to bring someone with them—she was unsure that the three of them would be able to take care of themselves on the journey that confronted them.

She wondered, briefly, if it were simply the door that she had opened, that had taken her to him, which had allowed him to notice her, or if there was, somehow, more to it than that.

The Marquis raised an eyebrow: he was detached, removed, a creature of pure irony. "My dear young lady," he said. "We are not bringing a passenger along on this expedition."

"Don't patronize me, de Carabas," said Door. She sounded tired. "And I think I can decide who comes with us. You *are* working for me, aren't you? Or is it the other way around?" Her sorrow and exhaustion had drained her of her patience. She needed de Carabas—she couldn't afford to drive him away—but she had reached her limit.

De Carabas stared at her, coldly angry. "He is *not* coming with us," he stated, flatly. "Anyway, he's probably dead by now."

RICHARD WAS NOT DEAD. He was sitting in the dark, on a ledge, on the side of a storm drain, wondering what to do, wondering how much further out of his depth he could possibly get. His life so far, he decided, had prepared him perfectly for a job in

securities, for shopping at the supermarket, for watching football on the telly on the weekends, for turning on a heater if he got cold. It had magnificently failed to prepare him for a life as an un-person on the roofs and in the sewers of London, for a life in the cold and the wet and the dark.

A light glimmered. Footsteps came toward him. If, he decided, it was a bunch of murderers, cannibals, or monsters, he would not even put up a fight. Let them end it all for him; he'd had enough. He stared down into the dark, to the place where his feet should be. The footsteps came closer.

"Richard?" The voice was Door's. He jumped. Then he studiously ignored her. *If it wasn't for you,* he thought . . .

"Richard?"

He didn't look up. "What?" he said.

"Look," she said. "You really wouldn't be in this mess if it weren't for me." *You can say that again,* he thought. "And I really don't think you'll be any safer with us. But. Well." She stopped. A deep breath. "I'm sorry. I really am. Are you coming?"

He looked at her then: a small elfin girl with huge, opal-colored eyes staring at him urgently from a heart-shaped, pale face. *Okay,* he said to himself, *I guess I'm not quite ready to just give up and die.* "Well, I don't have anywhere else to be right now," he said, with a studied unconcern that bordered on hysteria. "Why not?"

Her face changed. She threw her arms around his chest and hugged him, tightly. "And we will try to get you back home again," she said. "Promise. Once we've found what I'm looking for." He wondered if she meant it, suspected, for the first time, that what she was offering might be impossible. But he pushed

that thought out of his head. They began to walk down the tunnel. Richard could see Hunter and the Marquis waiting for them at the tunnel's mouth. The Marquis looked as if he had been forced to swallow a pulped lemon.

"What *are* you looking for, anyway?" asked Richard, cheering up a little.

Door took a deep breath, and answered after a long pause. "It's a long story," she said, solemnly. "Right now we're looking for an angel named Islington." It was then that Richard began to laugh; he couldn't help himself. There was hysteria in there, certainly, but there was also the exhaustion of someone who had managed, somehow, to believe several dozen impossible things in the last twenty-four hours, without ever getting a proper breakfast. His laughter echoed down the tunnels.

"An angel?" he said, giggling helplessly. "Called Islington?"

"We've got a long way to go," said Door.

And Richard shook his head, and felt wrung out, and emptied, and flayed. "An angel," he whispered, hysterically, to the tunnels and the dark. "An angel."

THERE WERE CANDLES ALL over the Great Hall: candles stood by the iron pillars that held the roof up; candles waited by the waterfall that ran down one wall and into the small rock pool below; candles clustered on the sides of the rock wall; candles huddled on the floor; candles were set into candlesticks by the huge door that stood between two dark iron pillars. The door was built of polished black flint set into a silver base that had tarnished, over the centuries, almost to black in its turn. The can-

dles were unlit; but as the tall form walked past, they flickered into flame. No hand touched them; no fires touched their wicks.

The figure's robe was simple, and white, or more than white. A color, or an absence of all colors, so bright as to be startling. Its feet were bare on the cold rock floor of the Great Hall. Its face was pale and wise, and gentle; and, perhaps, a little lonely.

It was very beautiful.

Soon every candle in the Hall was burning. It paused by the rock pool; knelt beside the water, cupped its hands, lowered them into the clear water, raised them, and drank. The water was cold, but very pure. When it had finished drinking the water it closed its eyes for a moment, as if in benediction. Then it stood up, and walked away, back through the Hall, the way it had come; and the candles went out as it passed, as they had done for tens of thousands of years. It had no wings; but still, it was, unmistakably, an angel.

Islington left the Great Hall; and the last of the candles went out, and the darkness returned.

6

R ICHARD WROTE A DIARY entry in
his head.

Dear Diary, he began. *On Fri-
day I had a job, a fiancée, a home,
and a life that made sense. (Well, as much as any
life makes sense.) Then I found an injured girl
bleeding on the pavement, and I tried to be a Good
Samaritan. Now I've got no fiancée, no home, no
job, and I'm walking around a couple of hundred
feet under the streets of London with the projected
life expectancy of a suicidal mayfly.*

"This way," said the Marquis, gesturing el-
egantly, his filthy lace cuff flowing.

"Don't all these tunnels look the same?"
asked Richard, tabling his diary entry for the
moment. "How can you tell which is which?"

"You can't," said the Marquis, sadly. "We're hopelessly lost. We'll never be seen again. In a couple of days we'll be killing each other for food."

"Really?" He hated himself for rising to the bait, even as he said it.

"No." The Marquis's expression said that torturing this poor fool was too easy to even be amusing. Richard found that he cared less and less what these people thought of him, however. Except, perhaps, for Door.

He went back to writing his mental diary. *There are hundreds of people in this other London. Thousands maybe. People who come from here, or people who have fallen through the cracks. I'm wandering around with a girl called Door, her bodyguard, and her psychotic grand vizier. We slept last night in a small tunnel that Door said was once a section of Regency sewer. The bodyguard was awake when I went to sleep, and awake when they woke me up. I don't think she ever sleeps. We had some fruitcake for breakfast; the Marquis had a large lump of it in his pocket. Why would anyone have a large lump of fruitcake in his pocket? My shoes dried out mostly while I slept.*

I want to go home. Then he mentally underlined the last sentence three times, rewrote it in huge letters in red ink, and circled it, before putting a number of exclamation marks next to it in his mental margin.

At least the tunnel they were now walking down was dry. It was a high-tech tunnel: all silvery pipes and white walls. The Marquis and Door walked together, in front. Richard tended to stay a couple of paces behind them. Hunter moved about: sometimes she was behind them, sometimes to one side of them or

to the other, often a little way in front, merging with the shadows. She made no sound when she moved, which Richard found rather disconcerting.

There was a crack of light ahead of them. "There we go," said the Marquis. "Bank station. Good place to start looking."

"You're out of your mind," said Richard. He did not mean it to be heard, but the most sotto of voces carried and echoed in the darkness.

"Indeed?" said the Marquis. The ground began to rumble: an Underground train was somewhere close at hand.

"Richard, just leave it," said Door.

But it was coming out of his mouth: "Well," he said. "You're both being silly. There are no such things as angels."

The Marquis nodded, said, "Ah. Yes. I understand you now. There are no such things as angels. Just as there is no London Below, no rat-speakers, no shepherds in Shepherd's Bush."

"There are *no* shepherds in Shepherd's Bush. I've been there. It's just houses and stores and roads and the BBC. That's all," pointed out Richard, flatly.

"There are shepherds," said Hunter, from the darkness just next to Richard's ear. "Pray you never meet them." She sounded perfectly serious.

"Well," said Richard, "I still don't believe that there are flocks of angels wandering about down here."

"There aren't," said the Marquis. "Just one." They had reached the end of the tunnel. There was a locked door in front of them. The Marquis stood back. "My lady?" he said to Door. She rested a hand on it, for a moment. The door opened, silently.

"Maybe," Richard said, persisting, "we're thinking of dif-

ferent things. The angels I have in mind are all wings, haloes, trumpets, peace-on-earth-goodwill-unto-men."

"That's right," said Door. "You got it. Angels."

They went through the door. Richard shut his eyes involuntarily at the sudden flood of light: it stabbed into his head like a migraine. As his eyes became used to the light, Richard found, to his surprise, that he knew where he was: they were in the long pedestrian tunnel that links Monument and Bank Tube stations. There were commuters wandering through the tunnels, none of whom gave the four of them even a first look. The perky wail of a saxophone echoed along the tunnel: Burt Bacharach and Hal David's "I'll Never Fall in Love Again," being played more or less competently. Richard successfully fought the urge to hum along. They walked toward Bank station.

"Who are we looking for again, then?" he asked, more or less innocently. "The Angel Gabriel? Raphael? Michael?"

They were passing a Tube map. The Marquis tapped Angel station with one long dark finger: Islington.

Richard had passed through Angel station hundreds of times. It was in trendy Islington, a district filled with antiques shops and places to eat. He knew very little about angels, but he was almost certain that Islington's tube stop was named after a pub, or a landmark. He changed the subject. "You know, when I tried to get on a Tube train a couple of days ago, it wouldn't let me."

"You just have to let them know who's boss, that's all," said Hunter, softly, from behind him.

Door chewed her lower lip. "This train we're looking for will let us on," she said. "If we can find it." Her words were almost drowned out by music coming from somewhere nearby. They went down a handful of steps and turned a corner.

The saxophone player had his coat in front of him, on the floor of the tunnel. On the coat were a few coins, which looked as if the man had placed them there himself to persuade passersby that everyone was doing it. Nobody was fooled.

The saxophone player was extremely tall; he had shoulder-length, dark hair and a long, forked dark beard, which framed deep-set eyes and a serious nose. He wore a ragged T-shirt, and oil-stained blue jeans. As the travelers reached him, he stopped playing, shook the spit from the saxophone mouthpiece, replaced it, and went into the old Julie London song "Cry Me a River."

Now, you say you're sorry . . .

Richard realized, with surprise, that the man could see them—and also that he was doing his best to pretend that he couldn't. The Marquis stopped in front of him. The wail of the saxophone trailed off in a nervous squeak. The Marquis flashed a cold grin. "It's Lear, isn't it?" he asked.

The man nodded, warily. His fingers stroked the keys of his saxophone. "We're after Earl's Court," continued the Marquis. "Would you happen to have such a thing as a train timetable about your person?"

Richard was beginning to catch on. He assumed that the Earl's Court to which he referred wasn't the familiar Tube station he had waited in innumerable times, reading a paper, or just daydreaming. The man named Lear moistened his lips with the tip of his tongue. "'S not impossible. What'd be in it for me, if I did?"

The Marquis thrust his hands deep into the pockets of his coat. Then he smiled, like a cat who had just been entrusted with

the keys to a home for wayward but plump canaries. "They say," he said, idly, as if he were simply passing the time, "that Merlin's master Blaise once wrote a reel so beguiling that it would charm the coins from the pockets of anyone who heard it."

Lear's eyes narrowed. "That'd be worth more than just a timetable," he said. "If you actually had it."

The Marquis did a perfectly good impression of someone re-alizing, *My, it would, wouldn't it?* "Well, then," he said, magnani-mously, "I suppose you would have to owe me, wouldn't you?"

Lear nodded, reluctantly. He fumbled in his back pocket, pulled out a much-folded scrap of paper, and held it up. The Mar-quis reached for it. Lear moved his hand away. "Let me hear the reel first, you old trickster," he said. "And it had better work."

The Marquis raised an eyebrow. He darted a hand into one of the inside pockets of his coat; when he pulled it out again it was holding a penny whistle and a small crystal ball. He looked at the crystal ball, made the kind of "hmmm" noise that means "Ah, so that's where that went," and put it away again. Then he flexed his fingers, put the penny whistle to his lips, and began to play an odd, rollicking tune that leapt and twisted and sang. It made Richard feel as if he were thirteen years old again, listening to his best friend's transistor radio at school in the lunch hour, lis-tening to the Top Twenty, back when pop music had mattered as it only can in your early teenage years: the Marquis' reel was everything he had ever wanted to hear in a song . . .

A handful of coins chinked onto Lear's coat, thrown by pass-ersby, who walked on with a smile on their faces and a spring in their step. The Marquis lowered his penny whistle. "I owe you, then, you old rascal," said Lear, nodding.

"Yes. You do." The Marquis took the paper—the timetable—from Lear, and scanned it, and nodded. "But a word to the wise. Don't overuse it. A little goes a very long way."

And the four of them walked away, down the long corridor, surrounded by posters advertising films and underwear, and the occasional official-looking notices warning buskers away from the station, listening to the sob of the saxophone, and to the sound of money landing on a coat.

The Marquis led them to a Central Line platform. Richard walked over to the edge of the platform and looked down. He wondered, as he always did, which one the live rail was, and decided, as he always did, that it was the one farthest from the platform, with the large whitish porcelain insulators between it and the ground; and then he found himself smiling, involuntarily, at a tiny dark gray mouse who was bravely prowling the tracks, three feet below him, in a mousy quest for abandoned sandwiches and dropped potato chips.

A voice came over the loudspeaker, that formal, disembodied male voice that warned, "Mind the Gap." It was intended to keep unwary passengers from stepping into the space between the train and the platform. Richard, like most Londoners, barely heard it anymore—it was like aural wallpaper. But, suddenly, Hunter's hand was on his arm. "Mind the Gap," she said urgently, to Richard. "Stand back over there. By the wall."

"What?" said Richard.

"I *said*," said Hunter, "mind the—"

And then it erupted over the side of the platform. It was diaphanous, dreamlike, a ghost-thing, the color of black smoke, and it welled up like silk underwater, and, moving astonishingly

fast while still seeming to drift almost in slow motion, it wrapped itself tightly around Richard's ankle. It stung, even through the fabric of his Levi's. The thing pulled him toward the edge of the platform, and he staggered.

He realized, as if from a distance, that Hunter had pulled out her staff, and was smacking the tentacle with it, hard, repeatedly.

There was a faraway screaming noise, thin and mindless, like an idiot child deprived of its toy. The smoke tentacle let go of Richard's ankle, and slid back over the edge of the platform, and it was gone. Hunter took Richard by the scruff of the neck and pulled him toward the back wall, where Richard slumped against it. He was trembling, and the world seemed suddenly utterly unreal. The color had been sucked from his jeans wherever the thing had touched him, making them look as if they'd been ineptly tie-dyed. He pulled up the trouser leg: tiny purple welts were coming up on the skin of his ankle and calf. "What . . . ," he tried to say, but nothing came out. He swallowed, and tried again. "What was that?"

Hunter looked down at him impassively. Her face could have been carved from brown wood. "I don't think it has a name," she said. "They live in the gaps. I did warn you."

"I've . . . never seen one before."

"You weren't part of the Underside before," said Hunter. "Just wait by the wall. It's safer."

The Marquis was checking the time on a large gold pocket watch. He returned it to his waistcoat pocket, consulted the paper Lear had given him and nodded, satisfied. "We're in luck," he pronounced. "The Earl's Court train should be coming through here in about half an hour."

"Earl's Court station isn't on the Central Line," pointed out Richard.

The Marquis stared at Richard, openly amused. "What a refreshing mind you have, young man," he said. "There really is nothing quite like total ignorance, is there?"

The warm wind began to blow. An Underground train pulled up at the station. People got off and other people got on, going about the business of their lives, and Richard watched them with envy. *"Mind the Gap,"* intoned a recorded voice. *"Stand clear of the doors. Mind the Gap."* Door took one look at Richard. Then, worried about what she was seeing, she walked over to him, and she took his hand. He was very pale, and his breath was coming shallow and fast. *"Mind the Gap,"* boomed the recorded voice again. "I'm fine," lied Richard bravely, to no one in particular.

THE CENTRAL WELL OF Mr. Croup and Mr. Vandemar's hospital was a dank and cheerless place. Ragged grass grew up through the abandoned desks, rubber tires, and bits of office furniture. The overall impression given by the area was that a decade before (perhaps out of boredom, perhaps out of frustration, perhaps even as a statement, or as performance art) a number of people had thrown the contents of their offices out of their windows, high above, and they had left them there to rot.

There was broken glass there, as well, broken glass in abundance. There were also several mattresses. For no easily explicable reason, some of these mattresses had at some point been set on fire. No one knew why; no one cared. Grass grew up through the springs. An entire ecology had evolved around the ornamental fountain in the center of the well, which had for a long time been

neither particularly ornamental nor a fountain. A cracked and leaking water pipe nearby had, with the aid of some rainwater, transformed it into a breeding ground for a number of little frogs who plopped about cheerfully, rejoicing in their freedom from any non-airborne natural predators. Crows and blackbirds and even occasional seagulls, on the other hand, regarded the place as a cat-free delicatessen with a special on frogs.

Slugs sprawled indolently under the springs of the burnt mattresses; snails left slime trails across the broken glass. Large black beetles scuttled industriously over the smashed gray plastic telephones and mysteriously mutilated Barbie dolls.

Mr. Croup and Mr. Vandemar had come up for a change of air. They were walking slowly around the perimeter of the central yard, broken glass crunching beneath their feet; they looked like shadows in their frayed black suits. Mr. Croup was in a cold fury. He was walking twice as fast as Mr. Vandemar, circling him, and almost dancing in his anger. At times, as if unable to contain the rage inside, Mr. Croup would fling himself at the hospital wall, physically attack it with his fists and feet, as if it were a poor substitute for a real person. Mr. Vandemar, on the other hand, simply walked. It was too consistent, too steady and inexorable a walk to be described as a stroll: Death walks like Mr. Vandemar. Mr. Vandemar watched Mr. Croup, impassively, as Mr. Croup kicked a sheet of glass which had been leaning against a wall. It shattered with a satisfying crash.

"I, Mister Vandemar," said Mr. Croup, surveying the wreckage, "I, for one, have had almost as much as I'm willing to take. Almost. Pussyfooting, trifling, lollygagging, shilly-shallying . . . whey-faced toad—I could pop out his eyes with my thumbs . . ."

Mr. Vandemar shook his head. "Not yet," he said. "He's our

boss. For this job. After we've been paid, maybe we could have some fun on our own time."

Mr. Croup spat on the ground. "He's a worthless, conniving dunderhead . . . We should butcher the bitch. Annul, cancel, inhume and amortize her."

A telephone began to ring, loudly. Mr. Croup and Mr. Vandemar looked around, puzzled. Eventually Mr. Vandemar found the telephone, halfway down a pile of rubble on top of a scree of water-stained medical records. Broken wires trailed from the back of it. He picked it up and passed it to Mr. Croup. "For you," he said. Mr. Vandemar did not like telephones.

"Mister Croup here," said Croup. Then, obsequiously, "Oh. It's you, sir . . ." A pause. "At present, as you requested, she is walking around, free as a daisy. I'm afraid your bodyguard idea went down like a dead baboon . . . Varney? Yes, he's quite dead." Another pause.

"Sir, I am commencing to have certain conceptual problems with the role of myself and my partner in these shenanigans." There was a third pause, and Mr. Croup went paler than pale. "Unprofessional?" he asked, mildly. "Us?" He curled his hand into a fist, which he slammed, rather hard, into the side of a brick wall. There was no change, however, in his tone of voice as he said, "Sir. Might I with due respect remind you that Mister Vandemar and myself burned down the City of Troy? We brought the Black Plague to Flanders. We have assassinated a dozen kings, five popes, half a hundred heroes and two accredited gods. Our last commission before this was the torturing to death of an entire monastery in sixteenth-century Tuscany. We are *utterly* professional."

Mr. Vandemar, who had been amusing himself by catching

little frogs, and seeing how many he could stuff into his mouth at a time before he was forced to start chewing, said, with his mouth full, "I liked doing that . . ."

"My point?" asked Mr. Croup, and he flicked some imaginary dust from his threadbare black suit, ignoring the real dust as he did so. "My point is that we are assassins. We are cutthroats. We kill." He listened to something, then, "Well, what about the Upworlder? Why can't we kill him?" Mr. Croup twitched, and he spat once more, and he kicked the wall, as he stood there holding the rust-stained half-broken telephone.

"*Scare her?* We're cutthroats, not scarecrows." A pause. He took a deep breath. "Yes, I understand, but I don't like it." But the person at the other end of the phone had hung up. Mr. Croup looked down at the telephone. Then he hefted it in one hand and proceeded methodically to smash it to shards of plastic and metal by banging it against the wall.

Mr. Vandemar walked over. He had found a large black slug with a bright orange underbelly, and he was chewing it, like a fat licorice cigar. The slug, which was not very bright, was trying to crawl away down Mr. Vandemar's chin. "Who was that?" asked Mr. Vandemar.

"Who the hell do you think it was?"

Mr. Vandemar chewed, thoughtfully, then sucked the slug into his mouth, like a strand of thick, glutinous, black-and-orange spaghetti. "A scarecrow man?" he ventured.

"Our employer."

"That was going to be my next guess."

"Scarecrows," spat Mr. Croup, disgusted. He was moving from a red rage to an oily gray sulk.

Mr. Vandemar swallowed the contents of his mouth, and wiped his lips on his sleeve. "Best way to scare crows," said Mr. Vandemar, "you just creep up behind them and put your hand round their little crow necks and squeeze until they don't move anymore. That scares the stuffing out of them."

And then he was silent; and from far above they heard the sound of crows flying, cawing angrily.

"Crows. Family *Corvidae*. Collective noun," intoned Mr. Croup, relishing the sound of the word: "a murder."

RICHARD WAITED AGAINST THE wall, next to Door. She said very little; she chewed her fingernails, ran her hands through her reddish hair until it was sticking up in all directions, then tried to push it back down again. She was certainly unlike anyone he had ever known. When she noticed him looking at her she shrugged and shimmied down further into her layers of clothes, deeper into her leather jacket. Her face looked out at the world from inside the jacket. The expression on her face made Richard think of a beautiful homeless child he had seen, the previous winter, behind Covent Garden: he had not been certain whether it was a girl or a boy. Its mother was begging, pleading with the passersby for coins to feed the child, and the infant that she carried in her arms. But the child stared out at the world, and said nothing, although it must have been cold and hungry. It just stared.

Hunter stood by Door, looking back and forth down the platform. The Marquis had told them where to wait, and had slipped away. From somewhere, Richard heard a baby begin to

cry. The Marquis slipped out of an exit-only door, and walked toward them. He was chewing on a piece of candy.

"Having fun?" asked Richard. A train was coming toward them, its approach heralded by a gust of warm wind.

"Just taking care of business," said the Marquis. He consulted the piece of paper, and his watch. He pointed to a place on the platform. "This should be the Earl's Court train. Stand behind me here, you three." Then, as the Underground train—a rather boring-looking, normal train, Richard was disappointed to observe—rumbled and rattled its way into the station, the Marquis leaned across Richard, and said to Door, "My lady? There is something that perhaps I should have mentioned earlier."

She turned her odd-colored eyes on him. "Yes?"

"Well," he said, "the Earl might not be *entirely* pleased to see me."

The train slowed down and stopped. The carriage that had pulled up in front of Richard was quite empty: its lights were turned off; it was bleak and empty and dark. From time to time Richard had noticed carriages like this one, locked and shadowy, on Tube trains, and had wondered what purpose they served. The other doors on the train hissed open, and passengers got on and got off. The doors of the darkened carriage remained closed. The Marquis drummed on the door with his fist, an intricate rhythmic rap. Nothing happened. Richard was just wondering if the train would now pull out without them on it, when the door of the dark carriage was pushed open from the inside. It opened about six inches, and an elderly, bespectacled face peered out at them.

"Who knocks?" he said.

Through the opening, Richard could see flames burning, and people, and smoke inside the car. Through the glass in the doors, however, he still saw a dark and empty carriage. "The Lady Door," said the Marquis, smoothly, "and her companions."

The door slid open all the way, and they were in Earl's Court.

7

———※———

THERE WAS STRAW SCATTERED on the floor, over a layer of rushes. There was an open log fire, sputtering and blazing in a large fireplace. There were a few chickens, strutting and pecking on the floor. There were seats with hand-embroidered cushions on them, and there were tapestries covering the windows and the doors.

Richard stumbled forward as the train lurched out of the station. He reached out, grabbed hold of the nearest person, and regained his balance. The nearest person happened to be a short, gray, elderly man-at-arms, who would have looked, Richard decided, exactly like a recently retired government employee, were it not for the tin hat, the surcoat, the rather clum-

sily knitted chain mail, and the spear; instead he looked like a recently retired government employee who had, somewhat against his will, been dragooned into his local amateur dramatic society, where he had been forced to play a man-at-arms.

The little gray man blinked shortsightedly at Richard, as Richard grabbed him, and then he said, lugubriously, "Sorry about that."

"My fault," said Richard.

"I know," said the man.

An enormous Irish wolfhound padded down the aisle, and stopped beside a lute player, who sat on the floor picking at a gladsome melody in a desultory fashion. The wolfhound glared at Richard, snorted with disdain, then lay down and went to sleep. At the far end of the carriage an elderly falconer, with a hooded falcon on his wrist, was exchanging pleasantries with a small knot of damozels of a certain age. Some passengers obviously stared at the four travelers; others, just as obviously, ignored them. It was, Richard realized, as if someone had taken a small medieval court and put it, as best they could, in one carriage of an Underground train.

A herald raised his bugle to his lips and played a tuneless blast, as an immense, elderly man, in a huge fur-lined dressing gown and carpet slippers, staggered through the connecting door to the next compartment, his arm resting on the shoulder of a jester in shabby motley. The old man was larger than life in every way: he wore an eye patch over his left eye, which had the effect of making him look slightly helpless and unbalanced, like a one-eyed hawk. There were fragments of food in his red-gray beard, and what appeared to be pajama pants were visible at the bottom of his shabby fur gown.

That, thought Richard, correctly, *must be the Earl.*

The Earl's jester, an elderly man with a pinched, humorless mouth and a painted face, looked like he had fled from a life as an all-round entertainer near the bottom of the bill on the Victorian music halls a hundred years before. He led the Earl to a throne-like carved wooden seat, in which, a trifle unsteadily, the Earl sat down. The wolfhound got up, padded down the length of the carriage, and settled itself at the Earl's slippered feet.

Earl's Court, thought Richard. *Of course.* And then he began to wonder whether there was a Baron in Barons Court tube station, or a Raven in Ravenscourt, or . . .

The little old man-at-arms coughed asthmatically, and said, "Right then, you lot. State your business." Door stepped forward. She held her head up high, suddenly seeming taller and more at ease than Richard had previously seen her, and she said, "We seek an audience with His Grace the Earl."

The Earl called down the carriage. "What did the little girl say, Halvard?" he asked. Richard wondered if he were deaf.

Halvard, the elderly man-at-arms, shuffled around, and cupped his hand to his mouth. "They seek an audience, Your Grace," he shouted, over the rattle of the train.

The Earl pushed aside his thick fur cap and scratched his head, meditatively. He was balding underneath his cap. "They do? An audience? How splendid. Who are they, Halvard?"

Halvard turned back to them. "He wants to know who you all are. Keep it short, though. Don't go on."

"I am the Lady Door," announced Door. "The Lord Portico was my father."

The Earl brightened at this, leaned forward, peered through

the smoke with his one good eye. "Did she say she was Portico's oldest girl?" he asked the jester.

"Yus, Your Grace."

The Earl beckoned to Door. "Come here," he said. "Come-come-come. Let me look at you." She walked down the swaying carriage, grabbing the thick rope straps that hung from the ceiling as she went, to keep her balance. When she stood before the Earl's wooden chair she curtseyed. He scratched at his beard, and stared at her. "We were all quite devastated to hear of your father's unfortunate—" said the Earl, and then he interrupted himself, and said, "Well, all your family, it was a . . ." And he trailed off, and said, "You know I had warmest regards for him, did a bit of business together . . . Good old Portico . . . full of ideas . . ." He stopped. Then he tapped the jester on the shoulder, and whispered, in a querulous boom, loud enough that it could be heard easily over the noise of the train, "Go and make jokes at them, Tooley. Earn your keep."

The Earl's fool staggered up the aisle with an arthritic mop and a rheumatic mow. He stopped in front of Richard. "And who might you be?" he asked.

"Me?" said Richard. "Um. Me? My name? It's Richard. Richard Mayhew."

"*Me?*" squeaked the Fool, in an elderly, rather theatrical imitation of Richard's Scottish accent. "*Me?* Um. *Me?* La, nuncle. "'Tis not a man, but a mooncalf." The courtiers sniggered, dustily.

"And I," de Carabas told the jester, with a blinding smile, "call myself the Marquis de Carabas." The Fool blinked.

"De Carabas the thief?" asked the jester. "De Carabas the

body snatcher? De Carabas the traitor?" He turned to the courtiers around them. "But this cannot be de Carabas. For why? Because de Carabas has long since been banished from the Earl's presence. Perhaps it is instead a strange new species of *stoat,* who grew particularly large." The courtiers tittered uneasily, and a low buzz of troubled conversation began. The Earl said nothing, but his lips were pressed together tightly, and he had begun to tremble.

"I am called Hunter," said Hunter to the jester.

The courtiers were silent then. The jester opened his mouth, as if he were going to say something, and then he looked at her, and he closed his mouth again. A hint of a smile played at the corner of Hunter's perfect lips. "Go on," she said. "Say something funny."

The jester stared at the trailing toes of his shoes. Then he muttered, "My hound hath no nose."

The Earl, who had been staring at the Marquis de Carabas like a slow-burning fuse, pop-eyed, white-lipped, unable to believe the evidence of his senses, now exploded to his feet, a gray-bearded volcano, an elderly berserker. His head brushed the roof of the carriage. He pointed at the Marquis, and shouted, spittle flying, "I will not stand for it, I will not. Make him come forward."

Halvard waggled a gloomy spear at the Marquis, who sauntered to the front of the train, until he stood, beside Door, in front of the Earl's throne. The wolfhound growled in the back of its throat.

"You," said the Earl, stabbing the air with a huge, knotted finger. "I know you, de Carabas. I haven't forgotten. I may be old, but I haven't forgotten."

The Marquis bowed. "Might I remind Your Grace," he said, urbanely, "that we had a deal? I negotiated the peace treaty between your people and the Raven's Court. And in return you agreed to provide a little favor." *So there is a raven's court,* thought Richard. He wondered what it was like.

"A little favor?" said the Earl. He turned a deep beetroot color. "Is that what you call it? I lost a dozen men to your foolishness in the retreat from White City. I lost an eye."

"And if you don't mind my saying so, Your Grace," said the Marquis, graciously, "that is a very fetching patch. It sets off your face perfectly."

"I swore . . . ," fulminated the Earl, beard bristling, "I swore . . . that if you ever set foot in my domain I would . . ." He trailed off. Shook his head, confused, and forgetful. Then he continued. "It'll come back to me. I do not forget."

"He might not be entirely pleased to see you?" whispered Door to de Carabas.

"Well, he's not," he muttered back.

Door stepped forward once more. "Your Grace," she said, loudly, clearly, "de Carabas is here with me as my guest and my companion. For the fellowship there has ever been between your family and mine, for the friendship between my father and—"

"He abused my hospitality," boomed the Earl. "I swore that . . . if he ever again entered my domain I would have him gutted and dried . . . like, like something that's been . . . um . . . gutted, first, and then . . . um . . . dried . . ."

"Perchance—a kipper, my lord?" suggested the jester.

The Earl shrugged. "It is of no matter. Guards, seize him."

And they did. While neither of the guards would ever see sixty again, each of them was holding a crossbow, pointed at the Marquis, and their hands did not tremble, neither with age nor fear. Richard looked at Hunter. She seemed untroubled by this, watching it almost with amusement, like someone watching a piece of drama played out for their benefit.

Door folded her arms, and stood taller, putting her head back, raising her pointed chin. She looked less like a ragged street pixie; more like someone used to getting her own way. The opal eyes flashed. "Your Grace, the Marquis is with me as my companion, on my quest. Our families have been friends for a long time now—"

"Yes. They have," interrupted the Earl, helpfully. "Hundreds of years. Hundreds and hundreds. Knew your grandfather, too. Funny old fellow. Bit vague," he confided.

"But I am forced to say that I will take an act of violence against my companion as an act of aggression against myself and my house." The girl stared up at the old man. He towered over her. They stood for some moments, frozen. He tugged on his red and gray beard, agitatedly, then he thrust out his lower lip like a small child. "I will not have him here," he said.

The Marquis took out the golden pocket watch he had found in Portico's study. He examined it, carelessly. Then he turned to Door, and said, as if none of the events around them had occurred, "My lady, I will obviously be of more use to you off this train than on. And I have other avenues to explore."

"No," she said. "If you go, we all go."

"I don't think so," said the Marquis. "Hunter will look after you as long as you stay in London Below. I'll meet you at the

next market. Don't do anything too stupid in the meantime." The train was coming into a station.

Door fixed the Earl with her look: there was something more ancient and powerful in those huge opal-colored eyes in their pale heart-shaped face than her young years would have seemed to allow. Richard noticed that the room fell quiet whenever she spoke. "Will you let him go in peace, Your Grace?" she asked.

The Earl ran his hands over his face, rubbed his good eye and his eye patch, then looked back at her. "Just make him go," said the Earl. He looked at the Marquis. "Next time"—he ran a thick old finger across his Adam's apple—"kipper."

The Marquis bowed low. "I'll see myself out," he said to the guards, and stepped toward the open door. Halvard raised his crossbow, pointed it toward the Marquis' back. Hunter reached out her hand, and pushed the end of the crossbow back down toward the floor. The Marquis stepped onto the platform, turned and waved an ironic good-bye flourish at them. The door hissed closed behind him.

The Earl sat down on his huge chair at the end of the carriage. He said nothing. The train rattled and lurched through the dark tunnel. "Where are my manners?" muttered the Earl to himself. He looked at them with one staring eye. Then he said it again, in a desperate boom that Richard could feel in his stomach, like a bass drum beat. *Where are my manners?* He motioned one of the elderly men-at-arms to him. "They will be hungry after their journey, Dagvard. Thirsty too, I shouldn't wonder."

"Yes, Your Grace."

"Stop the train!" called the Earl. The doors hissed open and Dagvard scuttled off onto a platform. Richard watched the

people on the platform. No one came into their carriage. No one seemed to notice that anything was at all odd, or in any way unusual.

Dagvard walked over to a vending machine on the side of the platform. He took off his helmet. Then he rapped, with one mailed glove, on the side of the machine. "Orders from the Earl," he said. "Choc'lits." A ratcheting whirr came from deep in the guts of the machine, and it began to spit out dozens of Cadbury Fruit and Nut chocolate bars, one after another. Dagvard held his metal helmet below the opening to catch them. The doors began to close. Halvard put the handle of his pike between the doors, and they opened again, and began bumping open and shut on the pike handle. *"Please stand clear of the doors,"* said a loudspeaker voice. *"The train cannot leave until the doors are all closed."*

The Earl was staring at Door lopsidedly, with his one good eye. "So. What brings you here to me?" he asked.

She licked her lips. "Well, indirectly, Your Grace, my father's death."

He nodded, slowly. "Yes. You seek vengeance. Quite right too." He coughed, then recited, in a basso profundo, *"Brave the battling blade, flashes the furious fire, steel sword sheathed in hated heart, crimsons the . . . the . . . something. Yes."*

"Vengeance?" Door thought for a moment. "Yes. That was what my father said. But I just want to understand what happened, and to protect myself. My family had no enemies." Dagvard staggered back onto the train then, his helmet filled with chocolate bars and cans of Coke; the doors were permitted to close, and the train moved off once more.

Lear's coat, still on the floor of the tunnel, was covered in coins and banknotes now, but it was also covered with shoes. Shoes worn on feet, shoes which were kicking the coins, smearing and tearing the banknotes, ripping the fabric of the coat. There was money underfoot, and no one seemed to notice. Lear had begun to cry. "Please. Why won't you leave me alone?" he begged. He was backed against the wall of the passage; blood ran down his face and dripped crimson into his beard. His saxophone hung limply, awkwardly, on his chest, dented and scraped.

He was surrounded by a small crowd of people—more than twenty, less than fifty—every one of them shoving and pushing, in a mindless mob, their eyes blank and staring, each man and woman fighting and clawing in order desperately to try to give Lear their money. There was blood on the tiled wall, where Lear had knocked his head. Lear flailed out at one middle-aged woman, her purse wide open, a fistful of five-pound notes thrust out at him. She clawed at his face in her eagerness to give him her money. He twisted to avoid her fingernails, and fell to the tunnel floor.

Someone trod on his hand. His face was pushed into a slurry of coins. He began to sob, and to curse. "I told you not to overuse it," said an elegant voice, nearby. "Naughty."

"Help me," gasped Lear.

"Well, there *is* a counter-charm," admitted the voice, almost reluctantly.

The crowd was pressing closer now. A flung fifty-pence coin opened Lear's cheek. He curled into a fetal ball, hugging him-

self, burying his face in his knees. "Play it, damn you," sobbed Lear. "Whatever you want . . . Just make them stop . . ."

A penny-whistle piping began softly, and echoed down the passage. A simple phrase, repeated over and over, slightly different every time: the de Carabas variations. The footsteps were moving away. Shuffling, at first, then picking up pace: moving away from him. He opened his eyes. The Marquis de Carabas was leaning against the wall, playing the penny whistle. When he saw Lear looking at him he took the whistle from his lips, replaced it in an inside pocket of his coat. He tossed Lear a lace-edged handkerchief of patched linen. Lear wiped the blood from his forehead and face. "They would have killed me," he said, accusingly.

"I *did* warn you," said de Carabas. "Just count yourself lucky I was coming back this way." He helped Lear into a sitting position. "Now," he said. "I think you owe me another favor."

Lear picked up his coat—torn and muddy and imprinted with the marks of many feet—from the passage floor. He suddenly felt very cold, and he wrapped the shredded coat around his shoulders. Coins fell and notes fluttered to the floor. He let them lie. "Was I really lucky? Or did you set me up?"

The Marquis looked almost offended. "I don't know how you could even bring yourself to think such a thing."

"'Cos I know you. That's how. So what is it this time? Theft? Arson?" Lear sounded resigned, and a little sad. And then, "Murder?"

De Carabas reached down and took back his handkerchief. "Theft, I'm afraid. You were right the first time," he said, with a smile. "I find myself in rather urgent need of a piece of T'ang dynasty sculpture." Lear shivered. Then, slowly, he nodded.

RICHARD WAS HANDED A bar of vending-machine-sized Cadbury Fruit and Nut chocolate, and a large silver goblet, ornamented around the rim with what appeared to Richard to be sapphires. The goblet was filled with Coca-Cola. The jester, whose name appeared to be Tooley, cleared his throat, loudly. "I would like to propose a toast to our guests," he said. "A child, a bravo, a fool. May they each get what they deserve."

"Which one am I?" whispered Richard to Hunter.

"The fool, of course," she said.

"In the old days," said Halvard dismally, after sipping his Coke, "we had wine. I prefer wine. It's not as sticky."

"Do all the machines just give you things like that?" asked Richard.

"Oh yes," said the old man. "They listen to the Earl, y'see. He rules the Underground. The bit with the trains. He's lord of the Central, the Circle, the Jubilee, the Victorious, the Bakerloo—well, all of them except the Underside Line."

"What's the Underside Line?" asked Richard.

Halvard shook his head, and pursed his lips. Hunter brushed Richard's shoulder with her fingers. "Remember what I told you about the shepherds of Shepherd's Bush?"

"You said I didn't want to meet them, and there were some things I was probably better off not knowing."

"Good," she said. "So now you can add the Underside Line to the list of things you're better off not knowing."

Door came back down the carriage toward them. She was smiling. "The Earl's agreed to help us," she said. "Come on. He's

meeting us in the library." Richard was almost proud of the way he didn't say "What library?" or point out that you couldn't put a library on a train. Instead he followed Door toward the Earl's empty throne, and round the back of it, and through the connecting door behind it, and into the library. It was a huge stone room, with a high wooden ceiling. Each wall was covered with shelves. Each shelf was laden with objects: there were books, yes. But the shelves were filled with a host of other things: tennis rackets, hockey sticks, umbrellas, a spade, a notebook computer, a wooden leg, several mugs, dozens of shoes, pairs of binoculars, a small log, six glove puppets, a lava lamp, various CDs, records (LPs, 45s and 78s), cassette tapes and eight-tracks, dice, toy cars, assorted pairs of dentures, watches, flashlights, four garden gnomes of assorted sizes (two fishing, one of them mooning, the last smoking a cigar), piles of newspapers, magazines, grimoires, three-legged stools, a box of cigars, a plastic nodding-head Alsatian, socks . . . The room was a tiny empire of lost property.

"This is his real domain," muttered Hunter. "Things lost. Things forgotten."

There were windows, set in the stone wall. Through them, Richard could see the rattling darkness and the passing lights of the Underground tunnels. The Earl was sitting on the floor with his legs splayed, patting the wolfhound and scratching it underneath the chin. The jester stood beside him, looking embarrassed. The Earl clambered to his feet when he saw them. His forehead creased. "Ah. There you are. Now, there was a reason I asked you here, it'll come to me . . ." He tugged at his red-gray beard, a tiny gesture from such a huge man.

"The Angel Islington, Your Grace," said Door, politely.

"Oh yes. Your father had a lot of ideas, you know. Asked me about them. I don't trust change. I sent him to Islington." He stopped. Blinked his one eye. "Did I tell you this already?"

"Yes, Your Grace. And how can *we* get to Islington?"

He nodded as if she had said something profound. "Only once by the quick way. After that you have to go the long way down. Dangerous."

Door said, patiently, "And the quick way is?"

"No, no. Need to be an opener to use it. Only good for Portico's family." He rested a huge hand on her shoulder. Then his hand slid up to her cheek. "Better off staying here with me. Keep an old man warm at night, eh?" He leered at her, and touched her tangle of hair with his old fingers. Hunter took a step toward Door. Door gestured with her hand: *No. Not yet.*

Door looked up at the Earl, and said, "Your Grace, I *am* Portico's oldest daughter. How do I get to the Angel Islington?" Richard found himself amazed that Door was able to keep her temper in the face of the Earl's obviously losing battle with temporal drift.

The Earl winked his single eye in a solemn blink: an old hawk, his head tipped on one side. Then he took his hand from her hair. "So you are. So you are. Portico's daughter. How is your dear father? Keeping well, I hope. Fine man. Good man."

"How do we get to the Angel Islington?" said Door, but there was a tremble in her voice.

"Hmm? Use the Angelus, of course."

Richard found himself imagining the Earl sixty, eighty, five hundred years ago: a mighty warrior, a cunning strategist, a great lover of women, a fine friend, a terrifying foe. There was still the wreckage of that man in there somewhere. That was

what made him so terrible, and so sad. The Earl fumbled on the shelves, moving pens and pipes and peashooters, little gargoyles and dead leaves. Then, like an aged cat stumbling on a mouse, he seized a small, rolled-up scroll, and handed it to the girl. "Here y'go, lassie," said the Earl. "All in here. And I suppose we'd better drop you off where you need to go."

"You'll drop us off?" asked Richard. "In a train?"

The Earl looked around for the source of the sound, focused on Richard, and smiled enormously. "Oh, think nothing of it," he boomed. "Anything for Portico's daughter." Door clutched the scroll tightly, triumphantly.

Richard could feel the train beginning to slow, and he, and Door, and Hunter were led out of the stone room, and back into the carriage. Richard peered out at the platform, as they slowed down.

"Excuse me. What station is this?" he asked. The train had stopped, facing one of the station signs: BRITISH MUSEUM, it said. Somehow, this was an oddity too many. He could accept the Mind the Gap Thing, and the Earl's Court, and even the strange library. But damn it, like all Londoners, he knew his Tube map, and this was going too far. "There isn't a British Museum station," said Richard, firmly.

"There isn't?" boomed the Earl. "Then, mm, then you must be very careful as you get off the train." And he guffawed, delightedly, and tapped his jester on the shoulder. "Hear that, Tooley? I am as funny as you are."

The jester smiled as bleak a smile as ever was seen. "My sides are splitting, my ribs are cracking, and my mirth is positively uncontainable, Your Grace," he said.

The doors hissed open. Door smiled up at the Earl. "Thank

you," she said. "Off, off," said the vast old man, shooing Door and Richard and Hunter out of the warm, smoky carriage onto the empty platform. And then the doors closed, and the train moved away, and Richard found himself staring at a sign which, no matter how many times he blinked—nor even if he looked away from it and looked back suddenly to take it by surprise—still obstinately persisted in saying:

BRITISH MUSEUM

8

I T WAS EARLY EVENING, and the cloud-
less sky was transmuting from royal blue
to a deep violet, with a smudge of fire-
orange and lime-green over Paddington,
four miles to the west, where, from Old Bailey's
perspective anyway, the sun had recently set.

Skies, thought Old Bailey, in a satisfied sort
of a way. *Never a two of them alike. Not by day nor
not by night, neither.* He was a bit of a connoisseur
of skies, was Old Bailey, and this was a good 'un.
The old man had pitched his tent for the night
on a roof opposite St. Paul's Cathedral, in the
center of the City of London.

He was fond of St. Paul's, and it, at least,
had changed little in the last three hundred
years. It had been built in white Portland stone,

which had, before it was even completed, begun to turn black from the soot and the filth in the smoky London air, and now, following the cleaning of London in the 1970s, it was more or less white again; but it was still St. Paul's. He was not sure that the same could be said for the rest of the City of London: he peered over the roof, stared away from his beloved sky, down to the sodium-lit pavement below. He could see security cameras affixed to a wall, and a few cars, and one late office worker, locking a door and then walking toward the Tube. *Brrr.* Even the thought of going underground made Old Bailey shudder. He was a roof man and proud of it, had fled the world at ground level so long ago . . .

Old Bailey remembered when people had actually *lived* here in the City, not just worked; when they had lived and lusted and laughed, built ramshackle houses one leaning against the next, each house filled with noisy people. Why, the noise and the mess and the stinks and the songs from the alley across the way (then known, at least colloquially, as Shitten Alley) had been legendary in their time, but no one lived in the City now. It was a cold and cheerless place of offices, of people who worked in the day and went home to somewhere else at night. It was not a place for living anymore. He even missed the stinks.

The last smudge of orange sun faded into nocturnal purple. The old man covered the cages, so the birds could get beauty sleep. They grumbled, then slept. Old Bailey scratched his nose, after which he went into his tent, and fetched a blackened stew-pot, some water, some carrots and potatoes, and salt, and a well-hanged pair of dead, plucked starlings. He walked out onto the roof, lit a small fire in a soot-blackened coffee can, and was put-

ting his stew on to cook when he became aware that someone was watching him from the shadows by a chimney stack.

He picked up his toasting fork and waved it threateningly at the chimney stack. "Who's there?"

The Marquis de Carabas stepped out of the shadows, bowed perfunctorily, and smiled gloriously. Old Bailey lowered his toasting fork. "Oh," he said. "It's you. Well, what do you want? Knowledge? Or birds?"

The Marquis walked over, picked a slice of raw carrot from Old Bailey's stew, and munched it. "Information, actually," he said.

Old Bailey chortled. "Hah," he said. "There's a turn-up for the books. Ehh?" Then he leaned toward the Marquis. "What'll you trade for it?"

"What do you need?"

"Maybe I should do what you do. I should ask for another favor. An investment for one day down the road." Old Bailey grinned.

"Much too expensive, in the long run," said the Marquis, without humor.

Old Bailey nodded. Now the sun had gone down, it was getting very cold, very fast. "Shoes, then," he said. "And a balaclava helmet." He inspected his fingerless gloves: they were more hole than glove. "And new gloveses. It's going to be a bastard winter."

"Very well. I'll bring them to you." The Marquis de Carabas put his hand into an inside pocket, and produced, like a magician producing a rose from thin air, the black animal figure he had taken from Portico's study. "Now. What can you tell me about this?"

Old Bailey pulled on his glasses. He took the object from de Carabas. It was cold to the touch. He sat down on an air-conditioning unit, then, turning the black obsidian statue over and over in his hand, he announced: "It's the Great Beast of London." The Marquis said nothing. His eyes flickered from the statue to Old Bailey, impatiently.

Old Bailey, enjoying the Marquis' minor discomfort, continued, at his own pace. "Now, they say that back in first King Charlie's day—him as got his head all chopped off, silly bugger—before the fire and the plague, this was, there was a butcher lived down by the Fleet Ditch, had some poor creature he was going to fatten up for Christmas. (Some says it was a piglet, and some says it wusn't, and there's some—and I list meself as one of them—that wusn't never properly certain.) One night in December the beast runned away, ran into the Fleet Ditch, and vanished into the sewers. And it fed on the sewage, and it grew, and it grew. And it got meaner, and nastier. They'd send in hunting parties after it, from time to time."

The Marquis pursed his lips. "It must have died three hundred years ago."

Old Bailey shook his head. "Things like that, they're too vicious to die. Too old and big and nasty."

The Marquis sighed. "I thought it was just a legend," he said. "Like the alligators in the sewers of New York City."

Old Bailey nodded, sagely: "What, the big white buggers? They're down there. I had a friend lost a head to one of them." A moment of silence. Old Bailey handed the statue back to the Marquis. Then he raised his hand, and snapped it, like a crocodile head, at de Carabas. "It was okay," gurned Old Bailey with a grin that was most terrible to behold. "He had another."

The Marquis sniffed, uncertain whether or not Old Bailey was pulling his leg. He made the statue of the Beast vanish inside his coat once more.

"Hang on," said Old Bailey. He went back inside his brown tent, and returned holding the ornate silver box the Marquis had given him on their previous meeting. He held it out to the Marquis. "How about this then?" he asked. "Are you ready to take it back? It fair gives me the creepy shivers, having it around."

The Marquis walked to the edge of the roof, dropped the eight feet to the next building. "I'll take it back when all this is over," he called. "Let us hope that you don't have to use it."

Old Bailey leaned over. "How will I know, if I do?"

"You'll know," called the Marquis. "And the rats will tell you what to do with it." And with that he was slipping down the side of the building, using drainpipes and ledges as handholds.

"Hope I never finds out, that's all I can say," said Old Bailey to himself. Then a thought struck him. "Hoy," he called out to the night and the City. "Don't forget the shoeses and the gloveses!"

THE ADVERTISEMENTS ON THE walls were for refreshing and health-giving malted drinks, for two-shilling day excursions by train to the seaside, for kippered herrings, moustache wax and bootblack. They were smoke-blackened relics of the late twenties or the early thirties. Richard stared at them in disbelief. It seemed completely abandoned: a forgotten place. "It *is* British Museum station," admitted Richard. "But . . . but there never *was* a British Museum station. This is all wrong."

"It was closed down in about 1933, and sealed off," said Door.

"How bizarre," said Richard. It was like walking through history. He could hear trains echoing through tunnels nearby, felt the push of air as they passed. "Are there many stations like this?"

"About fifty," said Hunter. "They aren't all accessible, though. Not even to us."

There was a movement in the shadows at the edge of the platform. "Hello," said Door. "How are you?" She went down into a crouch. A brown rat stepped out into the light. It sniffed at Door's hand.

"Thank you," said Door, cheerfully. "I'm glad *you* aren't dead, too."

Richard edged over. "Um, Door. Could you tell the rat something for me?"

The rat turned its head toward him. "Miss Whiskers says that if there's anything you've got to say to her, you can tell it to her yourself," said Door.

"Miss Whiskers?"

Door shrugged. "It's a literal translation," she said. "It sounds better in rat."

Richard did not doubt it. "Um. Hello . . . Miss Whiskers . . . Look, there was one of your rat-speaker people, a girl named Anaesthesia. She was taking me to the market. We were crossing this bridge in the dark, and she just never made it across."

The rat interrupted him, with a sharp *squee*. Door began to talk, hesitantly, like a simultaneous translator. "She says . . . that the rats do not blame you for the loss. Your guide was . . . mm . . . taken by the night . . . as tribute."

"But—"

The rat squeaked again. "Sometimes they come back . . . ," said Door. "She has taken note of your concern . . . and thanks you for it." The rat nodded to Richard, blinked her bead-black eyes, then leapt to the floor, and scurried back into the dark. "Nice rat," said Door. Her disposition seemed to have improved remarkably, now she had the scroll. "Up there," she said, indicating an archway effectively blocked by an iron door.

They walked over to it. Richard pushed against the metal. It was bolted from the other side. "Looks like it's been sealed up," said Richard. "We'll need special tools."

Door smiled, suddenly; her face seemed to be illuminated. For a moment, her elfin face became beautiful. "Richard," she said. "My family. We're openers. It's our Talent. Look . . ." She reached out a grubby hand, touched the door. For a long moment nothing happened, then there was a loud crash from the other side of the door, and a *chunk* from their side. Door pushed against the door and, with a fierce squeal from the rusted hinges, it opened. Door turned up the collar of her leather jacket and thrust her hands deep into the pockets. Hunter shone her flashlight into the blackness beyond the doorway: a flight of stone steps, going up, into the dark. "Hunter. Can you take the rear?" asked Door. "I'll go on in front. Richard can take the middle."

She walked up a couple of steps. Hunter stayed where she was. "Lady?" said Hunter. "You are going to London Above?"

"That's right," said Door. "We're going to the British Museum."

Hunter bit her lower lip. Then she shook her head. "I must stay in London Below," she said. There was a tremble in her

voice. Richard realized that this was the first time he had ever seen Hunter display any emotion other than effortless competence or, occasionally, tolerant amusement.

"Hunter," said Door, bewildered. "You're my bodyguard."

Hunter looked ill at ease. "I am your bodyguard in London Below," she said. "I cannot go with you to London Above."

"But, you have to."

"My lady, I cannot. I thought you understood. The Marquis knows." *Hunter will look after you as long as you stay in London Below,* thought Richard. *Yes.*

"No," said Door, her pointed chin pushed out and up, her odd-colored eyes narrowed. "I don't understand. What is it?" she added, scornfully. "Some kind of curse or something?" Hunter hesitated, licked her lips, then nodded. It was as if she were admitting to having some socially embarrassing disease.

"Look, Hunter," Richard heard his own voice saying, "don't be silly." For a moment he thought she was about to hit him, which would have been bad, or even to start crying, which would have been much, much worse. Then she took a deep breath, and said, in measured tones, "I will walk by your side when you are in London Below, my lady, and I shall guard your body from all harm that might befall you. But do not ask me to follow you to London Above. I cannot." She folded her arms beneath her breasts, planted her legs a little apart, and looked for all the underworld like a statue of a woman not going anywhere, cast in brass and in bronze and in burnt caramel.

"Right," said Door. "Come on, Richard." And she set off up the steps.

"Look," said Richard. "Why don't we stay down here? We

can find the Marquis, and then all set off together, and—" Door was disappearing into the darkness above him. Hunter was planted at the foot of the stairs.

"I shall wait here until she returns," Hunter told him. "You may go, or stay, as you will."

Richard chased Door up the steps, as fast as he could, in the dark. Soon he saw her lamplight above him. "Wait," he panted. "Please." She stopped, and waited for him to catch up. And then, when he had caught up, and was standing next to her on a claustrophobically small landing, she waited for him to catch his breath. "You can't just go running off like that," said Richard. Door said nothing; the line of her lips became slightly more compressed; the angle of her chin was ever-so-slightly raised. "She's your bodyguard," he pointed out.

Door began to walk up the next flight of steps. Richard followed her. "Well, we'll be back soon enough," said Door. "She can start guarding me again then."

The air was close, dank and oppressive. Richard wondered how you could tell if the air was bad, in the absence of a canary, and contented himself with hoping that it wasn't. "I think the Marquis probably did know. About her curse, or whatever it is," he said.

"Yes," she said. "I expect he did."

"He . . ." Richard began. "The Marquis. Well, you know, to be honest, he seems a little bit dodgy to me."

Door stopped. The steps dead-ended in a rough brick wall. "Mm," she agreed. "He's a little bit dodgy in the same way that rats are a little bit covered in fur."

"Then why go to him for help? Wasn't there someone else

who could have helped you, someone else you could have sent me to find?"

"We'll talk about it later." She opened the scroll the Earl had given her, glanced over the spidery archaic handwriting, then rolled it back up. "We'll be fine," she said, decisively. "It's all in here. We've just got to get into the British Museum. We find the Angelus, we get out. Easy. Nothing to it. A doddle. Close your eyes."

Richard closed his eyes, obediently. "Nothing to it," he repeated. "When people say that in films, it always means that something awful is going to happen."

He felt a breeze against his face. Something in the quality of the darkness beyond his closed eyelids changed. "So what's your point?" asked Door. The acoustics had altered as well: they were in a bigger room. "You can open your eyes now."

He opened his eyes. They were on the other side of the wall, he assumed, in what appeared to be a junk room. Not just any old junk room, though: there was something rather strange and special about the quality of this junk. It was the kind of magnificent, rare, strange and expensive junk one would only expect to see somewhere like . . .

"Are we in the British Museum?" he asked.

She frowned, and seemed to be thinking, or listening. "Not exactly. We're very near. I think this must be some kind of storage space or something." She reached up to touch the fabric of a suit of antique clothing, displayed on a wax dummy.

"I wish we'd stayed back with the bodyguard," said Richard.

Door tipped her head on one side, looked at him gravely. "And what do you need guarding from, Richard Mayhew?"

"Nothing," he admitted. And then they turned the corner, and he said, "Well . . . maybe them," and, at the same time, Door said, "Shit." The reason Richard said "Maybe them" and the reason Door said "Shit" was this: Mr. Croup and Mr. Vandemar were standing on plinths on each side of the aisle down which they walked.

They reminded Richard horridly of an exhibition of contemporary art Jessica had once taken him to: an exciting young artist had put on an exhibition which announced that it would be about breaking down all the Taboos of Art, and to this end the artist had embarked on a campaign of systematic grave robbery, and had displayed the thirty most interesting results of his depredations in glass cases. The exhibit was closed after the artist sold *Stolen Cadaver Number 25* to an advertising agency for a six-figure sum, and the relatives of Stolen Cadaver Number 25, seeing a photo of the sculpture in the *Sun,* had sued both for a share of the proceeds and to change the name of the art piece to *Edgar Fospring, 1919–1987, Loving Husband, Father and Uncle. Rest in Peace, Daddy.* Richard had stared at the glass-bound corpses in their stained suits and damaged dresses with horror: he had hated himself for looking, but had not been able to turn away.

Mr. Croup smiled like a snake with a crescent moon stuck in its mouth, and his resemblance to Stolen Cadavers numbers 1 to 30 was, if anything, increased by this. "What?" said the smiling Mr. Croup. "No Mister 'I'm So Clever and Know Everything' Marquis? No 'Oh, didn't I tell you? Whoops! I can't go upstairs?' Hunter?" He paused, for dramatic effect. There was something of the rotted ham about Mr. Croup. "So paint me gray and call

me a dire wolf if it isn't two little lost lambs, out on their own, after dark."

"You could call me a wolf too, Mister Croup," said Mr. Vandemar, helpfully.

Mr. Croup clambered down from his plinth. "A gentle word in your woolly ears, little lambkins," he said. Richard looked around them. There had to be somewhere they could run. He reached down, clasped Door's hand, looked around, desperately.

"No, please. Stay just where you are," said Mr. Croup. "We like you like that. And we don't want to have to hurt you."

"We do," said Mr. Vandemar.

"Well, yes, Mister Vandemar, once you put it like that. We want to hurt you both. We want to hurt you rather a lot. But that's not why we're here right now. We're here to make things more interesting. You see, when things get dull, my partner and I become restive and, hard as you may find this to believe, we lose our sunny and delightful dispositions."

Mr. Vandemar showed them his teeth, demonstrating his sunny and delightful disposition. It was unquestionably the most horrible thing that Richard had ever seen.

"Leave us alone," said Door. Her voice was clear and steady.

Richard squeezed her hand. If she could be brave, so could he. "If you want to hurt her," he said, "you'll have to kill me first."

Mr. Vandemar seemed genuinely pleased by this. "All right," he said. "Thanks."

"And we'll hurt you, too," said Mr. Croup.

"Not yet, though," said Mr. Vandemar.

"You see," explained Mr. Croup, in a voice like rancid butter, "right now, we're just here to worry you."

Mr. Vandemar's voice was a night wind blowing over a desert of bones. "Make you suffer," he said. "Spoil your day."

Mr. Croup sat down at the base of Mr. Vandemar's plinth. "You visited Earl's Court today," he said, in what Richard suspected he fondly imagined were light and conversational tones.

"So?" said Door. She was edging away from them, now.

Mr. Croup smiled. "How did we know that? How did we know where to find you now?"

"Can get to you any time at all," said Mr. Vandemar, almost in a whisper.

"You've been sold out, little ladybird," said Mr. Croup to Door and, Richard realized, to Door alone. "There's a traitor in your nest. A cuckoo."

"Come on," she said, and she ran. Richard ran with her, through the hall filled with junk, toward a door. At Door's touch, it opened.

"Bid them farewell, Mister Vandemar," said Mr. Croup's voice, from behind them.

"Bye-bye," said Mr. Vandemar.

"No no," corrected Mr. Croup. *"Au revoir."* He made a noise then—the *cuck-koo cuck-koo* that a cuckoo might make if it were five and a half feet high, and had a weakness for human flesh—while Mr. Vandemar, truer to his nature, threw back his bullet head and howled like a wolf, ghostly and feral and mad.

THEY WERE OUTSIDE, IN the open air, at night, running down a sidewalk in Bloomsbury's Russell Street. Richard thought his heart would pound its way through his chest. A large black car went by. The British Museum was on the other side of some high

black-painted railings. Discreet concealed lights illuminated the outside of the high white Victorian building, the huge pillars of the facade, the steps up to the front door. This was the repository of so many of the world's treasures, looted and found and rescued and donated over hundreds of years.

They reached a gate in the railings. Door grabbed it with both hands, and pushed against it. Nothing happened. "Can't you make it open?" asked Richard.

"What does it look like I'm trying to do?" she snapped back, an unfamiliar edge to her voice. A few hundred feet down the pavement, at the main gate, large cars were drawing up, couples in smart clothes were climbing out, walking along the drive toward the museum.

"Down there," said Richard. "The main gate."

Door nodded. She looked behind them. "Those two don't seem to be following us," she said. They hurried toward the main gate.

"Are you all right?" asked Richard. "What happened just then?"

Door hunched deep into her leather jacket. She was looking paler than usual, which was extremely pale indeed, and there were dark semicircles beneath her eyes. "I'm tired," she said, flatly. "Opened too many doors today. Takes a lot out of me, each time. I need a little time to recover. Something to eat, and I'll be fine."

There was a guard at the gate, minutely examining the engraved invitations that each of the well-shaven men in dinner jackets and the fragrant women in evening dresses needed to present, then ticking their names off on a list, before allowing them through. A uniformed policeman beside him surveyed the

guests implacably. Richard and Door walked through the gate, and no one glanced at them twice. There was a line of people standing on the stone steps that led up to the museum doors, and Richard and Door joined the queue. A white-haired man, accompanied by a woman bravely wearing a mink coat, joined the line immediately and neatly behind them. A thought struck Richard. "Can they see us?" he asked.

Door turned to the gentleman behind them in the line. She stared up at him. "Hello," she said.

The man looked around, a puzzled expression on his face, as if he were unsure what had attracted his attention. Then he caught sight of Door, standing just in front of him. "Hello . . . ?" he said.

"I'm Door," she told him. "This is Richard."

"Oh . . . ," said the man. Then he fumbled in an inner pocket, pulled out a cigar case, and forgot all about them.

"There. See?" said Door.

"I think so," he replied. They said nothing for some time, as the queue moved slowly toward the single open glass door at the museum's main entrance. Door looked at the writing on her scroll, as if she needed to reassure herself of something. Then Richard said, "A traitor?"

"They were just winding us up," said Door. "Trying to upset us."

"Doing a bloody good job of it too," said Richard. And they walked through the open door, and then they were in the British Museum.

Mr. Vandemar was hungry, so they walked back through Trafalgar Square.

"Scare her," muttered Mr. Croup, disgustedly. "*Scare her.* That we should be brought to this."

Mr. Vandemar had found half a prawn and lettuce sandwich in a waste bin, and was gently tearing it into small pieces, which he was tossing down onto the flagstones in front of him, attracting a small flock of peckish late-night pigeons. "Should have followed my idea," said Mr. Vandemar. "Would have scared her lots more if I'd pulled his head off while she wasn't looking, then put my hand up through his throat and wiggled my fingers about. They always scream," he confided, "when the eyeballs fall out." He demonstrated with his right hand, stabbing up with his fingers, and then wiggling them about.

Mr. Croup was having none of it. "Why get so squeamish at this stage in the game?" he asked.

"I'm not squeamish, Mister Croup," said Mr. Vandemar. "I like it when the eyeballs fall out. Peepers and tarriwags." More gray pigeons out past their bedtimes strutted over to peck at the fragments of bread and prawn, and to disdain the lettuce.

"Not you," said Mr. Croup. "The governor. Kill her, kidnap her, scare her. Why doesn't he make up his mind?"

Mr. Vandemar had run out of the sandwich he had been using as bait, and now he made a dash into the crowd of pigeons, who took to the wing with some clacking noises and the occasional grumbling coo. "Well caught, Mister Vandemar," said Mr. Croup, approvingly. Mr. Vandemar was holding a surprised and upset pigeon, which grumbled and fidgeted in his grasp, and pecked ineffectually at his fingers.

Mr. Croup sighed, dramatically. "Well, anyway. We've certainly put the cat amongst the pigeons now," he said, with relish. Mr. Vandemar held the pigeon up to his face. There was a crunching noise, as he bit off its head, and commenced to chew.

THE SECURITY GUARDS WERE directing the museum's guests to a hallway that seemed to be functioning as some kind of holding area. Door ignored the guards entirely and set off into the museum halls with Richard trailing along behind her. They went through the Egyptian rooms, up several flights of back stairs, and into a room marked EARLY ENGLISH.

"According to this scroll thingie," she said, "the Angelus is in this room somewhere." Then Door looked down at her scroll some more, and looked around the hall, more carefully. She made a face. "Tch," she explained, and took off back down the stairs, the way they had come. Richard had an intense feeling of déjà vu, before realizing that, yes, of course this felt familiar: it was how he had spent his weekends in the Jessica days. Which were starting to seem, already, like things that had happened to someone else a long, long time ago.

"The Angelus wasn't in that room, then?" asked Richard.

"No, it wasn't there," said Door, a little more fiercely than Richard felt the question had actually warranted.

"Oh," he said. "I only wondered." They went into another room. Richard wondered if he were starting to hallucinate from a surfeit of Earl's Court sugar, or from sensory deprivation. "I can hear music," he said. It sounded like a string quartet.

"The party," said Door.

Right. The people in the dinner jackets they had queued up with. No, the Angelus didn't seem to be here either. Door walked into the next hall along, and Richard trailed in her wake. He wished he could be of more use. "This Angelus," he said. "What does it look like?"

For a moment he thought she was going to reprimand him simply for asking. But she stopped, rubbed her forehead. "This just says it's got a picture of an angel on it. But it can't be that hard to find. After all," she added, hopefully, "how many things with angels on them are there here?"

9

⸻

ESSICA WAS UNDER A little pressure. She was worried, and nervous, and jittery. She had cataloged the collection, arranged with the British Museum to host the exhibition, organized the Restoration of the Prime Exhibit, assisted in hanging and exhibiting the collection, and had put together the list of invitees to the Fabulous Launch. It was just as well she didn't have a boyfriend, she would tell her friends. There'd be no time for one even if she had one. Still, it *would* be nice, she thought, when she got a moment: someone to go to galleries with on the weekends. Someone to . . .

No. She did not go to that place in her head. She could no more pin it down than she could put her finger on a bead of mercury, and she re-

focused on the exhibition. Even now, at the last minute, there were so many things that could go wrong. Many a horse had fallen at the final hurdle. Many an overconfident general had seen certain victory turn to defeat in the closing minutes of a battle. Jessica was simply going to ensure that nothing went wrong. She was wearing a green silk dress, an off-the-shoulder general marshalling her troops, and stoically pretending that Mr. Stockton was not half an hour late.

Her troops consisted of a headwaiter, a dozen serving staff, three women from the caterers, a string quartet, and her assistant, a young man named Clarence. Jessica was convinced that Clarence had only got his job because he was a) openly gay, and b) just as openly black; and thus it was a source of general irritation to her that he was by far the most efficient, competent and best assistant she had had to date.

She inspected the drinks table. "We're fine for champagne? Yes?" The headwaiter pointed to the crate of champagne beneath the table. "And sparkling mineral water?" Another nod. Another crate. Jessica pursed her lips. "What about *still* mineral water? Bubbles aren't everybody's cup of tea, you know." They had plenty of still mineral water. Good.

The string quartet were warming up. They were not quite loud enough to drown the noise coming from the hallway outside. It was the noise of a small but affluent crowd: the grumbling of ladies in mink coats and men, who, were it not for the NO SMOKING signs on the walls—and perhaps the advice of their doctors—would be smoking cigars; the grumbling of journalists and celebrities who could smell the canapés, vol-au-vents, sundry nibbles, and free champagne.

Clarence was talking to someone on his mobile phone, a slim-line piece of fold-out engineering that made the *Star Trek* communicators look bulky and old-fashioned. He turned it off, put it into the Armani pocket of his Armani suit without disturbing the line. He smiled, reassuringly. "Jessica, Mister Stockton's driver's phoned from the car. They're still running a couple of minutes late. Nothing to worry about."

"Nothing to worry about," echoed Jessica. Doomed. *Doomed*. The whole thing was going to be a disaster. *Her* disaster. She picked up a glass of champagne from the table, emptied it, and handed the empty glass to the wine waiter.

Clarence tipped his head on one side, listening to the grumbling reverberation from the hallway outside. He looked at his watch, then looked at Jessica questioningly, a captain querying his general. *Into the Valley of Death, then, boss?*

"Mister Stockton is on his way, Clarence," she said, calmly. "He has requested a private viewing before the event begins."

"Shall I go out and see how they're doing?"

"No," said Jessica, decisively. Then, just as decisively, "Yes." Food and drink dealt with, Jessica turned to the string quartet, and asked them, for the third time that evening, exactly what they planned to play.

Clarence opened the double doors. It was worse than he had thought: there had to be more than a hundred people in the hall. And they weren't just people. They were People. Some of them were even Personalities.

"Excuse me," said the Chairman of the Arts Council. "The invitations said eight o'clock sharp. It's twenty past eight already."

"We'll just be a few more minutes," reassured Clarence, smoothly. "Security arrangements."

A woman in a hat bore down on him. Her voice was stentorian, bullying and decidedly parliamentary. "Young man," she announced. "Do you know who I am?"

"Not really, no," lied Clarence, who knew exactly who all of them were. "Hold on a sec. I'll see if anyone in here does." He shut the door behind him. "Jessica? They're going to riot."

"Don't exaggerate, Clarence." She was moving around the room like a green silk whirlwind, positioning her serving staff, with their trays of canapés or drinks, in strategic corners of the hall; checking the public-address system, the podium, the curtain and the pull-rope. "I can see the headlines now," said Clarence, unfolding an imaginary newspaper. "GERITOL BILLIONAIRES CRUSH MARKETING BABE IN MUSEUM CANAPÉ DASH HORROR."

Somebody began knocking at the door. The volume in the hallway began to increase. Somebody was saying, very loudly, "Excuse me. Um. Excuse me." Someone else was informing the world that it was a disgrace, quite simply a disgrace, no other word for it. "Executive decision," said Clarence, suddenly. "I'm letting them in."

Jessica shouted, "No! If you—"

But it was too late. The doors were open, and the horde was pushing its way into the hall. The expression on Jessica's face morphed from one of horror to one of charmed delight. She shimmered toward the door. "Baroness," she said, with a happy smile. "I can't tell you how delighted we are that you were able to come to our little exhibition this evening. Mister Stockton's been unavoidably delayed, but he'll be here momentarily. Please,

have some canapés . . ." Over the Baroness's mink-draped shoulder, Clarence winked at her, cheerfully. Jessica ran through all the bad words she knew in her head. As soon as the Baroness had headed for the vol-au-vents, Jessica walked over to Clarence and, in a whisper, and still smiling, called him several of them.

RICHARD FROZE. A SECURITY guard was coming straight toward them, the beam of his flashlight flashing from side to side. He looked around for somewhere to hide.

Too late. Another guard was coming toward them, past the huge statues of dead Greek gods, flashlight beam swinging. "All right?" called the first guard. The other guard kept coming toward Richard and Door, and stopped just beside them.

"I suppose," she said. "I've already had to stop a couple of tosspots in suits from carving their initials on the Rosetta Stone. I hate these functions."

The first guard shone his flashlight straight into Richard's eyes, then let the beam slide off, skittering over shadows. "I keep telling you," he said, with the satisfied relish of any true prophet, "it's 'The Masque of the Red Death' all over again. A decadent elite party while civilization crumbles about their ears." He picked his nose, wiped it on the leather sole of his well-polished black boot.

The second guard sighed. "Thank you, Gerald. Right, back on patrol."

The guards walked out of the hall together. "Last one of these things we found someone had puked in a sarcophagus," said one of the guards, and then the door closed behind them.

"If you're part of London Below," said Door to Richard, in a

conversational voice, as they walked, side by side, into the next hall, "they normally don't even notice you exist unless you stop and talk to them. And even then, they forget you pretty quickly."

"But *I* saw you," said Richard. It had been bothering him for a while.

"I know," said Door. "Isn't that odd?"

"Everything's odd," said Richard, with feeling. The string music was getting louder. The surges of anxiety were somehow worse up here in London Above, where he was forced to reconcile these two universes. At least below, he could proceed dreamlike, putting one foot in front of the other like a sleepwalker.

"The Angelus is through there," announced Door, interrupting his reverie and pointing to the direction from which the music was coming.

"How do you know?"

"I know," she said, with utter certainty. "Come on." They stepped out of the darkness into a lighted corridor. There was a huge sign hanging across the corridor. It said:

<div align="center">

ANGELS OVER ENGLAND

AN EXHIBITION AT THE BRITISH MUSEUM

Sponsored by Stocktons PLC

</div>

They crossed the corridor, and walked through an open door, into a large room, in which a party was going on.

THERE WAS A STRING quartet playing, and a number of serving staff were providing a roomful of well-dressed people with food

and drink. There was a small stage in one corner of the room, with a podium on it, beside a high curtain.

The room was completely filled with angels.

There were statues of angels on tiny plinths. There were paintings of angels on the walls. There were angel frescoes. There were huge angels and tiny angels, stiff angels and amiable angels, angels with wings and haloes and angels with neither, warlike angels and peaceable angels. There were modern angels and classical angels. Hundreds upon hundreds of angels of every size and shape. Western angels, Middle Eastern angels, Eastern angels. Michelangelo angels. Joel-Peter Witkin angels, Picasso angels, Warhol angels. Mr. Stockton's angel collection was "indiscriminate to the point of trashiness, but certainly impressive in its eclecticism," in the words of the *Time Out* review.

"Would you think," Richard asked, "that I was being picky if I pointed out that trying to find something with an angel on it in here is going to be like trying to find a needle in an oh my god it's Jessica." Richard felt the blood drain from his face. Until now he had thought that that was simply a figure of speech. He hadn't thought it actually happened in real life.

"Someone you knew?" asked Door.

Richard nodded. "She was my. Well. We were going to be married. We've been together for a couple of years. She was with me when I found you. She was the one on the. She left that message. On the answering machine." He pointed across the room.

Jessica was making animated conversation with Lord Lloyd Webber, Sir Bob Geldof, and a bespectacled gentleman whom she strongly suspected of being a Saatchi. Every few minutes she checked her watch, and glanced toward the door.

"Her?" said Door, remembering the woman. Then, obviously feeling that she should say something nice about someone Richard had cared for, she said, "Well, she's very . . ." And she paused, and thought, and then said, ". . . clean."

Richard stared across the room. "Will she . . . is she going to be upset that we're here?"

"I doubt it," said Door. "Frankly, unless you do something stupid, like talk to her, she probably won't even notice you." And then, with more enthusiasm, she said, "Food!" She descended on the canapés like a small, smut-nosed, pixie-faced, red-haired, big-brown-leather-jacketed girl who hadn't eaten properly in ages. Enormous quantities of food were immediately crammed into her mouth, masticated and swallowed, while, at the same time, the more substantial sandwiches were wrapped in paper napkins, and placed into her pockets. Then, with a paper plate heaped high with chicken legs, melon slices, mushroom vol-au-vents, caviar puffs and small venison sausages, she began to circle the room, staring intently at each and every angelic artifact.

Richard trailed along behind her, with a Brie and fennel sandwich and a glass of freshly squeezed orange juice.

JESSICA WAS DEEPLY PUZZLED. She had noticed Richard, and having noticed him, she had noticed Door. There was something familiar about them both: it was like a tickle at the back of her head, impossible to place, utterly irritating.

It reminded Jessica of something her mother had once told her about, of how Jessica's mother had, one evening, encoun-

tered a woman she had known all her life—had been to school with, had served on the parish council with, had run the coconut shy at the village fête with—and how her mother, encountering the woman at a party, had suddenly realized that she was unable to recall the woman's name, although she knew the woman had a husband in publishing named Eric and a golden retriever named Major. It had left Jessica's mother quite disgruntled.

It was driving Jessica to distraction. "Who are those people?" she asked Clarence.

"Them? Well, he's the new editor of *Vogue,* she's the arts correspondent of the *New York Times.* The one between them is Kate Moss, I think . . ."

"No, not them," said Jessica. "*Them.* There."

Clarence looked in the place that she was pointing. "Hm? Oh. *Them.*" He couldn't understand how he had failed to see them before. Old age, he thought; he would soon be twenty-three. "Journalists?" he said, without much conviction. "They do look rather trendoid. Grunge chic? Please. I know I invited *The Face* . . ."

"I *know* him," said Jessica, frustrated. Then Mr. Stockton's chauffeur phoned from Holborn to say that he was almost at the British Museum, and Richard slid out of her head, like mercury trickling through her fingers.

"See anything?" asked Richard.

Door shook her head, and swallowed a mouthful of hastily chewed chicken leg. "It's like playing 'Spot the Pigeon' in Trafalgar Square," she said. "There's nothing that *feels* like the Angelus. The paper said I'd know it if I saw it." And she wandered off, inspecting angels, pushing her way past a Captain of Industry,

the Deputy Leader of the Opposition, and the Highest-Paid Call Girl in the South of England.

Richard turned away, and found himself face-to-face with Jessica. Her hair was piled on her head, and it framed her face perfectly in corkscrews of chestnut curls. She was very beautiful. She was smiling at him; it was the smile that did it. "Hello, Jessica," he said. "How are you?"

"Hello. You won't believe this," she said, "but my assistant failed to make a note of your newspaper, Mister uh."

"Paper?" said Richard.

"Did I say newspaper?" said Jessica, with a tinkling, sweet, and self-deprecating laugh. "Magazine . . . television station. You *are* with the media?"

"You're looking very fine, Jessica," said Richard.

"You have the advantage of me," she said, smiling roguishly.

"You're Jessica Bartram. You're a marketing executive at Stocktons. You're twenty-six. Your birthday is April the twenty-third, and in the throes of extreme passion you have a tendency to hum the Monkees song 'I'm a Believer' . . ."

Jessica was no longer smiling. "Is this some kind of joke?" she asked, coldly.

"Oh, and we've been engaged for the last eighteen months," said Richard.

Jessica smiled nervously. Perhaps this really was some kind of joke: one of those jokes that everyone else seemed to get and she never did. "I rather think I'd know if I'd been engaged to someone for eighteen months, Mister um," said Jessica.

"Mayhew," said Richard helpfully. "Richard Mayhew. You chucked me, and I don't exist anymore."

Jessica waved, urgently, at no one in particular all the way across the room. "Be right there," she called, desperately, and she began to back away.

"I'm a believer," sang Richard, cheerfully, *"I couldn't leave her if I tried . . ."*

Jessica snatched a glass of champagne from a passing tray, downed it in a gulp. At the far end of the room she could see Mr. Stockton's chauffeur, and where Mr. Stockton's chauffeur was . . .

She headed toward the doors. "So who was he?" asked Clarence, edging alongside her.

"Who?"

"Your mystery man."

"I don't know," she admitted. Then she said, "Look, maybe you ought to call security."

"Okay. Why?"

"Just . . . Just get me security," and then Mr. Arnold Stockton entered the hall, and everything else went out of her head.

Expansive, he was, and expensive, a Hogarth cartoon of a man, enormous of girth, many-chinned and broad-stomached. He was over sixty; his hair was gray and silver, and it was cut too long in the back, because it made people uncomfortable that his hair was too long, and Mr. Stockton liked making people uncomfortable. Compared to Arnold Stockton, Rupert Murdoch was a shady little piker, and the late Robert Maxwell was a beached whale. Arnold Stockton was a pit bull, which was how caricaturists often chose to draw him. Stocktons owned

a little bit of everything: satellites, newspapers, record com-
panies, amusement parks, books, magazines, comics, television
stations, film companies.

"I'll make the speech now," said Mr. Stockton, to Jessica,
by way of introduction. "Then I'll bugger off. Come back some
other time, when there aren't all these stuffed shirts about."

"Right," said Jessica. "Yes. The speech now. Of course."

And she led him up onto the little stage, up to the podium.
She tinked her fingernail against a glass, for silence. Nobody
heard her, so she said, "Excuse me," into the microphone. This
time the conversation quieted. "Ladies and gentlemen. Honored
guests. I'd like to welcome all of you to the British Museum,"
she said, "to the Stocktons-sponsored exhibition 'Angels over
England,' and to the man behind it all, our Chief Executive and
Chairman of the Board, Mister Arnold Stockton." The guests
applauded, none of them in any doubt as to who had assembled
the collection of angels, nor, for that matter, who paid for their
champagne.

Mr. Stockton cleared his throat. "Right," he said. "This
won't take long. When I was a small boy, I used to come to the
British Museum on Saturdays, because it was free, and we didn't
have much money. But I'd come up the big steps to the museum,
and I'd come down to this room round the back and look up at
this angel. It was like it knew what I was thinking."

Just at that moment, Clarence came back in, a couple of secu-
rity guards beside him. He pointed to Richard, who had stopped
to listen to Mr. Stockton's speech. Door was still examining ex-
hibits. "No, *him*," Clarence kept saying to the guards, in an un-
dertone. "No, look, just there. Yes? *Him*."

"Anyway. Like anything that's not looked after," continued Mr. Stockton, "it decayed, fell apart under the stresses and strains of modern times. Went rotten. Went bad. Well, it's taken a shitload of money"—he paused, to let it sink in: if he, Arnold Stockton, thought it was a shitload, then a shitload it certainly was—"and a dozen craftsmen have spent a great deal of time restoring it and fixing it up. After this the exhibition'll be going to America, and then around the world, so it maybe can inspire some other little penniless bugger to start his own communications empire."

He looked around. Turned to Jessica, muttered, "What do I do now?" She pointed to the pull-rope, at the side of the curtain. Mr. Stockton pulled the rope. The curtain billowed and opened, revealing an old door behind it.

Again, there was a small flurry of activity in Clarence's corner of the room. "No. *Him*," said Clarence. "For heaven's sake. Are you blind?"

It looked like it had once been the door to a cathedral. It was the height of two men, and wide enough for a pony to walk through. Carved into the wood of the door, and painted with red and white and gold leaf, was an extraordinary angel. It stared out at the world with blank medieval eyes. There was an impressed gasp from the guests, then they began to applaud.

"*The Angelus*." Door tugged at Richard's sleeve. "That's it! Richard, come on." She ran for the stage.

"Excuse me, sir," said a guard to Richard. "Might we see your invitation?" said another, taking Richard firmly but discreetly by the arm. "And do you have any identification?"

"No," said Richard.

Door was up on the stage. Richard tried to yank free and follow her, hoping that the guards would forget about him. They didn't: now that he had been brought to their attention they were going to proceed to treat him as they might any other shabby, unwashed, somewhat unshaven gatecrasher. The guard who was holding Richard increased his grip on his arm, muttering, "None of that."

Door paused on the stage, wondering how to make the guards let Richard go. Then she did the only thing she could think of. She went over to the microphone, went up on tiptoes, and she screamed, as loud as she possibly could, into the public-address system. She had a remarkable scream: it could, with no artificial assistance, go through your head like a new power drill with a bone-saw attachment. And amplified . . . It was simply unearthly.

A waitress dropped her tray of drinks. Heads turned. Hands covered ears. All conversation stopped. People stared at the stage in puzzlement and horror. And Richard made a break for it. "Sorry," he said to the stunned guard, as he yanked his arm out of the man's grip, and fled. "Wrong London." He reached the stage, grabbed Door's outstretched left hand. Her right hand touched the Angelus, the enormous cathedral door. Touched it, and *opened* it.

This time no one dropped any drinks. They were frozen, staring, utterly overwhelmed—and, momentarily, blinded. The Angelus had opened, and light, from behind the door, had flooded the room with radiance. People covered their eyes, then, hesitantly, opened them again, and simply stared. It was as if fireworks had been let off in the room. Not indoor fireworks, strange crawling things that sputter and smell bad; nor even the kind of fireworks that you let off in your back garden; but the kind of

industrial-strength fireworks that get fired up high enough to cause a potential menace to the airways: the kind of fireworks that end a day at Walt Disney World, or that give the fire marshals headaches at Pink Floyd concerts. It was a moment of pure magic.

The audience stared, entranced and amazed. The only noise to be heard was the gentle, gasping almost-groan of wonderment people make when they watch fireworks: the sound of awe. Then a grubby young man and a smut-faced girl in a huge leather jacket walked into the light show, and vanished. The door closed behind them. The light show was over.

And everything was normal again. The guests, and guards, and serving staff, blinked, shook their respective heads, and, having dealt with something entirely outside of their experience, agreed, somehow, without a word, that it had simply never happened. The string quartet began to play once more.

Mr. Stockton walked off, nodding brusquely to various acquaintances as he did so. Jessica walked over to Clarence. "What," she asked, quietly, "are those security guards doing in here?"

The guards in question were standing amongst the guests, looking around as if they were themselves unsure what they were doing there. Clarence began to explain just what the guards were doing there; and then he realized he had absolutely no idea. "I'll deal with it," said Clarence, efficiently.

Jessica nodded. She looked out over her party, and smiled benignly. It was all going rather well.

RICHARD AND DOOR WALKED into the light. And then it was dark, and chill, and Richard was blinking at the retinal afterimage of the light, which left him almost blinded: a ghostly series of

orange-green splotches that slowly faded, as his eyes accustomed themselves to the darkness that surrounded them.

They were in a huge hall, carved from rock. Iron pillars, black and rust-dusted, held up the roof, went off into the distant dark, perhaps for miles. From somewhere he could hear the gentle splash of water: a fountain, perhaps, or a spring. Door was still holding his hand, tightly. In the distance, a tiny flame flickered and flared. And another, and then another: it was a host of candles, flickering into flame, Richard realized. And walking toward them, through the candles, was a tall figure, dressed in a simple white robe.

The figure seemed to be moving slowly, but it must have been walking very fast, as it was only seconds before it was standing beside them. It had golden hair, and a pale face. It was not much taller than Richard, but it made him feel like a little child. It was not a man; it was not a woman. It was very beautiful. Its voice was quiet. It said, "The Lady Door, yes?"

Door said, "Yes."

A gentle smile. It nodded its head to her, almost humbly. "It is an honor finally to meet you and your companion. I am the Angel Islington." Its eyes were clear and wide. Its robes were not white, as Richard had initially thought: they seemed to have been woven from *light*.

Richard did not believe in angels. He never had believed in angels. He was damned if he was going to start now. Still, it was much easier not to believe in something when it was not actually looking directly at you, and saying your name. "Richard Mayhew," it said. "You, too, are welcome here, in my halls." It turned away. "Please," it said. "Follow me."

Richard and Door followed the angel through the caverns. The candles extinguished themselves behind them.

THE MARQUIS DE CARABAS strode through the empty hospital, broken glass and old syringes crunching beneath his square-toed black motorcycle boots. He stepped through a double door that led into a back staircase. He went down the stairs, to the cellars beneath the hospital.

He walked through the rooms beneath the building, stepping fastidiously around the heaps of moldering rubbish. He walked through the showers and the toilets, down an old iron staircase, through a wet, swampy place; and then he pulled open a half-rotted wooden door, and went inside. He looked around the room in which he found himself; he inspected, with magnificent disdain, the half-eaten kitten and the heap of razor blades. Then he cleared the debris off a chair, and sat down, comfortably, luxuriantly, in the dankness of the cellar, and he closed his eyes.

Eventually the door to the cellar was opened and people came in.

The Marquis de Carabas opened his eyes, and yawned. Then he flashed Mr. Croup and Mr. Vandemar a huge smile.

"Hello, boys," said de Carabas. "I thought it high time I came down here to talk to you in person."

10

⁕

"**D**O YOU DRINK WINE?" it asked.

Richard nodded.

"I had a little wine once," said Door, hesitantly. "My father. He. At dinner. Would let us taste it."

The Angel Islington lifted the bottle: it looked like some kind of decanter. Richard wondered if the bottle was made of glass; it refracted and reflected the candlelight so strangely. Perhaps it was some kind of crystal, or one huge diamond. It even made it seem that the wine inside was glowing, as if it were made of light.

The angel took the top off the crystal, and poured an inch of the liquid inside it into a

wineglass. It was a white wine, but a wine unlike any Richard had ever seen. It threw light around the caverns, like sunlight on a swimming pool.

Door and Richard sat around an age-blackened wooden table, on huge wooden chairs, and said nothing. "This wine," said Islington, "is the last bottle of its kind. I was given a dozen bottles by one of your ancestors."

It handed the glass to Door, and began to pour another inch of the glowing wine from the decanter into another glass. It did this reverently, almost lovingly, like a priest performing a ritual. "It was a welcome gift. This was, oh, thirty, forty thousand years ago. Quite a while ago, at any rate." It passed the wineglass to Richard. "I suppose that you could accuse me of squandering something I should treasure," it told them. "But I receive guests so rarely. And the way here is hard."

"The Angelus . . . ," murmured Door.

"You traveled here using the Angelus, yes. But that way only works once for each traveler." The angel raised its glass high, staring at the light. "Drink it carefully," it advised them. "It is most potent." It sat down at the table, between Richard and Door. "When one tastes it," it said, wistfully, "I like to imagine that one is actually tasting the sunlight of bygone days." It held up its glass. "A toast: to former glories."

"Former glories," chorused Richard and Door. And then, a little warily, they tasted the wine, sipping it, not drinking.

"It's amazing," said Door.

"It really is," said Richard. "I thought old wines turned to vinegar when they were exposed to air."

The angel shook its head. "Not this one. It is all a matter of

the type of grape and the place it was grown. This kind of grape, alas, perished when the vineyard vanished beneath the waves."

"It's magical," said Door, sipping the liquid light. "I've never tasted anything like it."

"And you never will again," said Islington. "There is no more wine from Atlantis."

Somewhere inside Richard a small reasonable voice pointed out that there never was an Atlantis, and, thus emboldened, went on to state that there were no such things as angels, and that for that matter most of his experiences of the last few days had been impossible. Richard ignored it. He was learning, awkwardly, to trust his instincts, and to realize that the simplest and most likely explanations for what he had seen and experienced recently were the ones that had been offered to him—no matter how unlikely they might seem. He opened his mouth and tasted the wine once more. It made him feel *happy*. It made him think of skies bigger and bluer than any he had ever seen, a golden sun hanging huge in the sky; everything simpler, everything *younger* than the world he knew.

There was a waterfall to the left of them; clear water ran down the rock, and collected in the rock pool. To the right of them was a door, set between two iron pillars: the door was made of polished flint set in a metal that was almost black in color.

"You really claim to be an angel?" Richard asked. "I mean, you've actually met God and everything?"

Islington smiled tolerantly. "I claim nothing, Richard," it said. "But I am an angel."

"You honor us," said Door.

"No. You do me much honor by coming here. Your father was a good man, Door, and a friend to me. I was deeply saddened by his death."

"He said . . . in his journal . . . he said I should come to you. He said I could trust you."

"I only hope that I can be worthy of that trust." The angel sipped its wine. "London Below is the second city that I have cared for. The first sank beneath the waves, and there was nothing I could do to prevent it. I know what pain is, and loss. You have my sympathies. What would you like to know?"

Door paused. "My family . . . they were killed by Croup and Vandemar. But—who ordered it? I want . . . I want to know *why*."

The angel nodded. "Many secrets find their way down to me," it said. "Many rumors, and half-truths, and echoes." Then it turned to Richard. "And you? What do you want, Richard Mayhew?"

Richard shrugged. "I want my life back. And my flat. And my job."

"That can happen," said the angel.

"Yeah. Right," said Richard, flatly.

"Do you doubt me, Richard Mayhew?" asked the Angel Islington.

Richard looked into its eyes. They were a luminescent gray in color, eyes as old as the universe, eyes that had seen galaxies congeal from stardust ten million million years ago; and Richard shook his head. Islington smiled at him, kindly. "It will not be easy, and you and your companions will face some very real difficulties, both in the task, and in the return. But there could be a way that we can learn: a key to all of our problems."

It got up, and walked over to a small rock shelf, where it picked up a figurine, one of several on the shelf. It was a small black statuette depicting some kind of animal, made of volcanic glass. The angel handed it to Door. "This will bring you safely through the last stage of your journey back to me," it said. "The rest is up to you."

"What do you want us to do?" asked Richard.

"The Black Friars are custodians of a key," it said. "Bring it to me."

"And you can use it to find out who killed my family?" asked Door.

"I hope so," said the angel. Richard finished his glass of wine. He felt it warming him, running through him. He had the strange feeling that if he looked down at his fingers he would be able to see the wine glowing through them. As if he were made of light . . .

"Good luck," whispered the Angel Islington. There was a rushing sound, like a wind soughing across a lost forest, or the beating of mighty wings.

RICHARD AND DOOR WERE sitting on the floor in a room in the British Museum, staring up at a carved painting of an angel on a cathedral door. The room was dark and empty. The party had been over for a long time. The sky outside was beginning to lighten. Richard stood up, then leaned down, and helped Door up.

"Black Friars?" he asked.

Door nodded.

Richard had crossed Blackfriars Bridge in the City of London many times, and he had often passed through Blackfriars station, but he was learning by now not to assume anything.

"Place or people?" he asked.

"People."

Richard walked over to the Angelus. He ran a finger down its painted robe. "Do you think he can really do it? Get me my life back?"

"I've never heard of such a thing. But I don't think he would have lied to us. He is an angel."

Door opened her hand, looked at the statue of the Beast. "My father had one of these," she said, sadly. She put it deep in one of the pockets of her brown leather jacket.

"Well," said Richard. "We're not going to get the key back lollygagging around here, are we?" They walked through the empty museum corridors.

"So what do you know about this key then?" asked Richard.

"Nothing," said Door. They had reached the main doors of the museum. "I've heard of the Black Friars, but I've never actually had anything to do with them." She pressed her fingers against a seriously locked glass door, which swung open at her touch.

"A bunch of monks . . . ," said Richard, thoughtfully. "I bet if we just tell them it's for an angel, a real one, they'll give us the sacred key, and—and throw in the magic tin opener and the amazing whistling corkscrew, as a surprise bonus." He began to laugh. He wondered if the wine was still affecting him.

"You're in good spirits," said Door.

He nodded, enthusiastically. "I'm going to go home. Ev-

erything is going to be normal again. Boring again. Wonderful again." Richard looked at the stone steps that led up to the British Museum, and decided that they were made to be danced down by Fred Astaire and Ginger Rogers. And seeing that neither of them happened to be available, he began to dance down the steps, doing what he fondly imagined was an amazing Fred Astaire impersonation, while humming something approximately half-way between "Puttin' on the Ritz" and "Top Hat, White Tie, and Tails." "Ya-ta-ta-da-da-ta-ta-ya," he sang, soft-shoeing down the steps and up again.

Door stood at the top of the steps, staring at him in horror. Then she began to giggle, helplessly. He looked up at her, and doffed his imaginary white silk top hat to her, mimed tossing it high in the air, catching it, and putting it back on his head.

"Twit," said Door, and smiled at him. In response, Richard grabbed her hand, and continued dancing up and down the steps. Door hesitated for a moment, then she, too, began to dance. She danced much better than Richard did. At the bottom of the steps they tumbled, breathless and exhausted and giggling, into each other's arms.

Richard felt his world spin.

He felt her heart beating against his chest. The moment began to transmute, and he wondered if there was something he should do. He wondered if he should kiss her. He wondered if he wanted to kiss her, and he realized that he truly did not know. He looked into her opal-colored eyes. Door put her head on one side, and pulled free. She pulled up the collar on her brown leather jacket, pulled it around her: armor and protection.

"Let's go and find our bodyguard," said Door. And they

walked away together, down the sidewalk, toward British Museum Station, stumbling only a little from time to time.

"WHAT," ASKED MR. CROUP, "do you want?"

"What," asked the Marquis de Carabas, a little more rhetorically, "does anyone want?"

"Dead things," suggested Mr. Vandemar. "Extra teeth."

"I thought perhaps we could make a deal," said the Marquis.

Mr. Croup began to laugh. It sounded like a piece of blackboard being dragged over the nails of a wall of severed fingers. "Oh, Messire Marquis. I think I can confidently state, with no risk of contradiction from any parties here present, that you have taken leave of whatever senses you are reputed to have had. You are," he confided, "if you will permit the vulgarism, completely off your head."

"Say the word," said Mr. Vandemar, who was now standing behind the Marquis' chair, "and it'll be off his neck before you can say Jack Ketch."

The Marquis breathed heavily on his fingernails, and polished them on the lapel of his coat. "I have always felt," he said, "that violence is the last refuge of the incompetent, and empty threats the final sanctuary of the terminally inept."

Mr. Croup glared. "What are you doing here?" he hissed.

The Marquis de Carabas stretched, like a big cat: a lynx, perhaps, or a huge black panther; and at the end of the stretch he was standing up, with his hands thrust deep in the pockets of his magnificent coat. "You are," he said, idly and conversation-

ally, "I understand, Mister Croup, a collector of T'ang dynasty figurines."

"How did you know that?"

"People tell me things. I'm approachable." The Marquis' smile was pure, untroubled, guileless: the smile of a man selling you a used Bible.

"Even if I were . . . ," began Mr. Croup.

"If you were," said the Marquis de Carabas, "you might be interested in *this*." He took one hand out of his pocket, and displayed it to Mr. Croup. Until earlier that evening it had sat in a glass case in the vaults of one of London's leading merchant banks. It was listed in certain catalogs as *The Spirit of Autumn (Grave Figure)*. It was roughly eight inches high: a piece of glazed pottery that had been shaped and painted and fired while Europe was in the Dark Ages, six hundred years before Columbus's first voyage.

Mr. Croup hissed, involuntarily, and reached for it. The Marquis pulled it out of reach, cradled it to his chest. "No no," said the Marquis. "It's not as simple as that."

"No?" asked Mr. Croup. "But what's to stop us taking it, and leaving bits of you all over the Underside? We've never dismembered a marquis before."

"Have," said Mr. Vandemar. "In York. In the fourteenth century. In the rain."

"He wasn't a marquis," said Mr. Croup. "He was the Earl of Exeter."

"And Marquis of Westmorland." Mr. Vandemar looked rather pleased with himself.

Mr. Croup sniffed. "What's to stop us hacking you into as

many pieces as we hacked the Marquis of Westmorland?" he asked.

De Carabas took his other hand out of his pocket. It held a small hammer. He tossed the hammer in the air, like a barman in a movie about cocktail making, and caught it by the handle, ending with the hammer poised over the china figurine. "Oh, please," he said. "No more silly threats. I think I'd feel better if you were both standing back over there."

Mr. Vandemar shot a look at Mr. Croup, who nodded, almost imperceptibly. There was a tremble in the air, and Mr. Vandemar was standing beside Mr. Croup, who smiled like a skull. "I have indeed been known to purchase the occasional T'ang piece," he admitted. "Is that for sale?"

"We don't go in so much for buying and selling here in the Underside, Mister Croup. Barter. Exchange. That's what we look for. But yes, indeed, this desirable little piece is certainly up for grabs."

Mr. Croup pursed his lips. He folded his arms. He unfolded them. He ran one hand through his greasy hair. Then, "Name your price," said Mr. Croup. The Marquis let himself breathe a deep, relieved, and almost audible sigh. It was possible that he was going to be able to pull this whole grandiose ruse off, after all. "First, three answers to three questions," he said.

Croup nodded. "Each way. We get three answers too."

"Fair enough," said the Marquis. "Secondly, I get safe conduct out of here. And you agree to give me at least an hour's head start."

Croup nodded violently. "Agreed. Ask your first question." His gaze was fixed on the statue.

"First question. Who are you working for?"

"Oh, that's an easy one," said Mr. Croup. "That's a simple answer. We are working for our employer, who wishes to remain nameless."

"Hmph. Why did you kill Door's family?"

"Orders from our employer," said Mr. Croup, his smile becoming more foxy by the moment.

"Why didn't you kill Door, when you had a chance?"

Before Mr. Croup could answer, Mr. Vandemar said, "Got to keep her alive. She's the only one that can open the door."

Mr. Croup glared up at his associate. "That's it," he said. "Tell him everything, why don't you?"

"I wanted a turn," muttered Mr. Vandemar.

"Right," said Mr. Croup. "So you've got three answers, for all the good that will do you. My first question: why are you protecting her?"

"Her father saved my life," said the Marquis, honestly. "I never paid off my debt to him. I prefer debts to be in my favor."

"I've got a question," said Mr. Vandemar.

"As have I, Mr. Vandemar. The Upworlder, Richard Mayhew. Why is he traveling with her? Why does she permit it?"

"Sentimentality on her part," said the Marquis de Carabas. He wondered, as he said it, if that was the whole truth. He had begun to wonder whether there might, perhaps, be more to the Upworlder than met the eye.

"Now me," said Mr. Vandemar. "What number am I thinking of?"

"I beg your pardon?"

"What number am I thinking of?" repeated Mr. Vandemar. "It's between one and a lot," he added, helpfully.

"Seven," said the Marquis. Mr. Vandemar nodded, impressed. Mr. Croup began, "Where is the—" but the Marquis shook his head. "Uh-uh," he said. "Now we're getting greedy."

There was a moment of utter silence, in that dank cellar. Then once more water dripped, and maggots rustled; and the Marquis said, "An hour's head start, remember."

"Of course," said Mr. Croup.

The Marquis de Carabas tossed the figurine to Mr. Croup, who caught it eagerly, like an addict catching a plastic baggie filled with white powder of dubious legality. And then, without a backward glance, the Marquis left the cellar.

Mr. Croup examined the figurine minutely, turning it over and over in his hands, a Dickensian curator of the Museum of the Damned, contemplating a prize exhibit. His tongue flicked out, from time to time, like a snake's. A perceptible flush appeared on his pallid cheeks. "Oh, fine, fine," he whispered. "T'ang dynasty indeed. Twelve hundred years old, the finest pottery figurines ever made on this earth. This was created by Kai Lung, finest of potters: there is not a twin to it in existence. Examine the color of the glaze; the sense of proportion; the life . . ." He was smiling now, like a baby; the innocent smile looked lost and confused on the shady terrain of Mr. Croup's face. "It adds a little wonder and beauty to the world."

And then he grinned, too widely, and lowered his face to the figurine, and crushed its head in his teeth, chomping and chewing wildly, swallowing in lumps. His teeth ground the china to a fine powder which dusted the lower part of his face.

He gloried in its destruction, throwing himself into it with the strange madness and uncontrolled bloodlust of a fox in a

henhouse. And then, when the statue was nothing but dust, he turned to Mr. Vandemar. He seemed strangely mellow, almost languid. "How long did we say we'd give him?"

"An hour."

"Mmm. And how long has it been?"

"Six minutes."

Mr. Croup lowered his head. He ran a finger across his chin, licked the powdered clay from his fingertip. "You follow him, Mister Vandemar," said Mr. Croup. "I need a little more time in which to savor the occasion."

HUNTER COULD HEAR THEM walking down the steps. She was standing in the shadows, with her arms folded, in the same position she had been in when they left her. Richard was humming, loudly. Door was giggling, helplessly; then she would stop, and tell Richard to be quiet. Then she would start giggling again. They walked past Hunter without noticing her.

She stepped out of the shadows, and said, "You have been gone for eight hours." It was a statement of fact, without reproach or curiosity.

Door blinked at her. "It didn't *seem* that long." Hunter said nothing.

Richard grinned blearily at her. "Don't you want to know what happened? Well, we got ambushed by Mister Croup and Mister Vandemar. Unfortunately we didn't have a bodyguard around. Still, I gave them a good seeing to."

Hunter raised a perfect eyebrow. "I am in awe of your pugilistic talents," she said coolly.

Door giggled. "He's kidding. Actually—they killed us."

"As an expert in the termination of bodily functions," Hunter said, "I must beg to differ. You are neither of you dead. At a guess, you are both very drunk."

Door stuck her tongue out at her bodyguard. "Nonsense. Touched hardly a drop. *That* much." She held out two fingers to show how tiny an amount "that much" was.

"Just went to a party," said Richard, "and saw Jessica and saw a real angel and got a little black piggywiggy and came back here."

"Just a little drink," continued Door, intently. "Old, old drink. Tiiiiny little drink. Very small. Almost not there." She began to hiccup. Then she giggled again. A hiccup interrupted her, and she sat down suddenly on the platform. "I think maybe we are a bit smashed," she said, soberly. Then she closed her eyes, and began, solemnly, to snore.

THE MARQUIS DE CARABAS was running through the underways as if all the hounds of Hell had his scent and were on his trail. He was splashing through six gray inches of the Tyburn, the hangman's river, kept safe in the darkness in a brick sewer beneath Park Lane, on its way south to Buckingham Palace. He had been running for seventeen minutes.

Thirty feet below Marble Arch, he paused. The sewer divided into two branches. The Marquis de Carabas ran down the left-hand branch.

Several minutes later, Mr. Vandemar walked through the sewer. And when he reached the junction he, too, paused for a

few moments, sniffing the air. And then he, too, walked down the left-hand branch.

HUNTER DROPPED RICHARD MAYHEW'S unconscious body into a pile of straw, with a grunt. He rolled in the straw, said something that sounded like "Forthril bjugly mobble wug" and went back to sleep. She put Door down in the straw next to him, more gently. Then she stood beside Door, in the dark stables under the ground, on guard still.

THE MARQUIS DE CARABAS was exhausted. He leaned against the tunnel wall, and stared at the steps that went up ahead of him. Then he pulled out the golden pocket watch, and looked at the time. Thirty-five minutes had passed since he had fled the hospital cellar.

"Is it an hour yet?" asked Mr. Vandemar. He was sitting on the steps ahead of the Marquis, picking his nails with a knife.

"Not even close," gasped the Marquis.

"Felt like an hour," said Mr. Vandemar, helpfully.

There was a shiver in the world, and Mr. Croup stood behind the Marquis de Carabas. He still had powder on his chin. De Carabas stared at Mr. Croup. He turned back to look at Mr. Vandemar. And then, spontaneously, the Marquis de Carabas began to laugh. Mr. Croup smiled. "You find us funny, Messire Marquis, do you not? A source of amusement. Is that not so? With our pretty clothes, and our convoluted circumlocutions—"

Mr. Vandemar murmured, "I haven't got a circumlo—"

"—and our little sillinesses of manner and behavior. And perhaps we are funny."

Mr. Croup raised one finger then, and waggled it at de Carabas. "But you must never imagine," he continued, "that just because something is funny, Messire Marquis, it is not dangerous."

And Mr. Vandemar threw his knife at the Marquis, hard and accurately. It hit him, hilt first, on the temple. His eyes rolled up in his head, and his knees buckled. "Circumlocution," said Mr. Croup to Mr. Vandemar. "It's a way of speaking around something. A digression. Verbosity."

Mr. Vandemar picked up the Marquis de Carabas by his waistband, and dragged him up the stairs, his head bump-bump-bumping on each step as they went, and Mr. Vandemar nodded. "I wondered," he said.

WATCHING THEIR DREAMS, NOW, as they sleep.

Hunter sleeps standing up.

In her dream, Hunter is in the undercity beneath Bangkok. It is partly a maze, and partly a forest, for the wilderness of Thailand has retreated deep beneath the ground, under the airport and the hotels and the streets. The world smells of spice and dried mango, and it also smells, not unpleasantly, of sex. It is humid, and she is sweating. It is dark, broken by phosphorescent patches on the wall, greenish-gray funguses that give light enough to fool the eye, light enough to walk by.

In her dream Hunter moves silent as a ghost through the wet tunnels, pushing her way through vegetation. She holds a

weighted throwing stick in her right hand; a leather shield covers her left forearm.

She smells it, in her dream, acrid and animal, and she pauses beside a wall of ruined masonry, and she waits, part of the shadows, one with the darkness. Hunting, like life, Hunter believes, consists chiefly of waiting. In Hunter's dream, however, she does not wait. Upon her arrival, it comes through the underbrush, a fury of brown and of white, undulating gently, like a wet-furred snake, its red eyes bright and peering through the darkness, its teeth like needles, a carnivore and a killer. The creature is extinct in the world above: it bears a similar relationship to the mink, and to the weasel, to that which a timber wolf bears to a Yorkshire terrier. It weighs almost three hundred pounds, and is a little over fifteen feet long, from the tip of its nose to the tip of its tail.

As it passes her, she hisses like a snake, and, momentarily, old instincts kicking in, it freezes. And then it leaps at her, nothing but hate and sharp teeth. She remembers, then, in her dream, that this had happened before, and that when it had happened, that time in the past, she had pushed the leather arm shield into its mouth, and crushed its skull with the leaden throwing stick, taking care not to damage the pelt. She had given the Great Weasel's pelt to a girl who had caught her eye, who had been appropriately grateful.

But, now, in her dream, that is not happening. Instead, the weasel is reaching out a forepaw toward her, and she is dropping her throwing stick, and taking its paw. And then and there, in the undercity beneath Bangkok, they are dancing together, in one intricate unending dance: and Hunter is watching them

from outside herself, and she is admiring the elaborate movements they make as they move, tail and legs and arms and fingers and eyes and hair all tumbling and twisting powerfully and strangely into the underneath and out across forever.

There is a tiny noise in the waking world, a dreaming whimper from the child Door, and Hunter moves from sleeping to waking fluidly and instantly; she is alert once more, and on guard. She forgets her dream entirely upon waking.

DOOR IS DREAMING OF her father.

In her dream, he is showing her how to open things. He picks up an orange, and gestures: in one smooth movement it inverts, and twists: the orange flesh is on the outside, now, and the skin is in the center, on the inside. *One must always maintain parity,* her father tells her, peeling off an inside-out orange segment for her. *Parity, symmetry, topology: these will be our subjects for the months to come, Door. But the most important thing for you to understand is this: all things want to open. You must feel that need, and use it.* Her father's hair is brown and thick, as it was a decade before his death, and he has an easy smile, which she remembers, but which time had diminished as the years went on.

In her dream, he passes her a padlock. She takes it from him. Her hands are the size and shape of her hands today, although she knows that, in truth, this occurred when she was a tiny child, that she is taking moments and conversations and lessons from over a dozen years, and is compressing them into one lesson. *Open it,* he tells her.

She holds it in her hand, feeling the cold metal, feeling the

weight of the lock in her hands. Something is bothering her. There is something she has to know. Door learned to open some time after she learned to walk. She remembers her mother holding her tightly, opening a door from Door's bedroom to the playroom, remembers watching her brother Arch separating linked silver rings, joining them back together.

She tries to open the padlock. She fumbles at it with her fingers, and with her mind. Nothing happens. She throws the padlock down onto the floor and begins to cry. Her father reaches down and picks up the padlock, puts it back into her hand. His long finger brushes away a tear from her cheek.

Remember, he tells her, *the padlock wants to open. All you have to do is let it do what it wants.*

It sits there in her hand, cold and inert and heavy. And then, suddenly, she understands, and, somewhere in her heart, she lets it be what it wants to be. There is a loud click, and the padlock opens. Her father is smiling.

There, she says.

Good girl, says her father. *That's all there is to opening. Everything else is just technique.*

She realizes what it is that is bothering her. *Father?* she asks. *Your journal. Who put it away? Who could have hidden it?* But he is receding from her, and already she is forgetting. She calls to him, but he cannot hear her, and although she can hear his voice in the distance, she can no longer make out what he is saying.

In the waking world, Door whimpers softly. Then she rolls over, cradles her arm around her face, snorts once, twice, then sleeps once more, sleeps without dreaming.

RICHARD KNOWS IT WAITS for them. Each tunnel he goes down, each turning, each branch he walks, the feeling grows in urgency and weight. He knows it is there, waiting, and the sense of impending catastrophe increases with every step. He knows that it should have been a relief when he turns the final corner, and sees it standing there, framed in the tunnel, waiting for him. Instead he feels only dread. In his dream it is the size of the world: there is nothing left in the world but the Beast, its flanks steaming, broken spars and juts of old weapons prickled from its hide. There is dried blood on its horns and on its tusks. It is gross, and vast, and evil.

And then it charges.

He raises his hand (but it isn't his hand) and he throws the spear at the creature.

He sees its eyes, red and vicious and gloating, as they float toward him, all in a fraction of a second that becomes a tiny forever. And then it is upon him . . .

The water was cold, and it hit Richard's face like a slap. His eyes jerked open, and he caught his breath. Hunter was looking down at him. She was holding a large wooden bucket. It was empty. He reached up one hand. His hair was soaked, and his face was wet. He wiped the water from his eyes, and shivered with cold.

"You didn't have to do that," said Richard. His mouth tasted like several small animals had been using it as a restroom before liquefying into something vaguely green. He tried to stand, and then sat down again, suddenly. "Ooh," he explained.

"How's your head?" asked Hunter, professionally.

"It's been better," said Richard.

Hunter picked up another wooden bucket, this one filled with water, and hauled it across the stable floor. "I don't know what you drank," she said. "But it must have been potent." Hunter dipped her hand into the bucket, and flicked it at Door's face, spraying her with water. Door's eyes flickered.

"No wonder Atlantis sank," muttered Richard. "If they all felt like this in the morning it was probably a relief. Where are we?"

Hunter flicked another handful of water at Door's face. "In the stables of a friend," she said. Richard looked around. The place did look a little like a stable. He wondered if it was for horses—what kind of horses would live beneath the ground? There was a device painted on the wall: the letter S (or was it a snake? Richard could not tell) circled by seven stars.

Door reached a tentative hand up to her head and touched it, experimentally, as if she were unsure just what she might find. "Ooh," she said, in a near-whisper. "Temple and Arch. Am I dead?"

"No," said Hunter.

"Pity."

Hunter helped her to a standing position. "Well," said Door, sleepily, "he did warn us it was strong." And then Door woke up completely, very hard, very fast. She grabbed Richard's shoulder, pointed to the device on the wall, the snaky S with the stars surrounding it. She gasped, and looked for all the world like a small mouse that had just realized it had wandered into a cattery. "Serpentine," she said to Richard, to Hunter. "That's Serpentine's crest. Richard, get up! We have to run—before she finds out we're here—"

"And do you think," asked a dry voice from the doorway, "that you could enter Serpentine's house without Serpentine knowing, child?"

Door pushed herself back against the wood of the stable wall. She was trembling. Richard realized, through the pounding in his head, that he had never seen Door so actually and obviously scared before.

Serpentine stood in the doorway. She was wearing a white leather corset, and high white leather boots, and the remains of what looked like it had once, long ago, been a silk-and-lace confection of a white wedding dress, now shredded and dirt-stained and torn. She towered above them all: her shock of graying hair brushed the door lintel. Her eyes were sharp, and her mouth was a cruel slash in an imperious face. She looked at Door as if she took terror as her due; as if she had become so used to fear that she now expected it, even liked it.

"Calm yourself," said Hunter.

"But she's Serpentine," wailed Door. "Of the Seven Sisters."

Serpentine inclined her head, cordially. Then she stepped out of the doorway, and walked toward them. Behind her was a thin woman with a severe face, and long dark hair, wearing a black dress pinched wasp-thin at the waist. The woman said nothing. Serpentine walked over to Hunter. "Hunter worked for me long ago," said Serpentine. She reached out a white finger, and gently stroked Hunter's brown cheek with it, a gesture of affection and possession. And then, "You've kept your looks better than I, Hunter." Hunter looked down. "Her friends are my friends, child," said Serpentine. "You are Door?"

"Yes," said Door, dry-mouthed.

Serpentine turned on Richard. "And what are you?" she asked, unimpressed.

"Richard," said Richard.

"I am Serpentine," she told him, graciously.

"So I gathered," said Richard.

"There is food waiting for all of you," said Serpentine, "should you wish to break your fast."

"Oh god, no," whimpered Richard politely. Door said nothing. She was still backed against the wall, still trembling gently, like a leaf in an autumn breeze. The fact that Hunter had clearly brought them here as a safe haven was doing nothing to assuage her fear.

"What is there to eat?" asked Hunter.

Serpentine looked at the wasp-waisted woman in the doorway. "Well?" she asked. The woman smiled the chilliest smile Richard had ever seen cross a human face, then she said, "Fried eggs poached eggs pickled eggs curried venison pickled onions pickled herrings smoked herrings salted herrings mushroom stew salted bacon stuffed cabbage mutton hotpot calves'-foot jelly—"

Richard opened his mouth to plead with her to stop, but it was too late. He was suddenly, violently, awfully sick.

He wanted someone to hold him, to tell him that everything would be all right, that he'd soon be feeling better; someone to give him an aspirin and a glass of water, and show him back to his bed. But nobody did; and his bed was another life away. He washed the sick from his face and hands with water from the bucket. Then he washed out his mouth. Then, swaying gently, he followed the four women to breakfast.

———————

"PASS THE CALVES'-FOOT JELLY," said Hunter, with her mouth full.

Serpentine's dining room was on what appeared to be the smallest Underground platform that Richard had ever seen. It was about twelve feet long, and much of that space was taken up with a dinner table. A white damask cloth was laid on the table, and a formal silver dinner service on that. The table was piled high with evil-smelling foodstuffs. The pickled quails' eggs, thought Richard, smelled the worst.

His skin felt clammy, and his eyes felt like they had been put in wrong, while his skull gave him the general impression that someone had removed it while he had slept, and swapped it for one two or three sizes too small. An Underground train went past a few feet from them; the wind of its passage whipped at the table. The noise of its passage went through Richard's head like a hot knife through brains. Richard groaned.

"Your hero is unable to hold his wine, I see," observed Serpentine, dispassionately.

"He's not my hero," said Door.

"I'm afraid he is. You learn to recognize the type. Something in the eyes, perhaps." She turned to the woman in black, who appeared to be some kind of majordomo. "A restorative for the gentleman." The woman smiled thinly, and glided away.

Door picked at a mushroom dish. "We are very grateful for all this, Lady Serpentine," she said.

Serpentine sniffed. "Just Serpentine, child. I have no time for silly honorifics and imaginary titles. So. You're Portico's oldest girl."

"Yes."

Serpentine dipped her finger in the briny sauce that held what appeared to be several small eels. She licked her finger, nodded approvingly. "I had little time for your father. All that foolishness about uniting the Underside. Stuff and nonsense. Silly man. Just asking for trouble. The last time I saw your father, I told him that if he ever came back here, I'd turn him into a blindworm." She turned to Door. "How is your father, by the way?"

"He's dead," said Door.

Serpentine looked perfectly satisfied. "See?" she said. "My point exactly." Door said nothing. Serpentine picked at something that was moving in her gray hair. She examined it minutely, then crushed it between finger and thumb, and dropped it onto the platform. Then she turned to Hunter, who was demolishing a small hill of pickled herrings. "You're Beast-hunting then?" she said. Hunter nodded, her mouth full. "You'll need the spear, of course," said Serpentine.

The wasp-waisted woman was now standing next to Richard, holding a small tray. On the tray was a small glass, containing an aggressively emerald-colored liquid. Richard stared at it, then looked at Door.

"What are you giving him?" asked Door.

"Nothing that will hurt him," said Serpentine, with a frosty smile. "You are guests."

Richard knocked back the green liquid, which tasted of thyme and peppermint and winter's mornings. He felt it go down, and prepared himself to try to stop it coming back up again. Instead he took a deep breath, and realized, with a little surprise, that his head no longer hurt; and that he was starving.

OLD BAILEY WAS NOT, intrinsically, one of those people put in the world to tell jokes. Despite this handicap, he persisted in telling jokes. The jokes he persisted in telling tended to be shaggy-dog stories of inordinate length, which would end in a sad pun, although, often as not, Old Bailey would be unable to remember it by the time he got there. The only public for Old Bailey's jokes consisted of a small captive audience of birds, who, particularly the rooks, viewed his jokes as deep and philosophical parables containing some deep and penetrating insights into what it meant to be human, and who would actually ask him, from time to time, to tell them another of his amusing stories.

"All right, all right, all right," Old Bailey was saying. "Stop me if you've heard this one before. There was a man walked into a bar. No, he wasn't a man. That's the joke. Sorry. He was a horse. A horse . . . no . . . a piece of string. Three pieces of string. Right. Three pieces of string walk into a bar."

A huge old rook croaked a question. Old Bailey rubbed his chin, then shrugged. "They just do. It's a joke. They can walk in the joke. He asks for a drink for himself and one for each of his friends. And the barman says, we 'don't serve pieces of string here.' To one of the pieces of string. So. It goes back to its friends and says they 'don't serve strings here.' And it's a joke, so the middle one does it too, three of them, you see, then the last one, he ties himself around the middle and he pulls the end of him all out. And he orders a drink." The rook croaked again, sagely. "Three drinks. Right. And the barman says, here, 'Aren't you one of those pieces of string?' And he says, the piece of string, he

says, no. 'I'm a frayed knot.' 'Afraid not,' y'see, 'a frayed knot.' Pun. Very, very funny."

The starlings made polite noises. The rooks nodded their heads, put their heads on one side. Then the oldest rook cawed at Old Bailey. "Another? I'm not made of hilarity, y'know. Let me think . . ."

There was a noise from the tent, a deep, pulsing noise, like the beating of a distant heart. Old Bailey hurried into his tent. The noise was coming from an old wooden chest in which Old Bailey kept those things he prized. He opened the chest. The throbbing noise became much, much louder. The small silver box was sitting on the top of Old Bailey's treasures. He reached down one gnarly hand and picked it up. A red light rhythmically pulsed and glowed inside it, like a heartbeat, and shone out through the silver filigree, and through the cracks and fastenings. "He's in trouble," said Old Bailey.

The oldest rook cawed a question. "No. It's not a joke. It's the Marquis," said Old Bailey. "He's in deep trouble."

RICHARD WAS HALFWAY THROUGH his second plate of breakfast when Serpentine pushed her chair back from the table.

"I think I have had my fill of hospitality," she said. "Child, young man, good day. Hunter . . ." She paused. Then she ran one claw-like finger along the line of Hunter's jaw. "Hunter, you are always welcome here." She nodded to them, imperiously, and stood up, and walked away, followed by her wasp-waisted butler.

"We should leave now," said Hunter. She stood up from the table, and Door and, more reluctantly, Richard followed her.

They walked along a corridor that was too thin to allow more than one of them to pass at a time. They went up some stone steps. They crossed an iron bridge in the darkness, while Underground trains echoed by beneath them. Then they entered what seemed like an endless network of underground vaults that smelled of damp and decay, of brick and stone and time. "That was your old boss, eh? She seemed nice enough," said Richard to Hunter. Hunter said nothing.

Door, who had been somewhat subdued, said, "When they want to make children behave themselves in the Underside, they tell them, 'Behave, or Serpentine will take you.'"

"Oh," said Richard. "And you worked for her, Hunter?"

"I worked for all the Seven Sisters."

"I thought that they hadn't spoken to each other for, oh, at least thirty years," said Door.

"Quite possibly. But they were still talking then."

"How old *are* you?" asked Door. Richard was pleased she had asked; he would never have dared.

"As old as my tongue," said Hunter, primly, "and a little older than my teeth."

"Anyway," said Richard, in the untroubled tone of voice of one whose hangover has left him, and who knew that, somewhere far above them, someone was having a beautiful day. "That was okay. Nice food. And no one was trying to kill us."

"I'm sure that will remedy itself as the day goes on," said Hunter, accurately. "Which way to the Black Friars, my lady?"

Door paused and concentrated. "We'll go the river way," she said. "Over here."

"Is HE COMING ROUND yet?" asked Mr. Croup.

Mr. Vandemar prodded the Marquis' prone body with one long finger. The breathing was shallow. "Not yet, Mister Croup. I think I broke him."

"You must be more careful with your toys, Mister Vandemar," said Mr. Croup.

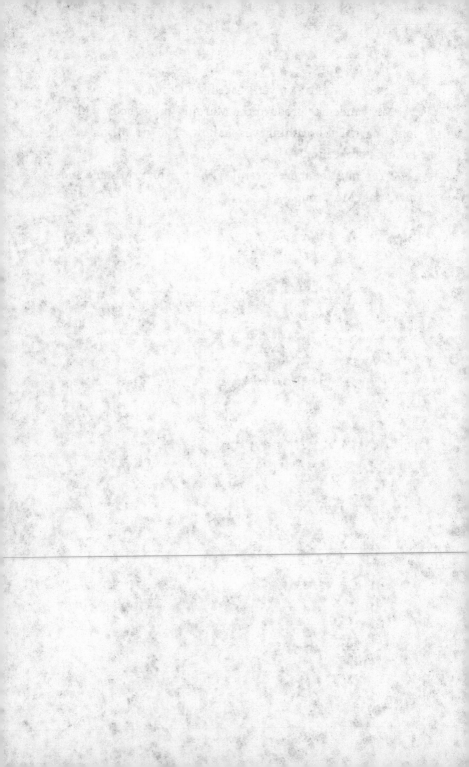

11

"SO WHAT ARE YOU after?" Richard asked Hunter. The three of them were walking, with extreme care, along the bank of an underground river. The bank was slippery, a narrow path along dark rock and sharp masonry. Richard watched with respect as the gray water rushed and tumbled, within arm's reach. This was not the kind of river you fell into and got out of again; it was the other kind.

"After?"

"Well," he said. "Personally, I'm trying to get back to the real London, and my old life. Door wants to find out who killed her family. What are you after?" They edged along the bank, a step at a time, Hunter in the lead. She

said nothing in reply. The river slowed, and fed into a small underground lake. They walked beside the water, their lamps reflecting in the black surface, their reflections smudged by the river mist. "So what is it?" asked Richard. He did not expect any kind of answer.

Hunter's voice was quiet and intense. She did not break her step as she spoke. "I fought in the sewers beneath New York with the great blind white alligator-king. He was thirty feet long, fat from sewage and fierce in battle. And I bested him, and I killed him. His eyes were like huge pearls in the darkness." Her strangely accented voice echoed in the underground, twined in the mist, in the night beneath the Earth.

"I fought the bear that stalked the city beneath Berlin. He had killed a thousand men, and his claws were stained brown and black from the dried blood of a hundred years, but he fell to me. He whispered words in a human tongue as he died." The mist hung low on the lake. Richard fancied that he could see the creatures she spoke of, white shapes writhing in the vapor.

"There was a black tiger in the undercity of Calcutta. A man-eater, brilliant and bitter, the size of a small elephant. A tiger is a worthy adversary. I took him with my bare hands." Richard glanced at Door. She was listening to Hunter intently: this was news to her too, then. "And I shall slay the Beast of London. They say his hide bristles with swords and spears and knives stuck in him by those who have tried and failed. His tusks are razors, and his hooves are thunderbolts.

"I will kill him, or I will die in the attempt."

Her eyes shone as she spoke of her prey. The river mist had become a thick yellow fog.

A bell was struck, a little way away, three times, the sound carrying across the water. The world began to lighten. Richard thought he could see the squat shapes of buildings around them. The yellow-green fog became thicker: it tasted of ash, and soot, and the grime of a thousand urban years. It clung to their lamps, muffling the light.

"What is this?" he asked.

"London fog," said Hunter.

"But they stopped years ago, didn't they? Clean Air Act, all that?" Richard found himself remembering the Sherlock Holmes books of his childhood. "What did they call them again?"

"Pea-soupers," said Door. "London Particulars. Thick yellow river-fogs, mixed with coal-smoke and whatever rubbish was going into the air for the last five centuries. Hasn't been one in the Upworld for, oh, forty years now. We get the ghosts of them down here. Mm. Not ghosts. More like echoes." Richard breathed in a strand of the yellow-green fog, and began to cough. "That doesn't sound good," said Door.

"Fog in my throat," said Richard. The ground was becoming stickier, muddier: it sucked at Richard's feet as he walked. "Still," he said, to reassure himself, "a little fog never hurt anyone."

Door looked up at him with big pixie eyes. "There was one in 1952 that they reckon killed four thousand people."

"People from here?" he asked. "Under London?"

"Your people," said Hunter. Richard was willing to believe it. He thought about holding his breath, but the fog was getting thicker. The ground was becoming mushier. "I don't understand," he asked. "Why do you have fogs down here, when we don't have them up there anymore?"

Door scratched her nose. "There are little bubbles of old time in London, where things and places stay the same, like bubbles in amber," she explained. "There's a lot of time in London, and it has to go somewhere—it doesn't all get used up at once."

"I may still be hungover," sighed Richard. "That almost made sense."

THE ABBOT HAD KNOWN that this day would bring pilgrims. The knowledge was a part of his dreams; it surrounded him, like the darkness. So the day became one of waiting, which was, he knew, a sin: moments were to be experienced; waiting was a sin against both the time that was still to come, and against the moments one was currently disregarding. Still, he was waiting. Through each of the day's services, through their scant meals, the Abbot was listening intently, waiting for the bell to sound, waiting to know who and how many.

He found himself hoping for a clean death. The last pilgrim had lasted for almost a year, a gibbering, screaming thing. The Abbot regarded his blindness neither as a blessing nor as a curse: it simply *was;* but even so, he had been grateful he had never been able to see the poor creature's face. Brother Jet, who had cared for the creature, still woke in the night, screaming, with its twisted face before him.

The bell tolled late in the afternoon, three times. The Abbot was in the shrine, on his knees, contemplating their charge. He pulled himself to his feet, and made his way to the corridor, where he waited. "Father?" The voice was that of Brother Fuliginous.

"Who guards the bridge?" the Abbot asked him. His voice was surprisingly deep and melodious for such an old man.

"Sable," came the reply from the darkness. The Abbot reached out a hand, grasped the young man's elbow, and walked beside him, slowly, through the corridors of the abbey.

THERE WAS NO SOLID ground; there was no lake. Their feet were splashing and squishing through some kind of marsh, in the yellow fog. "This," announced Richard, "is disgusting." It was seeping through his shoes, invading his socks, and making a much closer acquaintance with his toes than Richard was entirely happy with.

There was a bridge ahead of them, rising up out of the marsh, and a figure, dressed in black, waited at the foot of the bridge. He wore the black robes of a Dominican monk. His skin was the dark brown of old mahogany. He was a tall man, and he held a wooden staff as tall as he was. "Hold fast," he called. "Tell me your names, and your stations."

"I am the Lady Door," said Door. "I am Portico's daughter, of the House of the Arch."

"I am Hunter. I am her bodyguard."

"Richard Mayhew," said Richard. "Wet."

"And you wish to pass?"

Richard stepped forward. "Yes, we do actually. We're here for a key." The monk said nothing. He lifted his staff, and pushed Richard gently in the chest with it. Richard's feet slid out from under him, and he landed in the muddy water—or, to be fractionally more accurate, the watery mud. The monk waited a few

moments, to see if Richard would swing up and begin to fight. Richard didn't.

Hunter did.

Richard pulled himself up from the mud, and, mouth open, watched his first quarterstaff fight. The monk was good. He was bigger than Hunter, and, Richard suspected, stronger. Hunter, on the other hand, was faster than the monk. The wooden staves clacked and whapped in the mist.

The monk's staff made sudden contact with Hunter's midriff. She stumbled in the mud. He came in close—too close, as he discovered that her stumble had been a feint, and her staff slammed into him, hard and precisely, on the backs of his knees, and his legs no longer held his weight. The man tumbled into the wet mud, and Hunter rested the tip of her staff on the back of his neck.

"Enough," called a voice from the bridge.

Hunter took a step back. She stood beside Richard and Door once more. She had not even broken a sweat. The big monk got up from the mud. His lip was bleeding. He bowed low to Hunter, then walked to the foot of the bridge.

"Who are they, Brother Sable?" called the voice.

"The Lady Door, Lord Portico's daughter, of the House of the Arch; Hunter, her bodyguard; and Richard Mayhew Wet, their companion," said Brother Sable, through bruised lips. "She bested me in fair fight, Brother Fuliginous."

"Let them come up," said the voice.

Hunter led the way up the bridge. At the apex of the bridge, another monk was waiting for them: Brother Fuliginous. He was younger, and smaller, than the first monk they had met, but

he was dressed the same way. His skin was a deep, rich brown. There were other black-clad figures, just on the borders of the visible, further into the yellow fog. These were the Black Friars, then, Richard realized. The second monk stared at the three of them for a second, and then recited:

"I turn my head, and you may go where you want.

I turn it again, you will stay till you rot.

I have no face, but I live or die

By my crooked teeth—who am I?"

Door took a step forward. She licked her lips and half closed her eyes. "I turn my head . . . ," she said, puzzling to herself. "Crooked teeth . . . go where you . . ." Then a smile spread over her face. She stared up at Brother Fuliginous. "A key," she said. "The answer is, you're a key."

"A wise one," acknowledged Brother Fuliginous. "That's two steps taken. One more to take."

A very old man stepped out of the yellow fog and walked cautiously toward them, his gnarled hand holding on to the stone side of the bridge. He stopped when he reached Brother Fuliginous. His eyes were a glaucous blue-white, thick with cataracts. Richard liked him on sight. "How many of them are there?" he asked the younger man, in a deep and reassuring voice.

"Three, Father Abbot."

"And has one of them bested the first gatekeeper?"

"Yes, Father Abbot."

"And did one of them answer the second gatekeeper correctly?"

"Yes, Father Abbot."

There was regret in the old man's voice. "So, one of them is

left to face the Ordeal of the Key. Let him or her stand forward now."

Door said, "Oh no."

Hunter said, "Let me take his place. I will face the ordeal."

Brother Fuliginous shook his head. "We cannot permit that."

When Richard was a small boy he had been taken, as part of a school trip, to a local castle. With his class he had climbed the many steps to the highest point in the castle, a partly ruined tower. They had clustered together at the top, while the teacher pointed out to them the whole of the countryside, spread out below. Even at that age, Richard had not been very good with heights. He had clutched the safety rail, and screwed up his eyes, and tried not to look down. The teacher had told them that the drop from the top of the old tower to the bottom of the hill it overlooked was three hundred feet; then she told them that a penny, dropped from the top of the tower, would have enough force to penetrate the skull of a man at the bottom of the hill, that it would crack a skull like a bullet. That night Richard lay in bed, unable to sleep for imagining the penny falling with the power of a thunderbolt. Still looking like a penny, but such a murderous penny, when it dropped . . .

An ordeal.

The penny dropped for Richard. It was a thunderbolt sort of a penny.

"Hang on a sec," he said. "Back up. Mm-mm: ordeal. Someone's got an ordeal waiting for them. Somebody who didn't have a little fight down in the mud, and didn't get to answer the little riddle . . ." He was babbling. He could hear himself babbling, and he just didn't care.

"This ordeal of yours," Richard asked the Abbot. "How

much of an ordeal is it? Is this the kind of ordeal like going to visit a rather ill-tempered elderly female relative is an ordeal, or is this kind of ordeal more like a plunging your hand into scalding water to see how fast it takes off the skin sort of ordeal?"

"This way now," said the Abbot.

"You don't want him," said Door. "Take one of us."

"Three of you come. There are three tests. Each of you faces one test: that is fair," said the Abbot. "If he passes the ordeal, he will return to you."

A light breeze eased the fog. The other dark figures were holding crossbows. Each crossbow was pointed at Richard, or Hunter, or Door. The friars closed ranks, cutting Richard off from Hunter and from Door. "We're looking for a key," said Richard to the Abbot, in a low voice.

"Yes," said the Abbot, placidly.

"It's for an angel," explained Richard.

"Yes," said the Abbot. He reached out a hand, found the crook of Brother Fuliginous' arm.

Richard lowered his voice. "Look, you can't say no to an angel, especially a man of the cloth like yourself . . . Why don't we just skip the ordeal bit? If you could just hand it over, I can tell them we ordealed."

The Abbot began to walk down the curve of the bridge. There was a door open at the bottom. Richard followed him. Sometimes there is nothing you can do. "When our order was founded," said the Abbot, "we were entrusted with the key. It is one of the holiest, and the most powerful, of all sacred relics. We must pass it on, but only to the one who passes the ordeal, and proves worthy."

They walked through winding narrow corridors, Richard

leaving a trail of wet mud behind him. "If I fail the ordeal, then we don't get the key, do we?"

"No, my son."

Richard thought about this for a moment. "Could I come back later for a second go?"

Brother Fuliginous coughed. "Not really, my son," said the Abbot. "If that should happen, you will in all probability be"—he paused, and then said—"beyond caring. But do not fret, perhaps you will be the one to win the key, eh?" There was a ghastly attempt at reassurance in his voice, which was more terrifying than any kind of attempt to scare could have been.

"You would kill me?"

The Abbot stared ahead with blue-milk eyes. There was a touch of reproof in his voice. "We are holy men," he said. "No, it is the ordeal that kills you."

They walked down a flight of steps, into a low crypt-like room with oddly decorated walls. "Now," said the Abbot. "Smile!"

There was the electric fizz of a camera flash going off, blinding Richard for a moment. When he could see again, Brother Fuliginous had lowered a battered old Polaroid camera, and was yanking out the photograph. The friar waited until it had developed, and then he pinned it to the wall. "This is our wall of those who failed," sighed the Abbot, "to ensure that they are none of them forgotten. That is our burden also: memorial."

Richard stared at the faces. A few Polaroids; twenty or thirty other photographic snapshots, some sepia prints and daguerreotypes; and, after that, pencil sketches, and watercolors, and miniatures. They went all the way along one wall. The friars had been at this a very long time.

DOOR SHIVERED. "I'M SO stupid," she muttered. "I should have known. Three of us. I should never have come straight here."

Hunter's head was moving from side to side. She had noted the position of each of the friars and each of the crossbows; she had calculated the odds of getting Door over the side of the bridge first unharmed, then with only minor injuries, and lastly with major injury to herself, but only minor injury to Door. She was now recalculating. "And what would you have done differently if you *had* known?" she asked.

"I wouldn't have brought *him* here for a start," said Door. "I'd have found the Marquis."

Hunter put her head on one side. "You trust him?" she asked, directly, and Door knew she was talking of de Carabas, not Richard.

"Yes," said Door. "I more or less trust him."

Door had been five years old for just two days. The market was being held in the Gardens at Kew on that day, and her father had taken her with him, as a birthday treat. It was her first market. They were in the butterfly house, surrounded by brightly colored wings, iridescent weightless things that entranced and fascinated her, when her father crouched down beside her. "Door?" he said. "Turn around slowly, and look over there, by the door."

She turned, and looked. A dark-skinned man wearing a big coat, his black hair tied behind him in a long ponytail, was standing by the door, talking to two golden-skinned twins, a young man and a young woman. The young woman was crying, in the way that grown-ups cry, keeping it inside as much as they can, and hating it when it still pushes

out at the edges, making them ugly and funny-looking on the way. Door turned back to the butterflies. "You saw him?" asked her father. She nodded. "He calls himself the Marquis de Carabas," he said. "He's a fraud and a cheat and possibly even something of a monster. If you're ever in trouble, go to him. He will protect you, girl. He has to."

Door looked back at the man. He had a hand on the shoulder of each of the twins, and was leading them from the room; but he glanced back over his shoulder, as he left, and he looked straight at her, and smiled an enormous smile; and then he winked at her.

The friars who surrounded them were dark ghosts in the fog. Door raised her voice. "Excuse me, brother," she called to Brother Sable. "But our friend, who's gone to get the key. If he fails, what happens to us?"

He took a step toward them, hesitated, and then said, "We escort you away from here, and we let you go."

"What about Richard?" she asked. Beneath his cowl, she could see him shaking his head, sadly, finally. "I should have brought the Marquis," said Door; and she wondered where he was, and what he was doing.

THE MARQUIS DE CARABAS was being crucified on a large X-shaped wooden construction Mr. Vandemar had knocked together from several old pallets, part of a chair, a wooden gate, and something that appeared to be a cartwheel. He had also used most of a large box of rusting nails. Mr. Croup had supervised the construction, and made useful suggestions, between scavenging about the hospital, looking for useful implements. Now, Mr. Vandemar was up a ladder, hauling the whole construction around, Marquis and all. "A little bit up," called Mr. Croup, who

was down at ground level. "Little to the left. Yes. That'll do it. Lovely."

It had been a very long time since they had crucified anybody.

The Marquis de Carabas's arms and legs were spread into a wide X shape. Nails went into his hands and feet. He was also roped around the waist. He was, to all intents and purposes, unconscious. The whole construction dangled in the air, from several ropes, in a room that had once been the hospital staff cafeteria. On the ground below, Mr. Croup had assembled a large mound of sharp objects, ranging from razors and kitchen knives to abandoned scalpels and lancets, and a number of interesting things Mr. Vandemar had found in the former Dental Wing. There was even a poker, from the furnace room.

"Why don't you see how he's doing, Mister Vandemar?" asked Mr. Croup.

Mr. Vandemar reached out his hammer, and prodded the Marquis experimentally with it.

The Marquis de Carabas was not a good man, and he knew himself well enough to be perfectly certain that he was not a brave man. He had long since decided that the world, Above or Below, was a place that wished to be deceived, and, to this end, he had named himself from a lie in a fairy tale, and created himself—his clothes, his manner, his carriage—as a grand joke.

There was a dull pain at his wrists and his feet, and he was finding it harder and harder to breathe. There was nothing more to be gained by feigning unconsciousness, and he raised his head, as best he could, and spat a gob of scarlet blood into Mr. Vandemar's face.

It was a brave thing to do, he thought. And a stupid one. Per-

haps they would have let him die quietly, if he had not done that. Now, he had no doubt, they would hurt him more.

And perhaps his death would come the quicker for it.

THE OPEN KETTLE WAS boiling fiercely. Richard watched the bubbling water, and the thick steam, and wondered what they were going to do with it. His imagination was able to provide any number of answers, most of which would have been unimaginably painful, none of which turned out to be correct.

The boiling water was poured into a pot, to which Brother Fuliginous added three spoons of dried shredded leaves. The resultant liquid was poured from the pot through a tea strainer, into three china cups. The Abbot raised his blind head, sniffed the air, and smiled. "The first part of the Ordeal of the Key," he said, "is the nice cup of tea. Do you take sugar?"

"No, thank you," said Richard, warily.

Brother Fuliginous added a little milk to the tea, and passed a cup and saucer to Richard. "Is it poisoned?" he asked.

The Abbot looked almost offended. "Good gracious, no."

Richard sipped the tea, which tasted more or less exactly like tea always tasted. "But this is part of the ordeal?"

Brother Fuliginous took the Abbot's hands and placed a cup of tea in them. "In a manner of speaking," said the Abbot. "We always like to give the seekers a cup of tea before they start. Part of the ordeal for us. Not for you." He sipped his own tea, and a beatific smile spread across his ancient face. "Rather nice tea, all things considered."

Richard put down his teacup, almost untouched. "Would you mind then," he asked, "if we just got on with the ordeal?"

"Not at all," said the Abbot. "Not at all." He stood up, and the three of them walked toward a door, at the far end of the room.

"Is there . . ." Richard paused, trying to decide what he was trying to ask. Then he said, "Is there anything you can tell me about the ordeal?"

The Abbot shook his head. There really was nothing to say: he led the seekers to the door. And then he would wait, for an hour, or two, in the corridor outside. Then he would go back in, and remove the remains of the seeker from the shrine, and inter it in the vaults. And sometimes, which was worse, they would not be dead, although you could not call what was left of them *alive,* and those unfortunates the Black Friars cared for as best they could.

"Right," said Richard. And he smiled, unconvincingly, and added, "Well, lead on, Macduff."

Brother Fuliginous pulled back the bolts on the door. They opened with a crash, like twin gunshots. He pulled the door open. Richard stepped through it. Brother Fuliginous pushed the door closed behind him, and swung the bolts back into place. He led the Abbot back to his chair, and placed the cup of tea back in the old man's hand. The Abbot sipped his tea, in silence. And then he said, with honest regret in his voice, "It's 'Lay on, Macduff,' actually. But I hadn't the heart to correct him. He sounded like such a nice young man."

12

R ICHARD MAYHEW WALKED DOWN
the Underground platform. It was
a District Line station: the sign
said BLACKFRIARS. The platform was
empty. Somewhere in the distance an Under-
ground train roared and rattled, driving a ghost
wind along the platform, which scattered a copy
of the tabloid the *Sun* into its component pages,
four-color breasts and black and white invec-
tive scurrying and tumbling off the platform
and down onto the rails.

Richard walked the length of the platform.
Then he sat down on a bench, and waited for
something to happen.

Nothing happened.

He rubbed his head, and felt slightly sick.

There were footsteps on the platform, near him, and he looked up to see a prim little girl walking past him, hand in hand with a woman who looked like a larger, older version of herself. They glanced at him, and then, rather obviously, looked away. "Don't get too near to him, Melanie," advised the woman, in a very audible whisper.

Melanie looked at Richard, staring in the way children stare, without embarrassment or self-consciousness. Then she looked back at her mother. "Why do people like that stay alive?" she asked, curiously.

"Not enough guts to end it all," explained her mother.

Melanie risked another glance at Richard. "Pathetic," she said. Their feet pattered away down the platform, and soon they were gone. He wondered if he had imagined it. He tried to remember why he was standing on this platform. Was he waiting for a Tube train? Where was he going? He knew the answer was somewhere in his head, somewhere close at hand, but he could not touch it, could not bring it back from the lost places. He sat there, alone and wondering. Was he dreaming? With his hands he felt the hard red plastic seat beneath him, stamped the platform with mud-encrusted shoes (where had the mud come from?), touched his face . . . No. This was no dream. Wherever he was, was real. He felt odd: detached, and depressed, and horribly, strangely saddened. Someone sat down next to him. Richard did not look up, did not turn his head.

"Hullo," said a familiar voice. "How are you, Dick? You all right?"

Richard looked up. He felt his face creasing into a smile, hope hitting him like a blow to the chest. "Garry?" he asked, scared. Then, "You can see me?"

Garry grinned. "You always were a kidder," he said. "Funny man, funny."

Garry was wearing a suit and tie. He was clean shaven, and had not a hair out of place. Richard realized what he must look like: muddy, unshaven, rumpled... "Garry? I ... listen, I know what I must look like. I can explain." He thought for a moment. "No ... I can't. Not really."

"It's okay," said Garry reassuringly. His voice was soothing, sane. "Not sure how to tell you this. Bit awkward." He paused. "Look," he explained. "I'm not really here."

"Yes, you are," said Richard.

Garry shook his head, sympathetically. "No," he said. "I'm not. I'm you. Talking to yourself."

Richard wondered vaguely if this was one of Garry's jokes. "Maybe this will help," said Garry. He raised his hands to his face, pushed at it, molded, shaped. His face oozed like warm Silly Putty.

"Is that better?" said the person who had been Garry, in a voice that was jarringly familiar. Richard knew the new face: he had shaved it most weekday mornings since he had left school; he had cleaned its teeth, squeezed its spots, and, on occasion, wished it looked more like Tom Cruise's, or John Lennon's or anyone else's, really. It was, of course, his face. "You're sitting on Blackfriars station at rush hour," said the other Richard, casually. "You're talking to yourself. And you know what they say about people who talk to themselves. It's just you're starting to edge a little closer to sanity, now."

The damp, muddy Richard stared into the face of the clean, well-dressed Richard, and he said, "I don't know who you are or what you're trying to do. But you aren't even very convincing: you don't even look like me." He was lying, and he knew it.

His other self smiled encouragingly, and shook his head. "I'm you, Richard," he said. "I'm whatever's left of your sanity . . ."

It was not the embarrassing echo of his voice he heard on answering machines, on tapes and home videos, that horrid parody of a voice that passed for his: the man spoke with Richard's true voice, the voice he heard in his head when he spoke, resonant and real.

"Concentrate!" shouted the man with Richard's face. "Look at this place, try to see the people, try to see the truth . . . you're already the closest you've been in a week to reality . . ."

"This is bullshit," said Richard, flatly, desperately. He shook his head, denying everything his other self was saying, but, still, he looked at the platform, wondering what it was he was meant to be seeing. Then something flickered, at the corner of his vision; he followed it with his head, but it was gone.

"Look," whispered his double. "See."

"See what?" He was standing on an empty, dimly lit station platform, a lonely mausoleum of a place. And then . . .

The noise and the light struck him like a bottle across the face: he was standing on Blackfriars station, in the middle of the rush hour. People bustled by him: a riot of noise and light, of shoving, moving humanity. There was an Underground train waiting at the platform, and, reflected in its window, Richard could see himself. He looked crazy; he had a week's growth of beard; food was crusted around his mouth and in his beard; one eye had recently been blackened, and a boil, an angry red carbuncle, was coming up on the side of his nose; he was filthy, covered in a black, encrusted dirt which filled his pores and lived

under his fingernails; his eyes were red and bleary, his hair was matted and snarled. He was a crazy homeless person, standing on a platform of a busy Underground station, in the heart of the rush hour.

Richard buried his face deep in his hands.

When he raised his face, the other people were gone. The platform was dark again, and he was alone. He sat down on a bench, and closed his eyes. A hand found his hand, held it for some moments, and then squeezed it. A woman's hand: he could smell a familiar perfume.

The other Richard sat on his left, and now Jessica sat on his right, holding his hand in hers, looking at him compassionately. He had never seen that expression on her face before.

"Jess?" he said.

Jessica shook her head. She let go of his hand. "I'm afraid not," she said. "I'm still you. But you have to listen, darling. You're the closest to reality you've been—"

"You people keep saying, the closest to reality, the closest to sanity, I don't know what you—" He paused. Something came back to him, then. He looked at the other version of himself, at the woman he had loved. "Is this part of the ordeal?" he demanded.

"Ordeal?" asked Jessica. She exchanged a concerned glance with the-other-Richard-who-wasn't-him.

"Yes. Ordeal. With the Black Friars who live under London," Richard said. As he said it, it became more real. "There's a key I have to get for this angel called Islington. If I get him the key, he'll send me home again . . ." His mouth dried up, and he could talk no longer.

"Listen to yourself," said the other Richard, gently. "Can't you tell how ridiculous all this sounds?"

Jessica looked as if she were trying not to cry. Her eyes glistened. "You're not going through an ordeal, Richard. You—you had some kind of nervous breakdown. A couple of weeks ago. I think you just cracked up. I broke off our engagement—you'd been acting so strangely, it was like you were a different person, I—I couldn't cope . . . Then you vanished . . ." The tears began to run down her cheeks, and she stopped talking to blow her nose on a tissue.

The other Richard began to speak. "I wandered, alone and crazy, through the streets of London, sleeping under bridges, eating food from bins and skips. Shivering and lost and alone. Muttering to myself, talking to people who weren't there . . ."

"I'm so sorry, Richard," said Jessica. She was crying, now, her face contorted and unattractive. Her mascara was beginning to run, and her nose was red. He had never seen her hurting before, and he realized how much he wanted to take her pain away. Richard reached out for her, to try to hold her, to comfort and reassure her, but the world slid and twisted and changed . . .

Someone stumbled into him, cursed and walked away. Richard was lying prone on the platform, in the rush-hour glare. The side of his face was sticky and cold. He pulled his head up off the ground. He had been lying in a pool of his own vomit. At least, he hoped it was his own. Passersby stared at him with revulsion, or, after one flick of the eyes, did not look at him again.

He wiped at his face with his hands, and tried to get up, but could no longer remember how. Richard began to whimper. He shut his eyes tightly, and he kept them shut. When he opened

them, thirty seconds, or an hour, or a day later, the platform was in semidarkness. He climbed to his feet. There was nobody there. "Hello?" he called. "Help me. Please."

Garry was sitting on the bench, watching him. "What, you still need someone to tell you what to do?" Garry got up, and walked over to where Richard was standing. "Richard," he said, urgently. "I'm you. The only advice I can give you is what you're telling yourself. Only, maybe you're too scared to listen."

"You aren't me," said Richard, but he no longer believed it.

"Touch me," said Garry.

Richard reached a hand out: his hand pushed into Garry's face, squashing and distorting it, as if it were pushing into warm bubblegum. Richard felt nothing in the air around his hand. He pulled his fingers out of Garry's face.

"See?" said Garry. "I'm not here. All there is, is you, walking up and down the platform, talking to yourself, trying to get up the courage to . . ."

Richard had not meant to say anything; but his mouth moved and he heard his voice saying: "Trying to get up the courage to do what?"

A deep voice came over the loudspeaker, and echoed, distorted, down the platform. *"London Transport would like to apologize for the delay. This is due to an incident at Blackfriars station."* "To do that," said Garry, inclining his head. "Become an incident at Blackfriars station. To end it all. Your life's a joyless, loveless, empty sham. You've got no friends—"

"I've got you," whispered Richard.

Garry appraised Richard with frank eyes. "I think you're an arsehole," he said, honestly. "A complete joke."

"I've got Door, and Hunter and Anaesthesia."

Garry smiled. There was real pity in the smile, and it hurt Richard more than hatred or enmity could ever have done. "More imaginary friends? We all used to laugh at you round the office for those trolls. Remember them? On your desk." He laughed. Richard started to laugh too. It was all too horrible: there was nothing else to do but laugh. After some time he stopped laughing. Garry put his hand into his pocket and produced a small plastic troll. It had frizzy purple hair, and it had once sat on the top of Richard's computer screen. "Here," said Garry. He tossed the troll to Richard. Richard tried to catch it; he reached out his hands, but it fell through them as if they were not there. He went down onto his hands and knees on the empty platform, fumbling for the troll. It seemed to him, then, as if it were the only fragment he had of his real life: that if he could only get the troll back, perhaps he could get everything back . . .

Flash.

It was rush hour again. A train disgorged hundreds of people onto the platform, and hundreds of others tried to get on, and Richard was down on his hands and knees, being kicked and buffeted by the commuters. Somebody stepped on his fingers, hard. He screamed shrilly, and stuck his fingers into his mouth, instinctively, like a burned child; they tasted disgusting. He did not care: he could see the troll at the platform's edge, now only ten feet away, and he crawled, slowly, on all fours, through the crowd, across the platform. People swore at him; they got in his way; they buffeted him. He had never imagined that ten feet could be such a long distance to travel.

Richard heard a high-pitched voice giggling, as he crawled,

and he wondered who it could belong to. It was a disturbing giggle, nasty and strange. He wondered what manner of crazy person could giggle like that. He swallowed, and the giggling stopped, and then he knew.

He was almost at the edge of the platform. An elderly woman stepped onto the train, and as she did so, her foot knocked the purple-haired troll down into the darkness, down into the gap between the train and the platform. "No," said Richard. He was still laughing, an awkward, wheezing laugh, but tears stung his eyes, and spilled down his cheeks. He rubbed his eyes with his hands, making them sting even more.

Flash.

The platform was deserted and dark again. He climbed to his feet, and walked, unsteadily, the last few feet, to the edge of the platform. He could see it there, down on the tracks, by the third rail: a small splash of purple, his troll. He looked ahead of him: there were enormous posters stuck to the wall on the other side of the tracks. The posters advertised credit cards and sports shoes and holidays in Cyprus. As he looked the words on the posters twisted and mutated.

New messages:

END IT ALL

was one of them.

PUT YOURSELF OUT OF YOUR MISERY.

BE A MAN—DO YOURSELF IN.

HAVE A FATAL ACCIDENT TODAY.

He nodded. He was talking to himself. The posters did not really say that. Yes, he was talking to himself; and it was time that he listened. He could hear the rattling of a train, not far away, coming toward the station. Richard clenched his teeth, and swayed back and forth, as if he were still being buffeted by commuters, although he was alone on the platform.

The train was coming toward him, its headlights shining out from the tunnel like the eyes of a monstrous dragon in a childhood nightmare. And he understood then just how little effort it would take to make the pain stop—to take all the pain he ever had had, all the pain he ever would have, and make it all go away forever and ever. He pushed his hands deep into his pockets, and took a deep breath. It would be so easy. A moment of pain, and then it would all be over and done . . .

There was something in his pocket. He felt it with his fingers: something smooth and hard and roughly spherical. He pulled it out of his pocket, and examined it: a quartz bead. He remembered picking it up, then. He had been on the far side of Night's Bridge. The bead had been part of Anaesthesia's necklace.

And from somewhere, in his head or out of it, he thought he heard the rat-girl say, "Richard. Hold on." He did not know if there was anyone helping him at that moment. He suspected that he was, truly, talking to himself. That this was the real him speaking and he was, finally, listening.

He nodded, and put the bead back into his pocket. And he stood on the platform and waited for the train to come in. It arrived at the platform, slowed, came to a full stop.

The train doors hissed open. The carriage was filled with

every manner and kind of people, all of whom were, unmistakably, quite dead. There were fresh corpses, with ragged cuts in their throats or bullet holes in their temples. There were old, desiccated bodies. There were strap-hanging cadavers, covered with cobwebs, and messy, cancerous things lolling in their seats. Each corpse seemed, as much as one could tell, to have died by its own hand. Some were male and some were female. Richard thought he had seen some of those faces, pinned to a long wall; but he could no longer remember where he had seen them, could not remember when. The carriage smelled like a morgue might do, at the end of a long hot summer during the course of which the refrigeration equipment had failed for good.

Richard had no idea who he was anymore; no idea what was or what was not true; nor whether he was brave or cowardly, mad or sane, but he knew the next thing he had to do. He stepped onto the train, and all the lights went out.

THE BOLTS WERE DRAWN back. Two loud bangs echoed through the room. The door to the tiny shrine was pushed open, letting in lamplight from the hall outside.

It was a small room with a high arched ceiling. A silver key hung from a thread, attached to the highest point of the ceiling. The wind caused by the opening of the door made the key swing back and forth, and then spin slowly, first one way, and then the other. The Abbot held Brother Fuliginous's arm, and the two men walked into the shrine, side by side. Then the Abbot let go of the brother's arm, and said: "Take the body, Brother Fuliginous."

"But. But, Father . . ."

"What is it?"

Brother Fuliginous went down on one knee. The Abbot could hear fingers against cloth and skin. "He's not dead."

The Abbot sighed. It was an evil thing to think, he knew, but he honestly felt it was so much kinder if they died outright. This was so much worse. "One of those, eh?" he said. "Ah well, we will look after the poor creature until it passes on to its ultimate reward. Lead it to the infirmary."

And a weak voice said, quietly, but firmly, "I am not a poor creature." The Abbot heard someone stand up, heard Brother Fuliginous's sharp intake of breath. "I . . . I think I got through it," said Richard Mayhew's voice, suddenly uncertain. "Unless this is more of the ordeal."

"No, my son," said the Abbot. There was something in his voice that might have been awe, and might have been regret.

There was silence. "I . . . I think I will have that cup of tea now, if you don't mind," said Richard.

"Of course," said the Abbot. "This way." Richard stared at the old man. The glaucous eyes gazed out at nothing at all. He seemed pleased that Richard was alive, but . . .

"Excuse me, sir?" said Brother Fuliginous, respectfully, to Richard, breaking his train of thought. "Don't forget your key."

"Oh. Yes. Thanks." He had forgotten about the key. He reached out and closed his hand upon the cold silver key, rotating slowly on its thread. He tugged, and the thread snapped easily.

Richard opened his hand, and the key stared up at him from his palm. "By my crooked teeth," asked Richard, remembering, "who am I?"

He put it into his pocket, next to the small quartz bead, and together they left that place.

THE FOG HAD BEGUN to thin. Hunter was pleased. She was confident now that, should it become necessary, she could get the Lady Door away from the friars entirely unharmed, and get herself away with only minor flesh wounds.

There was a flurry of movement on the far side of the bridge. "Something's happening," said Hunter to Door, under her breath. "Get ready to make a run for it."

The friars drew back. Richard Mayhew, the Upworlder, came toward them through the fog, walking beside the Abbot. Richard looked different, somehow . . . Hunter scrutinized him, trying to work out what had changed. His center of balance had moved lower, become more centered. No . . . it was more than that. He looked less boyish. He looked as if he had begun to grow up.

"Still alive then?" said Hunter. He nodded, put his hand into his pocket, and pulled out a silver key. He tossed it to Door, who caught it, then flung herself at him, wrapping her arms around him, squeezing him as tightly as she could.

Then Door let go of Richard and ran to the Abbot. "I can't tell you how much this means to us," she said to him.

He smiled, weakly but graciously. "May the Temple and the Arch be with you all, on your journey through the Underside," he said.

Door curtseyed, and then, clutching the key tightly in her hand, she went back to Richard, and to Hunter. The three trav-

elers walked down the bridge, and away. The friars stood on the bridge until they were out of sight, lost in the old fog of the world beneath the world.

"We have lost the key," said the Abbot to himself, as much as to any of them. "God help us all."

13

THE ANGEL ISLINGTON WAS dreaming a dark and rushing dream.

Huge waves were rising and crashing over the city; the night sky was rent with forks of white lightning from horizon to horizon; the rain fell in sheets, the city trembled; fires started near the great amphitheater and spread, quickly, through the city, defying the storm. Islington was looking down on everything from far above, hovering in the air, as one hovers in dreams, as it had hovered in those long-ago times. There were buildings in that city that were many hundreds of feet high, but they were dwarfed by the gray-green Atlantic waves. And then it heard the people scream. There were four million people in Atlantis, and,

in its dream, Islington heard each and every one of their voices, clearly and distinctly, as, one by one, they screamed, and choked, and burned, and drowned, and died. The waves swallowed the city, and, at length, the storm subsided.

When dawn broke, there was nothing to indicate there had ever been a city there at all, let alone an island twice the size of Greece. Nothing of Atlantis remained but the water-bloated bodies of children, of women and of men, floating on the cold morning waves; bodies at which the seagulls, gray and white, were already beginning to pick, with their cruel beaks.

And Islington woke. It was standing in the octagon of iron pillars, beside the great black door made of flint and tarnished silver. It touched the cold smoothness of the flint, the chill of the metal. It touched the table. It ran its finger lightly along the walls. Then it walked through the chambers of its hall, one after another, touching things, as if to reassure itself of their existence, to convince itself it was here, and now. It followed patterns, as it walked, smooth channels its bare feet had worn, over the centuries, in the rock. It stopped when it reached the rock pool, kneeling down and letting its fingers touch the cold water.

There was a ripple in the water, which began with its fingertips and echoed out to the edges. The reflections in the pool, of the angel itself and the candle-flames that framed it, shimmered and transformed. It was looking into a cellar. The angel concentrated for a moment; it could hear a telephone ring, somewhere in the distance.

Mr. Croup walked over to the telephone, and picked up the handpiece. He looked rather pleased with himself. "Croup and Vandemar," he barked. "Eyes gouged, noses twisted, tongues pierced, chins cleft, throats slit."

"Mister Croup," said the angel. "They now have the key. I want the girl called Door kept safe on her journey back to me."

"Safe," repeated Mr. Croup, unimpressed. "Right. We'll keep her safe. What a marvelous idea—such originality. Positively astounding. Most people would be content with hiring assassins for executions, sly killings, vile murders even. Only you, sir, would hire the two finest cutthroats in the whole of space and time, and then ask them to ensure a little girl remains unharmed."

"See that she is, Mister Croup. Nothing is to hurt her. Permit her to be harmed in any way and you will displease me deeply. Do you understand?"

"Yes." Croup shifted uncomfortably.

"Is there anything else?" asked Islington.

"Yes, sir." Croup coughed, into his hand. "Do you remember the Marquis de Carabas?"

"Of course."

"I take it that there is no such similar prohibition on extirpating the Marquis . . . ?"

"Not any longer," said the angel. "Just protect the girl."

It removed its hand from the water. The reflection was now merely candle-flames, and an angel, of astonishing, perfectly androgynous beauty. The Angel Islington stood up, and returned to its inner chambers, to await its eventual visitors.

"WHAT DID HE SAY?" asked Mr. Vandemar.

"He said, Mister Vandemar, that we should feel free to do whatsoever we wished to the Marquis."

Vandemar nodded. "Did that include killing him painfully?" he asked, a little pedantically.

"Yes, Mister Vandemar, I would say, on reflection, it did."

"That's good, Mister Croup. Wouldn't like another telling-off." He looked up at the bloody thing hanging above them. "Better get rid of the body, then."

ONE OF THE FRONT wheels on the supermarket shopping cart squeaked, and had a pronounced tendency to pull to the left. Mr. Vandemar had found the metal cart on a grassed-in traffic island, near the hospital. It was, he had realized on seeing it, just the right size for moving a body. He could have carried the body, of course; but then it could have bled on him, or dripped other fluids. And he only had the one suit. So he pushed the shopping cart with the body of the Marquis de Carabas in it through the storm drain, and it went *squee, squee* and pulled to the left. He wished that Mr. Croup would push the shopping cart, for a change. But Mr. Croup was talking. "You know, Mister Vandemar," he was saying, "I am currently too overjoyed, too delighted, not to mention too utterly and illimitably ecstatic, to grouse, gripe or grumble—having finally been permitted to do what we do best—"

Mr. Vandemar negotiated a particularly awkward corner. "Kill someone, you mean?" he asked.

Mr. Croup beamed. "Kill someone I mean indeed, Mister Vandemar, brave soul, glittering, noble fellow. However, by now you must have sensed a lurking 'but' skulking beneath my happy, blithe and chipper exterior. A minuscule vexation, like the teeniest lump of raw liver sticking to the inside of my boot. You must, I have no doubt, be saying to yourself, 'All is not well in Mister Croup's breast. I shall induce him to unburden himself to me.'"

Mr. Vandemar pondered this, while he forced open the round iron door between the storm drain and the sewer, and clambered through. Then he manhandled the wire cart with the Marquis de Carabas's body in it through the doorway. And then, more or less certain that he had been thinking nothing of the sort, he said, "No."

Mr. Croup ignored this, and continued, "And, were I then, in response to your pleadings, to divulge to you what vexes me, I would confess that my soul is irked by the necessity to hide our light under a bushel. We should be hanging the former Marquis' sad remains from the highest gibbet in London Below. Not tossing it away, like a used . . ." He paused, searching for the exact simile.

"Rat?" suggested Mr. Vandemar. "Budgerigar? Spleen?" *Squee, squee* went the wheels of the shopping cart.

Mr. Croup did not like any of them. "Ah well," he said. In front of them was a deep channel of brown water. Drifting on the water's surface were off-white suds of foam, used condoms and occasional fragments of toilet paper. Mr. Vandemar stopped the shopping cart. Mr. Croup leaned down, and picked up the Marquis' head by the hair, and hissed into its dead ear, "The sooner this business is over and done with, the happier I'll be. There's other times and other places that would properly appreciate two pair of dab hands with the garroting wire and the boning knife."

Then he stood up. "Good night, good Marquis. Don't forget to write."

Mr. Vandemar tipped over the cart, and the Marquis' corpse tumbled out and splashed into the brown water below them. And then, because he had come to dislike it intensely, Mr. Vandemar pushed the shopping cart into the sewer as well, and watched the current carry it away.

Then Mr. Croup held his lamp up high, and he stared up at the place in which they stood. "It is saddening to reflect," said Mr. Croup, "that there are folk walking the streets above who will never know the beauty of these sewers, Mister Vandemar. These red-brick cathedrals beneath their feet."

"Craftsmanship," agreed Mr. Vandemar.

They turned their backs on the brown water, and made their way back into the tunnels. "With cities, as with people, Mister Vandemar," said Mr. Croup, fastidiously, "the condition of the bowels is all-important."

DOOR TIED THE KEY around her neck with a piece of string that she found in one of the pockets of her leather jacket. "That's not going to be safe," said Richard. The girl made a face at him. "Well," he said. "It's not."

She shrugged. "Okay," she said. "I'll get a chain for it when we get to the market." They were walking through a maze of caves, deep tunnels hacked from the limestone that to Richard felt almost prehistoric.

Richard chuckled. "What's so funny?" Door asked.

He grinned. "I was just thinking of the expression on the Marquis' face, when we tell him we got the key from the friars without his help."

"I'm sure he'll have something sardonic to say about it," she said. "And then, back to the angel. By the 'long and dangerous way.' Whatever that is."

Richard found himself about to say, "I'm sure it'll be long and dangerous," and made himself not say it. Instead he admired

the paintings on the cave walls. Russets and ochers and siennas outlined charging boars and fleeing gazelles, woolly mastodons and giant sloths: he imagined that the paintings had to be thousands of years old, but then they turned a corner, and he noticed that, in the same style, there were lorries, house cats, cars and—markedly inferior to the other images, as if only glimpsed infrequently, and from a long way away—airplanes.

None of the paintings were very high off the ground. He wondered if the painters were a race of subterranean Neanderthal pygmies. It was as likely as anything else in this strange world. "So where is the next market?" he asked.

"No idea," said Door. "Hunter?"

Hunter slipped out of the shadows. "I don't know."

A small figure dashed past them, going back the way they had come. A few moments later another couple of tiny figures came toward them in full pursuit. Hunter whipped out a hand as they passed, snagging a small boy by the ear. "Ow," he said, in the manner of small boys. "Let me go! She stole my paintbrush."

"That's right," said a piping voice from further down the corridor. "She did."

"I didn't," came an even higher and more piping voice, from even further down the corridor.

Hunter pointed to the paintings on the cave wall. "You did these?" she asked.

The boy had the towering arrogance only seen in the greatest of artists and all nine-year-old boys. "Yeah," he said, truculently. "Some of them."

"Not bad," said Hunter. The boy glared at her.

"Where's the next Floating Market?" asked Door.

"Belfast," said the boy. "Tonight."

"Thanks," said Door. "Hope you get your paintbrush back. Let him go, Hunter."

Hunter let go of the boy's ear. He did not move. He looked her up and down, then made a face, to indicate that he was, without any question at all, unimpressed. "*You're* Hunter?" he asked. She smiled down at him, modestly. He sniffed. "*You're* the best body-guard in the Underside?"

"So they tell me."

The boy reached one hand back and forward again, in one smooth movement. He stopped, puzzled, and opened his hand, examined his palm. Then he looked up at Hunter, confused. Hunter opened her hand to reveal a small flick-knife with a wicked blade. She held it up, out of the boy's reach. He wrinkled his nose. "How'd you do that?"

"Scram," said Hunter. She closed the knife, and tossed it back to the boy, who took off down the corridor without a backward glance, in pursuit of his paintbrush.

THE BODY OF THE Marquis de Carabas drifted east, through the deep sewer, facedown.

London's sewers had begun their lives as rivers and streams, flowing north to south (and, south of the Thames, south to north) carrying garbage, animal carcasses, and the contents of chamber pots into the Thames, which would, if it felt like it, carry the offending substances out to sea. This system had more or less worked for many years, until, in 1858, the enormous volume of effluent produced by the people and industries of London,

combined with a rather hot summer, produced a phenomenon known at the time as the Great Stink: the Thames itself had become an open sewer. People who could leave London left it; the ones who stayed wrapped cloths doused in carbolic around their faces and tried not to breathe through their noses. Parliament was forced to recess early in 1858, and the following year it ordered that a program of sewer building begin. The thousands of miles of sewers that were built were constructed with a gentle slope from the west to the east, and, somewhere beyond Greenwich, they were pumped into the Thames Estuary, and the sewage was swept off into the North Sea. It was this journey that the body of the late Marquis de Carabas was making, traveling west to east, toward the sunrise and the sewage works.

Rats on a high brick ledge, doing the things that rats do when no people are watching, saw the body go by. The largest of them, a big black male, chittered. A smaller brown female chittered back, then she leapt down from the ledge onto the Marquis' back, and rode it down the sewer a little way, sniffing at the hair and the coat, tasting the blood, and then, precariously, leaning over, and scrutinizing what could be seen of the face.

She hopped off the head into the filthy water, and swam industriously to the side, where she clambered up the slippery brickwork. She hurried back along a beam, and rejoined her companions.

"BELFAST?" ASKED RICHARD.

Door smiled, impishly, and would say nothing more than, "You'll see," when he pressed her about it.

He changed his tack. "How do you know that kid was telling you the truth about the market?" he asked.

"It's not something anyone down here ever lies about. I . . . don't think we can lie about it." She paused. "The market's special."

"How did that kid know where it was?"

"Someone told him," said Hunter.

Richard brooded on this for a moment. "How did they know?"

"Someone told them," explained Door.

"But . . ." He wondered who chose the locations in the first place, how the knowledge was spread, trying to frame the question in such a way that he did not sound stupid.

A rich female voice asked from the darkness, "Hss. Any idea when the next market is?"

She stepped into the light. She wore silver jewelry, and her dark hair was perfectly coiffed. She was very pale, and her long dress was jet-black velvet. Richard knew immediately that he had seen her before, but it took him a few moments to place her: the first Floating Market, that was it—in Harrods. She had smiled at him.

"Tonight," said Hunter. "Belfast."

"Thank you," said the woman. She had the most amazing eyes, thought Richard. They were the color of foxgloves.

"I'll see you there," she said, and she looked at Richard as she said it. Then she looked away, a little shyly; she stepped into the shadows, and she was gone.

"Who was that?" asked Richard.

"They call themselves Velvets," said Door. "They sleep down here during the day, and walk the Upworld at night."

"Are they dangerous?" asked Richard.

"Everybody's dangerous," said Hunter.

"Look," said Richard. "Going back to the market. Who decides where it gets held, and when? And how do the first people find out where it's being held?" Hunter shrugged. "Door?" he asked.

"I've never thought about it." They turned a corner. Door held up her lamp. "Not bad at all," said Door.

"And fast, too," said Hunter. She touched the painting on the rock wall with her fingertip. The paint was still wet. It was a painting of Hunter and Door and Richard. It was not flattering.

THE BLACK RAT ENTERED the lair of the Golden deferentially, his head lowered, ears back. He crawled forward, squeeing and chittering.

The Golden had made their lair in a pile of bones. This pile of bones had once belonged to a woolly mammoth, back in the cold times when the great hairy beasts walked across the snowy tundra of the South of England as if, in the opinion of the Golden, they owned the place. This particular mammoth, at least, had been disabused of that idea rather thoroughly and quite terminally by the Golden.

The black rat made its obeisance at the base of the bone pile. Then he lay on his back with his throat exposed, closed his eyes and waited. After a while a chittering from above told him that he could roll over.

One of the Golden crawled out of the mammoth skull, on the top of the heap of bones. It crawled along the old ivory tusk, a golden-furred rat with copper-colored eyes, the size of a large house cat.

The black rat spoke. The Golden thought, briefly, and chattered an order. The black rat rolled on his back, exposing his throat again, for a moment. Then a twist and a wriggle and he was on his way.

There had been Sewer Folk before the Great Stink, of course, living in the Elizabethan sewers, or the Restoration sewers, or the Regency sewers, as more and more of London's waterways were forced into pipes and covered passages, as the expanding population produced more filth, more rubbish, more effluent; but after the Great Stink, after the great program of Victorian sewer building, that was when they came into their own. They could be found anywhere in the length and breadth of the sewers, but they made their permanent homes in some of the church-like red-brick vaults toward the east, at the confluence of many of the churning foamy waters. There they would sit, rods and nets and improvised hooks beside them, and watch the surface of the brown water.

They wore clothes—brown and green clothes, covered in a thick layer of something that might have been mould and might have been a petrochemical ooze, and might, conceivably, have been something much worse. They wore their hair long and matted. They smelled more or less as one would imagine. Old storm lanterns were hung about the tunnel. Nobody knew what the Sewer Folk used for fuel, but their lanterns burned with a rather noxious blue and green flame.

It was not known how the Sewer Folk communicated amongst themselves. In their few dealings with the outside

world, they used a kind of dumb-show. They lived in a world of gurgles and drips, the men, the women, and the silent little sewer children.

Dunnikin spotted something in the water. He was the chief of the Sewer Folk, the wisest and the oldest. He knew the sewers better than their original builders. Dunnikin reached for a long shrimping net; one practiced hand-movement and he was fishing out a rather bedraggled mobile telephone from the water. He walked over to a small heap of rubbish in the corner, and put the telephone down with the rest of their haul. The day's catch so far consisted of: two odd gloves, a shoe, a cat skull, a copy of *Fiesta,* a sodden packet of cigarettes, an artificial leg, a dead cocker spaniel, a pair of antlers (mounted), and the bottom half of a perambulator.

It had not been a good day. And tonight was a market night, in the open air. So Dunnikin kept his eyes on the water. You never knew what would turn up.

OLD BAILEY WAS HANGING his washing out to dry. Blankets and sheets fluttered and blew in the wind on the top of Centre Point, the ugly and distinctive sixties skyscraper that marks the eastern end of Oxford Street, far above Tottenham Court Road station. Old Bailey did not care very much for Centre Point itself, but, as he'd often tell the birds, the view from the top was without compare, and, furthermore, the top of Centre Point was one of the few places in the West End of London where you did not have to look at Centre Point itself.

The wind ripped feathers from Old Bailey's coat and blew

them away, off over London. He did not mind. As he also often told his birds, there were more where those came from.

A large black rat crawled out through a ripped air-vent cover, looked around, then came over to Old Bailey's bird-spattered tent. It ran up the side of the tent, then along the top of Old Bailey's washing line. It squealed at him, urgently.

"Slower, slower," said Old Bailey. The rat repeated itself, at a lower pitch, but just as urgently. "Bless me," said Old Bailey. He ran into his tent, and returned with weapons—his toasting fork, and a coal shovel. Then he hurried back into the tent again, and came out with some bargaining tools. And then he walked back into the tent for the last time, and opened his wooden chest, and pocketed the silver box. "I really don't have time for this tom-foolery," he told the rat, on his final exit from the tent. "I'm a very busy man. Birds don't catch themselves, y'know."

The rat squeaked at him. Old Bailey was unfastening the coil of rope around his middle. "Well," he told the rat, "there's others could get the body. I'm not as young as I was. I don't like the underplaces. I'm a roof man, I am, born and bred."

The rat made a rude noise.

"More haste, less speed," replied Old Bailey. "I'm goin'. Young whippersnapper. I knew your great-great-grandfather, young feller-me-rat, so don't you try putting on airs . . . Now, where's the market going to be?" The rat told him. Then Old Bailey put the rat in his pocket, and climbed over the side of the building.

SITTING ON THE LEDGE beside the sewer, in his plastic lawn chair, Dunnikin was overcome by a presentiment of wealth and

prosperity. He could feel it drifting from west to east, toward them.

He clapped his hands, loudly. Other men ran to him, and the women, and the children, seizing hooks and nets and lines as they did so. They assembled along the slippery sewer ledge, in the sputtering green light of their lanterns. Dunnikin pointed, and they waited, in silence, which is how the Sewer Folk wait.

The body of the Marquis de Carabas came floating facedown along the sewer, the current carrying him slow and stately as a funeral barge. They pulled it in with their hooks and their nets, in silence, and soon had it up on the ledge. They removed the coat, the boots, the gold pocket watch, and the contents of the coat pockets, although they left the rest of the clothes on the corpse.

Dunnikin beamed at the loot. He clapped again, and the Sewer Folk began to ready themselves for the market. Now they truly had something of value to sell.

"ARE YOU SURE THE Marquis will be at the market?" Richard asked Door, as the path began, slowly, to climb.

"He won't let us down," she said, as confidently as she could. "I'm sure he'll be there."

14

HMS *BELFAST* IS A gunship of 11,000 tons, commissioned in 1939, which saw active service in the Second World War. Since then it has been moored on the south bank of the Thames, in postcard land, between Tower Bridge and London Bridge, opposite the Tower of London. From its deck one can see St. Paul's Cathedral, and the gilt top of the column-like Monument to the Great Fire of London, erected, as so much of London was erected, by Christopher Wren. The ship serves as a floating museum, as a memorial, as a training ground.

There is a walkway onto the ship from the shore, and they came down the walkway in their twos and threes, and in their dozens. They

set up their stalls as early as they could, all the tribes of London Below, united both by the Market Truce and by a mutual desire to pitch their own stalls as far as possible from the Sewer Folk's stall.

It had been agreed well over a century before that the Sewer Folk could only set up a stall at those markets held in the open air. Dunnikin and his folk dumped their booty in a large pile on a rubber sheet, beneath a large gun tower. Nobody ever came to the Sewer Folk's stall immediately, but toward the end of the market they would come, the bargain hunters, the curious, and those few fortunate individuals blessed with no sense of smell.

Richard and Hunter and Door pushed their way through the crowds on the deck. Richard realized that he had somehow lost the need to stop and stare. The people here were no less strange than at the last Floating Market, but, he supposed, he was every bit as strange to them, wasn't he? He looked around, scanning the faces in the crowd as they walked, hunting for the Marquis' ironic smile. "I don't see him," he said.

They were approaching a smith's stall, where a man who could easily have passed for a small mountain, if one were to overlook the shaggy brown beard, tossed a lump of red molten metal from a brazier onto an anvil. Richard had never seen a real anvil before. He could feel the heat from the molten metal and the brazier from a dozen feet away.

"Keep looking. De Carabas'll turn up," said Door, looking behind them. "Like a bad penny." She thought for a moment, and added, "What exactly is a bad penny anyway?" And then, before Richard could answer, she squealed, "Hammersmith!"

The bearded mountain man looked up, stopped hitting the

molten metal, and roared, "By the Temple and the Arch. Lady Door!" Then he picked her up, as if she weighed no more than a mouse.

"Hullo, Hammersmith," said Door. "I hoped you'd be here."

"Never miss a market, lady," he thundered, cheerfully. Then he confided, like an explosion with a secret, "This's where the business is, y'see. Now," he said, recollecting the cooling lump of metal on his anvil, "just you wait here a moment." He put Door down at eye level, on the top of his booth, seven feet above the deck.

He banged the lump of metal with his hammer, twisting it as he did so with implements Richard assumed, correctly, were tongs. Under the hammer blows it changed from a shapeless blob of orange metal into a perfect black rose. It was a work of astonishing delicacy, each petal perfect and distinct. Hammersmith dipped the rose into a bucket of cold water beside the anvil; it hissed and steamed. Then he pulled it out of the bucket, wiped it, and handed it to a fat man in chain mail who was standing, patiently, to one side; the fat man professed himself well satisfied, and gave Hammersmith, in return, a green plastic Marks and Spencer shopping bag, filled with various kinds of cheese.

"Hammersmith?" said Door, from her perch. "These are my friends."

Hammersmith enveloped Richard's hand in one several sizes up. His handshake was enthusiastic, but very gentle, as if he had, in the past, had a number of accidents shaking hands, and had practiced it until he got it right. "Charmed," he boomed.

"Richard," said Richard.

Hammersmith looked delighted. "Richard! Fine name! I had a horse called Richard." He let go of Richard's hand, turned to Hunter, and said, "And you are . . . Hunter? Hunter! As I live, breathe and defecate! It is!" Hammersmith blushed like a schoolboy. He spat on his hand, and attempted, awkwardly, to plaster his hair back. Then he stuck his hand out, and realized that he had just spat on it, and he wiped it on his leather apron, and shifted his weight from foot to foot.

"Hammersmith," said Hunter, with a perfect caramel smile.

"Hammersmith?" asked Door. "Will you help me down?"

He looked shamefaced. "Beg pardon, lady," he said, and lifted her down. It came to Richard then that Hammersmith had known Door as a small child, and he found himself feeling unaccountably jealous of the huge man. "Now," Hammersmith was saying to Door. "What can I do for you?"

"Couple of things," she said. "But first of all—" She turned to Richard. "Richard? I've got a job for you."

Hunter raised an eyebrow. "For him?"

Door nodded. "For both of you. Will you go and find us some food? Please?"

Richard felt oddly proud. He had proved himself in the ordeal. He was One of Them. He would Go, and he would Bring Back Food. He puffed out his chest.

"I am your bodyguard. I stay by your side," said Hunter.

Door grinned. Her opal-colored eyes flashed. "In the market? It's okay, Hunter. Market Truce holds. No one's going to touch me here. And Richard needs looking after more than I do." Richard deflated, but no one was watching.

"And what if someone violated the Truce?" asked Hunter.

Hammersmith shivered, despite the heat of his brazier. "Violate the Market Truce? Brrrr."

"It's not going to happen. Go on. Both of you. Curry, please. And get me some poppadoms, please. Spicy ones."

Hunter ran her hand through her hair. Then she turned and walked off into the crowd, and Richard went with her. "So what would happen if someone violated Market Truce?" asked Richard, as they pushed through the crowds.

She thought about this for a moment. "The last time it happened was about three hundred years ago. A couple of friends got into an argument over a woman, in the market. A knife was pulled and one of them died. The other fled."

"What happened to him? Was he killed?"

Hunter shook her head. "Quite the opposite. He still wishes he had been the one to have died."

"He's still alive?"

Hunter pursed her lips. "Ish," she said, after a while. "Alive-ish."

A moment passed. *"Phew,"* Richard said, thinking he was going to be ill. "What's that—that stink?"

"Sewer Folk."

Richard averted his head, and tried not to breathe through his nose until they were well away from the Sewer Folk's stall.

"Any sign of the Marquis yet?" he asked. Hunter shook her head. She could have reached out her hand and touched him. They went up a gangplank, toward the food stalls, and more welcoming aromas.

OLD BAILEY FOUND THE Sewer Folk with little difficulty, following his nose.

He knew what he had to do, and he took a certain pleasure in making a bit of a performance of it, ostentatiously examining the dead cocker spaniel, the artificial leg, and the damp and moldering portable telephone, and shaking his head dolorously at each of them. Then he made a point of noticing the Marquis' body. He scratched his nose. He put on his spectacles and peered at it. He nodded to himself, glumly, hoping to give the vague impression of being a man in need of a corpse who was disappointed by the selection but was going to have to make do with what they had. Then he beckoned to Dunnikin, and pointed to the corpse.

Dunnikin opened his hands wide, smiled beatifically, and gazed up toward the heavens, conveying the bliss with which the Marquis' remains had entered their life. He put a hand to his forehead, lowered it, and looked devastated, in order to convey the tragedy that losing such a remarkable corpse would be.

Old Bailey put a hand in his pocket, and produced a half-used stick of deodorant. He handed it to Dunnikin, who squinted at it, licked it, and handed it back, unimpressed. Old Bailey pocketed it. He looked back at the corpse of the Marquis de Carabas, half-dressed, barefoot, still damp from its journey through the sewers. The body was ashen, drained of blood from many cuts, small and large, and the skin was wrinkled and prune-like from its time in the water.

Then he pulled out a bottle, three-quarters filled with a yellow liquid, and passed it to Dunnikin. Dunnikin looked at it suspiciously. The Sewer Folk know what a bottle of Chanel No. 5 looks like, and they gathered around Dunnikin, staring. Carefully, self-importantly, he unscrewed the top of the bottle, and

dabbed the tiniest amount on his wrist. Then, with a gravity the finest Parisian *parfumier* would have envied, Dunnikin sniffed. He nodded his head, enthusiastically, and approached Old Bailey to embrace him and conclude the deal. The old man averted his face, and held his breath until the embrace was concluded.

Old Bailey held up one finger, and tried his best to mime that he was not so young as once he was and that, dead or not, the Marquis de Carabas was a bit on the heavy side. Dunnikin picked his nose thoughtfully, and then, with a hand gesture indicating not only magnanimity but also a foolish and misplaced generosity that would, obviously, send him, Dunnikin, and the rest of the Sewer Folk, to the poor house, he had one of the younger Sewer Folk tie the corpse to the bottom half of the old perambulator.

The old roof-man covered the body with a cloth, and he pulled it away from the Sewer Folk, across the crowded deck.

"ONE PORTION OF VEGETABLE curry, please," said Richard, to the woman at the curry stall. "And, um, I was wondering. The meat curry. What kind of meat is it, then?" The woman told him. "Oh," said Richard. "Right. Um. Just better make that vegetable curries all round."

"Hello again," said a rich voice beside him. It was the pale woman they had met in the caves, with the black dress and the foxglove-colored eyes.

"Hullo," said Richard, with a smile. "—Oh, and some poppadoms, please.—You, um, here for curry?"

She fixed him with her violet eyes, and said, in mock Bela

Lugosi, "I do not eat . . . curry." And then she laughed, a lavish, delighted laugh, and Richard found himself realizing how long it had been since he had shared a joke with a woman.

"Oh. Um. Richard. Richard Mayhew." He stuck out his hand. She touched it with her own hand, in something a little like a handshake. Her fingers were very cold, but then, late at night, at the end of autumn, on a ship out on the Thames, everything is very cold.

"Lamia," she said. "I'm a Velvet."

"Ah," he said. "Right. Are there a lot of you?"

"A few," she said.

Richard collected the containers with the curry in. "What do you do?" he asked.

"When I'm not looking for food," she said, with a smile, "I'm a guide. I know every inch of the Underside."

Hunter, who Richard could have sworn was over on the other side of the stall, was standing next to Lamia. She said, "He's not yours."

Lamia smiled sweetly. "I'll be the judge of that," she said.

Richard said, "Hunter, this is Lamia. She's a Velcro."

"Vel-vet," corrected Lamia, sweetly.

"She's a guide."

"I'll take you wherever you want to go."

Hunter took the bag with the food in it from Richard. "Time to go back," she said.

"Well," said Richard. "If we're off to see the you-know-what, maybe she could help."

Hunter said nothing; instead, she looked at Richard. Had she looked at him that way the day before, he would have dropped

the subject. But that was then. "Let's see what Door thinks," said Richard. "Any sign of the Marquis?"

"Not yet," said Hunter.

OLD BAILEY HAD DRAGGED the corpse down the gangplank tied to its pram base, like a ghastly Guy Fawkes, one of the effigies that, not so very long ago, the children of London had wheeled and dragged around in early November, displaying them to passersby before their flaming demise on the bonfires of the fifth of November, Bonfire Night. He pulled the corpse over Tower Bridge, and, muttering and complaining, he hauled it up the hill past the Tower of London. He made his way west toward Tower Hill station and stopped a little before the station, beside a large gray jut of wall. It wasn't a roof, thought Old Bailey, but it would do.

It was one of the last remnants of the London Wall. The London Wall, according to tradition, was built on the orders of the Roman Emperor Constantine the Great, in the third century A.D., at the request of his mother Helena, who was actually from London and was sick of potentates and civic leaders from all over the Empire mentioning to her, in an offhanded manner, how big the city walls were where they were from, and asking what the city walls were like in her part of the world. When it was finished it had enclosed the small city completely; it was thirty feet high, and eight feet wide, and was, unarguably, the London Wall.

It was no longer thirty feet high, the ground level having risen since Constantine's mother's day (most of the original Lon-

don Wall is fifteen feet below street level today), and it no longer
enclosed the city. But it was still an imposing lump of wall. Old
Bailey nodded vigorously to himself. He fastened a length of rope
to the pram base, and he scrambled up the wall; then, grunting
and "bless-me"-ing, he hauled the Marquis up to the top of the
wall. He untied the body from the pram wheels, and laid it gen-
tly out on its back, arms at its sides. There were wounds on the
body that were still oozing. It was very dead.

"You stupid bugger," whispered Old Bailey, sadly. "What did
you want to get yourself killed for, anyway?"

The moon was bright and small and high in the cold night,
and autumn constellations speckled the blue-black sky like the
dust of crushed diamonds. A nightingale fluttered onto the wall,
examined the corpse of the Marquis de Carabas, and chirruped
sweetly. "None of your beak," said Old Bailey, gruffly. "You
birds don't smell like flipping roses, neither." It chirped a melo-
dious nightingale obscenity at him, and flew off into the night.

Old Bailey reached into his pocket and pulled out the black
rat, who had gone to sleep. It stared about it sleepily, then
yawned, displaying a vast and ratty expanse of piebald tongue.
"Personally," said Old Bailey to the black rat, "I'll be happy if
I never smell anything ever again." He put it down by his feet
on the stones of London Wall, and it chittered at him, and ges-
tured with its front paws. Old Bailey sighed. Carefully, he took
the silver box out from his pocket, and, from an inner pocket, he
pulled the toasting fork.

He placed the silver box on de Carabas's chest, then, ner-
vously, he reached out the toasting fork, and flipped open the
lid of the box. Inside the silver box, on a nest of red velvet, was

a large duck's egg, pale blue-green in the moonlight. Old Bailey raised the toasting fork, screwed up his eyes, and smashed the egg.

There was a *whup* as it imploded.

There was a great stillness for several seconds after that; then the wind began. It had no direction, but seemed somehow to be coming from everywhere, a swirling sudden gale. Fallen leaves, newspaper pages, all the city's detritus blew up from the ground and was driven through the air. The wind touched the surface of the Thames and carried the cold water into the sky in a fine and driving spray. It was a mad wind, a dangerous, crazy wind. The stall-holders on the deck of the *Belfast* cursed it and clutched their possessions to stop them blowing away.

And then, when it seemed that the wind would become so strong it would blow the world away and blow the stars away and send the people tumbling through the air like so many desiccated autumn leaves—

Just then—

—it was over, and the leaves, and the papers, and the plastic shopping bags, tumbled to the earth, and the road, and the water.

High on the remnant of the London Wall, the silence that followed the wind was, in its way, as loud as the wind had been. It was broken by a cough; a horrid, wet coughing. This was followed by the sound of someone awkwardly rolling over; and then the sound of someone being terribly and obscenely sick.

The Marquis de Carabas vomited sewer water over the side of the London Wall, staining the gray stones with brown foulness. It took a long time to purge the water from his body. And

then he said, in a hoarse voice that was little more than a grinding whisper, "I think my throat's been cut. Have you anything to bind it with?"

Old Bailey fumbled in his pockets, and pulled out a grubby length of cloth. He passed it to the Marquis, who wrapped it around his throat a few times and then tied it tight. Old Bailey found himself reminded, incongruously, of the high-wrapped Beau Brummel collars of the Regency dandies.

"Anything to drink?" croaked the Marquis.

Old Bailey pulled out his hip-flask, and unscrewed the top, and passed it to the Marquis, who swigged back a mouthful, then winced with pain, and coughed weakly. The black rat, who had watched all this with interest, now began to climb down the fragment of wall and away. It would tell the Golden: all favors had been repaid, all debts were done.

The Marquis gave Old Bailey back his hip-flask. Old Bailey put it away. "How are ye feeling?" he asked.

"I've felt better." The Marquis sat up, shivering. His nose was running, and his eyes flickered about: he was staring at the world as if he had never seen it before.

"What did you have to go and get yourself killed for, anyway, that's what I want to know," asked Old Bailey.

"Information," whispered the Marquis. "People tell you so much more when they know you're just about to be dead. And then they talk around you, when you are."

"Then you found out what you wanted to know?"

The Marquis fingered the wounds in his arms and his legs. "Oh yes. Most of it. I have more than an inkling of what this affair is actually about." Then he closed his eyes once more, and

wrapped his arms about himself, and swayed, slowly, back and forth.

"What's it like then?" asked Old Bailey. "Being dead?"

The Marquis sighed. And then he twisted his lips up into a smile, and with a glitter of his old self, he replied, "Live long enough, Old Bailey, and you can find out for yourself."

Old Bailey looked disappointed. "Bastard. After all I done to bring you back from that dread bourne from which there is no returning. Well, usually no returning."

The Marquis de Carabas looked up at him. His eyes were very white in the moonlight. And he whispered, "What's it like being dead? It's very cold, my friend. Very dark, and very cold."

DOOR HELD UP THE chain. The silver key hung from it, red and orange in the light of Hammersmith's brazier. She smiled. "Fine work, Hammersmith."

"Thank you, lady."

She hung the chain around her neck, and hid the key away inside her layers of clothes. "What would you like in return?"

The smith looked abashed. "I hardly want to presume upon your good nature . . . ," he mumbled.

Door made her "get on with it" face. He bent down, and produced a black box from beneath a pile of metalworking tools. It was made of dark wood, inlaid with ivory and mother-of-pearl, and was the size of a large dictionary. He turned it over and over in his hands. "It's a puzzle-box," he explained. "I took it in return for some smithing a handful of years back. I can't get it to open, though I've tried ever-so."

Door took the box, and ran her fingers over the smooth surface. "I'm not surprised you haven't been able to open it. The mechanism's all jammed. It's completely fused shut."

Hammersmith looked glum. "So I'll never find out what's in it."

Door made an amused face. Her fingers explored the surface of the box. A rod slid out of the side of the box. She half-pushed the rod back into the box, then twisted. There was a clunk from deep inside it, and a door opened in the side. "Here," said Door.

"My lady," said Hammersmith. He took the box from her, and pulled the door open all the way. There was a drawer inside the box, which he pulled open. The small toad, in the drawer, croaked and looked about itself with copper eyes, incuriously. Hammersmith's face fell. "I was hoping it would be diamonds and pearls," he said.

Door reached out a hand, and stroked the toad's head. "He's got pretty eyes," she said. "Keep him, Hammersmith. He'll bring you luck. And thank you again. I know I can rely on your discretion."

"You can rely on me, lady," said Hammersmith, earnestly.

THEY SAT TOGETHER ON the top of the London Wall, not speaking. Old Bailey slowly lowered the pram wheels to the ground below them.

"Where's the market?" asked the Marquis.

Old Bailey pointed to the gunship. "Over there."

"Door and the others. They'll be expecting me."

"You aren't in any condition to go anywhere."

The Marquis coughed, painfully. It sounded, to Old Bailey, like there was still plenty of sewer in his lungs. "I've made a long enough journey today," de Carabas whispered. "A little further won't hurt." He examined his hands, flexed the fingers slowly, as if to see whether or not they would do as he wished. And then he twisted his body around, and began, awkwardly, to climb down the side of the wall. But before he did so, he said, hoarsely and perhaps a little sadly, "It would seem, Old Bailey, that I owe you a favor."

WHEN RICHARD RETURNED WITH the curries, Door ran to him and threw her arms around him. She hugged him tightly, and even patted his bottom, before seizing the paper bag from him, and pulling it open with enthusiasm. She took a container of vegetable curry, and began, happily, to eat.

"Thanks," said Door, with her mouth full. "Any sign of the Marquis yet?"

"None," said Hunter.

"Croup and Vandemar?"

"No."

"Yummy curry. This is really good."

"Got the chain all right?" asked Richard. Door pulled the chain up from around her neck, enough to show it was there, and she let it fall again, the weight of the key pulling it back down.

"Door," said Richard, "this is Lamia. She's a guide. She says she can take us anywhere in the Underside."

"Anywhere?" Door munched a poppadom.

"Anywhere," said Lamia.

Door put her head on one side. "Do you know where the Angel Islington is?"

Lamia blinked, slowly, long lashes covering and revealing her foxglove-colored eyes. "Islington?" she said. "You can't go there . . ."

"Do you know?"

"Down Street," said Lamia. "The end of Down Street. But it's not safe."

Hunter had been watching this conversation, arms folded and unimpressed. Now she said, "We don't need a guide."

"Well," said Richard, "I think we do. The Marquis isn't around anywhere. We know it's going to be a dangerous journey. We have to get the . . . the thing I got . . . to the Angel. And then he'll tell Door about her family, and he'll tell me how to get home."

Lamia looked up at Hunter with delight. "And he can give you brains," she said, cheerfully, "and me a heart."

Door wiped the last of the curry from her bowl with her fingers, and licked them. "We'll be fine, just the three of us, Richard. We cannot afford a guide."

Lamia bridled. "I'll take my payment from him, not you."

"And what payment would your kind demand?" asked Hunter.

"That," said Lamia with a sweet smile, "is for me to know and him to wonder."

Door shook her head. "I really don't think so."

Richard snorted. "You just don't like it that I'm sorting everything out for once, instead of following blindly behind you going where I'm told."

"That's not it at all."

Richard turned to Hunter. "Well, Hunter. Do you know the way to Islington?" Hunter shook her head.

Door sighed. "We should get a move on. Down Street, you say?"

Lamia smiled with plum-colored lips. "Yes, lady."

BY THE TIME THE Marquis reached the market they were gone.

15

THEY WALKED OFF THE ship, down the long gangplank and onto the shore, where they went down some steps, through a long, unlit underpass, and up again. Lamia strode confidently ahead of them. She brought them out in a small, cobbled alley. Gaslights burned and sputtered on the walls.

"Third door along," she said.

They stopped in front of the door. There was a brass plate on it, which said:

THE ROYAL SOCIETY
FOR THE PREVENTION OF CRUELTY
TO HOUSES.

And beneath that, in smaller letters:

DOWN STREET. PLEASE KNOCK.

"You get to the street through the house?" asked Richard.

"No," said Lamia. "The street is in the house."

Richard knocked on the door. Nothing happened. They waited, and they shivered from the early-morning cold. Richard knocked again. Finally, he rang the doorbell. The door was opened by a sleepy-looking footman, wearing a powdered, crooked wig and scarlet livery. He looked at the motley rabble on his doorstep with an expression that indicated that they had not been worth getting out of bed for.

"Can I help you?" said the footman. Richard had been told to fuck off and die with more warmth and good humor.

"Down Street," said Lamia, imperiously.

"This way," sighed the footman. "If you'll wipe your feet."

They walked through an impressive lobby. Then they waited while the footman lit each of the candles on a candelabra, of the sort normally only seen on paperback book covers, where it is traditionally clutched by a young lady in a flowing nightdress who is fleeing from the kind of manor house that only has one light on anywhere, burning in an attic window.

They went down some impressive, richly carpeted stairs. They went down a flight of less impressive, less richly carpeted stairs. They went down a flight of entirely unimpressive stairs carpeted in a threadbare brown sacking, and, finally, they went down a flight of drab wooden stairs with no carpet on them at all.

At the bottom of those stairs was an antique service elevator, with a sign on it. The sign said:

OUT OF ORDER.

The footman ignored the sign, and pulled open the wire outer door with a metallic thud. Lamia thanked him, politely, and stepped into the elevator. The others followed. The footman turned his back on them. Richard watched him through the wire mesh, clutching his candelabra, going back up the wooden stairs.

There was a short row of black buttons on the wall of the elevator. Lamia pressed the bottom-most button. The metal lattice door closed automatically, with a bang. A motor engaged, and the elevator began, slowly, creakily, to descend. The four of them stood close-packed in the elevator. Richard realized that he could smell each of the women in the elevator with him: Door smelled mostly of curry; Hunter smelled, not unpleasantly, of sweat, in a way that made him think of great cats in cages at zoos; while Lamia smelled, intoxicatingly, of honeysuckle and lily of the valley and musk.

The elevator continued to descend. Richard was sweating, in a clammy cold sweat, and digging his fingernails deep into his palms. In the most conversational tones he could muster, he said, "Now would be a very bad time to discover that one was claustrophobic, wouldn't it?"

"Yes," said Door.

"Then I won't," said Richard.

And they went down.

Finally, there was a jerk, and a clunk, and a ratcheting noise, and the elevator stopped. Hunter pulled open the door, looked about, and then stepped out onto a narrow ledge.

Richard looked out of the open elevator door. They were hanging in the air, at the top of something that reminded Richard of a painting he had once seen of the Tower of Babel, or rather of how the Tower of Babel in the painting might have looked were it inside out: it was an enormous and ornate spiral path, carved out of rock, which went down and down around a central well. Lights flickered dimly, here and there in the walls, beside the paths, and, far, far below them, tiny fires were burning. It was at the top of the central well, a few thousand feet above solid ground, that the elevator was hanging. It swayed a little.

Richard took a deep breath, and followed the others onto the wooden ledge. Then, although he knew it was a bad idea, he looked down. There was nothing but a wooden board between him and the rock floor, thousands of feet below. There was a long plank stretched between the ledge on which they stood and the top of the rocky path, twenty feet away. "And I suppose," he said, with a great deal less insouciance than he imagined, "this wouldn't be a good time to point out that I'm really crap at heights."

"It's safe," said Lamia. "Or it was the last time I was here. Watch." She walked across the board, a rustle of black velvet. She could have balanced a dozen books on her head, and never dropped one. When she reached the stone path at the side, she stopped, and turned, and smiled at them encouragingly. Hunter followed her across, then turned, and waited beside her on the edge.

"See?" said Door. She reached out a hand, squeezed Richard's arm. "It's fine."

Richard nodded, and swallowed. *Fine.*

Door walked across. She did not seem to be enjoying herself; but she crossed, nonetheless. The three women waited for Richard, who stood there. Richard noticed after a while that he did not seem to be starting to walk across the wooden plank, despite any "Walk!" commands he sent to his legs.

Far above them, a button was pressed: Richard heard the thunk and the distant grinding of an elderly electric motor. The door of the elevator slammed closed behind him, leaving Richard standing, precariously, on a narrow wooden platform, no wider than a plank itself.

"Richard!" shouted Door. "Move!"

The elevator began to ascend. Richard stepped off the shaking platform, and onto the wooden board; then his legs turned to jelly beneath him, and he found himself on all fours on the plank, holding on for dear life. There was a tiny, rational part of his mind that wondered about the elevator: who had called it back up, and why? The rest of his mind, however, was engaged in telling all his limbs to clutch the plank rigidly, and in screaming, at the top of its mental voice, "I don't want to die." Richard closed his eyes as tightly as he could, certain that if he opened them, and saw the rock wall below him, he would simply let go of the plank, and fall, and fall, and—

"I'm not scared of falling," he told himself. "The bit I'm scared of is the bit where you stop falling, and start being dead." But he knew he was lying to himself. It was the fall he was scared of—afraid of flailing and tumbling helplessly through the air,

down to the rock floor far below, knowing there was nothing he could do to save himself, no miracle that would save him . . .

He slowly became aware that someone was talking to him.

"Just climb along the plank, Richard," someone was saying.

"I . . . can't," he whispered.

"You went through worse than this to get the key, Richard," someone said. It was Door talking.

"I'm really not very good at heights," he said, obstinately, his face pressed against the wooden board, his teeth chattering. Then, "I want to go home." He felt the wood of the plank pressing against his face. And then the plank began to shake.

Hunter's voice said, "I'm really not sure how much weight the board will bear. You two put your weight here." The plank vibrated as someone moved along it, toward him. He clung to it, with his eyes closed. Then Hunter said, quietly, confidently, in his ear, "Richard?"

"Mm."

"Just edge forward, Richard. A bit at a time. Come on . . ." Her caramel fingers stroked his white-knuckled hand, clasping the plank. "Come on."

He took a deep breath, and inched forward. And froze again. "You're doing fine," said Hunter. "That's good. Come on." And, inch by inch, creep by crawl, she talked Richard along the plank, and then, at the end of the plank, she simply picked him up, her hands beneath his arms, and placed him on solid ground.

"Thank you," he said. He could not think of anything else to say to Hunter that would be big enough to cover what she had just done for him. He said it again. "Thank you." And then he said, to all of them, "I'm sorry."

Door looked up at him. "It's okay," she said. "You're safe now." Richard looked at the winding spiral road beneath the world, going down, and down; and he looked at Hunter and Door and Lamia; and he laughed until he wept.

"What," Door demanded, when, at length, he had stopped laughing, "is so funny?"

"Safe," he said, simply. Door stared at him, and then she, too, smiled. "So where do we go now?" Richard asked.

"Down," said Lamia. They began to walk down Down Street. Hunter was in the lead, with Door beside her. Richard walked next to Lamia, breathing in the lily of the valley, honey-suckle scent of her, and enjoying her company.

"I really appreciate you coming with us," he told her. "Being a guide. I hope it's not going to be bad luck for you or anything."

She fixed him with her foxglove-colored eyes. "Why should it be bad luck?"

"Do you know who the rat-speakers are?"

"Of course."

"There was a rat-speaker girl named Anaesthesia. She. Well, we got to be sort of friends a bit, and she was guiding me somewhere. And then she got stolen. On Night's Bridge. I keep wondering what happened to her."

She smiled at him sympathetically. "My people have stories about that. Some of them may even be true."

"You'll have to tell me about them," he said. It was cold. His breath was steaming in the chilly air.

"One day," she said. Her breath did not steam. "It's very good of you, taking me with you."

"Least we could do."

Door and Hunter went around the curve in front of them,

and were lost to sight. "You know," said Richard, "the other two are getting a bit ahead of us. We might want to hurry."

"Let them go," she said, gently. "We'll catch up."

It was, thought Richard, peculiarly like going to a movie with a girl as a teenager. Or rather, like walking home afterward: stopping at bus shelters, or beside walls, to snatch a kiss, a hasty fumble of skin and a tangle of tongues, then hurrying on to catch up with your mates and her friends . . .

Lamia ran a cold finger down his cheek. "You're so warm," she said, admiringly. "It must be wonderful to have so much warmth."

Richard tried to look modest. "It's not something I think about much, really," he admitted. He heard, distantly, from above, the metallic slam of the elevator door.

Lamia looked up at him, pleadingly, sweetly. "Would you give me some of your heat, Richard?" she asked. "I'm so cold."

Richard wondered if he should kiss her. "What? I . . ."

She looked disappointed. "Don't you like me?" she asked. He hoped, desperately, that he had not hurt her feelings.

"Of course I like you," he heard his voice saying. "You're very nice."

"And you aren't using all your heat, are you?" she pointed out, reasonably.

"I suppose not . . ."

"And you said you'd pay me for being your guide. And it's what I want, as my payment. Warmth. Can I have some?"

Anything she wanted. Anything. The honeysuckle and the lily of the valley wrapped around him, and his eyes saw nothing but her pale skin and her dark plum-bloom lips, and her

jet-black hair. He nodded. Somewhere inside him something was screaming; but whatever it was, it could wait. She reached up her hands to his face and pulled it gently down toward her. Then she kissed him, long and languorously. There was a moment of initial shock at the chill of her lips, and the cold of her tongue, and then he succumbed to her kiss entirely.

After some time, she pulled back.

He could feel the ice on his lips. He stumbled back against the wall. He tried to blink, but his eyes felt as if they were frozen open. She looked up at him, and smiled delightedly; her skin was flushed and pink, and her lips were scarlet; her breath steamed in the cold air. She licked her red lips with a warm crimson tongue. His world began to go dark. He thought he saw a black shape at the edge of his vision.

"More," she said. And she reached out to him.

HE WATCHED THE VELVET pull Richard to her for the first kiss, watched the rime and the frost spread over Richard's skin. He watched her pull back, happily. And then he walked up behind her, and, as she moved in to finish what she had begun, he reached out and seized her, hard, by the neck, and lifted her off the ground.

"Give it back," he rasped in her ear. "Give him back his life." The Velvet reacted like a kitten who had just been dropped into a bathtub, wriggling and hissing and spitting and scratching. It did her no good: she was held tight by the throat.

"You can't make me," she said, in decidedly unmusical tones.

He increased the pressure. "Give him his life back," he told

her, hoarsely and honestly, "or I'll break your neck." She winced. He pushed her toward Richard, frozen and crumpled against the rock wall.

She took Richard's hand, and breathed into his nose and mouth. Vapor came from her mouth, and trickled into his. The ice on his skin began to thaw, the rime on his hair to vanish.

He squeezed her neck again. "All of it, Lamia."

She hissed then, extremely grudgingly, and opened her mouth once more. A final puff of steam drifted from her mouth to his, and vanished inside him. Richard blinked. The ice on his eyes had melted to tears, and were running down his cheeks. "What did you do to me?" he asked.

"She was drinking your life," said the Marquis de Carabas, in a hoarse whisper. "Taking your warmth. Turning you into a cold thing like her."

Lamia's face twisted, like a tiny child deprived of a favorite toy. Her foxglove eyes flashed. "I need it more than he does," she wailed.

"I thought you liked me," said Richard, stupidly.

The Marquis picked Lamia up, one-handed, and brought her face close to his. "Go near him again, you or any of the Velvet Children, and I'll come by day to your cavern, while you sleep, and I'll burn it to the ground. Understand?"

She nodded. He let go of her, and she dropped to the floor. Then she pulled herself up to her full size, which was not terribly tall, threw back her head, and spat, hard, into the Marquis' face. Lamia picked up the front of her black velvet dress, and ran up the slope, and away, her footsteps echoing through the winding rock path of Down Street, while her ice-cold spittle ran

down the Marquis' cheek. He wiped it away with the back of his hand.

"She was going to kill me," stammered Richard.

"Not immediately," said the Marquis, dismissively. "You would have died eventually, though, when she finished eating your life."

Richard stared at the Marquis. His skin was filthy, and he seemed ashen beneath the dark of his skin. His coat was gone: instead, he wore an old blanket wrapped about his shoulders, like a poncho, with something bulky—Richard could not tell what—strapped beneath it. He was barefoot, and, in what Richard took to be some kind of bizarre fashion affectation, there was a discolored cloth wrapped all the way around his throat.

"We were looking for you," said Richard.

"And now you've found me," croaked the Marquis, drily.

"We were expecting to see you at the market."

"Yes. Well. Some people thought I was dead. I was forced to keep a low profile."

"Why . . . why did some people think you were dead?"

The Marquis looked at Richard with eyes that had seen too much and gone too far. "Because they killed me," he said. "Come on, the others can't be too far ahead."

Richard looked over the side of the path, across the central well. He could see Door and Hunter, across the well, on the level below. They were looking around—for him, he assumed. He called to them, shouted and waved, but the sound did not carry. The Marquis laid a hand upon Richard's arm. "Look," he said. He pointed to the level beneath Door and Hunter. Something moved. Richard squinted: he could make out two figures, stand-

ing in the shadows. "Croup and Vandemar," said the Marquis. "It's a trap."

"What do we do?"

"Run!" said the Marquis. "Warn them. I can't run yet . . . Go, damn you!"

And Richard ran. He ran as fast as he could, as hard as he could, down the sloping stone road under the world. He felt a sudden stabbing pain in his chest: a stitch. And he pushed himself on, and still he ran.

He turned a corner, and he saw them all. "Hunter! Door!" he gasped, breathless. "Stop! Watch out!"

Door turned. Mr. Croup and Mr. Vandemar stepped out from behind a pillar. Mr. Vandemar yanked Door's hands behind her back, and bound them in one movement, with a nylon strip. Mr. Croup was holding something long and thin in a brown cloth cover, like the kind Richard's father had used to carry his fishing rods in. Hunter stood there, her mouth open. Richard shouted, "Hunter. Quickly."

She nodded, spun around, and kicked out one foot, in a smooth, almost balletic motion.

Her foot caught Richard squarely in the stomach. He fell to the floor several feet away, winded and breathless and hurt. "Hunter?" he gasped.

"I'm afraid so," said Hunter, and she turned away. Richard felt sick and saddened. The betrayal hurt him as much as the blow.

Mr. Croup and Mr. Vandemar ignored Richard and Hunter entirely. Mr. Vandemar was trussing Door's arms, while Mr. Croup stood and watched. "Don't think of us as murderers

and cutthroats, Miss," Mr. Croup was saying, conversationally. "Think of us as an escort service."

"Only without the bosoms," said Mr. Vandemar. He sounded ever-so-slightly embarrassed.

Mr. Croup turned to Mr. Vandemar. "*Escort* in the sense of accompany, Mister Vandemar. Ensure our fair lady gets where she's going in safety. I am comparing you neither to a lady of the evening, nor to a common street harlot."

Mr. Vandemar was unmollified. "Said we were an escort service," he muttered. "Know what that is."

"Strike it from the record, Mister Vandemar. I misspoke myself. Let us from henceforth be chaperones. Guards. Accompanists."

Mr. Vandemar scratched his nose with a raven-skull ring. "All right," he said.

Hunter stood beside the rock face, looking at none of them, and Richard lay on the rock floor and writhed and tried, somehow, to suck air back into his lungs. Mr. Croup turned back to Door, and smiled, showing many teeth. "You see, Lady Door, we are going to make sure you get safely to your destination."

Door ignored him. "Hunter," she called, "what's happening?" Hunter did not move, nor did she answer.

Mr. Croup beamed, proudly. "Before Hunter agreed to work for you, she agreed to work for our principal. Taking care of you."

"We told you," crowed Mr. Vandemar. "We told you one of you was a traitor." He threw back his head, and howled like a wolf.

"I thought you were talking about the Marquis," said Door.

Mr. Croup scratched his head of orange hair, theatrically. "Talking of the Marquis, I wonder where he is. He's a bit *late*, isn't he, Mister Vandemar?"

"Very *late* indeed, Mister Croup. As *late* as he possibly could be."

Mr. Croup coughed sententiously and delivered his punch line. "Then from now on, we'll have to call him the *late* Marquis de Carabas. I'm afraid he's ever-so-slightly—"

"Dead as a doornail," finished Mr. Vandemar.

Richard finally managed to get enough air into his lungs to gasp, "You traitorous bitch."

Hunter glanced at the ground. "No hard feelings," she whispered.

"The key you obtained from the Black Friars," said Mr. Croup to Door. "Who has it?"

"I do," gasped Richard. "You can search me, if you like. Look." He fumbled in his pockets—noticing something hard and unfamiliar in his back pocket, but there was no time to investigate that now—and he pulled out the front-door key of his old flat. He dragged himself to his feet and staggered over to Mr. Croup and Mr. Vandemar. "Here."

Mr. Croup reached over, and took the key from him. "Good gracious me," he said, scarcely glancing at it. "I find myself utterly taken in by his cunning ploy, Mister Vandemar." He passed the key to Mr. Vandemar, who held it up between finger and thumb, and crushed it like brass foil. "Fooled again, Mister Croup," he said.

"Hurt him, Mister Vandemar," said Mr. Croup.

"With pleasure, Mister Croup," said Mr. Vandemar, and he

kicked Richard in the kneecap. Richard fell to the ground, in agony. As if from a long way away, he could hear Mr. Vandemar's voice; it appeared to be lecturing him. "People think it's how hard you kick that hurts," Mr. Vandemar's voice was saying. "But it's not how hard you kick. It's where. I mean, this's really a very gentle kick"—something slammed into Richard's left shoulder. His left arm went numb, and a purple-white blossom of pain opened up in his shoulder. It felt like his whole arm was on fire, and freezing, as if someone had jabbed an electrical prod deep into his flesh, and turned up the current as high as it would go. He whimpered. And Mr. Vandemar was saying, ". . . but it hurts just as much as *this*—which is much harder"— and the boot rammed into Richard's side like a cannonball. He could hear himself screaming, and sobbing, and he wished that he knew how to make himself stop.

"I've got the key," he heard Door say.

"If only you had a Swiss Army knife," Mr. Vandemar told Richard, helpfully, "I could show you what I do with all the bits. Even the bottle opener, and the thing for getting stones out of horses' hooves."

"Leave him, Mister Vandemar. There will be time enough for Swiss Army knives. Does she have the token?" Mr. Croup fumbled in Door's pockets, and took out the carved obsidian figure: the tiny Beast the angel had given her.

Hunter's voice was low and resonant. "What about me? Where's my payment?"

Mr. Croup sniffed. He tossed her the fishing-rod case. She caught it one-handed. "Good hunting," said Mr. Croup. Then he and Mr. Vandemar turned and walked off down the twisting

slope of Down Street, with Door between them. Richard lay on the floor and watched them go, with a terrible feeling of despair spreading outward from his heart.

Hunter knelt on the ground, and began to undo the straps on the case. Her eyes were wide and shining. Richard ached. "What is it?" he asked. "Thirty pieces of silver?" She pulled it, slowly, from its fabric cover, her fingers caressing it, stroking it, loving it. "A spear," she said, simply.

It was made of a bronze-colored metal; the blade was long and it curved like a kris, sharp on one side, serrated on the other; there were faces carved into the side of the haft, which was green with verdigris, and decorated with strange designs and odd curlicues. It was about five feet long, from the tip of the blade to the end of the haft. Hunter touched it, almost fearfully, as if it were the most beautiful thing she had ever seen.

"You sold Door out for a spear," said Richard. Hunter said nothing. She wetted a fingertip with her pink tongue, then gently ran it across the side of the head of the spear, testing the edge on the blade; and then she smiled, as if she were satisfied with what she felt. "Are you going to kill me?" Richard asked. He was surprised to find himself no longer scared of death—or at least, he realized, he was not scared of that death.

She turned her head, then, and looked at him. She looked more alive than he had ever seen her; more beautiful, and more dangerous. "And what kind of challenge would I have, hunting you, Richard Mayhew?" she asked, with a vivid smile. "I have bigger game to kill."

"This is your Great-Beast-of-London-hunting spear, isn't it?" he said.

She looked at the spear in a way that no woman had ever looked at Richard. "They say that nothing can stand against it."

"But Door trusted you. *I* trusted you."

She was no longer smiling. "Enough."

Slowly, the pain was beginning to abate, dwindling to a dull ache in his shoulder and his side and his knee. "So who are you working for? Where are they taking her? Who's behind all this?"

"Tell him, Hunter," rasped the Marquis de Carabas. He was holding a crossbow pointed at Hunter. His bare feet were planted on the ground, his face was implacable.

"I wondered whether you were as dead as Croup and Vandemar claimed you were," said Hunter, barely turning her head. "You struck me as a hard man to kill."

He inclined his head, in an ironic bow, but his eyes did not move, and his hands remained steady. "And you strike me that way too, dear lady. But a crossbow bolt to the throat and a fall of several thousand feet may prove me wrong, eh? Put the spear down and step back." She placed the spear on the floor, gently, lovingly; then she stood up and stepped back from it. "You may as well tell him, Hunter," said the Marquis. "I know; I found out the hard way. Tell him who's behind all this."

"Islington," she said.

Richard shook his head, as if he were trying to brush away a fly. "It can't be," he said. "I mean, I've met Islington. He's an angel." And then, almost desperately, he asked, "Why?"

The Marquis' eyes had not left Hunter, nor had the point of the crossbow wavered. "I wish I knew. But Islington is at the bottom of Down Street, and at the bottom of this mess. And be-

tween us and Islington is the labyrinth and the Beast. Richard, take the spear. Hunter, walk in front of me, please."

Richard picked up the spear, and then, awkwardly, using the spear to lean on, he pulled himself up to a standing position. "You want her to come with us?" he asked, puzzled.

"Would you prefer her behind us?" asked the Marquis, drily.

"You could kill her," said Richard.

"I will, if there are no other alternatives," said the Marquis, "but I would hate to remove an option before it was entirely necessary. Anyway, death is so final, isn't it?"

"Is it?" asked Richard.

"Sometimes," said the Marquis de Carabas. And they went down.

16

THEY WALKED FOR HOURS in silence, following the winding stone road downward. Richard was still in pain; he was limping, and experiencing a strange mental and physical turmoil: feelings of defeat and betrayal roiled within him, which, combined with the near loss of his life to Lamia, the damage inflicted by Mr. Vandemar, and his experiences on the plank far above, left him feeling utterly wrecked. And, which made it worse, he was quite certain that all of his experiences of the last day paled into something rather small and insignificant when placed beside whatever the Marquis had experienced. So he said nothing.

The Marquis kept silent as every word he

uttered hurt his throat. He was content to let it heal, and to concentrate on Hunter. He knew that, should he let his attention flag for even a moment, she would know it, and she would be away, or she would turn on them. So he said nothing.

Hunter walked a little ahead of them. She, also, said nothing.

After some hours, they reached the bottom of Down Street. The street ended in a vast Cyclopean gateway—built of enormous rough stone blocks. *Giants built that gate,* thought Richard, half-remembered tales of long-dead kings of mythical London churning in his head, tales of King Bran and of the giants Gog and Magog, with hands the size of oak trees, and severed heads as big as hills. The portal itself had long since rusted and crumbled away. Fragments of it could be seen in the mud beneath their feet and dangling uselessly from a rusted hinge on the side of the gate. The hinge was taller than Richard.

The Marquis gestured for Hunter to stop. He moistened his lips, and said, "This gate marks the end of Down Street, and the beginning of the labyrinth. And beyond the labyrinth waits the Angel Islington. And in the labyrinth is the Beast."

"I still don't understand," said Richard. "Islington. I actually met him. It. Him. He's an angel. I mean, a real angel."

The Marquis smiled, without humor. "When angels go bad, Richard, they go worse than anyone. Remember, Lucifer used to be an angel."

Hunter watched Richard with nut-brown eyes. "The place you visited is Islington's citadel, and also its prison," she said. It was the first thing she had said in hours. "It cannot leave."

The Marquis addressed her directly. "I assume that the labyrinth and the Beast are there to discourage visitors."

She inclined her head. "So I would assume also."

Richard turned on the Marquis, all his anger and impotence and frustration spewing out of him in one angry blast. "Why are you even talking to her? Why is she still with us? She was a traitor—she tried to make us think that you were the traitor."

"And I saved your life, Richard Mayhew," said Hunter, quietly. "Many times. On the bridge. At the gap. On the board up there." She looked into his eyes, and it was Richard who looked away.

Something echoed through the tunnels: a bellow, or a roar. The hairs on the back of Richard's neck prickled. It was far away, but that was the only thing about it in which he could take any comfort. He knew that sound: he had heard it in his dreams, but now it sounded neither like a bull nor like a boar; it sounded like a lion; it sounded like a dragon.

"The labyrinth is one of the oldest places in London Below," said the Marquis. "Before King Lud founded the village on the Thames marshes, there was a labyrinth here."

"No Beast, though," said Richard.

"Not then."

Richard hesitated. The distant roaring began again. "I . . . I think I've had dreams about the Beast," he said.

The Marquis raised an eyebrow. "What kind of dreams?"

"Bad ones," said Richard.

The Marquis thought about this, eyes flickering. And then he said, "Look, Richard. I'm taking Hunter. But if you want to wait here, well, no one could accuse you of cowardice."

Richard shook his head: sometimes there is nothing you can do. "I'm not turning back. Not now. They've got Door."

"Right," said the Marquis. "Well then. Shall we go?"

Hunter's perfect caramel lips twisted into a sneer. "You'd have to be mad to go in there," she said. "Without the angel's token you could never find your way. Never get past the boar."

The Marquis reached his hand under his poncho blanket, and produced the little obsidian statue he had taken from Door's father's study. "One of these, you mean?" he asked. The Marquis felt, then, that much of what he had gone through in the previous week was made up for by the expression on Hunter's face. They went through the gate, into the labyrinth.

DOOR'S ARMS WERE BOUND behind her back, and Mr. Vandemar walked behind her, one huge beringed hand resting on her shoulder, pushing her along. Mr. Croup scuttled on ahead of them, holding the obsidian talisman he had taken from her on high, and peering edgily from side to side, like a particularly pompous weasel on its way to raid the henhouse.

The labyrinth itself was a place of pure madness. It was built of lost fragments of London Above: alleys and roads and corridors and sewers that had fallen through the cracks over the millennia, and entered the world of the lost and the forgotten. The two men and the girl walked over cobbles, and through mud, and through dung of various kinds, and over rotting wooden boards. They walked through daylight and night, through gaslit streets, and sodium-lit streets, and streets lit with burning rushes and links. It was an ever-changing place: and each path divided and circled and doubled back on itself.

Mr. Croup felt the tug of the talisman, and let it take him

where it wanted to go. They walked down a tiny alleyway, which had once been part of a Victorian "rookery" (a slum comprised in equal parts of theft and penny gin, of twopenny-halfpenny squalor and threepenny sex), and they heard it, snuffling and snorting somewhere nearby. And then it bellowed, deep and dark. Mr. Croup hesitated, before hurrying forward, up a short wooden staircase; and then, at the end of the alley, he stopped, squinting about him, before he led them down some steps into a long stone tunnel that had once run across the Fleet Marshes, in the Templars' time.

Door said, "You're afraid, aren't you?"

He glared at her. "Hush your tongue."

She smiled, although she did not feel like smiling. "You're scared that your safe-conduct token won't get you past the Beast. What are you planning now? To kidnap Islington? Sell both of us to the highest bidder?"

"Quiet," said Mr. Vandemar. But Mr. Croup simply chuckled; and Door knew then that the Angel Islington was not her friend.

She began to shout. "Hey! Beast! We're over here! Yoo-hoo! Mister Beast!" Mr. Vandemar cuffed her head, and knocked her against the wall. "Said to be quiet," he told her, calmly. She tasted blood in her mouth, and spat scarlet on the mud. Then she opened her mouth to begin shouting once more. Mr. Vandemar, anticipating this, had taken a handkerchief from his pocket and forced it into her mouth. She tried to bite his thumb as he did so, but it made no appreciable impression on him.

"Now you'll be quiet," he told her.

Mr. Vandemar was very proud of his handkerchief, which

was spattered with green and brown and black and had origi-
nally belonged to a rather overweight snuff-dealer in the 1820s,
who had died of apoplexy and been buried with his handkerchief
in his pocket. Mr. Vandemar still occasionally found fragments
of snuff-merchant in it, but it was, he felt, a fine handkerchief
for all that.

They continued in silence.

IN ITS ROCK HALL at the end of the labyrinth, which was its
citadel and its prison, the Angel Islington was doing something it
had not done in many thousands of years: it was singing. It had a
beautiful voice, melodious and sweet. Like all angels, it had per-
fect pitch. Islington was singing a song by Irving Berlin. And it
danced, gracefully, as it sang, executing slow and flawless moves
and steps, in its Great Hall filled with candles.

> *"Heaven,"* sang the angel, *"I'm in Heaven,*
> *and my heart beats so that I can hardly speak . . ."*

It ceased to dance when it reached the black door in its cham-
ber, the door made of flint and tarnished silver. It ran its fingers
slowly over the surface of the door, pressed its cheek to the door's
cold surface. And it continued, more quietly, to sing.

> *"Heaven . . .*
> *I'm in Heaven . . .*
> *I'm in Heaven . . .*
> *I'm in Heaven . . ."*

And then it smiled, gently and sweetly, and the smile of the Angel Islington was a monstrous thing to behold. It spoke the words, then, to itself, repeating them over and over, the syllables hanging bleakly in the air in the candlelit darkness of its chamber.

"I'm in Heaven," it said.

RICHARD MADE ANOTHER ENTRY in his mental diary. *Dear Diary,* he thought. *Today I've survived walking the plank, the kiss of death, and a lecture on kicking. Right now, I'm on my way through a labyrinth with a mad bastard who came back from the dead, and a bodyguard who turned out to be a . . . whatever the opposite of a bodyguard is. I am so far out of my depth that . . .* Metaphors failed him, then. He had gone beyond the world of metaphor and simile, into the place of things that *are,* and it was changing him.

They were wading through a narrow passage of wet, marshy ground, between dark stone walls. The Marquis held both the token and the crossbow, and he took care to walk, at all times, about ten feet behind Hunter. Richard, in the lead, was carrying Hunter's Beast spear, and a yellow flare the Marquis had produced from beneath his blanket, which illuminated the stone walls and the mud, and he walked well in front of Hunter. The marshland stank, and huge mosquitoes had begun to settle upon Richard's arms and legs and face, biting him painfully and raising huge, itching welts. Neither Hunter nor the Marquis had so much as mentioned the mosquitoes.

Richard was beginning to suspect that they were quite lost. It did not help his mood any that there were a large number of

dead people in the marsh: leathery preserved bodies, and dis-
colored skeletal bones, and pallid, water-swollen corpses. He
wondered how long the corpses had been there, and whether
they had been killed by the Beast, or by the mosquitoes. He said
nothing as they walked on for another five minutes and eleven
mosquito bites, and then he called out, "I think we're lost. We've
been through this way before."

The Marquis held up the token. "No. We're fine," he said.
"The token is leading us straight. Clever little thing."

"Yeah," said Richard, who was not impressed. "Very clever."

It was then that the Marquis stepped, barefoot, on the shat-
tered rib cage of a half-buried corpse, puncturing his heel,
and causing him to stumble. The little black statue went flying
through the air and tumbled into the black marsh with the satis-
fied plop of a leaping fish returning to the water. The Marquis
righted himself and pointed the crossbow at Hunter's back. He
could feel warmth and a sharp pain in the heel of his right foot.
He hoped he had not cut it too badly; he had little enough blood
to spare anymore.

"Richard," he called. "I dropped it. Can you come back
here?" Richard walked back, holding the flare high, hoping for
the glint of flame on obsidian, seeing nothing but wet mud. "Get
down into the mud and look," said the Marquis.

Richard groaned.

"You've dreamed of the Beast, Richard," said the Marquis.
"Do you really want to encounter it?"

Richard thought about this for not very long, then he pushed
the haft of the bronze spear into the surface of the marsh, and
stood the flare up into the mud beside it, illuminating the surface

of the marsh with a fitful amber light, and he got down on his hands and knees in the bog, searching for the statue. He ran his hands over the surface of the marsh, hoping not to encounter any dead faces or hands. "It's hopeless. It could be anywhere."

"Keep looking," said the Marquis.

Richard tried to remember how he usually found things. First he let his mind go as blank as he could, then he let his gaze wander over the surface of the marsh, purposelessly, idly. Something glittered on the boggy surface, five feet to his left. It was the Beast statue. "I can see it," called Richard.

He floundered toward it through the mud. The little glassy beast was head-down in a puddle of dark water. Perhaps the mud was disturbed by Richard's approach; more likely, as Richard was convinced forever after, it was just the sheer cussedness of the material world. Whatever the cause, he was almost next to the little statue when the marsh made a noise that sounded like a giant stomach rumbling, and a large bubble of gas floated up, and popped noxiously and obscenely beside the talisman, which vanished beneath the water.

Richard reached the place where the talisman had been, and pushed his arms deep into the mud, searching for it wildly, not caring what else his fingers might encounter. It was no use. It was gone forever. "What do we do now?" asked Richard.

The Marquis sighed. "Get back over here, and we'll figure out something."

Richard said, quietly, "Too late."

It was coming toward them so slowly, so ponderously, that he thought for a fragment of a second that it was old, sick, even dying. That was his first thought. And then he realized how

much ground it was covering as it approached, mud and foul water splashing up from its hooves as it ran, and he realized how wrong he had been in thinking it slow. Thirty feet away from them the Beast slowed, and stopped, with a grunt. Its flanks were steaming. It bellowed, in triumph, and in challenge. There were broken spears, and shattered swords, and rusted knives, bristling from its sides and back. The yellow flare light glinted in its red eyes, and on its tusks, and its hooves.

It lowered its massive head. It was some kind of boar, thought Richard, and then he realized that that had to be nonsense: no boar could be so huge. It was the size of an ox, of a bull elephant, of a lifetime. It stared at them, and it paused for a hundred years, which transpired in a dozen heartbeats.

Hunter knelt, in one fluid motion, and pulled up the spear from the Fleet Marsh, which released it with a sucking noise. And, in a voice that was pure joy, she said, "Yes. At last."

She had forgotten them all; forgotten Richard down in the mud, and the Marquis and his foolish crossbow, and the world. She was delighted and transported, in a perfect place, the world she lived for. Her world contained two things: Hunter, and the Beast. The Beast knew that too. It was the perfect match, the hunter, and the hunted. And who was who, and which was which, only time would reveal; time and the dance.

The Beast charged.

Hunter waited until she could see the white spittle dripping from its mouth, and as it lowered its head she stabbed up with the spear; but, as she tried to sink the spear into its side, she understood that she had moved just a fraction of a second too late, and the spear went tumbling out of her numbed hands, and a tusk sharper than the sharpest razor blade opened her side. And

as she fell beneath its monstrous weight, she felt its sharp hooves crushing down on her arm, and her hip, and her ribs. And then it was gone, vanished back into the darkness, and the dance was done.

MR. CROUP WAS MORE relieved than he would have admitted to be through the labyrinth. But he and Mr. Vandemar were through it, unharmed, as was their prey. There was a rock face in front of them, an oaken double door set in the rock face, and an oval mirror set in the right-hand door.

Mr. Croup touched the mirror with one grimy hand. The surface of the mirror clouded at his touch, seethed for a moment, bubbling and roiling like a vat of boiling quicksilver, and then was still. The Angel Islington looked out at them. Mr. Croup cleared his throat. "Good morning, sir. It is us, and we have the young lady you sent us to fetch for you."

"And the key?" The angel's gentle voice seemed to come from all around them.

"Hanging around her swan-like neck," said Mr. Croup, a little more anxiously than he intended to.

"Then enter," said the angel. The oak doors swung open at his words, and they went in.

IT HAD ALL HAPPENED so fast. The Beast had come out of the darkness, Hunter had snatched the spear, and it had charged her, and disappeared back into the darkness.

Richard strained to hear the Beast. He could hear nothing but, somewhere close to him, the slow *drip, drip* of water, and the

high, maddening whine of mosquitoes. Hunter lay on her back in the mud. One arm was twisted at a peculiar angle. He crawled toward her, through the mire. "Hunter?" he whispered. "Can you hear me?"

There was a pause. And then, a whisper so faint he thought for a moment he had imagined it. "Yes."

The Marquis was still some yards away, standing stock-still beside a wall. Now he called out, "Richard—stay where you are. The creature's just biding its time. It'll be back."

Richard ignored him. He spoke to Hunter. "Are you . . ." He paused. It seemed such a stupid thing to say. He said it anyway. "Are you going to be all right?" She laughed, then, with blood-flecked lips, and shook her head. "Are there any medical people down here?" he asked the Marquis.

"Not in the sense you're thinking of. We have some healers, a handful of leeches and chirurgeons . . ."

Hunter coughed, then, and winced. Bright red, arterial blood trickled from the corner of her mouth. The Marquis edged a little closer. "Do you keep your life hidden anywhere, Hunter?" he asked.

"I'm a hunter," she whispered, disdainfully. "We don't go in for that kind of thing . . ." She pulled air into her lungs with an effort, then exhaled, as if the simple effort of breathing were becoming too much for her. "Richard, have you ever used a spear?"

"No."

"Take it," she whispered.

"But—"

"Do it." Her voice was low and urgent. "Pick it up. Hold it at the blunt end."

Richard picked up the fallen spear. He held it at the blunt end. "I knew that bit," he told her.

A glimmer of a smile breathed across her face. "I know."

"Look," said Richard, feeling, not for the first time, like the only sensible person in a madhouse. "Why don't we just stay very quiet. Maybe it'll go away. We'll try to get you some help." And, not for the first time, the person he was talking to ignored him utterly.

"I did a bad thing, Richard Mayhew," she whispered, sadly. "I did a very bad thing. Because I wanted to be the one to kill the Beast. Because I needed the spear." And then, impossibly, she began to haul herself to her feet. Richard had not realized how badly she had been injured; nor could he now imagine what pain she must be in: he could see her right arm hanging uselessly, a white shard of bone protruding horribly from the skin. Blood ran from a cut in her side. Her rib cage looked *wrong*.

"Stop it," he hissed, futilely. "Get down."

With her left hand she pulled a knife from her belt, put it into her right hand, closed the nerveless fingers around the hilt. "I did a bad thing," she repeated. "And now I make amends."

She began humming, then. Humming high and humming low, until she found the note that made the walls and the pipes and the room reverberate, and she hummed that note until it felt like the entire labyrinth must be echoing to her hum. And then, sucking the air into her shattered rib cage, she shouted, "Hey. Big boy? Where are you?" There came no reply. No noise but the low drip of water. Even the mosquitoes were quiet.

"Maybe it's . . . gone away," said Richard, gripping the spear so tightly that it hurt his hands.

"I doubt it," muttered the Marquis.

"Come on, you bastard," Hunter screamed. "Are you scared?"

There was a deep bellow from in front of them, and the Beast came out of the dark, and it charged once more. This time there could be no room for mistakes. *The dance,* thought Hunter. *The dance is not yet over.*

As the Beast came toward her, its horns lowered, she shouted, "Now—Richard. Strike! Under and up! *Now!*" before the Beast hit her and her words turned into a wordless scream.

Richard saw the Beast come out from the darkness, into the light of the flare. It all happened very slowly. It was like a dream. It was like all his dreams. The Beast was so close he could smell the shit-and-blood animal stench of it, so close he could feel its warmth. And Richard stabbed with the spear, as hard as he could, pushing up into its side and letting it sink in.

A bellow, then, or a roar, of anguish, and hatred, and pain. And then silence.

He could hear his heart, thudding in his ears, and he could hear water dripping. The mosquitoes began to whine once more. He realized he was still holding tight to the haft of the spear, although the blade of it was buried deep within the body of the immobile Beast. He let go of it, and staggered around the beast, looking for Hunter. She was trapped beneath the Beast. It occurred to him that if he moved her, pulling her out from under it, he might cause her death, so instead he pushed, as hard as he could, against the warm dead flanks of the Beast, trying to move it. It was like trying to push-start a Sherman tank, but eventually, awkwardly, he tumbled it half-off her.

Hunter lay on her back, staring up at the darkness above

them. Her eyes were open, and unfocused, and Richard knew, somehow, that they saw nothing at all. "Hunter?" he said.

"I'm still here, Richard Mayhew." Her voice sounded almost detached. She made no effort to find him with her eyes, no effort to focus. "Is it dead?"

"I think so. It's not moving."

And then she laughed; it was a strange sort of laugh—as if she had just heard the funniest joke that ever the world told a hunter. And, between her spasms of laughter, and the wet, racking coughs that interrupted them, she shared the joke with him. "You killed the Beast," she said. "So now you're the greatest hunter in London Below. The Warrior . . ." And then she stopped laughing. "I can't feel my hands. Take my right hand." Richard fumbled under the Beast's body, and wrapped his hand around Hunter's chill fingers. They felt so small, suddenly. "Is there still a knife in my hand?" she whispered.

"Yes." He could feel it, cold and sticky.

"Take the knife. She's yours."

"I don't want your—"

"*Take her.*" He pried the knife free from her fingers. "She's yours now," whispered Hunter. Nothing was moving, save her lips; and her eyes were clouding. "She's always looked after me. Clean my blood off her, though . . . mustn't rust the blade . . . a hunter always looks after her weapons." She gulped air. "Now . . . touch the Beast's blood . . . to your eyes and tongue . . ."

Richard was not sure that he had heard her correctly, nor that he believed what he had heard. "What?"

Richard had not noticed the Marquis approach, but now he

spoke intently into Richard's ear. "Do it, Richard. She's right. It'll get you through the labyrinth. Do it."

Richard put his hand down to the spear, ran it up the haft until he felt the Beast's hide, and the warm stickiness of the Beast's blood. Feeling slightly foolish, he touched his hand to his tongue, tasting the salt of the creature's blood: it did not, to his surprise, revolt him. It tasted utterly natural, like tasting an ocean. He touched his bloody fingers to his eyes, where the blood stang like sweat.

Then, "I did it," he told her.

"That's good," whispered Hunter. She said nothing more.

The Marquis de Carabas reached out his hand, and closed her eyes. Richard wiped Hunter's knife on his shirt. It was what she had told him to do. It saved having to think.

"Better get a move on," said the Marquis, standing up.

"We can't just leave her here."

"We can. We can come back for the body later."

Richard polished the blade as hard as he could on his shirt. He was crying, now, but he had not noticed. "And if there isn't any later?"

"Then we'll just have to hope that someone disposes of all our remains. Including the Lady Door's. And she must be getting tired of waiting for us." Richard looked down. He wiped the last of her blood off Hunter's knife, and put it through his belt. Then he nodded. "You go," said de Carabas. "I'll follow as fast as I can."

Richard hesitated; and then, as best he could, he ran.

PERHAPS IT WAS THE Beast's blood that did it; he certainly had no other explanation. Whatever the reason, he ran straight and true through the labyrinth, which no longer held any mysteries for him. He felt that he knew every twist, every path, every alley and lane and tunnel of it. He ran, stumbling and falling, and still running, exhausted, through the labyrinth, his blood pounding in his temples. A rhyme coursed through his head, as he ran, pounding and echoing to the rhythm of his feet. It was something he had heard as a child.

> This aye night, this aye night
> Every night and all
> Fire and fleet and candlelight
> And Christ receive thy soul.

The words went around and around, dirge-like, in his head. *Fire and fleet and candlelight . . .*

At the end of the labyrinth was a sheer granite cliff, and set in the cliff were high wooden double-doors. There was an oval mirror hanging on one of the doors. The doors were closed. He touched the wood, and the door opened, silently, to his touch.

Richard went inside.

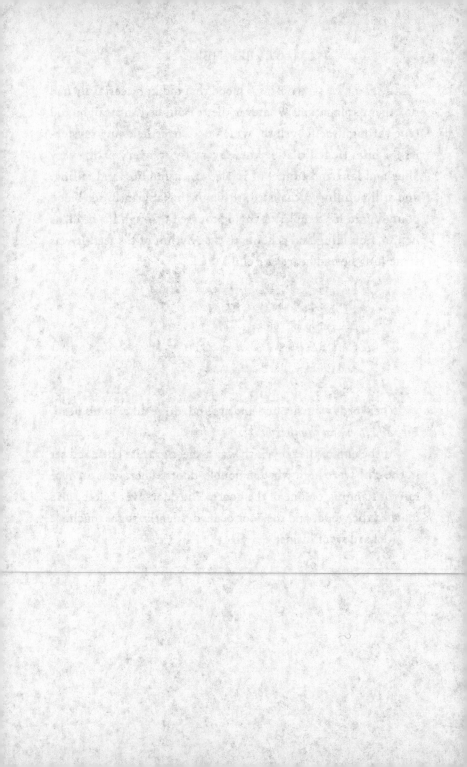

17

———✦———

RICHARD FOLLOWED THE PATH be-
tween the burning candles which
led him through the angel's vault to
the Great Hall. He reccognized his
surroundings: this was where they had drunk
Islington's wine: an octagon of iron pillars sup-
porting the stone roof above them, the huge
black stone and metal door, the old wooden
table, the candles.

Door was chained up, spread-eagled be-
tween two pillars beside the flint and silver
door. She stared at him as he came in, her odd-
colored pixie-eyes wide and scared. The Angel
Islington, standing beside her, turned and
smiled at Richard as he entered. That was the
most chilling thing of all: the gentle compas-
sion, the sweetness of that smile.

"Come in, Richard Mayhew. Come in," said the Angel Islington. "Dear me. You do look a mess." There was honest concern in its voice. Richard hesitated. "Please." The angel gestured, curling a white forefinger, urging him further in. "I think we all know each other. You know the Lady Door of course, and my associates, Mister Croup, Mister Vandemar." Richard turned. Croup and Vandemar were standing on each side of him. Mr. Vandemar smiled at him. Mr. Croup did not. "I was rather hoping you would show up," continued the angel. It tipped its head on one side, and asked, "By the bye, where is Hunter?"

"She's dead," said Richard. He heard Door gasp.

"Oh. The poor dear," said Islington. It shook its head sadly, obviously regretting the senseless loss of human life, the frailty of all mortals, born to suffer and to die.

"Still," said Mr. Croup chirpily. "Can't make an omelette without killing a few people."

Richard ignored them, as best he could. "Door? Are you all right?"

"More or less, thanks. So far." Her lower lip was swollen, and there was a bruise on her cheek.

"I am afraid," said Islington, "that Miss Door was proving a little intransigent. I was just discussing having Mister Croup and Mister Vandemar . . ." It paused. There were obviously some things it found distasteful actually to say.

"Torture her," suggested Mr. Vandemar, helpfully.

"We are," said Mr. Croup, "after all, famed across the entirety of creation for our skill in the excruciatory arts."

"Good at hurting people," clarified Mr. Vandemar.

The angel continued, staring intently at Richard as it spoke, as if it had heard neither of them. "But then, Miss Door does not strike me as someone who will easily change her mind."

"Give us time enough," said Mr. Croup. "We'd break her."

"Into little wet bits," said Mr. Vandemar.

Islington shook his head, and smiled indulgently at this display of enthusiasm. "No time," it said to Richard, "no time. However, she does strike me as someone who would indeed act to end the pain and suffering of a friend, a fellow mortal, such as yourself, Richard . . ." Mr. Croup hit Richard in the stomach, then: a vicious rabbit-punch to the gut, and Richard doubled up. He felt Mr. Vandemar's fingers on the back of his neck, pulling him back to a standing position.

"But it's wrong," said Door.

Islington looked thoughtful. "Wrong?" it said, puzzled and amused.

Mr. Croup pulled Richard's head close to his, and smiled his graveyard smile. "He's traveled so far beyond right and wrong he couldn't see them with a telescope on a nice clear night," he confided. "Now, Mister Vandemar, if you'll do the honors?"

Mr. Vandemar took Richard's left hand in his. He took Richard's little finger between his huge fingers, and bent it back until it broke. Richard cried out.

The angel turned, slowly. It seemed distracted by something. It blinked its pearl-gray eyes. "There's someone else out there. Mister Croup?" There was a dark shimmer where Mr. Croup had been, and he was there no longer.

THE MARQUIS DE CARABAS was flattened against the side of the red granite cliff, staring at the oak doors that led into Islington's dwelling.

Plans and plots whirled through his head, each scheme fizzling out uselessly as he imagined it. He had rather thought he would have known what to do when he got to this point, and he was discovering, to his disgust, that he had absolutely no idea. There were no more favors to call in, no levers to press or buttons to push, so he scrutinized the doors, and wondered whether they were guarded, whether the angel would know if they were opened. There had to be an obvious solution he was missing, if only he thought hard enough: perhaps something would occur to him. At least, he thought, slightly cheered, he had surprise on his side.

That was until he felt the cold point of a sharp knife placed on the side of his throat, and he heard Mr. Croup's oily voice whispering in his ear. "I already killed you once today," it was saying. "What does it take to teach some people?"

RICHARD WAS MANACLED AND chained between a pair of iron pillars when Mr. Croup returned, prodding the Marquis de Carabas with his knife. The angel looked at the Marquis, with disappointment on its face, then, gently, it shook its beautiful head. "You told me he was dead," it said.

"He is," said Mr. Vandemar.

"He was," corrected Mr. Croup.

The angel's voice was a fraction less gentle and less caring. "I will not be lied to," it said.

"We don't lie," said Mr. Croup, affronted.

"Do," said Mr. Vandemar.

Mr. Croup ran a grimy hand through his filthy orange hair, in exasperation. "Indeed we do. But not this time."

The pain in Richard's hand showed no indication of subsiding. "How can you behave like this?" he asked, angrily. "You're an angel."

"What did I tell you, Richard?" asked the Marquis, drily.

Richard thought. "You said, Lucifer was an angel."

Islington smiled superciliously. "Lucifer?" it said. "Lucifer was an idiot. It wound up lord and master of nothing at all."

The Marquis grinned. "And you wound up lord and master of two thugs and a roomful of candles?"

The angel licked its lips. "They told me it was my punishment for Atlantis. I told them there was nothing more I could have done. The whole affair was . . ." It paused, as if it were hunting for the correct word. And then it said, with regret, "Unfortunate."

"But millions of people were killed," said Door.

Islington clasped its hands in front of its chest, as if it were posing for a Christmas card. "These things happen," it explained, reasonably.

"Of course they do," said the Marquis, mildly, the irony implicit in his words, not in his voice. "Cities sink every day. And you had nothing to do with it?"

It was as if the lid had been pulled off something dark and writhing: a place of derangement and fury and utter viciousness; and, in a time of scary things, it was the most frightening thing Richard had seen. The angel's serene beauty cracked; its eyes

flashed; and it screamed at them, crazy-scary and uncontrolled, utterly certain in its rightness, *"They deserved it."*

There was a moment of silence. And then the angel lowered its head, and sighed, and raised its head, and said, very quietly and with deep regret, "Just one of those things." Then it pointed to the Marquis. "Chain him up," it said.

Croup and Vandemar fastened manacles around the Marquis' wrists, and chained the manacles securely to the pillars beside Richard. The angel had turned its attention back to Door. It walked over to her, reached out its hand, placed it beneath her pointed chin, and raised her head, to stare into her eyes. "Your family," it said, gently. "You come from a very unusual family. Quite remarkable."

"Then why did you have us killed?"

"Not all of you," it said. Richard thought it was talking about Door, but then it said, "There was always the possibility that you might not have . . . worked out as well as you did." It released her chin, and stroked her face with long, white fingers, and it said, "Your family can open doors. They can create doors where there were no doors. They can unlock doors that are locked. Open doors that were never meant to be opened." It ran its fingers down her neck, gently, as if it were caressing her, then closed its hand on the key about her neck. "When I was sentenced here, they gave me the door to my prison. And they took the key to the door, and put it down here too. An exquisite form of torture." It tugged, gently, on the chain, pulling it out from under Door's layers of silk and cotton and lace, revealing the silver key; and then it ran its fingers over the key, as if it were exploring her secret places.

Richard knew, then. "The Black Friars were keeping the key safe from you," he said.

Islington let go of the key. Door was chained up beside the door made of black flint and tarnished silver. The angel walked to it, and placed a hand on it, white against the blackness of the door. "From me," agreed Islington. "A key. A door. An opener of the door. There must be the three, you see: a particularly refined sort of joke. The idea being that when they decided I had earned forgiveness and my freedom, they would send me an opener, and give me the key. I just decided to take matters into my own hands, and will be leaving a little early."

It turned back to Door. Once more it caressed the key. Then it closed its hand about the key and tugged, hard. The chain snapped. Door winced. "I spoke first to your father, Door," the angel continued. "He worried about the Underside. He wanted to unite London Below, to unite the baronies and fiefdoms—perhaps even to forge some kind of bond with London Above. I told him I would help him, if he would help me. Then I told him the nature of the help I needed, and he laughed at me." It repeated the words, as if it still found them impossible to believe. "He laughed. At me."

Door shook her head. "You killed him because he turned you down?"

"I didn't kill him," Islington corrected her, gently. "I had him killed."

"But he told me I could trust you. He told me to come here. In his journal."

Mr. Croup began to giggle. "He didn't," he said. "He never did. That was us. What was it he actually said, Mister Vandemar?"

"Door, child, fear Islington," said Mr. Vandemar, with her father's voice. The voice was exact. "Islington's got to be behind all this. It's dangerous, Door—keep away from it—"

Islington caressed her cheek, with the key. "I thought my version would get you here a little faster."

"We took the journal," said Mr. Croup. "We fixed it, and we returned it."

"Where does the door lead to?" called Richard.

"Home," said the angel.

"Heaven?"

And Islington said nothing, but it smiled, in the manner of a cat who has not only devoured the cream and the canary, but also the chicken you were saving for dinner, and the crème brûlée that would have been dessert.

"So, you figure they won't notice you're back?" sneered the Marquis. "Just, 'Oh look, there's another angel, here, grab a harp and on with the hosannas'?"

Islington's gray eyes were bright. "Not for me the smooth agonies of adulation, of hymns and halos and self-seeking prayers," it said. "I have . . . my own agenda."

"Well, now you've got the key," said Door.

"And I have you," said the angel. "You're the opener. Without you the key is useless. Open the door for me."

"You killed her family," said Richard. "You've had her hunted through London Below. Now you want her to open a door for you so you can single-handedly invade Heaven? You're not much of a judge of character, are you? She'll never do it."

The angel looked at him, then, with eyes older than the Milky Way. Then it said, "Ah me," and turned its back, as if it

were ill-prepared to watch the unpleasantness that was about to occur.

"Hurt him some more, Mister Vandemar," said Mr. Croup. "Cut off his ear."

Mr. Vandemar raised his hand. It was empty. He jerked his arm, almost imperceptibly, and now he was holding a knife. "Told you one day you'd find out what your own liver tastes like," he said to Richard. "Today's going to be your lucky day." He slid the knife blade gently beneath Richard's earlobe. Richard felt no pain—perhaps, he thought, he had felt too much pain already that day, perhaps the blade was too sharp to hurt. But he felt the warm blood drip, wetly, from his ear down his neck. Door was watching him, and her elfin face and huge opal-colored eyes filled his vision. He tried to send her mental messages. *Hold out. Don't let them make you do this. I'll be fine.* Then Mr. Vandemar put a little pressure on the knife, and Richard began to scream.

"Stop them," said Door. "I'll open your door."

Islington gestured, curtly, and Mr. Vandemar sighed piteously and put his knife away. The warm blood dripped down Richard's neck, and pooled and puddled in the hollow of his clavicle. Mr. Croup walked over to Door, and unlocked the right-hand manacle. She stood there, rubbing her wrist, framed by the pillars. She was still chained to the pillar on the left, but she now had a certain amount of freedom of movement. She put her hand out for the key. "Remember," said Islington. "I have your friends."

Door looked at him with utter contempt, every inch Lord Portico's oldest daughter. "Give me the key," she said. The angel passed her the silver key.

"Door," called Richard. "Don't do it. Don't set it free. We don't matter."

"Actually," said the Marquis, "I matter very much. But I have to agree. Don't do it."

She looked from Richard to the Marquis, her eyes lingering on their manacled hands, on the heavy chains that bound them to the black iron pillars. She looked very vulnerable; and then she turned away, and walked to the limit of her own chain, until she stood in front of the black door made of flint and tarnished silver. There was no keyhole. She put the palm of her right hand on the door, and closed her eyes, let the door tell her where it opened, what it could do, finding those places inside herself that corresponded with the door. When she pulled her hand away, there was a keyhole that had not been there before. A white light lanced out from behind the keyhole, sharp and bright as a laser in the candlelit darkness of the hall.

The girl pushed the silver key into the keyhole. There was a pause, and then she turned it in the lock. Something went click, and there was a chiming noise, and suddenly the door was framed in light. "When I am gone," said the angel, very quietly, to Mr. Croup and Mr. Vandemar, with charm, and with kindness, and with compassion, "kill them all, howsoever you wish." It turned back to the door, which Door was pulling open: it was opening slowly, as if there were great resistance. She was sweating.

"So your employer's leaving," said the Marquis to Mr. Croup. "I hope you've both been paid in full."

Croup peered at the Marquis, and said, "What?"

"Well," said Richard, wondering what the Marquis was try-

ing to do, but willing to play along, "you don't think you're ever going to see him again, do you?"

Mr. Vandemar blinked, slowly, like an antique camera, and said, "What?"

Mr. Croup scratched his chin. "The corpses-to-be have a point," he said to Mr. Vandemar. He walked toward the angel, who stood, arms folded, in front of the door. "Sir? It might be wise for you to settle up, before you commence the next stage of your travels."

The angel turned, and looked down at him as if he were less important than the least speck of dirt. Then it turned away. Richard wondered what it was contemplating. "It is of no matter now," said the angel. "Soon, all the rewards your revolting little minds can conceive of will be yours. When I have my throne."

"Jam tomorrow, eh?" said Richard.

"Don't like jam," said Mr. Vandemar. "Makes me belch."

Mr. Croup waggled a finger at Mr. Vandemar. "He's welching out on us," he said. "You don't welch on Mister Croup and Mister Vandemar, me bucko. We collect our debts."

Mr. Vandemar walked over to where Mr. Croup was standing. "In full," he said.

"With interest," barked Mr. Croup.

"And meat hooks," said Mr. Vandemar.

"From Heaven?" called Richard, from behind them. Mr. Croup and Mr. Vandemar walked toward the contemplative angel. "Hey!" said Mr. Croup.

The door had opened, only a crack, but it was open. Light flooded through the crack in the door. The angel took a step forward. It was as if it were dreaming with its eyes wide open. The

light from the crack in the door bathed its face, and it drank it in like wine. "Have no fear," it said. "For when the vastness of creation is mine, and they gather about my throne to sing hosannas to my name, I shall reward the worthy and cast down those who are hateful in my sight."

And then it muttered something else, under its breath. Richard was never certain exactly what it had said, although, he later maintained, it had sounded a great deal like, "Bloody Gabriel, for a start."

With an effort, Door wrenched the black door fully open. The view through the door was blinding in its intensity: a swirling maelstrom of color and light. Richard squinted his eyes, and turned his head away from the glare, all vicious orange and retinal purple. *Is that what Heaven looks like? It seems more like Hell.*

And then he felt the wind.

A candle flew past his head, and vanished through the door. And then another. And then the air was filled with candles, all spinning and tumbling through the air, heading for the light. It was as if the whole room were being sucked through the door. It was more than a wind, though. Richard knew that. His wrists began to hurt where they were manacled—it was as if, suddenly, he weighed twice as much as he ever had before. And then his perspective changed. The view through the doorway—it was looking *down:* it was not merely the wind that was pulling everything toward the door. It was gravity. The wind was only the air in the hall being sucked into the place on the other side of the door. He wondered what was on the other side of the door— the surface of a star, perhaps, or the event horizon of a black hole, or something he could not even imagine.

Islington grabbed hold of the pillar beside the door, and held on desperately. "That's not Heaven," it shouted, gray eyes flashing, spittle on its perfect lips. "You mad little witch. What have you done?"

Door was clutching the chains that held her to the black pillar, white knuckled. There was triumph in her eyes. Mr. Vandemar had caught hold of a table leg, while Mr. Croup, in his turn, had caught hold of Mr. Vandemar. "It wasn't the real key," said Door, triumphantly, over the roar of the wind. "That was just a copy of the key I had Hammersmith make in the market."

"But it opened the door," screamed the angel.

"No," said the girl with the opal eyes, distantly. "I opened a door. As far and hard away as I could, I opened a door."

There was no longer any trace of kindness or compassion on the angel's face; only hatred, pure and honest and cold. "I will kill you," it told her.

"Like you killed my family? I don't think you're going to kill anyone anymore."

The angel was hanging on to the pillar with pale fingers, but its body was at a ninety-degree angle to the room, and was most of the way through the door. It looked both comical and dreadful. It licked its lips. "Stop it," it pleaded. "Close the door. I'll tell you where your sister is . . . She's still alive . . ."

Door flinched.

And Islington was sucked through the door, a tiny, plummeting figure, shrinking as it tumbled into the blinding gulf beyond. The pull was getting stronger. Richard prayed that his chains and manacles would hold: he could feel himself being sucked toward the opening, and, from the corner of his eye, he

could see the Marquis dangling from his chains, like a string-puppet being sucked up by a vacuum cleaner.

The table, the leg of which Mr. Vandemar was holding tightly, flew through the air and jammed in the open doorway. Mr. Croup and Mr. Vandemar were dangling out of the door. Mr. Croup, who was clinging, quite literally, to Mr. Vandemar's coattails, took a deep breath, and began slowly to clamber, hand over hand, up Mr. Vandemar's back. The table creaked. Mr. Croup looked at Door, and he smiled like a fox on really nasty drugs. "*I* killed your family," said Mr. Croup. "Not him. And now I'm—finally—going to finish the—"

It was at that moment that the fabric of Mr. Vandemar's dark suit gave way. Mr. Croup tumbled, screaming, into the void, clutching a long strip of black fabric. Mr. Vandemar looked down at the flailing figure of Mr. Croup as it fell away from them. He, too, looked over at Door, but there was no menace in his gaze. He shrugged, as best one can shrug while holding on to a table leg for dear life, and then he said, mildly, "Buh-bye," and he let go of the table leg.

Silently he plunged through the door, into the light, shrinking as he fell, heading for the tiny figure of Mr. Croup. Soon the two shapes merged into one little blob of blackness in a sea of churning purple and white and orange light, and then the black dot, too, was gone. It made some sort of sense, Richard thought: they were a team, after all.

It was getting harder to breathe. Richard felt giddy and light-headed. The table in the doorway splintered and was sucked away through the door. One of Richard's manacles popped open, and his right arm whipped free. He grabbed the chain holding

the left hand, and gripped it as tightly as he could, grateful that the broken finger was on the hand that was still in the manacle; even so, red and blue flashes of pain were shooting up his left arm. He could hear himself, distantly, shouting in pain.

He could not breathe. White blotches of light exploded behind his eyes. He could feel the chain beginning to give way . . .

The sound of the black door slamming closed filled his whole world. Richard fell violently back against the cold iron pillar, and slumped to the floor. There was silence, then, in the hall—silence, and utter darkness, in the Great Hall under the earth. Richard closed his eyes: it made no difference to the darkness, and he opened his eyes once more.

The hush was broken by the Marquis' voice, asking, drily, "So where did you send them?"

And then Richard heard a girl's voice talking. He knew it had to be Door's, but it sounded so young, like the voice of a tiny child at bedtime, at the end of a long and exhausting day. "I don't know . . . A long way away. I'm . . . very tired now. I . . ."

"Door," said the Marquis. "Snap out of it." It was good that he was saying it, thought Richard, somebody had to, and Richard could no longer remember how to talk. There was a click, then, in the darkness: the sound of a manacle opening, followed by the sound of chains falling against a metal pillar. Then the sound of a match being struck. A candle was lit: it burned weakly, and flickered in the thin air. *Fire and fleet and candlelight,* thought Richard, and he could not remember why.

Door walked, unsteadily, to the Marquis, holding her candle. She reached out a hand, touched his chains, and his manacles clicked open. He rubbed his wrists. Then she walked over

to Richard, and touched his single remaining manacle. It fell open. Door sighed, then, and sat down beside him. He reached out his good arm and cradled her head, holding her close to him. He rocked her slowly back and forth, crooning a wordless lullaby. It was cold, cold, there in the angel's empty hall; but soon the warmth of unconsciousness reached out and enveloped them both.

The Marquis de Carabas watched the sleeping children. The idea of sleep—of returning, even for a short time, to a state so horribly close to death—scared him more than he would have ever believed. But, eventually, even he put his head down on his arm, and closed his eyes.

And then there were none.

18

T HE LADY SERPENTINE, WHO was, but for Olympia, the oldest of the Seven Sisters, walked through the labyrinth beyond Down Street, her head held high, her white leather boots squashing through the dank mud. This was, after all, the furthest she had been from her house in over a hundred years. Her wasp-waisted majordomo, dressed from head to foot all in black leather, walked ahead of her, holding a large carriage lamp. Two of Serpentine's other women, similarly dressed, walked behind her at a respectful distance.

The ripped lace train of Serpentine's dress dragged in the mire behind her, but she paid it

no mind. She saw something glinting in the lamplight ahead of them, and, beside it, a dark and bulky shape.

"There it is," she said.

The two women who had been walking behind her hurried forward, splashing through the marsh, and as Serpentine's butler approached, bringing with her a swinging circle of warm light, the shapes resolved into objects. The light had been glinting from a long bronze spear. Hunter's body, twisted and bloody and wretched, lay on its back, half-buried in the mud, in a large pool of scarlet gore, its legs trapped beneath the body of an enormous boar-like creature. Her eyes were closed.

Serpentine's women hauled the body out from under the Beast, and laid it in the mud. Serpentine knelt in the wet mire, and ran one finger down Hunter's cold cheek, until it reached her blood-blackened lips, where she let it linger for some moments. Then she stood up. "Bring the spear," said Serpentine.

One of the women picked up Hunter's body; the other pulled the spear from the carcass of the Beast, and put it over her shoulder. And then the four figures turned, and went back the way they had come; a silent procession deep beneath the world. The lamplight flickered on Serpentine's ravaged face as she walked; but it revealed no emotion of any kind, neither happy nor sad.

19

FOR A MOMENT, UPON waking, he had no idea at all who he was. It was a tremendously liberating feeling, as if he were free to be whatever he wanted to be: he could be anyone at all—able to try on any identity; he could be a man or a woman, a rat or a bird, a monster or a god. And then someone made a rustling noise, and he woke up the rest of the way, and in waking he found that he was Richard Mayhew, whoever that was, whatever that meant. He was Richard Mayhew, and he did not know where he was.

There was crisp linen pressed against his face. He hurt all over; in some places—the little finger on his left hand, for example—more than others.

Someone was nearby. Richard could hear breathing, and the hesitant rustling noises of a person in the same room he was in, trying to be discreet. Richard raised his head, and discovered, in the raising, more places that hurt. Some of them hurt very badly. Far away—rooms and rooms away—people were singing. The song was so distant and quiet he knew he would lose it if he opened his eyes: a deep, melodious chanting . . .

He opened his eyes. The room was small, and dimly lit. He was on a low bed, and the rustling sound he had heard was made by a cowled figure in a black robe, with his back to Richard. The black figure was dusting the room, with an incongruously brightly colored feather duster. "Where am I?" asked Richard.

The black figure nearly dropped its feather duster, then it turned, revealing a very nervous, thin, dark brown face. "Would you like some water?" the Black Friar asked, in the manner of one who has been told that if the patient wakes up, he is to be asked if he would like some water, and has been repeating it to himself over and over for the last forty minutes to make sure that he didn't forget.

"I . . ." And Richard realized that he was most dreadfully thirsty. He sat up in the bed. "Yes, I would. Thank you very much." The friar poured some water from a battered metal jug into a battered metal cup, and passed it to Richard. Richard sipped the water slowly, restraining the impulse to gulp it down. It was crystal-cold and clear and tasted like diamonds and ice.

Richard looked down at himself. His clothes were gone. He had been dressed in a long robe, like one of the Black Friars' habits, but gray. His broken finger had been splinted and neatly bandaged. He raised a finger to his ear; there was a sticking plaster

on it, and what felt like stitches beneath the plaster. "You're one
of the Black Friars," said Richard.

"Yes, sir."

"How did I get here? Where are my friends?"

The friar pointed to the corridor, wordlessly and nervously.
Richard got out of the bed. He checked under his gray robe: he
was naked. His torso and legs were covered in a variety of deep
indigo and purple bruises, all of which seemed to have been
rubbed with some kind of ointment: it smelt like cough syrup
and buttered toast. His right knee was bandaged. He wondered
where his clothes were. There were sandals beside the bed, and
he put them on, then he walked out into the corridor. The Abbot
was coming down the passage toward him, holding on to the
arm of Brother Fuliginous, his blind eyes pearlescent in the
darkness beneath his cowl.

"You are awake, then, Richard Mayhew," said the Abbot.
"How do you feel?"

Richard made a face. "My hand . . ."

"We set your finger. It had been broken. We tended your
bruises and your cuts. And you needed rest, which we gave you."

"Where's Door? And the Marquis? How did we get here?"

"I had you brought here," said the Abbot. The two friars
began to walk down the corridor, and Richard walked with
them.

"Hunter," said Richard. "Did you bring back her body?"

The Abbot shook his head. "There was no body. Only the
Beast."

"Ah, um. My clothes . . ." They came to the door of a cell,
much like the one Richard had woken in. Door was sitting on

the edge of her bed, reading a copy of *Mansfield Park* that Richard was certain that the friars had not previously known that they had. She also wore a gray monk's robe, which was much, much too big for her, almost comically so. She looked up as they entered. "Hello," she said. "You've been asleep for ages. How are you feeling?"

"Fine, I think. How are you?"

She smiled. It was not a very convincing smile. "A bit shaky," she admitted. There was a loud rattling in the corridor, and Richard turned to see the Marquis de Carabas being wheeled toward them in a rickety and antique wheelchair. The wheelchair was being pushed by a large Black Friar. Richard wondered how the Marquis managed to make being pushed around in a wheelchair look a romantic and swashbuckling thing to do. The Marquis honored them with an enormous smile. "Good evening, friends," he said.

"Now," said the Abbot, "that you are all here, we must talk."

He led them to a large room, warmed by a roaring scrap wood fire. They arranged themselves around a table. The Abbot gestured for them all to sit down. He felt for his chair, and sat down in it. Then he sent Brother Fuliginous and Brother Tenebrae (who had been pushing the Marquis' bath chair) out of the room.

"So," said the Abbot. "To business. Where is Islington?"

Door shrugged. "As far away as I could send him. Halfway across space and time."

"I see," said the Abbot. And then he said, "Good."

"Why didn't you warn us about him?" asked Richard.

"That was not our responsibility."

Richard snorted. "What happens now?" he asked them all.

The Abbot said nothing.

"Happens? In what way?" asked Door.

"Well, you wanted to avenge your family. And you have. And you've sent everyone involved off to some distant corner of nowhere. I mean, no one's going to try and kill you anymore, are they?"

"Not for right now," said Door, seriously.

"And you?" Richard asked the Marquis de Carabas. "Have you got what you wanted?"

The Marquis nodded. "I believe so. My debt to Lord Portico has been paid in full, and the Lady Door owes me a significant favor."

Richard looked to Door. She nodded. "So what about me?" he asked.

"Well," said Door. "We couldn't have done it without you."

"That's not what I meant. What about getting me back home?"

The Marquis raised an eyebrow. "Who do you think she is— the Wizard of Oz? We can't send you home. This is your home."

Door said, "I tried to tell you that before, Richard."

"There has to be a way," said Richard, and he slammed his left hand down on the table, hard, for emphasis. And then he said, "Ow,"—because slamming your hand down on a table for emphasis is not a wise thing to do when you have a broken finger—but he said it very quietly, because he had gone through much worse.

"Where is the key?" asked the Abbot.

Richard inclined his head. "Door," he said.

She shook her pixie head. "I don't have it," she told him. "I slipped it back into your pocket at the last market. When you brought the curry."

Richard opened his mouth, and then he closed it again. Then he opened it and said, "You mean, when I told Croup and Vandemar that I had it, and they were welcome to search me . . . I had it?" She nodded. He remembered the hard object in his back pocket, on Down Street; remembered her hugging him on the ship . . . "Crumbs," he said.

The Abbot reached out. His wrinkled brown fingers picked up a small bell from the table, which he shook, summoning Brother Fuliginous. "Bring me the Warrior's trousers," he said. Fuliginous nodded and left.

"I'm no warrior," said Richard.

The Abbot smiled gently. "You killed the Beast," he explained, almost regretfully. "You are the Warrior."

Richard folded his arms, exasperated. "So, after all this, I still don't get to go home, but as a consolation prize I've made it onto some kind of archaic underground honors list?"

The Marquis looked unsympathetic. "You can't go back to London Above. A few individuals manage a kind of half-life—you've met Iliaster and Lear. But that's the best you could hope for, and it isn't a good life."

Door reached out a hand, and touched Richard's arm. "I'm sorry," she told him. "But look at all the good you've done. You got the key for us."

"Well," he asked, "what was the point of that? You just forged a new key—" Brother Fuliginous reappeared, carrying Richard's jeans; they were ripped, and covered in mud, and splashed with

dried blood, and they stank. The friar handed the trousers to the Abbot, who commenced to go through the pockets. Door smiled, sweetly. "I couldn't have had Hammersmith copy it without the original," she reminded him.

The Abbot cleared his throat. "You are all very stupid people," he told them, graciously, "and you do not know anything at all." He held up the silver key. It glinted in the firelight. "Richard passed the Ordeal of the Key. He is its master, until he returns it to our keeping. The key has power."

"It's the key to Heaven . . . ," said Richard, unsure of what the Abbot was getting at, of what point he was trying to make.

The old man's voice was deep and melodious. "The key is the key to all reality. If Richard wants to return to London Above, then the key will take him back to London Above."

"It's that simple?" asked Richard. The old man nodded his blind head, beneath the shadows of his cowl. "Then when could we do this?"

"As soon as you are ready," said the Abbot.

THE FRIARS HAD WASHED and repaired his clothes, and returned them to him. Brother Fuliginous led him through the abbey, up a vertiginous series of ladders and steps, up into the bell tower. There was a heavy wooden trapdoor in the top of the tower. Brother Fuliginous unlocked it, and the two men pushed through it, and found themselves in a narrow tunnel, thickly cobwebbed, with metal rungs set in the side of one wall. They climbed the rungs, going up for what seemed like thousands of feet, and came out on a dusty Underground station platform.

NIGHTINGALE LANE

said the old signs on the wall. Brother Fuliginous wished Richard
well, and told him to wait there, and he would be collected, and
then he clambered down the side of the wall, and he was gone.

Richard sat on the platform for twenty minutes. He won-
dered what kind of station this was: it seemed neither abandoned,
like British Museum, nor real, like Blackfriars: instead it was
a ghost station, an imaginary place, forgotten and strange. He
wondered why the Marquis had not said good-bye. When Rich-
ard had asked Door, she had said that she didn't know, but that
maybe good-byes were something else, like comforting people,
at which the Marquis wasn't much good. Then she told him that
she had something in her eye, and she gave him a paper with his
instructions on it, and she went away.

Something waved from the darkness of the tunnel: something
white. It was a handkerchief on a stick. "Hello?" called Richard.

The feather-wrapped roundness of Old Bailey stepped out
of the gloom, looking self-conscious and ill at ease. He was wav-
ing Richard's handkerchief, and he was sweating. "It's me little
flag," he said, pointing to the handkerchief.

"I'm glad it's come in useful."

Old Bailey grinned uneasily. "Right. Just wanted to say.
Something I got for you. Here you go." He thrust a hand into
a coat pocket, and pulled out a long black feather with a blue-
purple-green sheen to it; red thread had been wound around the
quill end of the feather.

"Um. Well, thanks," said Richard, unsure of what he ought
to do with it.

"It's a feather," explained Old Bailey. "And a good one. Me-

mento. Souvenir. Keepsake. And it's free. A gift. Me to you. Bit of
a thank-you."

"Yes. Well. Very kind of you."

Richard put it in his pocket. A warm wind blew through the
tunnel: a train was coming. "This'll be your train now," said Old
Bailey. "I don't take trains, me. Give me a good roof any day." He
shook Richard's hand, and fled.

The train pulled in at the station. Its headlights were turned
off, and there was nobody standing in the driver's compartment
in the front. It came to a full stop: all the carriages were dark,
and no doors opened. Richard knocked on the door in front of
him, hoping that it was the correct one. The door gaped open,
flooding the imaginary station with warm yellow light. Two
small, elderly gentlemen holding long, copper-colored bugles
stepped off the train and onto the platform. Richard recognized
them: Dagvard and Halvard, from Earl's Court; although he
could no longer recall, if he had ever known, which gentleman
was which. They put their bugles to their lips, and performed a
ragged, but sincere, fanfare. Richard got onto the train, and they
walked in behind him.

The Earl was sitting at the end of the carriage, petting the
enormous Irish wolfhound. The jester—Tooley, thought Rich-
ard, that was his name—stood beside him. Other than that, and
the two men-at-arms, the carriage was deserted. "Who is it?"
asked the Earl.

"It's him, sire," said his jester. "Richard Mayhew. The one
who killed the Beast."

"The Warrior?" The Earl scratched his red-gray beard,
thoughtfully. "Bring him here."

Richard walked down to the Earl's chair. The Earl eyed him

up and down pensively, and gave no indication that he remembered ever meeting Richard before. "Thought you'd be taller," said the Earl, at length.

"Sorry."

"Well, better get on with it." The old man stood up, and addressed the empty carriage. "Good evening. Here to honor young Mayflower. What was it the bard said?" And then he recited, in a rhythmic alliterative boom, *" 'Crimson the cuts in the carcass, Fast falls the foe, Dauntless devout defender, Bravest of boys . . .'* Not really a boy anymore, though, is he, Tooley?"

"Not particularly, Your Grace."

The Earl reached out his hand. "Give me your sword, boy."

Richard put his hand to his belt, pulled out the knife that Hunter had given him. "Will this do?" he asked.

"Yes-yes," said the old man, taking the knife from him.

"Kneel," said Tooley, in a stage whisper, pointing to the train floor. Richard went down on one knee; the Earl tapped him gently on each shoulder with the knife. "Arise," he bellowed, "Sir Richard of Maybury. With this knife I do give to you the freedom of the Underside. May you be allowed to walk freely, without let or hindrance . . . and so on and so forth . . . et cetera . . . blah blah blah," he trailed off, vaguely.

"Thanks," said Richard. "It's Mayhew, actually." But the train was coming to a stop.

"This is where you get off," said the Earl. He gave Richard his knife—Hunter's knife—once more, patted him on the back, and pointed toward the door.

THE PLACE THAT RICHARD got off was not an Underground station. It was aboveground, and it reminded Richard a little of St. Pancras station—there was something similarly oversized and mock-Gothic about the architecture. But there was also a wrongness that somehow marked it as part of London Below. The light was that strange, strained gray one only sees shortly before dawn and for a few moments after sunset, the times when the world washes out into gloom, and color and distance become impossible to judge.

There was a man sitting on a wooden bench, watching him; and Richard approached him, cautiously, unable to tell, in the mirk, who the man was, whether it was someone he had met before. Richard was still holding Hunter's knife—his knife— and now he gripped the hilt more tightly, for reassurance. The man looked up as Richard approached, and sprang to his feet. He tugged at his forelock, something Richard had previously only seen done on television adaptations of classic novels. He looked both comical and unpleasant. Richard recognized the man as the Lord Rat-speaker.

"Well-well. Yes-yes," said the rat-speaker, agitatedly, beginning in midsentence. "Just to say, the girl Anaesthesia. No hard feelings. The rats are your friends, still. And the rat-speakers. You come to us. We'll do you all right."

"Thanks," said Richard. *Anaesthesia will take him,* he thought. *She's expendable.*

The Lord Rat-speaker fumbled on the bench, and presented Richard with a black vinyl zip-up sports bag. It was extremely familiar. "It's all there. Everything. Take a look." Richard opened the bag. All his possessions were in there, including, on

the top of some neatly folded jeans, his wallet. He zipped the bag up, and threw it over his shoulder, and walked away from the man, without a thank-you or a backward glance.

Richard walked out of the station, and down some gray stone steps.

All was silent. All was empty. Dead autumn leaves blew across the forecourt, a flurry of yellow and ocher and brown, a sudden burst of muted color in the dim light. Richard crossed the forecourt, and walked down some steps into an underpass. There was a fluttering in the half-dark, and, warily, he turned. There were about a dozen of them, in the corridor behind him, and they slipped toward him almost silently, just a rustle of dark velvet, and, here and there, the clink of silver jewelry. The rustle of the leaves had been so much louder than these pale women. They watched him with hungry eyes.

He was scared, then. He had the knife, true, but he could no more fight with it than he could jump across the Thames. He hoped that, if they attacked, he might be able to scare them away with it. He could smell honeysuckle, and lily of the valley, and musk.

Lamia edged her way to the front of the Velvets, and stepped forward. Richard raised the knife, nervously, remembering the chilly passion of her embrace, how pleasant it was and how cold. She smiled at him, and inclined her head, sweetly. Then she kissed her fingertips, and blew the kiss toward Richard.

He shivered. Something fluttered in the darkness of the underpass; and when he looked again, there was nothing but shadows.

THROUGH THE UNDERPASS, AND Richard walked up some steps, and found himself at the top of a small grassy hill. It was dawn, and he could just make out details of the countryside around him: almost leafless oak, and ash, and beech trees, readily identifiable by the shapes of their trunks. A wide, clean river meandered gently through the green countryside. As he looked around, he realized that he was on an island of some kind—two smaller rivers ran into the larger one, cutting him, on his little hill, off from the mainland. He knew then, without knowing how, but with total certainty, that he was still in London, but London as it had been perhaps three thousand years ago, or more, before ever the first stone of the first human habitation was laid upon a stone.

He unzipped his bag, and put the knife away in it, beside his wallet. Then he zipped it up again. The sky was starting to lighten, but the light was odd. It was younger somehow than the sunlight he was familiar with—purer, perhaps. An orange-red sun rose in the east, where Docklands would one day be, and Richard watched the dawn breaking over forests and marshes that he kept thinking of as Greenwich and Kent and the sea.

"Hullo," said Door. He had not seen her approach. She was wearing different clothes beneath her battered brown leather jacket: they were still layered and ripped and patched, though, in taffeta and lace and silk and brocade. Her short red hair shone in the dawn like burnished copper.

"Hello," said Richard. She stood beside him, and twined her small fingers into his right hand, the hand that was holding the sports bag. "Where are we?" he asked.

"On the awesome and terrible island of Westminster," she

told him. It sounded as if she were quoting from somewhere, but he did not believe he had ever heard that phrase before. They began to walk together over the long grass, wet and white with melting frost. Their footprints left a dark green trail in the grass behind them, showing where they had come from.

"Look," said Door. "With the angel gone, there's a lot of sorting out to do in London Below. And there's only me to do it. My father wanted to unite London Below . . . I suppose I ought to try to finish what he started." They were walking north, away from the Thames, hand in hand. White seagulls wheeled and called in the sky above them. "Richard, you heard what Islington said to us about keeping my sister alive, just in case. I may not be the only one of my family left. And you've saved my life. More than once." She paused, and then, all in a rush, blurted, "You've been a really good friend to me, Richard. And I've sort of got to quite like having you around. Please don't go."

He squeezed her hand in his, gently. "Well," he said, "I've sort of got to quite like having you around, too. But I don't belong in this world. In my London . . . well, the most dangerous thing you ever have to watch out for is a taxi in a bit of a hurry. I like you too. I like you an awful lot. But I have to go home."

She looked up at him with her odd-colored eyes, green and blue and flame. "Then we won't ever see each other again," she said.

"I suppose we won't."

"Thanks for everything you did," she said, seriously. Then she threw her arms around him, and she squeezed him tightly enough that the bruises on his ribs hurt, and he hugged her back, just as tightly, making all of his bruises complain violently, and he simply didn't care.

"Well," he said, eventually. "It was very nice knowing you."
She was blinking hard. He wondered if she were going to tell
him again that she had something in her eye. Instead she said,
"Are you ready?"

He nodded.

"Have you got the key?"

He put down his bag, and rummaged in his back pocket with
his good hand. He took out the key, and handed it to her. She held
it out in front of her, as if it were being inserted in an imaginary
door. "Okay," she said. "Just walk. Don't look back."

He began walking down a small hill, away from the blue
waters of the Thames. A gray gull swooped past. At the bottom
of the hill, he looked back. She stood at the top of the hill, silhou-
etted by the rising sun. Her cheeks were glistening. The orange
sunlight gleamed on the key.

Door turned it, with one decisive motion.

THE WORLD WENT DARK, and a low roar filled Richard's head,
like the maddened growling of a thousand enraged beasts.

20

THE WORLD WENT DARK, and a low roar filled Richard's head, like the maddened growling of a thousand enraged beasts. He blinked at the darkness, held tight to his bag. He wondered if he had been foolish, putting the knife away. Some people brushed past him in the dark. Richard started away from them. There were steps in front of him, which Richard began to ascend, and, as he did so, the world began to resolve, to take shape and to re-form.

The growling was the roar of traffic, and he was coming out of an underpass in Trafalgar Square. The sky was the perfect untroubled blue of a television screen, tuned to a dead channel.

It was midmorning, on a warm October

day, and he stood in the square holding his bag and blinking at the sunlight. Black taxis and red buses and multicolored cars roared and careered about the square, while tourists threw handfuls of pigeon feed down for the legions of tubby pigeons and took their snapshots of Nelson's Column and the huge Landseer lions that flanked it. He walked through the square, wondering if he was real or not. The Japanese tourists ignored him. He tried talking to a pretty fair-haired girl, who laughed, and shook her head, and said something in a language Richard thought might have been Italian, but was actually Finnish.

There was a small child of indeterminate sex, staring at some pigeons while orally demolishing a chocolate bar. He crouched down next to it. "Um. Hello, kiddie," said Richard. The child sucked its chocolate bar intently, and gave no indication of recognizing Richard as another human being. "Hello," repeated Richard, a slight note of desperation creeping into his voice. "Can you see me? Kiddie? Hello?"

Two small eyes glared at him from a chocolate-covered face. And then its lower lip began to tremble, and the child fled, throwing its arms around the legs of the nearest adult female, and wailing, "Mu-um? This man's bothering me. He's bothering me, Mum."

The child's mother turned on Richard with a formidable scowl. "What are you doing," she demanded, "bothering our Leslie? There are places for people like you."

Richard began to smile. It was a huge and happy smile. You could not have killed that smile by hitting Richard over the back of the head with a brick. "I really am most frightfully sorry," he said, grinning like a Cheshire Cat. And then, clutching his bag,

he ran through Trafalgar Square, accompanied by bursts of sudden pigeons, who took to the air in startlement.

HE TOOK HIS CASH card out of his wallet, and he put it into the cash machine. It recognized his four-digit pin number, advised him to keep it a secret and not disclose it to anyone, and asked what kind of service he would like. He asked for cash, and it gave him cash in abundance. He punched the air in delight, and then, embarrassed, pretended that he had been hailing a cab.

A cab stopped for him—it stopped!—for him!—and he climbed in, and sat in the back, and beamed. He asked the driver to take him to his office. And when the cab driver pointed out that it would almost be quicker to walk, Richard grinned even wider, and said he did not care. And as soon as they were under way he asked—practically begged—the cab driver to regale him, Richard, with his opinions on Inner-City Traffic Problems, How Best to Deal with Crime, and Thorny Political Issues of the Day. The cab driver accused Richard of "taking the Mickey," and sulked for all of the five-minute journey up the Strand. Richard did not care. He tipped the man ridiculously anyway. And then he walked into his office.

As he entered the building, he felt the smile begin to leave his face. Each step he took left him more anxious, more uneasy. What if he still had no job? What did it matter if small, chocolate-covered children and cab drivers could see him, if it turned out that by some appalling mischance he remained invisible to his workmates?

Mr. Figgis, the security guard, looked up from a copy of

Naughty Teenage Nymphets, which he had hidden inside his copy of the *Sun,* and he sniffed. "Morning, Mister Mayhew," he said. It was not a welcoming "Morning." It was the kind of "Morning" that implied that the speaker really did not care if the recipient lived or died—nor indeed, for that matter, if it was even morning.

"Figgis!" exclaimed Richard, in delight. "And hello to you too, Mister Figgis, you exceptional security guard!"

Nobody had ever said anything remotely like that to Mr. Figgis before, not even naked ladies in his imagination; he stared suspiciously at Richard until he got into the elevator, and vanished from sight, then he returned his attention to the naughty teenage nymphets, none of whom, he was beginning to suspect, was ever likely to see twenty-nine again, lollipops or no lollipops.

Richard got out of the elevator, and walked, slightly hesitantly, down the corridor. *Everything will be all right,* he told himself, *if only my desk is there. If my desk is there, everything will be fine.* He walked into the large, open-plan office he had worked in for three years. People were working at desks, talking on telephones, rummaging through filing cabinets, drinking bad tea and worse coffee. It was his office.

And there was the place by the window, where his desk had once been, which was now occupied by a gray cluster of filing cabinets and a yucca plant. He was about to turn and run when someone handed him a cup of tea in a Styrofoam cup.

"The return of the prodigal, eh?" said Garry. "Here you go."

"Hello, Garry," said Richard. "Where's my desk?"

"This way," said Garry. "How was Majorca?"

"Majorca?"

"Don't you always go to Majorca?" asked Garry. They were walking up the back stairs that led to the fourth floor.

"Not this time," said Richard.

"I was going to say," said Garry. "Not much of a tan."

"No," agreed Richard. "Well. You know. I needed a change."

Garry nodded. He pointed to a door that had, for as long as Richard had been there, been the door to the executive files and supplies room. "A change? Well, you've certainly got one now. And may I be the first to congratulate you?"

The plaque on the door said:

R.O. Mayhew
Junior Partner.

"Lucky bastard," said Garry, affectionately.

He wandered off, and Richard went through the door, utterly bemused. The room was no longer an executive supplies and file room: it had been emptied of files and supplies, and painted in gray and black and white, and recarpeted, and in the center of the office was a large desk. He examined it: it was, unmistakably, his very own desk. His trolls had all been neatly put away in one of the desk drawers, and he took them all out, and arranged them around the office. He had his own window, with a nice view of the sludge-brown river and the South Bank of the Thames beyond. There was even a large green plant, with huge waxy leaves, of the kind that looks artificial but isn't. His old, dusty cream-colored computer terminal had been replaced with a much sleeker, cleaner black computer terminal, which took up less desk space.

He walked over to the window, and sipped his tea, staring out at the dirty brown river.

"You've found everything all right, then?" He looked up. Crisp and efficient, Sylvia, the MD's PA, was standing in the doorway. She smiled when she saw him.

"Um. Yes. Look, there are things I have to take care of at home . . . d'you think it'd be all right if I took the rest of the day off and—"

"Suit yourself. You aren't meant to be back in till tomorrow anyway."

"I'm not?" he asked. "Right."

Sylvia frowned. "What happened to your finger?"

"I broke it," he told her.

She looked at his hand with concern. "You weren't in a fight, were you?"

"Me?"

She grinned. "Just teasing. I suppose you shut it in a door. That's what my sister did."

"No," Richard began to admit, "I was in a fi—" Sylvia raised an eyebrow. "A door," he finished lamely.

He went to the building he had once lived in by taxi. He was not sure that he trusted himself to travel by the Underground. Not yet. Having no door key, he knocked at the door of his flat, and was more than disappointed when it was opened by the woman Richard last remembered meeting, or rather, failing to meet, in his bathroom. He introduced himself as the previous tenant, and quickly established that a) he, Richard, no longer lived there, and b) she, Mrs. Buchanan, had no idea what had happened to any of his personal possessions. Richard took some

notes, and then he said good-bye very nicely, and took another black taxi to go and see a man in a camel-hair coat.

The smooth man in the camel-hair coat was not wearing his camel-hair coat, and was, in fact, a good deal less smooth than the last time Richard had encountered him. They were sitting in his office, and he had listened to Richard's list of complaints with the expression of someone who has recently and accidentally swallowed whole a live spider, and has just begun to feel it squirm.

"Well, yes," he admitted, after looking at the files. "There does seem to have been some kind of problem, now you mention it. I can't quite see how it could have happened."

"I don't think it matters how it happened," said Richard, reasonably. "The fact of the matter is that while I was away for a few weeks, you let my flat to"—he consulted his notes—"George and Adele Buchanan. Who have no intention of leaving."

The man closed the file. "Well," he said. "Mistakes do happen. Human error. I'm afraid there's nothing we can do about it."

The old Richard, the one who had lived in what was now the Buchanans' home, would have crumbled at this point, apologized for being a nuisance, and gone away. Instead, Richard said, "Really? Nothing you can do about it? You let out a property I was legally renting from your company to someone else, and in the process lost all my personal possessions, and there's nothing you can do about it? Now, I happen to think, and I'm sure my lawyer will also think, that there is a great deal you can do about it."

The man without the camel-hair coat looked as if the spider was beginning to crawl back up his throat. "But we don't

have any other vacant flats like yours in the building," he said. "There's only the penthouse suite."

"That," Richard told the man, coldly, "would be fine . . ." The man relaxed. ". . . for living accommodation. Now," said Richard, "let's talk about compensation for my lost possessions."

THE NEW FLAT WAS much nicer than the one he had left behind. It had more windows, and a balcony, a spacious lounge and a proper spare bedroom. Richard prowled it, dissatisfied. The man-without-a-camel-hair-coat had, extremely grudgingly, had the flat furnished with a bed, a sofa, several chairs, and a television set.

Richard put Hunter's knife on the mantelpiece.

He bought a takeaway curry from the Indian restaurant across the road, and sat on the carpeted floor of his new flat, and ate it, and wondered if he had ever really eaten curry late at night in a street market held on the deck of a gunship moored by Tower Bridge. It did not seem very likely, now he came to think of it.

The doorbell rang. He got up and answered the door. "We found a lot of your stuff, Mr. Mayhew," said the man who was once more wearing his camel-hair coat. "Turned out it'd been put into storage. Right, bring the stuff in, lads."

A couple of burly men hauled in several large wooden packing cases, filled with Richard's stuff, and deposited them on the carpet in the middle of the living room.

"Thanks," said Richard. He reached into the first packing case, unwrapped the first paper-covered object, which turned

out to be a framed photograph of Jessica. He stared at it for some moments, and then he put it down again in the case. He found the packing case with his clothes in, and removed them from the case and put them away in his bedroom, but the other cases sat, untouched, in the middle of the living room floor. As the days went on, he felt increasingly guilty about not unpacking them. But he did not unpack them.

HE WAS IN HIS office, sitting at his desk, staring out of the window, when the intercom buzzed. "Richard?" said Sylvia. "The MD wants a meeting in his office in twenty minutes to discuss the Wandsworth Report."

"I'll be there," he said. Then, because he had nothing else to do for the next ten minutes, he picked up an orange troll and menaced a slightly smaller green-haired troll with it. "I am the greatest warrior of London Below. Prepare to die," he said, in a dangerous trollish voice, waggling the orange troll. Then he picked up the green-haired troll, and said, in a smaller trollish voice, "Aha! But first you shall drink the nice cup of tea . . ."

Someone knocked on the door, and, guiltily, he put down the trolls. "Come in." The door opened, and Jessica came in, and stood in the doorway. She looked nervous. He had forgotten quite how beautiful she was. "Hello, Richard," she said.

"Hello, Jess," said Richard, and then he corrected himself. "Sorry—Jessica."

She smiled, and tossed her hair. "Oh, Jess is fine," she said, and looked as if she almost meant it. "Jessica—Jess. Nobody's called me Jess for ages. I rather miss it."

"So," said Richard, "what brings, do I have the honor, you, um."

"Just wanted to see you really."

He was not sure what he ought to say. "That's nice," he said.

She closed the door to his office, and took a few steps toward him. "Richard. You know something strange? I remember calling the engagement off. But I hardly remember what we were arguing about."

"No?"

"It's not important, though. Is it?" She looked around the office. "You got a promotion?"

"Yes."

"I'm happy for you." She put a hand into the pocket of her coat, and pulled out a small brown box. She put it down on Richard's desk. He opened the box, although he knew what was inside it. "It's our engagement ring. I thought that, well, maybe, I'd give it back to you, and then, well, if things worked out, well, perhaps one day you'd give it back to me."

It glittered in the sunlight: the most money he had ever spent on anything. He closed the box, and gave it back to her. "You keep it, Jessica," he said. And then, "I'm sorry."

She bit her lower lip. "Did you meet someone?"

He hesitated. He thought of Lamia, and Hunter, and Anaesthesia, and even Door, but none of them were someones in the way that she meant. "No. No one else," he said. And then, realizing it was true as he said it, "I've just changed, that's all."

His intercom buzzed. "Richard? We're waiting for you." He pressed the button. "Be right down, Sylvia."

He looked at Jessica. She said nothing. Perhaps there was

nothing she could trust herself to say. She walked away, and she closed the door quietly behind her.

Richard picked up the papers he would need, with one hand. He ran the other hand across his face, as if he were wiping something away: sorrow, perhaps, or tears, or Jessica.

HE STARTED TAKING THE Tube again, to and from work, although he soon found that he had stopped buying newspapers to read on his journey in the morning and the evening, and instead of reading he would scan the faces of the other people on the train, faces of every kind and color, and wonder if they were all from London Above, wonder what went on behind their eyes.

During the evening rush hour, a few days after his encounter with Jessica, he thought he saw Lamia across the carriage, with her back to him, her dark hair piled high on her head and her dress long and black. His heart began to pound in his chest. He pushed his way toward her through the crowded compartment. As he got closer, the train pulled into a station, the doors hissed open, and she stepped off. But it was not Lamia. Just another young London Goth, he realized, disappointed, off for a night on the town.

ONE SATURDAY AFTERNOON HE saw a large brown rat, sitting on top of the plastic garbage cans at the back of Newton Mansions, cleaning its whiskers and looking as if it owned the world. At Richard's approach it leapt down onto the pavement,

and waited in the shadow of the garbage cans, staring up at him with wary bead-black eyes.

Richard crouched down. "Hello," he said, gently. "Do we know each other?" The rat made no kind of response that Richard was able to perceive, but it did not run away. "My name is Richard Mayhew," he continued, in a low voice. "I'm not actually a rat-speaker, but I, um, know a few rats, well, I've met some, and I wondered if you were familiar with the Lady Door . . ."

He heard a shoe scrape behind him, and he turned to see the Buchanans looking at him curiously. "Have you . . . lost something?" asked Mrs. Buchanan. Richard heard, but ignored, her husband's gruff whisper of "Just his marbles."

"No," said Richard, honestly, "I was, um, saying hello to a—" The rat scurried off and away.

"Was that a rat?" barked George Buchanan. "I'll complain to the council. It's a disgrace. But that's London for you, isn't it?"

Yes, agreed Richard. It was. It really was.

RICHARD'S POSSESSIONS CONTINUED TO sit untouched in the wooden packing cases in the middle of the living room floor.

He had not yet turned on the television. He would come home at night, and eat, then he would stand at the window, looking out over London, at the cars and the rooftops and the lights, as the late autumn twilight turned into night and the lights came on all over the city. He would watch until the city's lights began to be turned off, standing alone in his darkened flat. Eventually, reluctantly, he would undress, and climb into bed, and go to sleep.

Sylvia came into his office one Friday afternoon. He was opening envelopes, using his knife—Hunter's knife—as a letter opener. "Richard?" she said. "I was wondering. Are you getting out much, these days?" He shook his head. "Well, a bunch of us are going out this evening. Do you fancy coming along?"

"Um. Sure," he said. "Yes. I'd love it."

He hated it.

There were eight of them: Sylvia and her young man, who had something to do with vintage cars; Garry from Corporate Accounts, who had recently broken up with his girlfriend, due to what Garry persisted in describing as a slight misunderstanding (he had thought she would be rather more understanding about his sleeping with her best friend than she had in fact turned out to be when she found out); several perfectly nice people and friends of nice people; and the new girl from Computer Services.

First they saw a film at the huge screen of the Odeon, Leicester Square. The good guy won in the end, and there were plenty of explosions and flying objects on the way. Sylvia decided that Richard should sit next to the girl from Computer Services, as, she explained, she was new to the company, and did not know many people.

They walked down to Old Compton Street, on the edge of Soho, where the tawdry and the chic sit side by side, to the benefit of both, and they ate at La Reache, filling up on couscous and dozens of marvelous plates of small exotic nibbly bits which covered their table and spilled over onto an unused table nearby,

and they walked from there to a small pub Sylvia liked in nearby
Berwick Street, and they had a few drinks, and they chatted.

The new girl from Computer Services smiled at Richard a
lot, as the evening went on, and he had nothing at all to say to
her. He bought a round of drinks for the party, and the girl from
Computer Services helped him carry them from the bar back
to their table. Garry went off to the men's room, and the girl
from Computer Services came and sat next to Richard, taking
his place. Richard's head was filled with the clink of glasses, and
the blare of the jukebox, and the sharp smell of beer and spilt
Bacardi and cigarette smoke. He tried to listen to the conversa-
tions going on at the table, and he found that he could no longer
concentrate on what anyone was saying, and, which was worse,
that he was not interested in any of the bits he was able to hear.

And it came to him then, as clearly and as certainly as if he
had been watching it on the big screen at the Odeon, Leicester
Square: the rest of his life. He would go home tonight with the
girl from Computer Services, and they would make gentle love,
and tomorrow, it being Saturday, they would spend the morning
in bed. And then they would get up, and together they would re-
move his possessions from the packing cases, and put them away.
In a year, or a little less, he would marry the girl from Computer
Services, and get another promotion, and they would have two
children, a boy and a girl, and they would move out to the sub-
urbs, to Harrow or Croydon or Hampstead or even as far away
as distant Reading.

And it would not be a bad life. He knew that, too. Sometimes
there is nothing you can do.

When Garry came back from the toilet, he looked around

in puzzlement. Everyone was there except . . . "Dick?" he asked "Has anyone seen Richard?"

The girl from Computer Services shrugged.

GARRY WENT OUTSIDE, TO Berwick Street. The cold of the night air was like a splash of water to his face. He could taste winter in the air. He called, "Dick? Hey? Richard?"

"Over here."

Richard was leaning against a wall, in the shadows. "Just getting a breath of fresh air."

"Are you all right?" asked Garry.

"Yes," said Richard. "No. I don't know."

"Well," said Garry, "that covers your options. Do you want to talk about it?"

Richard looked at him seriously. "You'll laugh at me."

"I'll do that anyway."

Richard looked at Garry. Then Garry was relieved to see him smile, and he knew that they were still friends. Garry looked back at the pub. Then he put his hands into his coat pockets. "Come on," he said. "Let's walk. You can get it off your chest. *Then* I'll laugh at you."

"Bastard," said Richard, sounding a lot more like Richard than he had in recent weeks.

"It's what friends are for."

They began to amble off, under the streetlights. "Look, Garry," Richard began. "Do you ever wonder if this is all there is?"

"What?"

Richard gestured vaguely, taking in everything. "Work. Home. The pub. Meeting girls. Living in the city. Life. Is that all there is?"

"I think that sums it up, yes," said Garry.

Richard sighed. "Well," he said, "for a start, I didn't go to Majorca. I mean, I *really* didn't go to Majorca."

RICHARD TALKED AS THEY walked up and down the warren of tiny Soho back streets between Regent Street and the Charing Cross Road. He talked, and talked, beginning with finding a girl bleeding on the pavement, and trying to help, because he couldn't just leave her there, and what happened next. And when they got too cold to walk they went into an all-night greasy-spoon café. It was a proper one, the kind that cooked everything in lard, and served cups of serious tea in large chipped white mugs shiny with bacon grease. Richard and Garry sat and Richard talked while Garry listened, and then they ordered fried eggs and baked beans and toast and sat and ate them, while Richard continued to talk, and Garry continued to listen. They mopped up the last of their egg yolks with the toast. They drank more tea, until eventually Richard said, ". . . and then Door did something with the key, and I was back again. In London Above. Well, the real London. And, well, you know the rest."

There was a silence. "That's all," said Richard. He finished his tea.

Garry scratched his head. "Look," he said, at length. "Is this real? Not some kind of horrible leg-pull? I mean, somebody with a camera isn't about to leap out from behind the grill or something and tell me I'm on *Candid Camera*?"

"I sincerely hope not," said Richard. "You . . . do you be-lieve me?"

Garry looked at the bill on their table, counted out pound coins and dropped them onto the Formica, where they sat beside a plastic tomato ketchup container in the shape of an oversized tomato, old sauce caked black about its nozzle. "I believe that, well, *something* happened to you, obviously . . . Look, more to the point, do *you* believe it?"

Richard stared up at him. There were dark circles beneath Richard's eyes. "Do I believe it? I don't know anymore. I did. I was there. There was a bit in there when you turned up, you know."

"You didn't mention that before."

"It was a pretty horrid bit. You told me that I'd gone mad and I was just wandering around London hallucinating."

They walked out of the café, and walked south, toward Pic-cadilly. "Well," said Garry. "You must admit, it sounds more likely than your magical London underneath, where the people who fall through the cracks go. I've passed the people who fall through the cracks, Richard: they sleep in shop doorways all down the Strand. They don't go to a special London. They freeze to death in the winter."

Richard said nothing.

Garry continued. "I think maybe you got some kind of blow on the head. Or maybe some kind of shock when Jessica chucked you. For a while you went a little crazy. Then you got better."

Richard shivered. "You know what scares me? I think you could be right."

"So life isn't exciting?" continued Garry. "Great. Give me boredom. At least I know where I'm going to eat and sleep to-

night. I'll still have a job on Monday. Yeah?" He turned and looked at Richard.

Richard nodded, hesitantly. "Yeah."

Garry looked at his watch. "Bloody hell," he exclaimed. "It's after two o'clock. Let's hope there are still a few taxis about." They walked into Brewer Street, at the Piccadilly end of Soho, wandering past the lights of the peep shows and the strip clubs. Garry was talking about taxis. He was not saying anything original, or even interesting. He was simply fulfilling his obligation as a Londoner to grumble about taxis. ". . . had his light on and everything," he was saying, "I told him where I wanted to go, he said, sorry, I'm on my way home, I said, where do all you taxi drivers live anyway? And why don't any of you live near me? The trick is to get in first, then tell them you live south of the river, I mean, what was he trying to tell me? The way he was carrying on Battersea might as well have been in bloody Katmandu . . ."

Richard had tuned him out. When they reached Great Windmill Street, Richard crossed the road, and stared into the window of the Vintage Magazine Shop, examining the cartoonish models of forgotten film stars, and the old posters and comics and magazines on display. It had been a glimpse into a world of adventure and imagination. And it was not true. He told himself that.

"So, what do you think?" Garry asked.

Richard jerked back to the present. "Of what?"

Garry realized Richard had not heard a word he had said. He said it again. "If there aren't any taxis we could get night buses."

"Yeah," said Richard. "Great. Fine."

Garry grimaced. "You worry me."

"Sorry."

They walked down Great Windmill Street, toward Piccadilly. Richard thrust his hands deep into his pockets. He looked puzzled for a moment, and pulled out a rather crumpled black crow's feather, with red thread tied around the quill.

"What's that?" asked Garry.

"It's a—" He stopped. "It's just a feather. You're right. It's only rubbish." He dropped the feather in the gutter at the curb, and did not look back.

Garry hesitated. Then he said, picking his words with care, "Have you thought about seeing somebody?"

"See somebody? Look, I'm not crazy, Garry."

"Are you sure about that?" A taxi came toward them, yellow for-hire light burning.

"No," said Richard, honestly. "Here's a taxi. You take it. I'll take the next one."

"Thanks." Garry waved down the taxi, and climbed into the back before telling the driver that he wished to go to Battersea. He pulled down the window, and, as the taxi pulled out, he said, "Richard—this is reality. Get used to it. It's all there is. See you on Monday."

Richard waved at him, and watched the taxi drive away. Then he turned around, and walked slowly away from the lights of Piccadilly, back up toward Brewer Street. There was no longer a feather by the curb. Richard paused beside an old woman, fast asleep in a shop doorway. She was covered with a ripped old blanket, and her few possessions—two small junk-filled cardboard boxes, and a dirty, once-white umbrella—were tied to-

gether with string beside her, and the string was tied around her wrist, to stop anyone stealing them while she slept. She wore a woolen bobble hat, of no particular color.

He pulled out his wallet, found a ten-pound note, and bent down to slide the folded note into the woman's hand. Her eyes opened, and she jerked awake. She blinked at the money with old eyes. "What's this?" she said, sleepily, displeased at having been woken.

"Keep it," said Richard.

She unfolded the money, then pushed it up her sleeve. "Whatchyouwant?" she asked Richard, suspiciously.

"Nothing," said Richard. "I really don't want anything. Nothing at all." And then he realized how true that was; and how dreadful a thing it had become. "Have you ever got everything you ever wanted? And then realized it wasn't what you wanted at all?"

"Can't say that I have," she said, picking the grit from the corner of her eyes.

"I thought I wanted this," said Richard. "I thought I wanted a nice normal life. I mean, maybe I am crazy. I mean, maybe. But if this is all there is, then I don't want to be sane. You know?" She shook her head. He reached into his inside pocket. "You see this?" he said. He held up the knife. "Hunter gave this to me as she died," he told her.

"Don't hurt me," said the old lady. "I ain't done nuffing."

There was a strange intensity in his voice. "I wiped her blood from the blade. A hunter looks after her weapons. The Earl knighted me with it. He gave me the freedom of the Underside."

"I don't know anyfing about that," she said. "Please. Put it away. That's a good lad."

Richard hefted the knife. Then he lunged toward the brick wall, next to the doorway in which the woman had been sleeping. He slashed three times, scratching at the wall, once horizontally, twice vertically. "What you doin'?" asked the woman, warily.

"Making a door," he told her.

She sniffed. "You ought to put that thing away. If the police see you they'll run you in for offensive weapons."

Richard looked at the outline of a doorway he had scratched on the wall. He put his knife back into his pocket, and he began to hammer on the wall with his fists. "Hey! Is there anyone there? Can you hear me? It's me—Richard. Door? Someone?" He hurt his hands, but he kept banging and flailing at the brickwork.

And then the madness left him, and he stopped.

"Sorry," he said to the old lady.

She did not answer. She had either gone back to sleep or, more probably, pretended to go back to sleep. Elderly snores, real or feigned, came from the doorway. Richard sat down on the pavement, and wondered quite how someone could make such a mess of their life as he had made of his. Then he looked back at the doorway he had scratched on the wall.

There was a door-shaped hole in the wall, where he had scratched his outline. There was a man standing in the doorway, with his arms folded theatrically. He stood there until he was certain that Richard had seen him. And then he yawned hugely, covering his mouth with a dark hand.

The Marquis de Carabas raised an eyebrow. "Well?" he said, irritably. "Are you coming?"

Richard stared at him for a heartbeat.

Then Richard nodded, without trusting himself to speak, and stood up. And they walked away together through the hole in the wall, back into the darkness, leaving nothing behind them; not even the doorway.

AN ALTOGETHER DIFFERENT PROLOGUE, FOUR HUNDRED YEARS EARLIER

I T WAS THE MIDDLE of the sixteenth century, and it was raining in Tuscany: a cold, mean-spirited rain that turned the world gray.

A smudge of black smoke rose toward the early morning sky from the little monastery on the hill.

Two men sat on the hill, watching the building begin to burn.

"That, Mister Vandemar," said the smaller of them, waving a greasy hand toward the smoke, "is going to be a very fine conflagration, as soon as it conflagrates. Although a strict regard for truth would compel me to confess my doubt that any of the inhabitants are going to be in a position fully and entirely to appreciate it."

"Because of being dead, you mean, Mister Croup?" asked his companion. He was eating something that looked like it might once have been a puppy, using his knife to slice large chunks off the carcass and place them into his mouth.

"Because, as you so wisely point out, sage fellow, of being dead."

This is how you can tell the two speakers apart: firstly, Mr. Vandemar is two and a half heads taller than Mr. Croup.

For secondly, Mr. Croup has eyes of a faded, china blue, while Mr. Vandemar's eyes are brown.

For thirdly, while Mr. Vandemar fashioned the rings he wears on his right hand out of the skulls of four large ravens, Mr. Croup has no obvious jewelry.

For fourthly, Mr. Croup likes words, while Mr. Vandemar is always hungry.

The monastery caught, with a whoompf of air: it conflagrated.

"Don't like sage," said Mr. Vandemar. "Tastes funny."

Someone screamed; and there was a loud rumble, as the roof collapsed, and a roar of flames rose high.

"Somebody wasn't dead," said Mr. Croup.

"Is now," said Mr. Vandemar, and he ate another slice of raw puppy. He had found his lunch lying dead in a ditch, while they were walking away from the monastery. He liked the sixteenth century.

"What's next?" he asked.

Mr. Croup grinned, with teeth that looked like an accident in a graveyard. "About four hundred years from now," he said. "London Below."

Mr. Vandemar digested this along with some puppy. At length, he asked, "Kill people?"

"Oh yes," said Mr. Croup. "I certainly think I can guarantee that."

ACKNOWLEDGMENTS

MY THANKS TO ALL the readers of this book in its various drafts and versions for their input, suggestions and feedback—particularly to Steve Brust, Martha Soukup, Dave Langford, Gene Wolfe, Cindy Wall, Lorraine Garland and Kelli Bickman; to Doug Young and Sheila Ableman at BBC Books for their help and input, and to Jennifer Hershey and Lou Aronica at Avon Books. I would also like to thank all the people who came to my rescue whenever chunks of this novel devolved to their component electrons, and Norton Utilities.

I'd also like to thank Pete Atkins for his help in assembling this final draft of the text.

NEIL GAIMAN

HOW THE
MARQUIS GOT HIS
COAT BACK

———◆———

I started this story in 2002, and stopped almost immediately. I kept meaning to get back to it, but I never did.

In 2013 BBC's Radio 4 broadcast an adaptation of Neverwhere. *It was adapted by Dirk Maggs, and starred James McAvoy, Natalie Dormer, and Benedict Cumberbatch. They sent it to me to listen to.*

This is wonderful, *I thought.* I wish there was more of it.

So I finished the story about the Marquis and his coat. It takes place, in the book you just read, shortly after he loses his coat and his life.

It was good to be back. Good finally to encounter

*characters I had first imagined over twenty years ago. And you would
think it might have scratched my itch to return to London Below. And
it did, a little.*

But soon it will be time to go back for a much longer journey.

I T WAS BEAUTIFUL. I T was remarkable. It was unique. It
was the reason that the Marquis de Carabas was chained to a
pole in the middle of a circular room, far, far underground,
while the water level rose slowly higher and higher. It had
thirty pockets, seven of which were obvious, nineteen of which
were hidden, and four of which were more or less impossible to
find—even, on occasion, for the Marquis himself.

He had (we shall return to the pole, and the room, and the
rising water, in due course) once been given—although *given*
might be considered an unfortunate, if justified, exaggeration—a
magnifying glass, by Victoria herself. It was a marvelous piece of
work: ornate, gilt, with a chain and tiny cherubs and gargoyles,
and the lens had the unusual property of rendering transparent
anything you looked at through it. The Marquis did not know
where Victoria had originally obtained the magnifying glass,
before he pilfered it from her, to make up for a payment he felt
was not entirely what had been agreed—after all, there was only
one Elephant, and obtaining the Elephant's diary had not been
easy, nor had escaping the Elephant and Castle once it had been
obtained. The Marquis had slipped Victoria's magnifying glass
into one of the four pockets that practically weren't there at all,
and had never been able to find it again.

In addition to its unusual pockets, it had magnificent sleeves, an imposing collar, and a slit up the back. It was made of some kind of leather, it was the color of a wet street at midnight, and, more important than any of these things, it had style.

There are people who will tell you that clothes make the man, and mostly they are wrong. However, it would be true to say that when the boy who would become the Marquis put that coat on for the very first time, and stared at himself in the looking glass, he stood up straighter, and his posture changed, because he knew, seeing his reflection, that the sort of person who wore a coat like that was no mere youth, no simple sneak-thief and favor-trader. The boy wearing the coat, which was, back then, too large for him, had smiled, looking at his reflection, and remembered an illustration from a book he had seen, of a miller's cat standing on its two hind legs. A jaunty cat wearing a fine coat and big, proud boots. And he named himself.

A coat like that, he knew, was the kind of coat that could only be worn by the Marquis de Carabas. He was never sure, not then and not later, how you pronounced *Marquis de Carabas*. Some days he said it one way, some days the other.

The water level had reached his knees, and he thought, *This would never have happened if I still had my coat.*

IT WAS THE MARKET day after the worst week of the Marquis de Carabas's life and things did not seem to be getting any better. Still, he was no longer dead, and his cut throat was healing rapidly. There was even a rasp in his throat he found quite attractive. Those were definite upsides.

There were just as definite downsides to being dead, or at least, to having been recently dead, and missing his coat was the worst of them.

The Sewer Folk were not helpful.

"You sold my corpse," said the Marquis. "These things happen. You also sold my possessions. I want them back. I'll pay."

Dunnikin of the Sewer Folk shrugged. "Sold them," he said. "Just like we sold you. Can't go getting things back that you sold. Not good business."

"We are talking," said the Marquis de Carabas, "about my coat. And I fully intend to have it back."

Dunnikin shrugged.

"To whom did you sell it?" asked the Marquis.

The sewer dweller said nothing at all. He acted as if he had not even heard the question.

"I can get you perfumes," said the Marquis, masking his irritability with all the blandness he could muster. "Glorious, magnificent, odiferous perfumes. You know you want them."

Dunnikin stared, stony-faced, at the Marquis. Then he drew his finger across his throat. As gestures went, the Marquis reflected, it was in appalling taste. Still, it had the desired effect. He stopped asking questions; there would be no answers from this direction.

The Marquis walked over to the food court. That night, the Floating Market was being held in the Tate Gallery. The food court was in the Pre-Raphaelite room, and had already been mostly packed away. There were almost no stalls left: just a sad-looking little man selling some kind of sausage, and, in the corner, beneath a Burne-Jones painting of ladies in diaphanous robes walking downstairs, there were some Mushroom People,

with some stools, tables and a grill. The Marquis had once eaten one of the sad-looking man's sausages, and he had a firm policy of never intentionally making the same mistake twice, so he walked to the Mushroom People's stall.

There were three of the Mushroom People looking after the stall, two young men and a young woman. They smelled damp. They wore old duffel coats and army-surplus jackets, and they peered out from beneath their shaggy hair as if the light hurt their eyes.

"What are you selling?" he asked.

"The Mushroom. The Mushroom on toast. Raw the Mushroom."

"I'll have some of the Mushroom on toast," he said, and one of the Mushroom People—a thin, pale young woman with the complexion of day-old porridge—cut a slice off a puffball fungus the size of a tree stump. "And I want it cooked properly all the way through," he told her.

"Be brave. Eat it raw," said the woman. "Join us."

"I have already had dealings with the Mushroom," said the Marquis. "We came to an understanding."

The woman put the slice of white puffball under the portable grill.

One of the young men, tall, with hunched shoulders, in a duffel coat that smelled like old cellars, edged over to the Marquis, and poured him a glass of mushroom tea. He leaned forward, and the Marquis could see the tiny crop of pale mushrooms splashed like pimples over his cheek.

The Mushroom person said, "You're de Carabas? The fixer?"

The Marquis did not think of himself as a fixer. He said, "I am."

"I hear you're looking for your coat. I was there when the Sewer Folk sold it. Start of the last Market it was. On Belfast. I saw who bought it."

The hair on the back of the Marquis's neck pricked up. "And what would you want for the information?"

The Mushroom's young man licked his lips with a lichenous tongue. "There's a girl I like as won't give me the time of day."

"A Mushroom girl?"

"Would I were so lucky. If we were as one both in love and in the body of the Mushroom, I wouldn't have nothing to worry about. No. She's one of the Raven's Court. But she eats here sometimes. And we talk. Just like you and I are talking now."

The Marquis did not smile in pity and he did not wince. He barely raised an eyebrow. "And yet she does not return your ardor. How strange. What do you want me to do about it?"

The young man reached one gray hand into the pocket of his long duffel coat. He pulled out an envelope, inside a clear plastic sandwich bag.

"I wrote her a letter. More of a poem, you might say, although I'm not much of a poet. To tell her how I feels about her. But I don't know that she'd read it, if I gived it to her. Then I saw you, and I thought, if it was you as was to give it to her, with all your fine words and your fancy flourishes . . ." He trailed off.

"You thought she would read it and then be more inclined to listen to your suit."

The young man looked down at his duffel coat with a puzzled expression. "I've not got a suit," he said. "Only what I've got on."

The Marquis tried not to sigh. The Mushroom woman put a cracked plastic plate down in front of him, with a steaming

slice of grilled the Mushroom on it, soaking into a brown slice of crusty toast.

He poked at the Mushroom experimentally, making sure that it was cooked all the way through, and there were no active spores. You could never be too careful, and the Marquis considered himself much too selfish for symbiosis.

It was good. He chewed, and swallowed, though the food hurt his throat.

"So all you want is for me to make sure she reads your missive of yearning?"

"You mean my letter? My poem?"

"I do."

"Well, yes. And I want you to be there with her, to make sure she doesn't put it away unread, and I want you to bring her answer back to me." The Marquis looked at the young man. It was true that he had tiny mushrooms sprouting from his neck and cheeks, and his hair was heavy and unwashed, and there was a general smell about him of abandoned places, but it was also true that through his thick fringe his eyes were pale blue and intense, and that he was tall, and not unattractive. The Marquis imagined him washed and cleaned up and somewhat less fungal, and approved. "I put the letter in the sandwich bag," said the young man, "So it doesn't get wet on the way."

"Very wise. Now, tell me: who bought my coat?"

"Not yet, Mister Jumps-the-gun. You haven't asked about my true love. Her name is Drusilla. You'll know her because she is the most beautiful woman in all of the Raven's Court."

"Beauty is traditionally in the eye of the beholder. Give me more to go on."

"I told you. Her name's Drusilla. There's only one. And she

has a big red birthmark on the back of her hand that looks like a star."

"It seems an unlikely love pairing. One of the Mushroom's folk, in love with a lady of the Raven's Court. What makes you think she'll give up her life for your damp cellars and fungoid joys?"

The Mushroom youth shrugged. "She'll love me," he said. "Once she's read my poem." He twisted the stem of a tiny parasol mushroom growing on his right cheek, and when it fell to the table, he picked it up and continued to twist it between his fingers. "We're on?"

"We're on."

"The cove as bought your coat," said the Mushroom youth, "carried a stick."

"Lots of people carry sticks," said de Carabas.

"This one had a crook on the end," said the Mushroom youth. "Looked a bit like a frog, he did. Short one. Bit fat. Hair the color of gravel. Needed a coat and took a shine to yours." He popped the parasol mushroom into his mouth.

"Useful information. I shall certainly pass your ardor and felicitations on to the fair Drusilla," said the Marquis de Carabas, with a cheer that he most definitely did not feel.

De Carabas reached across the table, and took the sandwich bag with the envelope in it from the young man's fingers. He slipped it into one of the pockets sewn inside his shirt.

And then he walked away, thinking about a man holding a crook.

THE MARQUIS DE CARABAS wore a blanket as a substitute for his coat. He wore it swathed about him like hell's own poncho. It did not make him happy. He wished he had his coat. *Fine feathers do not make fine birds,* whispered a voice at the back of his mind, something someone had said to him when he was a boy; he suspected that it was his brother's voice, and he did his best to forget it had ever spoken.

A crook: the man who had taken his coat from the sewer people had been carrying a crook.

He pondered.

The Marquis de Carabas liked being who he was, and when he took risks he liked them to be calculated risks, and he was someone who double- and triple-checked his calculations.

He checked his calculations for the fourth time.

The Marquis de Carabas did not trust people. It was bad for business and it could set an unfortunate precedent. He did not trust his friends or his occasional lovers, and he certainly never trusted his employers. He reserved the entirety of his trust for the Marquis de Carabas, an imposing figure in an imposing coat, able to outtalk, outthink and outplan anybody.

There were only two sorts of people who carried crooks: bishops and shepherds.

In Bishopsgate, the crooks were decorative, nonfunctional, purely symbolic. And the bishops had no need of coats. They had robes, after all, nice, white, bishoppy robes.

The Marquis was not scared of the bishops. He knew the Sewer Folk were not scared of the bishops. The inhabitants of Shepherd's Bush were another matter entirely. Even in his coat, and at the best of times, at the peak of health and with a small

army at his beck and call, the Marquis would not have wanted to encounter the shepherds.

He toyed with the idea of visiting Bishopsgate, of spending a pleasant handful of days establishing that his coat was not there.

And then he sighed, dramatically, and went to the Guide's Pen, and looked for a bonded guide who might be persuaded take him to Shepherd's Bush.

HIS GUIDE WAS QUITE remarkably short, with fair hair cut close. The Marquis had first thought she was in her teens, until, after traveling with her for half a day, he had decided she was in her twenties. He had talked to half a dozen guides before he found her. Her name was Knibbs, and she had seemed confident, and he needed confidence. He told her the two places he was going, as they walked out of the Guide's Pen.

"So where do you want to go first, then?" she asked. "Shepherd's Bush, or Raven's Court?"

"The visit to Raven's Court is a formality; it is merely to deliver a letter. To someone named Drusilla."

"A love letter?"

"I believe so. Why do you ask?"

"I have heard that the fair Drusilla is most wickedly beautiful, and she has the unfortunate habit of reshaping those who displease her into birds of prey. You must love her very much, to be writing letters to her."

"I am afraid I have never encountered the young lady," said the Marquis. "The letter is not from me. And it doesn't matter which we visit first."

"You know," said Knibbs, thoughtfully, "just in case something dreadfully unfortunate happens to you when you get to the shepherds, we should probably do Raven's Court first. So the fair Drusilla gets her letter. I'm not saying that something horrible will happen to you, mind. Just that it's better to be safe than, y'know, dead."

The Marquis de Carabas looked down at his blanketed shape. He was uncertain. Had he been wearing his coat, he knew, he would not have been uncertain; he would have known exactly what to do. He looked at the girl and he mustered the most convincing grin he could. "Raven's Court it is, then," he said.

Knibbs had nodded, and set off on the path, and the Marquis had followed her.

The paths of London Below are not the paths of London Above: they rely to no little extent on things like belief and opinion and tradition as much as they rely upon the realities of maps.

De Carabas and Knibbs were two tiny figures walking through a high, vaulted tunnel carved from old, white stone. Their footsteps echoed.

"You're de Carabas, aren't you?" said Knibbs. "You're famous. You know how to get places. What exactly do you need a guide for?"

"Two heads are better than one," he told her. "So are two sets of eyes."

"You used to have a posh coat, didn't you?" she said.

"I did. Yes."

"What happened to it?"

He said nothing. Then he said, "I've changed my mind. We're going to Shepherd's Bush first."

"Fair enough," said his guide. "Easy to take you one place as another. I'll wait for you outside the shepherds' trading post, mind."

"Very wise, girl."

"My name's Knibbs," she said. "Not girl. Do you want to know why I become a guide? It's an interesting story."

"Not particularly," said the Marquis de Carabas. He was not feeling particularly talkative, and the guide was being well recompensed for her trouble. "Why don't we try to move in silence?"

Knibbs nodded, and said nothing as they reached the end of the tunnel, nothing as they clambered down some metal rungs set in the side of a wall. It was not until they had reached the banks of the Mortlake, the vast underground Lake of the Dead, and she was lighting a candle on the shore to summon the boatman, that she spoke again.

Knibbs said, "The thing about being a proper guide is that you're bonded. So people know you won't steer them wrong."

The Marquis only grunted. He was wondering what to tell the shepherds at the trading post, trying out alternate routes through possibility and through probability. He had nothing that the shepherds would want, that was the trouble.

"You lead them wrong, you'll never work as a guide again," said Knibbs, cheerfully. "That's why we're bonded."

"I know," said the Marquis. She was a most irritating guide, he thought. Two heads were only better than one if the other head kept its mouth shut and did not start telling him things he already knew.

"I got bonded," she said, "in Bond Street." She tapped the little chain around her wrist.

"I don't see the ferryman," said the Marquis.

"He'll be here soon enough. You keep an eye out for him in that direction, and halloo when you sees him. I'll keep looking over here. One way or another, we'll spot him."

They stared out over the dark water of the lake. Knibbs began to talk again. "Before I was a guide, when I was just little, my people trained me up for this. They said it was the only way that honor could ever be satisfied."

The Marquis turned to face her. She held the candle in front of her, at eye level. *Everything is off, here,* thought the Marquis, and he realized he should have been listening to her from the beginning. *Everything is wrong.* He said, "Who are your people, Knibbs? Where do you come from?"

"Somewhere you ain't welcome anymore," said the girl. "I was born and bred to give my fealty and loyalty to the Elephant and the Castle."

Something hard struck him on the back of the head then, hit him like a hammer blow, and lightning pulsed in the darkness of his mind as he crumpled to the floor.

THE MARQUIS DE CARABAS could not move his arms. They were, he realized, tied behind him. He was lying on his side.

He had been unconscious. If the people who did this to him thought him unconscious then he would do nothing to disabuse them of the idea, he decided. He let his eyes slit open the merest crack, to sneak a glance at the world.

A deep, grinding voice said, "Oh, don't be silly, de Carabas. I don't believe you're still out. I've got big ears. I can hear your

heartbeat. Open your eyes properly, you weasel. Face me like a man."

The Marquis recognized the voice, and hoped he was mistaken. He opened his eyes. He was staring at legs, human legs with bare feet. The toes were squat and pushed together. The legs and feet were the color of teak. He knew those legs. He had not been mistaken.

His mind bifurcated: A small part of it berated him for his inattention and his foolishness. Knibbs had *told* him, by the Temple and the Arch; he just had not listened to her. But even as he raged at his own foolishness, the rest of his mind took over, forced a smile, and said, "Why, this is indeed an honor. You really didn't have to arrange to meet me like this. Why, the merest inkling that your prominence might have had even the teeniest desire to see me would have—"

"Sent you scurrying off in the other direction as fast as your spindly little legs could carry you," said the person with the teak-colored legs. He reached over with his trunk, which was long and flexible, and a greenish-blue color, and which hung to his ankles, and he pushed the Marquis onto his back.

The Marquis began rubbing his bound wrists slowly against the concrete beneath them, while he said, "Not at all. Quite the opposite. Words cannot actually describe how much pleasure I take in your pachydermic presence. Might I suggest that you untie me, and allow me to greet you, man to—man to elephant?"

"I don't think so, given all the trouble I've been through to make this happen," said the other. He had the head of a greenish-gray elephant. His tusks were sharp and stained reddish brown at the tips. "You know, I swore when I found out what you had

done that I would make you scream and beg for mercy. And I swore I'd say no, to giving you mercy, when you begged for it."

"You could say yes, instead," said the Marquis.

"I couldn't say yes. Hospitality abused," said the elephant. "I never forget."

The Marquis had been commissioned to bring Victoria the Elephant's diary, when he and the world had been much younger. The Elephant ran his fiefdom arrogantly, sometimes viciously and with no tenderness or humor, and the Marquis had thought that the Elephant was stupid. He had even believed that there was no way that the Elephant would correctly identify his role in the disappearance of the diary. It had been a long time ago, though, when the Marquis was young and foolish.

"This whole spending years training up a guide to betray me just on the off chance I'd come along and hire her," said the Marquis. "Isn't that a bit of an overreaction?"

"Not if you know me," said the Elephant. "If you know me, it's pretty mild. I did lots of other things to find you too."

The Marquis tried to sit up. The Elephant pushed him back to the floor, with one bare foot. "Beg for mercy," said the Elephant.

That one was easy. "Mercy!" said the Marquis. "I beg! I plead! Show me mercy—the finest of all gifts. It befits you, mighty Elephant, as lord of your own demesne, to be merciful to one who is not even fit to wipe the dust from your excellent toes . . ."

"Did you know," said the Elephant, "that everything you say sounds sarcastic?"

"I didn't. I apologize. I meant every single word of it."

"Scream," said the Elephant.

The Marquis de Carabas screamed very loudly and very long. It is hard to scream when your throat has been recently cut, but he screamed as hard and piteously as he could.

"You even scream sarcastically," said the Elephant.

There was a large black cast-iron pipe jutting out from the wall. A wheel in the side of the pipe allowed whatever came out of the pipe to be turned on and turned off. The Elephant hauled on it with powerful arms, and a trickle of dark sludge came out, followed by a spurt of water.

"Drainage overflow," said the Elephant. "Now. Thing is, I do my homework. You keep your life well hidden, de Carabas. You have done all these years, since you and I first crossed paths. No point in even trying anything as long as you had your life elsewhere. I've had people all over London Below—people you've eaten with, people you've slept with or laughed with or wound up naked in the clock tower of Big Ben with—but there was never any point in taking it further, not as long as your life was still carefully tucked out of harm's way. Until last week, when the word under the street was that your life was out of its box. And that was when I put the word out, that I'd give the freedom of the Castle to the first person to let me see—"

"See me scream for mercy," said de Carabas. "You said."

"You interrupted me," said the Elephant, mildly. "I was going to say, I was going to give the freedom of the Castle to the first person to let me see your dead body."

He pulled the wheel the rest of the way and the spurt of water became a gush.

"I ought to warn you. There is," said de Carabas, "a curse on the hand of anyone who kills me."

"I'll take the curse," said the Elephant. "Although you're probably making it up. You'll like the next bit. The room fills with water, and then you drown. Then I let the water out, and I come in, and I laugh a lot." He made a trumpeting noise that might, de Carabas reflected, have been a laugh, if you were an elephant.

The Elephant stepped out of de Carabas's line of sight.

The Marquis heard a door bang. He was lying in a puddle. He writhed and wriggled, then got to his feet. He looked down: there was a metal cuff around his ankle, which was chained to a metal pole in the center of the room.

He wished he were wearing his coat: there were blades in his coat; there were picklocks; there were buttons that were nowhere nearly as innocent and buttonlike as they appeared to be. He rubbed the rope that bound his wrists against the metal pole, hoping to make it fray, feeling the skin of his wrists and palms rubbing off even as the rope absorbed the water and tightened about him. The water level continued to rise; already it was up to his waist.

De Carabas looked about the circular chamber. All he had to do was free himself from the bonds that tied his wrists—obviously by loosening the pole to which he was bound—and then he would open the cuff around his ankle, turn off the water, get out of the room, avoid a revenge-driven Elephant and any of his assorted thugs, and get away.

He tugged on the pole. It didn't move. He tugged on it harder. It didn't move some more.

He slumped against the pole, and he thought about death, a true, final death, and he thought about his coat.

A voice whispered in his ear. It said, "Quiet!"

Something tugged at his wrists, and his bonds fell away. It was only as life came back into his wrists that he realized how tightly he had been bound. He turned around.

He said, "What?"

The face that met his was as familiar as his own. The smile was devastating, the eyes were guileless and adventuresome.

"Ankle," said the man, with a new smile that was even more devastating than the previous one.

The Marquis de Carabas was not devastated. He raised his leg, and the man reached down, did something with a piece of wire, and removed the leg cuff.

"I heard you were having a spot of bother," said the man. His skin was as dark as the Marquis's own. He was less than an inch taller than de Carabas, but he held himself as if he were easily taller than anyone he was ever likely to meet.

"No. No bother. I'm fine," said the Marquis.

"You aren't. I just rescued you."

De Carabas ignored this. "Where's the Elephant?"

"On the other side of that door, with a number of the people working for him. The doors lock automatically when the hall is filled with water. He needed to be certain that he wouldn't be trapped in here with you. It was what I was counting on."

"Counting on?"

"Of course. I'd been following them for several hours. Ever since I heard that you'd gone off with one of the Elephant's plants. I thought, *Bad move,* I thought. *He'll be needing a hand with that.*"

"You *heard* . . . ?"

"Look," said the man, who looked a little like the Marquis

de Carabas, only he was taller, and perhaps some people—not the Marquis, obviously—might have thought him just a hair more attractive, "you don't think I was going to let anything happen to my little brother, did you?"

They were up to their waists in water. "I was fine," said de Carabas. "I had it all under control."

The man walked over to the far end of the room. He knelt down, fumbled in the water, then, from his backpack, he produced something that looked like a short crowbar. He pushed one end of it beneath the surface of the water. "Get ready," he said. "I think this should be our quickest way out of here."

The Marquis was still flexing his pins-and-needles cramping fingers, trying to rub life back into them. "What is it?" he said, trying to sound unimpressed.

The man said, "There we go," and pulled up a large square of metal. "It's the drain." De Carabas did not have a chance to protest, as his brother picked him up and dropped him down a hole in the floor.

Probably, thought de Carabas, *there are rides like this at funfairs.* He could imagine them. Upworlders might pay good money to take this ride, if they were certain they would survive it.

He crashed through pipes, swept along by the flow of water, always heading down and deeper. He was not certain he was going to survive the ride, and he was not having fun.

The Marquis's body was bruised and battered as he rode the water down the pipe. He tumbled out, facedown, onto a large metal grate, which seemed scarcely able to hold his weight. He crawled off the grate onto the rock floor beside it, and he shivered.

There was an unlikely sort of a noise, and it was immediately followed by his brother, who shot out of the pipe and landed on his feet, as if he'd been practicing. He smiled. "Fun, eh?"

"Not really," said the Marquis de Carabas. And then he had to ask. "Were you just going '*Whee!*'?"

"Of course! Weren't you?" asked his brother.

De Carabas got to his feet, unsteadily. He said only, "What are you calling yourself these days?"

"Still the same. I don't change."

"It's not your real name, Peregrine," said de Carabas.

"It'll do. It marks my territory and my intentions. You're still calling yourself a Marquis, then?" said Peregrine.

"I am, because I say I am," said the Marquis. He looked, he was sure, like a drowned thing, and sounded, he was certain, unconvincing. He felt small and foolish.

"Your choice. Anyway, I'm off. You don't need me anymore. Stay out of trouble. You don't actually have to thank me." His brother meant it, of course. That was what stung the hardest.

The Marquis de Carabas hated himself. He hadn't wanted to say it, but now it had to be said. "Thank you, Peregrine."

"Oh!" said Peregrine. "Your coat. Word on the street is, it wound up in Shepherd's Bush. That's all I know. So. Advice. Mean this most sincerely. I know you don't like advice. But, the coat? Let it go. Forget about it. Just get a new coat. Honest."

"Well then," said the Marquis.

"Well," said Peregrine, and he grinned, and shook himself like a dog, spraying water everywhere, before he slipped into the shadows and was gone.

The Marquis de Carabas stood and dripped balefully.

He had a little time before the Elephant discovered the lack of water in the room, and the lack of a body, and came looking for him.

He checked his shirt pocket: the sandwich bag was there, and the envelope appeared safe and dry inside it.

He wondered, for a moment, about something that had bothered him since the Market. Why would the Mushroom lad use him, de Carabas, to send a letter to the fair Drusilla? And what kind of letter could persuade a member of the Raven's Court, and one with a star on her hand at that, to give up her life at the court, and love one of the Mushroom folk?

A suspicion occurred to him. It was not a comfortable idea, nor a charitable one, but it was swept aside by more immediate problems.

He could hide: lie low, for a while. All this would pass. But there was the coat to think about. He had been rescued—rescued!—by his brother, something that would never have happened under normal circumstances. He could get a new coat. Of course he could. But it would not be *his* coat.

A shepherd had his coat.

The Marquis de Carabas always had a plan, and he always had a fallback plan; and beneath these plans he always had a real plan, one that he would not even let himself know about, for when the original plan and the fallback plan had both gone south.

Now, it pained him to admit to himself, he had no plan. He did not even have a normal, boring, obvious plan that he could abandon as soon as things got tricky. He just had a want, and it drove him as their need for food or love or safety drove those the Marquis considered lesser men.

He was planless. He just wanted his coat back.

The Marquis de Carabas began walking. He had an envelope containing a love poem in his pocket, he was wrapped in a damp blanket, and he hated his brother for rescuing him.

When you create yourself from scratch you need a model of some kind, something to aim towards or head away from—all the things you want to be, or intentionally want not to be.

The Marquis had known whom he had wanted not to be, when he was a boy. He had definitely not wanted to be like Peregrine. He had not wanted to be like anyone at all. He had, instead, wanted to be elegant, elusive, brilliant, and, above all things, he had wanted to be unique.

Just like Peregrine.

THE THING WAS, HE had been told, by a former shepherd, on the run, whom he had helped across the Tyburn River, to freedom, and to a short but happy life as a camp entertainer for the Roman Legion who waited there, beside the river, for orders that would never come, that the shepherds never *made* you do anything. They just took your natural impulses and desires and they pushed them, reinforced them, so you acted quite naturally, only you acted in the ways that they wanted.

He remembered that, and then he forgot it, because he was scared of being alone.

The Marquis had not known until just this moment quite how scared he was of being alone, and was surprised by how happy he was to see several other people walking in the same direction as he was.

"I'm glad you're here," one of them called.

"I'm glad you're here," called another.

"I'm glad I'm here too," said de Carabas. Where was he going? Where were they going? So good that they were all traveling the same way together. There was safety in numbers.

"It's good to be together," said a thin white woman, with a happy sort of a sigh. And it was.

"It's good to be together," said the Marquis.

"Indeed it is. It's good to be together," said his neighbor on the other side. There was something familiar about this person. He had huge ears, like fans, and a nose like a thick, gray-green snake. The Marquis began to wonder if he had ever met this person before, and was trying to remember exactly where, when he was tapped gently on the shoulder by a man holding a large stick with a curved end.

"We never want to fall out of step, do we?" said the man, reasonably, and the Marquis thought, *Of course we don't,* and he sped up a little, so he was back in step once more.

"That's good. Out of step is out of mind," said the man with the stick, and he moved on.

"Out of step is out of mind," said the Marquis, aloud, wondering how he could have missed knowing something so obvious, so basic. There was a tiny part of him, somewhere distant, that wondered what that actually meant.

They reached the place they were going, and it was good to be among friends.

Time passed strangely in that place, but soon enough the Marquis and his friend with the gray-green face and the long nose were given a job to do, a real job, and it was this: they dis-

posed of those members of the flock who could no longer move or serve, once anything that might be of use had been removed and reused. They removed the last of what was left, hair and tallow fat and all, then they dragged them to the pit, and dropped the remnants in. The shifts were long and tiring, and the work was messy, but the two of them did it together and they stayed in step.

They had been working proudly together for several days when the Marquis noticed an irritant. Someone appeared to be trying to attract his attention.

"I followed you," whispered the stranger. "I know you didn't want me to. But, well, needs must."

The Marquis did not know what the stranger was talking about.

"I've got an escape plan, as soon as I can wake you up," said the stranger. "Please wake up."

The Marquis was awake. Again, he found he did not know what the stranger was talking about. Why did the man think he was asleep? The Marquis would have said something, but he had to work. He pondered this, while dismembering the next former member of the flock, until he decided there was something he could say, to explain why the stranger was irritating him. He said it aloud. "It's good to work," said the Marquis.

His friend, with the long, flexible nose, and the huge ears, nodded his head at this.

They worked. After a while his friend hauled what was left of some former members of the flock over to the pit, and pushed them in. The pit went down a long way.

The Marquis tried to ignore the stranger, who was now standing behind him. He was quite put out when he felt some-

thing slapped over his mouth, and his hands being bound together behind his back. He was not certain what he was meant to do. It made him feel quite out of step with the flock, and he would have complained, would have called out to his friend, but his lips were now stuck together and he was unable to do more than make ineffectual noises.

"It's me," whispered the voice from behind him, urgently. "Peregrine. Your brother. You've been captured by the shepherds. We have to get you out of here." And then, "Uh-oh."

A noise in the air, like something barking. It came closer: a high yip-yipping that turned suddenly into a triumphant howl, and was answered by matching howls from around them.

A voice barked, "Where's your flockmate?"

A low, elephantine voice rumbled, "He went over there. With the other one."

"Other one?"

The Marquis hoped they would come and find him and sort this all out. There was obviously some sort of mistake going on. He wanted to be in step with the flock, and now he was out of step, an unwilling victim. He wanted to work.

"Lud's gate!" muttered Peregrine. And then they were surrounded by the shapes of people who were not exactly people: they were sharp of face, and dressed in furs. They spoke excitedly to each other.

The people untied the Marquis's hands, although they left the tape on his face. He did not mind. He had nothing to say.

The Marquis was relieved it was all over and looked forward to getting back to work, but, to his slight puzzlement, he, his kidnapper, and his friend with the huge long flexible nose were

walked away from the pit, along a causeway, and, eventually, into a honeycomb of little rooms, each room filled with people toiling away in step.

Up some narrow stairs. One of their escorts, dressed in rough furs, scratched at a door. A voice called, "Enter!" and the Marquis felt a thrill that was almost sexual. That voice. That was the voice of someone the Marquis had spent his whole life wanting to please. (His whole life went back, what? A week? Two weeks?)

"A stray lamb," said one of the escorts. "And his predator. Also his flockmate."

The room was large, and hung with oil paintings: landscapes, mostly, stained with age and smoke and dust. "Why?" said the man, sitting at a desk in the back of the room. He did not turn around. "Why do you bother me with this nonsense?"

"Because," said a voice, and the Marquis recognized it as that of his would-be kidnapper, "you gave orders that if ever I were to be apprehended within the bounds of the Shepherds' Bush, I was to be brought to you to dispose of personally."

The man pushed his chair back and got up. He walked towards them, stepping into the light. There was a wooden crook propped against the wall, and he picked it up as he passed. For several long moments he looked at them.

"Peregrine?" he said, at last, and the Marquis thrilled at his voice. "I had heard that you had gone into retirement. Become a monk or something. I never dreamed you'd dare to come back."

(Something very big was filling the Marquis's head. Something was filling his heart and his mind. It was something enormous, something he could almost touch.)

The shepherd reached out a hand and ripped the tape from the Marquis's mouth. The Marquis knew he should have been overjoyed by this, should have been thrilled to get attention from this man.

"And now I see . . . who would have thought it?" The shepherd's voice was deep and resonant. "He is here already. And already one of ours? The Marquis de Carabas. You know, Peregrine, I had been looking forward to ripping out your tongue, to grinding your fingers away while you watched, but think how much more delightful it would be if the last thing you ever saw was your own brother, one of our flock, as the instrument of your doom."

(An enormous thing filled the Marquis's head.)

The shepherd was plump, well-fed, and was excellently dressed. He had sandy-gray-colored hair and a harassed expression. He wore a remarkable coat, even if it was somewhat tight on him. The coat was the color of a wet street at midnight.

The enormous thing filling his head, the Marquis realized, was rage. It was rage, and it burned through the Marquis like a forest fire, devouring everything in its path with a red flame.

The coat. It was elegant. It was beautiful. It was so close that he could have reached out and touched it.

And it was unquestionably *his*.

The Marquis de Carabas did nothing to indicate that he had woken up. That would have been a mistake. He thought, and he thought fast, and what he thought had nothing to do with the room he was in. The Marquis had only one advantage over the shepherd and his dogs: he knew he was awake and in control of his thoughts, and they did not.

He hypothesized. He tested his hypothesis in his head. And then, he acted.

"Excuse me," he said, blandly. "But I'm afraid I do need to be getting along. Can we hurry this up? I'm late for something that's frightfully important."

The shepherd leaned on his crook. He did not appear to be concerned by this. He said only, "You've left the flock, de Carabas."

"It would appear so," said the Marquis. "Hello, Peregrine. Wonderful to see you looking so sprightly. And the Elephant. How delightful. The gang's all here." He turned his attention back to the shepherd. "Wonderful meeting you, delightful to spend a modicum of time as one of your little band of serious thinkers. But I really must be tootling off now. Important diplomatic mission. Letter to deliver. You know how it is."

Peregrine said, "My brother, I'm not sure that you understand the gravity of the situation here . . ."

The Marquis, who understood the gravity of the situation perfectly, said, "I'm sure these nice people"—he gestured to the shepherd and to the three fur-clad, sharp-faced sheepdog people who were standing about them—"will let me head out of here, leaving you behind. It's you they want, not me. And I have something extremely important to deliver."

Peregrine said, "I can handle this."

"You have to be quiet now," said the shepherd. He took the strip of tape he had removed from the Marquis's mouth and pressed it down over Peregrine's.

The shepherd was shorter than the Marquis, and fatter, and the magnificent coat looked faintly ridiculous on him. "Some-

thing important to deliver?" asked the shepherd, brushing dust from his fingers. "What exactly are we talking about here?"

"I am afraid I cannot possibly tell you that," said the Marquis. "You are, after all, not the intended recipient of this particular diplomatic communiqué."

"Why not? What's it say? Who's it for?"

The Marquis shrugged. His coat was so close that he could have reached out and stroked it. "Only the threat of death could force me even to show it to you," he said reluctantly.

"Well, that's easy. I threaten you with death. That's in addition to the death sentence you're already under as an apostate member of the flock. And as for laughing boy here"—the shepherd gestured with his crook towards Peregrine, who was not laughing—"he's tried to steal a member of the flock. That's a death sentence too, in addition to everything else we're planning to do to him."

The shepherd looked at the Elephant. "And, I know I should have asked before, but what in the Auld Witch's name is *this*?"

"I am a loyal member of the flock," said the Elephant, humbly, in his deep voice, and the Marquis wondered if he had himself sounded so soulless and flat when he had been part of the flock. "I have remained loyal and in step even when this one did not."

"And the flock is grateful for all your hard work," said the shepherd. He reached out a hand and touched the sharp tip of one Elephantine tusk, experimentally. "I've never seen anything like you before, and if I never see another one again it'll be too soon. Probably best if you die too."

The Elephant's ears twitched. "But I am of the flock . . ."

The shepherd looked up into the Elephant's huge face. "Better safe than sorry," he said. Then, to the Marquis: "Well? Where is this important letter?"

The Marquis de Carabas said, "It is inside my shirt. I must repeat that it is the most significant document that I have ever been charged to deliver. I must ask you not to look at it. For your own safety."

The shepherd tugged at the front of the Marquis's shirt. The buttons flew, and rattled off the walls onto the floor. The letter, in its sandwich bag, was in the pocket inside the shirt.

"This is most unfortunate. I trust you will read it aloud to us before we die," said the Marquis. "But whether or not you read it to us, I can promise that Peregrine and I will be holding our breath. Won't we, Peregrine?"

The shepherd opened the sandwich bag, then he looked at the envelope. He ripped it open and pulled a sheet of discolored paper from inside it. Dust came from the envelope as the paper came out. The dust hung in the still air in that dim room.

"'My darling beautiful Drusilla,'" read the shepherd, aloud. "'While I know that you do not presently feel about me as I feel about you . . .' What *is* this nonsense?"

The Marquis said nothing. He did not even smile. He was, as he had stated, holding his breath; he was hoping that Peregrine had listened to him; and he was counting, because at that moment counting seemed like the best possible thing that he could do to distract himself from needing to breathe. He would soon need to breathe.

Thirty-five . . . thirty-six . . . thirty-seven . . .

He wondered how long mushroom spores remained in the air.

Forty-three . . . forty-four . . . forty-five . . . forty-six . . .

The shepherd had stopped speaking.

The Marquis took a step backward, fearing a knife in his ribs or teeth in his throat from the rough-furred guard-dog men, but there was nothing. He walked backward, away from the dog-men, and the Elephant.

He saw that Peregrine was also walking backward.

His lungs hurt. His heart was pounding in his temples, pounding almost loudly enough to drown out the thin ringing noise in his ears.

Only when the Marquis's back was against a bookcase on the wall and he was as far as he could possibly get from the envelope did he allow himself to take a deep breath. He heard Peregrine breathe in too.

There was a stretching noise. Peregrine opened his mouth wide, and the tape dropped to the ground. "What," asked Peregrine, "was all that about?"

"Our way out of this room, and our way out of Shepherd's Bush, if I am not mistaken," said de Carabas. "As I so rarely am. Would you mind unbinding my wrists?"

He felt Peregrine's hands on his bound hands, and then the bindings fell away.

There was a low rumbling. "I'm going to kill somebody," said the Elephant. "As soon as I figure out who."

"Whoa, dear heart," said the Marquis, rubbing his hands together. "You mean *whom*." The shepherd and the sheepdogs were taking awkward, experimental steps towards the door. "And I can assure you that you aren't going to kill anybody, not as long as you want to get home to the castle safely."

The Elephant's trunk swished irritably. "I'm definitely going to kill *you*."

The Marquis grinned. "You are going to force me to say *pshaw*," he said. "Or *fiddlesticks*. Until this moment I have never had the slightest yearning to say *fiddlesticks*. But I can feel it right now welling up inside me—"

"What, by the Temple and the Arch, has got into you?" asked the Elephant.

"Wrong question. But I shall ask the right question on your behalf. The question is actually, what *hasn't* got into the three of us? It hasn't got into Peregrine and me because we were holding our breath. It hasn't got into you because, I don't know, probably because you're an elephant, with nice thick skin, more likely because you were breathing through your trunk, which is down at ground level—and what did get into our captors? And the answer is, what hasn't got into us are the selfsame spores that have got into our portly shepherd and his pseudocanine companions."

"Spores of the Mushroom?" asked Peregrine. "The Mushroom People's the Mushroom?"

"Indeed. That selfsame Mushroom," agreed the Marquis.

"Blimming heck," said the Elephant.

"Which is why," de Carabas told the Elephant, "if you attempt to kill me, or to kill Peregrine, you will not only fail but you will doom us all. Whereas if you shut up and we all do our best to look as if we are still part of the flock, then we have a chance. The spores will be threading their way into their brains now. And any moment now the Mushroom will begin calling them home."

A SHEPHERD WALKED, IMPLACABLY. He held a wooden crook. Three men followed him. One of those men had the head of an elephant; one was tall and ridiculously handsome; and the last of the flock wore a most magnificent coat. It fit him perfectly, and it was the color of a wet street at night.

The flock were followed by guard dogs, who moved as if they were ready to walk through fire to get wherever they believed that they were going.

It was not unusual in Shepherd's Bush to see a shepherd and part of his flock moving from place to place, accompanied by several of the fiercest sheepdogs (who were human, or had been, once). So when they saw a shepherd and three sheepdogs apparently leading three members of the flock away from Shepherd's Bush, none of the greater flock paid them any mind. The members of the flock who saw them simply did the same things they had always done, as members of the flock, and if they were aware that the influence of the shepherds had waned a little, then they patiently waited for another shepherd to come and to take care of them and to keep them safe from predators and from the world. It was a scary thing to be alone, after all.

Nobody noticed as they crossed the bounds of Shepherd's Bush, and still they kept on walking.

The seven of them reached the banks of the Kilburn, where they stopped, and the former shepherd and the three shaggy dog-men strode out into the water.

There was, the Marquis knew, nothing in the four men's heads at that moment but a need to get to the Mushroom, to

taste its flesh once more, to let it live inside them, to serve it, and to serve it well. In exchange, the Mushroom would fix all the things about themselves that they hated: it would make their interior lives much happier and more interesting.

"Should've let me kill 'em," said the Elephant as the former shepherd and sheepdogs waded away.

"No point," said the Marquis. "Not even for revenge. The people who captured us don't exist any longer."

The Elephant flapped his ears hard, then scratched them vigorously. "Talking about revenge, who the hell did you steal my diary for anyway?" he asked.

"Victoria," admitted de Carabas.

"Not actually on my list of potential thieves. She's a deep one," said the Elephant, after a moment.

"I'll not argue with that," said the Marquis. "Also, she failed to pay me the entire amount agreed. I wound up obtaining my own lagniappe to make up the deficit."

He reached a dark hand into the inside of his coat. His fingers found the obvious pockets, and the less obvious, and then, to his surprise, the least obvious of all. He reached inside it, and pulled out a magnifying glass on a chain. "It was Victoria's," he said. "I believe you can use it to see through solid things. Perhaps this could be considered a small payment against my debt to you . . . ?"

The Elephant took something out of its own pocket—the Marquis could not see what it was—and squinted at it through the magnifying glass. Then the Elephant made a noise halfway between a delighted snort and a trumpet of satisfaction. "Oh fine, very fine," it said. It pocketed both of the objects. Then it

said, "I suppose that saving my life outranks stealing my diary. And while I wouldn't have needed saving if I hadn't followed you down the drain, further recriminations are pointless. Consider your life your own once more."

"I look forward to visiting you in the Castle someday," said the Marquis.

"Don't push your luck, mate," said the Elephant, with an irritable swish of his trunk.

"I won't," said the Marquis, resisting the urge to point out that pushing his luck was the only way he had made it this far. He looked around and realized that Peregrine had slipped mysteriously and irritatingly away into the shadows, once more, without so much as a good-bye.

The Marquis hated it when people did that.

He made a small, courtly bow to the Elephant, and the Marquis's coat, his glorious coat, caught the bow, amplified it, made it perfect, and made it the kind of bow that only the Marquis de Carabas could ever possibly make. Whoever he was.

THE NEXT FLOATING MARKET was being held in Derry and Tom's Roof Garden. There had been no Derry and Tom's since 1973, but time and space and London Below had their own uncomfortable agreement, and the roof garden was younger and more innocent than it is today. The folk from London Above (they were young, and in an intense discussion, and they had stacked heels and paisley tops and bell-bottom flares, the men and the women) ignored the folk from London Below entirely.

The Marquis de Carabas strode through the roof garden as if he owned the place, walking swiftly until he reached the food court. He passed a tiny woman selling curling cheese sandwiches from a wheelbarrow piled high with the things, a curry stall, a short man with a huge glass bowl of pale white blind fish and a toasting fork, until, finally, he reached the stall that was selling the Mushroom.

"Slice of the Mushroom, well grilled, please," said the Marquis de Carabas.

The man who took his order was shorter than he was, and still somewhat stouter. He had sandy, receding hair and a harried expression.

"Coming right up," said the man. "Anything else?"

"No, that's all." And then, curiously, the Marquis asked, "Do you remember me?"

"I am afraid not," said the Mushroom man. "But I must say, that is a most beautiful coat."

"Thank you," said the Marquis de Carabas. He looked around. "Where is the young fellow who used to work here?"

"Ah. That is a most curious story, sir," said the man. He did not yet smell of damp, although there was a small encrustation of mushrooms on the side of his neck. "I am informed that somebody told the fair Drusilla, of the Court of the Raven, that our Vince had designs upon her, and had—you may not credit it, but I am assured that it is so—apparently sent her a letter filled with spores with the intention of making her his bride in the Mushroom."

The Marquis raised an eyebrow quizzically, although he found none of this surprising. He had, after all, told Drusilla

himself, and had even shown her the original letter. "Did she take well to the news?"

"I do not believe that she did, sir. I do not believe that she did. She and several of her sisters were waiting for Vince, and they all caught up with us on our way to the Market. She told him they had matters to discuss, of an intimate nature. He seemed delighted by this news, and went off with her, to find out what these matters were. I have been waiting for him to arrive at the Market and come and work all evening, but I no longer believe he will be coming." Then the man said, a little wistfully, "That is a very fine coat. It seems to me that I might have had one like it, in a former life."

"I do not doubt it," said the Marquis de Carabas, satisfied with what he had heard, cutting into his grilled slice of the Mushroom, "but this particular coat is most definitely mine."

As he made his way out of the Market, he passed a clump of people descending the stairs and he paused and nodded at a young woman of uncommon grace. She had the long orange hair and the flattened profile of a Pre-Raphaelite beauty, and there was a birthmark in the shape of a five-pointed star on the back of one hand. Her other hand was stroking the head of a large, rumpled owl, which glared uncomfortably out at the world with eyes that were, unusually for such a bird, of an intense, pale blue.

The Marquis nodded at her, and she glanced awkwardly at him, then she looked away in the manner of someone who had just begun to realize that she owed the Marquis a favor.

He nodded at her, amiably, and continued to descend.

Drusilla hurried after him. She looked as if she had something she wanted to say.

The Marquis de Carabas reached the foot of the stairs ahead of her. He stopped for a moment, and he thought about people, and about things, and about how hard it is to do anything for the first time. And then, clad in his fine coat, he slipped mysteriously, even irritatingly, into the shadows, without so much as a good-bye, and he was gone.

THE NEIL GAIMAN COLLECTION

NEVERWHERE

Richard Mayhew is a London businessman with a good heart and an ordinary life that is changed forever when he helps a young girl he finds injured on the street. His act of kindness catapults him into a world that is both familiar and threateningly bizarre.

"The chimerical stuff of nightmare and daydream."
— *USA Today*

STARDUST

Tristran Thorn dares to traverse the unexplored lands on the other side of the ancient wall that surrounds his tiny village to search for a fallen star—and win the heart of the girl he thinks he loves.

"A twisting, wondrous tale full of magic that only Neil Gaiman could have written."
— *Chicago Tribune*

AMERICAN GODS

In this unforgettable tale of monsters and men, mystery and magic, ex-con Shadow Moon becomes bodyguard, driver, and errand boy for the enigmatic Mr. Wednesday—and is put squarely in the path of an impending storm: an epic war between gods old and new.

"Dark fun, and nourishing to the soul."
— Michael Chabon

ANANSI BOYS

If his scoundrel of an estranged father hadn't dropped dead, Charlie Nancy would have no idea that his dad was Anansi, the powerful trickster spider-god, or that he has a brother who is also a god. Suddenly, Charlie's life has gotten very interesting . . . and downright dangerous.

"Thrilling, spooky, and wondrous."
— *Denver Post*

THE OCEAN AT THE END OF THE LANE

A man returns to his childhood home to attend a funeral and is drawn to the farm at the end of the road, where, when he was seven, he met a most remarkable girl. Now, decades later, as he sits by the pond (that she claimed was an ocean), the unremembered past comes flooding back.

"[Gaiman's] mind is a dark fathomless ocean, and every time I sink into it, this world fades, replaced by one far more terrible and beautiful in which I will happily drown."
— *New York Times Book Review*

THE NEIL GAIMAN READER

A representation of Neil Gaiman's groundbreaking, endlessly imaginative fiction, this captivating volume includes excerpts from his five novels for adults—*Neverwhere, Stardust, American Gods, Anansi Boys,* and *The Ocean at the End of the Lane*—and nearly fifty of his short stories.

> "Gaiman gives us permission to never let go of the world of wonder that we're all told at some time to leave behind."
> — Marlon James, from his foreword to *The Neil Gaiman Reader*

SMOKE AND MIRRORS

An elderly widow finds the Holy Grail beneath an old fur coat. A newlywed couple receives a gift that reveals a chilling alternate history of their marriage. Such imaginative gems and more await within this collection of short fiction from one of the most celebrated literary artists of our day.

> "Gaiman is a treasure-house of story,
> and we are lucky to have him."
> — Stephen King

FRAGILE THINGS

Two teenage boys crash a party and meet the girls of their dreams—and nightmares. A mysterious circus terrifies an audience before vanishing into the night. By turns delightful and disturbing, this critically acclaimed collection contains more than thirty pieces of short fiction.

> "Dazzling tales from a master of the fantastic."
> — *Washington Post Book World*

TRIGGER WARNING

Neil Gaiman's third collection of short fiction is a rich cornucopia of speculative explorations and magical realism, horror and ghost stories, fabulism and poetry—a treasury of delights that illuminates the genius of a master storyteller at the height of his powers.

> "Exciting, often musical writing."
> — *Boston Globe*

GOOD OMENS

According to *The Nice and Accurate Prophecies of Agnes Nutter, Witch*, the world will end on a Saturday. Next Saturday, in fact. However, a somewhat fussy angel and a fast-living demon—both of whom have lived amongst Earth's mortals since The Beginning and have grown rather fond of the lifestyle—are not actually looking forward to the coming Rapture. And someone seems to have misplaced the Antichrist . . .

THE QUITE NICE AND FAIRLY ACCURATE *GOOD OMENS* SCRIPT BOOK

Collected here are Neil Gaiman's complete original scripts for the smash-hit six-episode television series, based on the beloved novel he wrote with Terry Pratchett, offering readers deeper insight into Gaiman's brilliant adaptation of a classic comic masterwork.

MAKE GOOD ART

This striking volume, designed by renowned graphic artist Chip Kidd, contains the full text of Neil Gaiman's May 2012 commencement address delivered at Philadelphia's University of the Arts, in which he shared his thoughts about creativity, bravery, and strength. Above all, Gaiman encouraged the fledgling painters, musicians, writers, and dreamers to *make good art*.

ART MATTERS

A stunning and timely creative call to arms combining four extraordinary written pieces by Neil Gaiman illustrated with the striking artwork of Chris Riddell. Drawn from Gaiman's trove of published speeches, poems, and creative manifestos, *Art Matters* is an embodiment of this remarkable multimedia artist's vision—an exploration of how reading, imagining, and creating can transform the world and our lives.

THE VIEW FROM THE CHEAP SEATS

A fascinating collection of nonfiction pieces exploring myriad subjects ranging from art and artists to dreams, myths, and memories—all observed, explored, and presented in the inimitable Gaiman style. Insightful, incisive, witty, and wise, *The View from the Cheap Seats* offers a glimpse into the head and heart of one of the most acclaimed, beloved, and influential artists of our time.

THE ANNOTATED AMERICAN GODS

This comprehensively annotated volume of Neil Gaiman's masterwork *American Gods* features analysis from award-winning annotator and editor Leslie S. Klinger, whose incisive commentary identifies gods and supernatural beings, elucidates key phrases, and shows how Gaiman built his award-winning novel, giving readers unparalleled insight into the story as well as into Gaiman's creative process and authorial decisions. Carefully chosen illustrations complement and illuminate the narrative.

CORALINE

In Coraline's family's new flat there's a locked door. On the other side is a brick wall—until Coraline unlocks the door . . . and finds a passage to another flat in another house just like her own. Only different. There's another mother and father there who want Coraline to be their little girl. They want to change her and keep her with them . . . forever.

"A marvelously strange and scary book. . . . *Coraline* is the real thing."
— Philip Pullman, *The Guardian*

THE GRAVEYARD BOOK

A modern classic—winner of both the Newbery (US) and Carnegie (UK) Medals—this ingenious reimagining of Rudyard Kipling's *The Jungle Book* tells the story of Nobody Owens, a living, breathing boy who dwells in a graveyard, raised by a guardian who belongs neither to the world of the living nor to the realm of the dead. But flesh-and-blood danger waits just outside the cemetery walls: the man who murdered Bod's family will not rest until he finishes what he began so many years ago.

"*The Graveyard Book* is everything everyone loves about Neil Gaiman, only multiplied many times over."
— Joe Hill

THE TRUTH IS A CAVE IN THE BLACK MOUNTAINS

Beautifully illustrated by renowned artist Eddie Campbell, this four-color edition of Neil Gaiman's award-winning novelette brings to vivid life a haunting story of family, the otherworld, and a search for hidden treasure.

"[A] deceptively dark tale of how far men will go to achieve their heart's desire only to find that the achievement pales in comparison to the desiring."
— *Pittsburgh Post-Gazette*